The Lost Love Song

Minnie Darke

CORGI BOOKS

TRANSWORLD PUBLISHERS
61–63 Uxbridge Road, London W5 5SA
www.penguin.co.uk

Transworld is part of the Penguin Random House group of companies
whose addresses can be found at global.penguinrandomhouse.com

Originally published in Australia in 2020 by Michael Joseph,
a division of Penguin Random House Australia
First published in Great Britain in 2020 by Transworld Digital
and by Corgi Books
an imprint of Transworld Publishers

A CIP catalogue record for this book
is available from the British Library.

ISBN
9780552175982

Internal design by Post Prepress Australia
Typeset in Adobe Garamond 10.68/15.15pt by Post Prepress.
Sagrantino set by Jouve (UK), Milton Keynes.
Printed and bound in Great Britain by Clays Ltd, Elcograf S.p.A.

Penguin Random House is committed to a sustainable
future for our business, our readers and our planet. This book
is made from Forest Stewardship Council® certified paper.

1 3 5 7 9 10 8 6 4 2

You can cage the singer, but not the song.

Harry Belafonte

prelude

THE LOVE SONG began its life, not with a fanfare or a crash of cymbals, but instead with a knock at a door.

The door belonged to a room in the basement of the Conservatorium of Music, a graceful old building whose wide corridors and stairwells had been almost entirely emptied out by the January holidays and the heat. But even if this had been a busy day in the middle of semester, the sign on the door in question would still have been misleading. DEPARTMENT OF INFORMATION TECHNOLOGY, it read, even though the room beyond it had only a single occupant. His name was Arie Johnson, he was twenty-six years old, and at just before midday he was sitting at his computer without a clue in the world that he was never going to eat the slightly squashed ham and cheese sandwich he'd made for himself that morning. Or that his life was about to change forever.

When Arie heard the knock, he looked up to see Diana Clare standing in his doorway, but this alone was not enough to reveal to him the magnitude of what was about to happen. He observed that her long hair was piled up on top of her head like a bundle of fairy floss, and that the colour in her cheeks was high. This wasn't unreasonable, though, since the day's forecast was for a top of 34°C.

1

Until the previous day, Arie had known Diana only from a distance. Like most people, he'd seen her on posters and in write-ups in the arts section of newspapers. With the exception of one or two historical figures who had concert halls named after them, or whose statues struck dramatic bronze poses in the Conservatorium grounds, Diana Clare, piano prodigy, was almost certainly the institution's most famous graduate. It was her trademark to perform in a red sleeveless dress and an incongruous pair of Converse high-tops, her lips painted the colour of her gown. In the Conservatorium's main foyer there was a photograph of her playing – shoulders bare, expressive arms outstretched to the keys, head tipped back so that her ginger-blonde hair poured down towards the floor.

At twenty-five, Diana had already performed in some of the world's most famous concert halls, and now she was back at the Con for the summer to teach a series of masterclasses. The task of setting up her computer had fallen to Arie, and yesterday as he'd jogged up the stairs to the office she'd been allocated, he'd had such a clear mental picture of her that he was momentarily surprised not to find her in a red dress. Instead, she was wearing a denim pinafore and a shirt covered in tiny shamrocks, her hair pulled back into braids.

In photographs, Diana Clare was glamorous. Stunning. But Arie immediately liked the way she looked in person – her face densely freckled, her hands surprisingly small, her fingernails cut almost to the quick, her eyelashes so pale they were nearly invisible.

Still, Arie was nothing if not a realist. In school and through university, he'd been the guy all the girls described as 'totally adorable', meaning of course that they wanted him only as a confidant, a shoulder to cry on, and a handy target for their flirting practice.

2

For the whole time he worked on the cranky old iMac in Diana's office, she'd been sweet and attentive to him, but Arie was wise to this behaviour. In his experience, women often behaved this way while they were getting their tech problems fixed. It meant they were grateful; it did not mean they were romantically interested in him.

So, if Diana Clare was here in his office doorway on the day after he'd sorted out her password issues, network access and printing connection, the reason could only be professional. He gave her an apologetic frown.

'I'm guessing something's not working,' he said.

'Oh, no,' she said quickly. 'Everything's fine.'

Arie blinked. 'Okay, so . . . ?'

'The reason I stopped by . . .' she said, then paused. She took a breath and spoke again, all in a rush, 'Was to see if maybe you wanted to have lunch with me.'

Arie stared.

This was Diana Clare. *The* Diana Clare. This was the woman who played the piano with her whole body, as if nobody was watching, as if someone was pouring music in through the top of her head so that it sluiced through her, eddying in her shoulders and torso before being funnelled out through her fingers and onto the keys. And she had just suggested he go out to lunch with her.

Was she asking him out on a date? Was that the correct interpretation of the situation? His impulse was to Google it, but she was waiting for an answer, which meant that he was going to have to coordinate some kind of functional connection between his brain and his mouth.

'If you're not too busy, of course,' she prompted, but Arie's tongue seemed to have lost the ability to verb or noun. In fact, it seemed suddenly incapable of any kind of movement that pertained to speech.

If Diana hadn't looked so sincerely nervous, Arie might have thought he was being pranked. But if this wasn't a prank, there was only one other explanation: he was experiencing a real, live, actual miracle. Shouldn't there have been a beam of revelatory light streaming through a window? Arie guessed that wasn't really possible in a basement office.

'I'm sorry,' Diana said, taking a half-step backwards, 'if the invitation was unwelcome, or—'

Arie commanded his tongue to get its shit together.

'Lutch would be gates,' he managed.

Her features shifted into an expression of amusement. 'Did you just say something about Bill Gates?'

'Lunch,' Arie clarified. 'Lunch. Would be great.'

From there, things proceeded swiftly – *allegro* at the very least, and possibly even *presto*. Tuesday lunch at a café not far from the Conservatorium was followed by a Wednesday night pizza date, which concluded chastely (with a kiss in the back of a taxi), and in turn by a Friday night curry date, which did not.

Diana's place was a small flat on the ground floor of a once-stately home that had been chopped roughly into six separate dwellings. The tiny kitchen was a fire hazard, and the even tinier bathroom was a health risk, but as Diana led Arie through the front door, she explained that she was away so often it hardly seemed worth forking out for a nicer place. Plus, she told him, the flat's third room – the one that trebled as bedroom, dining room and living room – had a bay window.

4

'That's something you're going to need to know about me,' Diana said.

She was talking to him, Arie registered with astonishment, about the future, and as if that future might include him.

'What is?' he asked.

'That I'll always need a bay window.'

'Because?'

'The Steinway deserves nothing less,' she said, gesturing to her baby grand piano, which did look pleasing when framed by the angles of the window, even if the panes were curtained in shabby damask and the seat beneath the sill was covered with what looked to be a week's worth of Diana's unfolded laundry, breakfast dishes and coffee cups.

The Steinway seemed larger, Arie noticed, than Diana's bed, a single, which was pushed up against a wall and topped with a meringue of clothes and mismatched sheets. The bed may have been small, but Arie didn't mind, because it was there he learned Diana made love as wholeheartedly as she played the piano.

In those early months of his relationship with Diana, Arie wasn't the only one who regarded his good fortune as inexplicable. The Conservatorium's thrice-married music theory lecturer cornered Arie at the pub one Friday after work, raised a leery eyebrow and said, 'You clearly have hidden talents, Arie, my boy.' Meanwhile, Arie's best friend and flatmate, Richard, began making fairly regular jibes about catching sight of Arie in a Victoria Bitter commercial, walking under the banner for MEN WHO PUNCH ABOVE THEIR WEIGHT.

If Arie could brush off the obviously green-tinged comments of colleagues and friends, it was a little harder to dismiss the reaction of Diana's mother. The first time he met Belinda Clare, he felt as if he were being looked over by an off-duty parade sergeant who desperately wanted to tell him to pull his shoulders back. Or get a haircut. Perhaps it was because there was no father to meet that Diana's mother felt the need to be formidable.

'So, where *is* your father?' Arie asked Diana in those early days of telling each other about their lives.

'Absent,' Diana said, and that seemed to be all the answer she felt inclined to supply.

Belinda, in her mid-forties, had short fair hair that was just beginning to silver at the temples and the weary air of someone who'd never had the luxury of being careless. She lived an hour and a half's drive out of the city, in a weatherboard farmhouse with a long backyard, unmown grass, unpruned apricot trees and a view over densely forested hills.

Following a strained afternoon tea in a room whose walls were hung with portraits of Diana, and whose shelves displayed a small army of certificates earned by Diana and trophies won by Diana, Belinda took Arie out to the back shed to have him lift a box of empty jars down from a high shelf; the apricots, apparently, were ready for jam.

Belinda watched him with an intent and critical air while he unfolded the stepladder and edged out of storage the cardboard carton to which she'd pointed.

'So, what is it about *you* that makes her so happy?'

Arie, climbing back down the ladder with the box in his arms, hadn't the first clue how to answer this, but fortunately Belinda wasn't actually expecting a reply.

'You adore her?' she asked.

'Of course,' he said.

'I raised her to be adored,' she said.

'Well, that makes sense,' Arie said, and Belinda took the carton of jars out of his arms in a way that strongly suggested he couldn't be trusted to hold it any longer.

'Then I suppose you'll do,' she said. 'For now.'

Four weeks later Arie moved into Diana's flat, bringing his double bed with him. He and she marked the first night of living-togetherness by drinking raspberry gin and going to bed so early that they were both awake again before midnight and sitting naked at the piano, Diana between Arie's legs, her back against his chest, his arms folded around her swaying body as she played.

He hadn't the least idea if she was playing Mozart or Mendelssohn. He only knew that he was in love with this woman, who liked pizzas and curries even hotter than he did, who clutched at his hands during scary movies, and who found it more draining to spend an hour engaged in small talk at a cocktail party than she did to play a Rachmaninov concerto. She practised the piano for upwards of five hours a day, and although she usually came away from the keyboard listless and irritable, her moods were a bit like sun-showers – soon over with and forgotten.

No matter how deeply Arie pondered the question, he still had no idea why Diana seemed to be equally in love with him, and although he would have liked to be able to say that this was a mystery he was prepared to leave unsolved, just so long as it never ended, in truth it kept him up at night.

When Diana brought the music to a close, resolving the melody in a beautiful finishing chord, Arie felt her lean back into him with a sigh of pleasure. He rested his chin on her bare shoulder, his cheek against the briar-tangle of her hair.

'Why?' he asked.

'Why what?'

'Why me?'

This time her sigh sounded like exasperation.

'I'm not just fishing for compliments,' Arie hastened to add. 'I just really . . . I need to understand.'

'I don't get why you think it needs explanation.'

'Well, you're *you*, and I'm . . . so completely average. Look at me. Even my birthmark' – it was on his hip – 'is beige.'

Diana smiled while her hands moved over the keyboard, making the kinds of sounds that Arie had come to think of as the musical equivalent of doodling.

'Diana?'

'I don't know what you want me to say.'

'I don't understand why you're not moving in with . . . I don't know, the world's most gorgeous cello player.'

'Another *musician*?' Diana said, with a shudder of horror. 'Ugh. No thanks.'

'But why me?'

If Diana had been better with words, she might have been able to tell him all the many reasons why. She might have been able to say that in the moment she'd first met him, she'd liked the way his dark blond hair fell into his eyes, which were a rich shade of brown and full of something that she'd promised herself she would never again go without: kindness.

Perhaps she'd have told him that even if he did give off an air of geekiness in the rumpled blue shirt, cheap office pants and loose-laced Vans that he wore every day to work, this was more than compensated for by his complete lack of ego. She might have said that she loved the supple, olive-toned skin on his forearms and couldn't get enough of his hands, which were long and elegant, and – slightly irritatingly – looked more like a piano player's than her own. That she loved his voice, which reminded her of the viola: not extremely deep, but just nicely deeper than you might expect. That she trusted him not to cheat on her, and that she knew he'd never hold her back.

If Diana had been better with words, she might have been able to summarise all of this by saying that to her Arie was the most rare and beautiful of things: a duckling that had absolutely no idea it had already grown into a swan.

But words were not Diana's thing. Music was. So, as she thought of all her reasons for falling in love with Arie, her fingers made their way around the keyboard of the Steinway, trying out different combinations of notes.

'Okay,' she said at last. 'How about this?'

She took Arie's right hand in hers and placed his thumb on one of the ivory keys so that a single note rang out into the room. 'This is you. A for Arie,' and then she placed his ring finger on another key, 'and this is me. D for Diana. Play them together.'

He did, and together they made a solemn kind of sound. Serious and beautiful.

'Okay, now listen,' she said, and played three notes together in a chord. 'See the bottom note is D. Now listen.'

She shifted her hand to a different chord. 'Now the bottom note is A.'

Then she played the two chords again.

'Hear it? Hear how those two chords go together? The Diana chord, and then the Arie chord. When you put together chords like those two, one then the other, in this case the D then the A, it's called a plagal cadence.'

'Sorry. A what?'

'Plagal cadence,' she repeated. 'The interval between the bottom notes of the two chords is a fourth. Now, if the interval

9

between the bottom notes was a *fifth*, then that would be a perfect cadence. That would be where E goes to A. Listen. The D chord goes to the A chord, now the E chord goes to the A chord. Can you hear the difference?' But she didn't wait for him to answer. 'Perfect cadence, plagal cadence. Perfect cadence, plagal cadence. I like the plagal, personally. Can you think what it reminds you of?'

She played the two chords again and again, but Arie wasn't sure.

Diana went on, 'It's what you hear at church, when they sing the *Amen* at the end of a hymn. Listen.'

At first, he couldn't hear it, but then – as she sang along to the chords, 'A-men' – the music came into focus.

'You see? You see?' she asked.

'I think I do, actually.'

Diana let her fingers run all over the keyboard, unloosing a waterfall of music that ended up with the sound he now recognised as the plagal cadence.

'Do you know what I mean?' she asked.

'I am your *Amen*?' Arie asked.

'Yes, you are,' Diana said. 'And I am yours.'

And for seven years, this was absolutely true.

ONE

anniversary

NATURALLY, ARIE AND Diana bought a house with a bay window. It was a terrace house on a narrow street in the city's historic quarter – a neighbourhood of sandstone cottages, artfully painted weatherboards, beautifully curated vintage stores, tiny street-corner parks and perhaps the world's highest per-capita concentration of rustic bakery–cafés.

It was Arie who found the house. After being outbid at two auctions, he went on the offensive, walking the streets on weekends and knocking on doors until at last, in Tavistock Row, he came upon a house with a bay window and an owner who didn't laugh in his face when he asked if they were interested in selling.

The place retained every last bit of its shabby, unrenovated charm, and its location gave heft to the price, but Diana declared the bay window to be perfect. It was on the upper storey, in a room with polished floorboards and double doors of frosted glass. Diana painted the walls herself, in a shade of beige that she chose almost entirely because it was called Grand Piano, and she angled the Steinway so that the bay window was at her back and the morning sun fell on the keys while she practised.

In that house, on the seven-year anniversary of the day Arie and Diana had met, a packed suitcase stood ready at the base of the stairs. In the morning, Diana was going on tour. First stop Singapore, then onwards to the places whose winters made her think of snow domes: Paris and Salzburg, Prague and St Petersburg. She would be overseas for almost a month, so – as was customary on nights before she went away – Richard and Lenka came over for dinner.

Although Diana and Arie had a snug little dining room, meals with Richard and Lenka never made it out of the kitchen. As Arie loaded toppings onto his homemade pizzas and slid his creations in and out of the oven, Richard gave unsolicited advice from the other side of the bench. Diana, in bare feet and a gingham dress, leaned against the kitchen sink with a half-empty glass in hand, observing that Lenka, who was sitting on the kitchen's only stool, was yet to take a sip of the wine Diana had poured for her half an hour earlier. Questions were also raised by the width of the purple swing-top Lenka wore, and which Diana was fairly sure was brand new.

'I'm glad you're going away, actually, Di,' Richard said, with a grin.

Richard was the only person alive who was allowed to shorten Diana's name in this way. That she let him get away with it was a concession to the importance of his friendship with Arie, which dated back to grade eight, when Richard had arrived from the UK, thickly bespectacled, with a mouthful of braces and an accent that was interpreted as insufferably stuck-up. The braces and the accent were long gone, of course, and for some years the spectacles had been a good deal more Dolce & Gabbana than Coke bottle.

'Well, thanks for that charming sentiment, Richie-poo.' Just because she tolerated him calling her 'Di' didn't mean she wasn't going to fight back.

'He reckons he gets more work out of me when you're not

here,' Arie said, sprinkling a pizza with a liberal quantity of sliced jalapeños.

'I do,' Richard insisted. 'The only time you log more hours than me is when Di's overseas. I love it! Get to put my feet up for once.'

It was five years since Arie had quit his job at the Conservatorium to go into partnership with Richard in their own web development company. Bit by bit, as it had expanded and taken on more employees, Sonder Digital had colonised half the second floor of an old warehouse building in a semi-industrial corner of the city. Giving each other shit was a crucial part of the bond between the two programmers, who often spent their leisure time talking shop in a language that was as impenetrable to Diana and Lenka as computer code itself.

'He is so full of it,' Lenka said in her lightly accented English, although she didn't need to. The truth was that both Richard and Arie worked ridiculously long hours and cared equally deeply about the success of their business. To keep the staff happy and fulfilled, they'd instituted daily pep talks, regular team bonding activities and a monthly Hack Day, as well as fitting the office out with a table tennis set-up and a large fridge that was always generously stocked with kombucha.

Diana moved to Arie's side and swiped a slice of mozzarella from one of his pizzas.

'Pest,' he said, although he kissed her hair.

'You'll take care of him for me, won't you?' Diana asked Lenka. 'Make sure he doesn't get worked into the ground while I'm gone.'

'Don't worry. I'll feed him and water him. Make sure he occasionally gets fresh air and sunlight,' Lenka said. 'I promise.'

It wasn't always a done deal that the partners of long-standing best friends like Arie and Richard ended up being close friends

15

themselves, but Diana and Lenka were among the lucky ones, despite being about as different as two women could be. Diana, as a rule, did not cook. Neither did she fold laundry, put out garbage, clean ovens or scrub bathrooms. Lenka, on the other hand, was unable to leave her house until she had wiped the sink, straightened her already straight doona cover and plumped her couch cushions. Diana knew it wasn't fair to have been blessed with the ability to eat anything she wanted and remain stick thin, while Lenka had to restrict herself to a regimented diet in order to remain only as round as she already was.

Lenka was a psychologist, and Diana could imagine how reassuring her clients would find her forthright practicality. Lenka wasn't the slightest bit musical; instead she played several sports, the rougher the better. Although, tonight Diana found herself wondering for how much longer this would be true. She watched Richard take a slug of his boutique beer and run a hand through his close-cropped hair.

'So, um,' he said, 'we have news. It isn't really public yet, but that'll probably happen when you're away, Di, and . . . well, we wanted to tell you in person.'

Diana looked to Lenka.

'We're pregnant,' she announced.

In the cramped kitchen, there was an explosion of hugging, squealing and delight, along with all the usual questions. How far along? (Almost twelve weeks.) Will you find out the sex? (Absolutely.) How much leave will you take? (As much as I can get away with.) Diana poured Lenka's wine down the sink and fetched her a glass of sparkling mineral water.

'We were hoping,' Lenka said, 'that you two would be the baby's godparents.'

'Of course,' Arie said, glancing over at Diana. In the fleeting look that passed between them, Arie sensed some kind of uncertainty. But before he could study it, and before Richard or Lenka had noticed her reservation, Diana was once again bubbling over with happiness for her friends.

'Holy shit,' she said, clinking her glass against Lenka's, Arie's and Richard's. 'You guys are having a freaking *baby*!'

'Aren't you two celebrating tonight as well?' Lenka asked, trying to deflect some of the attention.

'We are,' Diana said, slipping her arm around Arie's waist. 'Seven years together. Seven years.'

'Is there a particular reason for that?' Diana asked.

It was past eleven, and for the last quarter of an hour Arie had been sitting shirtless against the pillows in the summer warmth of their bedroom. He was aware of every move Diana made as she padded around the bedroom in a pale pink wisp of a nightgown, dithering with her hand luggage and setting the alarm.

'A reason for what?' Arie asked.

Although there was a book open on his lap, Diana was fairly sure that in all the time it had taken her to check and double-check she had packed all her important things . . . passport, credit card, phone charger . . . he hadn't turned a single page. She sat beside him on the bed.

'For that little thundercloud over your head.'

'There's no thundercloud,' he said, without looking up from his page.

'Arie, it's right there,' Diana said, poking at the air just above his head. 'I can see it.'

'You're imagining it.'

17

'I don't think I am.'

Now he did look up. He closed his book, and sighed. 'Do you really want to do this? Right now? Tonight?'

Diana was surprised by the note of irritation in his tone. 'Well, it seems like you have something to say.' She set her jaw. 'So, let's hear it.'

'Okay then,' Arie said. 'Look at your hand. The left.'

Diana did as she was asked.

'What do you see?'

She saw freckles, two fine parallel scars from a rabbit scratch she'd sustained as a child, and short, slim fingers that right now had stored inside them one half of Prokofiev's *Concerto No. 2*, the one she would soon play with the Orchestre de Paris.

'I don't see anything.'

'That's right,' Arie said.

'O-o-oh. I get it. You're mad I'm not wearing my engagement ring.' The thing was, Diana never wore rings. Or bracelets, or a watch; they got in the way while she was playing. 'I hate wearing rings. You know that.'

Arie sat forward so that Diana could see every detail of the unmarked olive skin of his chest, the vulnerable dips on the insides of his collarbones, the smooth curves of his shoulders. She wished she had not taken his bait. If she'd just taken the book out of his hands, switched off the lamp and slid into bed beside him, by now they'd be making love the way they always did right before she went away – with an edge of sadness that gave it a delicious little bite.

'How long have you had the engagement ring that you hate wearing?' he asked.

'It must be . . . what? Three years?'

Arie had proposed to Diana in New York, on a blue-sky day

in August, in a rowboat in Central Park. With its bolted-on oars, the blunt-nosed little vessel hadn't been easy to manoeuvre, but somehow Arie had managed to paddle across the busy lake to the place where a jazz trio was playing under a pergola that jutted out into the water. He'd had high hopes for the ring in his pocket, having asked the jeweller to make it small enough, delicate enough, for a pianist to wear. But although Diana had received it – and his proposal – with nothing but joy and excitement, the ring had spent almost all of its life inside a velvet box. And no wedding had ever ensued.

'We've been engaged for nearly four and a half years,' Arie said.

'Well, that's pretty good going, isn't it?' Diana replied with brittle humour, hoping to get a laugh out of him. None came.

'Why aren't we married?'

Diana sighed. 'You know *why*. We just haven't got around to it yet. We never know when I'm going to be . . .'

'Actually, you're in control of your schedule. So *why* aren't we married?'

'Why do we have to be?'

'I hate it when you answer questions with questions.'

'I like being Diana Clare,' she said, aware of the pouty tone in her voice.

'Who says you'd have to change your name?'

'I like being *Miss* Clare. I hate Ms. It's clunky.'

'When you said yes, did you ever have any intention of marrying me?'

'Yes,' Diana said, without conviction.

'So are you ever going to marry me?'

'I'm never going to leave you,' Diana said.

'That's not what I asked.'

'Oh, Arie, I don't know.'

Arie heard the frustration in her voice and wished he hadn't bothered with the conversation. After seven years, he ought to have known better than to go head to head with Diana over an issue like this one; being challenged only made her obstinate.

'Well, I want you to think about it. While you're away. I want you to come home with a decision.'

Diana felt a chill ripple down her spine. 'Or *what*?'

'It isn't an ultimatum.'

'Feels like one.'

'It's time, Diana. It's time we took that step.'

'Weddings are tacky,' Diana said, in a way that was both dismissive and an invitation for Arie to disagree.

'It could be however you wanted it to be,' he said gently.

'But why is it necessary? You know I love you. I do. I *love* you. I've already said I want to be with you forever. We bought this house together. I'm not going anywhere.'

'Except, of course, you are,' Arie said.

There was a silence, in which Diana felt every mile of the distance she was about to travel, and every minute of all the hours that would pass before she would be home again.

'And, what was that thing you did? When Richard and Lenka asked us to be godparents?' Arie asked.

'What thing?'

'You know. That look you gave me.'

Diana sighed deeply. 'It was a really big question, and you just said *yes*, without even thinking about it. Being a godparent is a com*mit*ment.'

'So? They're our closest friends.'

'I don't like to say yes to anything unless I'm totally sure I'm going to be able to do it properly. Get it right.'

20

In this, Arie recognised the perfectionist tendencies that made her the pianist she was.

'Diana, everywhere I look, all around me, there are people going forwards,' he said. 'But we're not.'

Her eyes narrowed. 'Is this about having children? Is *that* what this is really all about?'

'I don't know,' Arie faltered. 'That's a whole other debate. But I'd like to get married. I want to . . . do the next thing. But you . . . it feels like you just want things to go on the way they are, forever.'

'Why is that so terrible?'

'Have you ever thought that maybe it's not what I want?'

Diana was not accustomed to Arie telling her what he wanted. The fact was, and Diana knew this, that what Arie usually wanted was to make *her* happy.

She got to her feet.

'Where are you going?' Arie asked, even though – as she walked out the bedroom door – he knew. A moment later he heard the lid of the Steinway being flung open. Then piano scales were coming through the walls – fierce, yet precise.

If, in one sense, the love song had begun seven years before with a knock at a door, in another sense it began that night in the piano room.

It was almost midnight by the time Diana had played enough scales to work her way through her annoyance, although quite why she was so annoyed she couldn't precisely say. Her feelings about weddings were complicated. There was embarrassment in the mix, certainly. The idea of dressing up in a particular kind of dress and saying a particular set of words . . . it all felt mawkish to her. Part of her felt that getting married involved making in public a promise that ought to be completely private. Another part almost, *almost*, liked the idea. But even if her feelings about weddings were complicated, her feelings about Arie were not. If she'd been better with words, she might have been able to tell him as much.

She sat at the piano, a sheen of sweat on her skin and the backs of her thighs clinging to the leather-topped stool. The bay window, its angled panes open in the hope of catching a cooling breeze, allowed in the scent of the jasmine that grew wild over the front of the house. As Diana took in the familiar pattern of the white keys and the black, she could feel the shape of the song inside her. Like any good love song, this one had two parts. As her fingers moved over the keys, they first invented the deeper part, the foundation, which consisted of sequences of chords, arranged in threes, rising and falling. Then they formed the melody, which came in over the top of the lower notes, sweet and sustained, swirling like icing on a cake.

After a while, Diana opened a manuscript book, black and leather-bound, and took up the pencil that she kept on the music desk of the piano. She played, and stopped, jotted down the notes she had just discovered, then played again. She scrubbed at certain notes with an eraser, wrote other notes in their place, then played again.

By the time Arie appeared in the doorway, squinting against the light, the song was almost finished. It needed only three or four more bars to be complete, but there could be no fudging, not when it came to an ending. Diana did not like songs to simply fade out. For her, one of the great pleasures of good music was an exquisitely resolved ending, when a final note or chord hung in the air and resonated in her chest so that she felt like crying. Not because she was sad, but because she was moved.

She looked at him – his chest bare, his pale blue cotton boxer shorts low on his hips. Every part of him, she knew and loved: the top right-hand quarter of his chest where she rested her head when she half woke in the mornings, edged closer and nudged her way into his arms; the ridiculously accentuated arches of his feet; the perfect flat whorl of his navel; the way his facial hair – on the rare occasion he let it grow – was a shade or two darker than the hair on his head; his sculpted lips.

'Come to bed,' he said, holding out a hand. 'You'll be so tired tomorrow.'

Diana closed the notebook on the piano desk, stood and stretched. Reaching the doorway, she took his hand and put her forehead against his chest.

'I'm sorry,' she said, her eyes on the floor.

'What was that thing you were playing?' he asked.

She looked up at him and shrugged. 'Just a . . . song.'

'It was beautiful.'

He was right. It was beautiful, but as Diana got up and went with him back to their bed, she still didn't know exactly how it ended.

how to end a love song

Two NIGHTS LATER, on the twenty-sixth floor of a glassy hotel in Singapore, Diana lay between the starched white sheets of a king-sized bed, not sleeping. Against her floor-to-ceiling windows, heavy droplets of monsoonal rain exploded into rivulets. The city beyond was a bright matrix of coloured lights and slashes of gleaming black water.

Diana's famous red dress was draped across a plush armchair and a pair of high-heeled shoes lay kicked off on the carpet. Diana didn't like performing in heels; she much preferred her trusty old Converse sneakers, but a newspaper arts reporter had offered the opinion that it was time – now that Diana was thirty-two – for her to 'relinquish the trappings of her wunderkind days'. Maturity, Diana thought, was enough to give you blisters.

The bedside clock announced the local time was just past midnight, which meant that back home it was past three. Even so, Diana was not the least bit sleepy. On a bench beyond the foot of the bed, its silhouette reflecting in a huge mirror, was the enormous bouquet she had been given at the end of tonight's performance. Tropical and lush, the arrangement was full of large-scale foliage and the pink orchids that were the Singaporean national flower. But, like pianos themselves, bouquets were hardly something that

24

could be taken on the road. Tomorrow, when the blooms hadn't even begun to wilt, she would leave her flowers behind in the hotel's ice bucket and hope that someone else would have a chance to enjoy them while she was making her way to Paris.

Diana wished she were not so very wide awake. Not now. She needed to be rested if she was going to arrive in the French capital ready to begin several days of demanding orchestral rehearsals for the Prokofiev concerto. For another half a deluded hour, she lay with her eyes closed and tried to sleep. But it was futile.

Switching on the light, she had to admit that the hotel room had been thoroughly Diana-fied. Her suitcase appeared to have coughed three-quarters of its contents out onto the floor, where there lay a tangled pile of garments and shoes, toiletries and sheet music. From the chaos, Diana tugged out a light dress and a pair of sandals, her notebook and a pencil that would have to do, even though it needed sharpening. Then she stepped out into the hallway and set off in search of the hotel's piano.

When it came to accommodation, the presence of a piano was Diana's only hard and fast requirement. Sometimes the instrument would turn out to be nothing more prepossessing than a tinny upright, tucked against a wall in the kind of parlour where guests were invited to have a late-night cup of cocoa. Other times, it would be a grand piano in pride of place in an echoing, marble-floored lobby. Here in Singapore, the piano she found was a glossy black Kawai, full sized and nearly new, occupying a commanding position on a balcony above the hotel's rattan-furnished lounge. It was cordoned off with red velvet ropes strung between chrome bollards, but its curved lid was propped, invitingly, open.

Diana could hear, drifting up from the room below, the chink of ice in substantial tumblers, streams of chatter and bursts of laughter. Over the railing she could see men in boat shoes and open-necked shirts toasting each other with beer bottles wedged with lemon. Women with the aura of off-the-leash flight attendants sipped cocktails, their bright dresses showing off the kind of flawless brown ankles and shoulders that made Diana envious.

The ropes and bollards, Diana decided, didn't apply to her. She stepped over a low loop of velvet, and sat down at the piano. By way of a few exploratory scales, she introduced herself to the instrument, which met her touch with a reassuringly warm, even sound. A good piano, in Diana's world, was one that allowed her to imagine its sound rising off it in a lovely round bubble. And this was a good piano – good enough that she briefly considered putting herself through the paces of the Prokofiev concerto. But, no. Sleep did not lie in that direction.

Tonight was a night for her almost-finished love song. She set her fingers on the keys and softly began, hoping that the momentum of the music would carry her all the way to the last, perfect note.

As she played, she thought of Arie, about how it felt to love him, and be loved by him. She thought about all the things that people, and sometimes even Arie himself, couldn't see, or didn't understand.

Diana had never wished for a man of a certain height, or with a particular angle to his jawline, or with a dazzling future in some particular high-calibre profession. What she'd been looking for was something infinitely more precious – a certain architecture of the heart. Immediately that she met Arie, she'd been able to sense it within him – like a pale marble palace with open walls. Stable but delicate, solid but airy. From the very first, she'd known that in him, she had found a place that she could trust without question, a place she could rest, a place where she would always be free.

Somehow her song had to convey all of this, as well as how

treasured she felt when he set down a cup of tea each morning at her bedside, and how she loved his voice, which was mellow and gentle and sexy, whether on the other end of a telephone or in her ear in the darkness, and how grateful she was each time he refused – with perfect diplomacy – to be goaded into an argument with her mother; and also how it felt each time she arrived home at the end of a tour, scanned the airport arrivals hall for his face in the crowd, and found it.

She thought about how it would be, at the end of this trip, to take him into the piano room and play her song for him, and how good it would feel when he understood that she had made up her mind.

Have I? she asked herself.

Yes, she thought, *yes*. She would marry him. Even though she was afraid, even though she wasn't sure she would always get every part of it right. If it really was so important to him, then she would do it. And with that, her hands mapped their way across the last short stretch of the melody. E chord to A chord. A perfect cadence. It was obvious really, she thought, as the rightness of the chord progression raised pinpricks of tears at the back of her eyes.

'Yes,' Diana murmured to herself. 'That's right.'

She lifted her hands from the keys and smiled as the final notes of her love song hovered in the muggy air of the hotel balcony.

A fact of Arie's life was that if Diana was at home, there was music. She liked it loud, and had once explained to Arie that for her there was such a thing as a perfect volume. The way she described it, it was as if the music were being siphoned into her skull, and as it got louder it took up more and more space, until there came a moment of equilibrium when the sound precisely occupied the contours of the bones, squeezing out all other thought.

For Diana, Arie had learned, music was an all-purpose medication. She used rousing music to stir herself to action, maudlin music to soothe herself in distress, violent music if she needed to vent, and bittersweet music if she felt like crying.

Usually, if Arie woke on a Sunday morning to find Diana's half of the bed empty, there would already be music somewhere in the house. Whether she was singing in the bathroom, playing the Steinway behind the frosted glass doors of the piano room, listening to the radio in the kitchen or cranking the stereo so that sound filtered into every room of the house, the nature of the music would tell Arie everything he needed to know about Diana's mood.

This particular Sunday morning, though, the house was quiet. The only accompaniment to Arie's solitary routine – make coffee, shower, shave, wander down to the bakery for a *pain au chocolat*, read the newspaper at the kitchen bench – was a tune he was humming, unsatisfactorily, to himself. It was that tune she'd been playing in the middle of the night when he'd gone into the piano room to coax her back to bed. He made a mental note to ask her again what it was. When she got home.

Travelling, for Diana, almost always brought on the slightly suspended feeling she had now, as she stood in the queue to board the Sunday night Air Pleiades Flight PQ108 from Singapore to Paris. No matter how far or how often she journeyed, travelling never made her feel that the world was small. Rather, it reminded her how vast and complicated the planet was – how many different people there were living inside their individual orbits, walking their particular streets, visiting their local shops, eating their accustomed foods, speaking their one or many languages.

Thinking of Arie, she took out her phone. The message she wrote was only one word long: *Sonder.*

It was Diana who'd come up with the name for Arie and Richard's business. Sonder – a word from the internet phenomenon the *Dictionary of Obscure Sorrows* – was a word to describe the sudden feeling or knowledge that everyone else around you was experiencing a reality as deep and complex as your own. It could happen in a busy street, or on a subway train, or – as it so often did for Diana – in an airport. All these people, and every single one of them full to the brim with pasts and futures, hopes and fears, friends and enemies, loves and losses.

She added an emoji to her message, the one of a smiling face with blushing cheeks, but then, calculating that it would be almost midnight back at home, and that Arie was likely to be asleep, she decided not to press send. She didn't want him sitting bolt upright in their bed and fumbling for his phone; she didn't want him worrying. She would send the message later, she thought, because in that moment Diana Clare was a woman who thought there was plenty of later to come.

She put her phone away and watched the people around her. Her attention was drawn to a small girl with large brown eyes and impossibly long black hair, who held tightly and proudly to the handle of her very own ladybird suitcase. She observed a handsome Nordic-looking couple who stood in the queue, each of them wearing a BabyBjörn carrier that held a small, white-haired baby. Each parent was clearly exhausted, but equally clearly on a mission to surmount their exhaustion without losing their shit.

Diana admired the flight attendants behind the check-in

booths, all of them with silver Pleiades constellation brooches pinned to their immaculate navy lapels. She had no way of knowing that they had all been away from home for the entire previous week, and that this was to be the last flight of their roster. Neither had she any way of knowing that they had arrived late at the airport, the crew bus having been delayed when a collision between a motorbike and a delivery van caused a pile-up on a rain-slicked freeway. With their beautifully pressed shirts and blouses, their polished black shoes, the women with their buns carefully sprayed, the men with their chins newly shaven, they concealed perfectly the rush they now faced to achieve an on-schedule departure time of 10.35 pm.

After flashing her passport and boarding pass, Diana made her way down the airbridge and stepped onto the plane. Inside, the air retained something of the warmth and humidity of the local conditions; Diana found it hard to believe that she would step off this plane into the pre-dawn of Charles de Gaulle Airport, where she would need her coat, scarf, hat and gloves. She was pleased to find she had been seated by a window, with a luxuriously empty seat next to her. Even better, the woman in the aisle seat, who wore a pair of expensive noise-cancelling headphones, showed no early signs of wanting to chat.

Beyond her porthole window, on the far side of a stretch of wet tarmac, lightning forked brightly on the horizon. Diana did not switch on her seat-back television, or open her novel to read. She tucked the airline's thin blue blanket around her, put her pillow against the arm of her seat to cushion her hip, and closed her eyes, so that she was already half asleep when the plane heaved itself up off the ground and into the air.

A flicked switch.

That's all it was, really – a switch flicked in the wrong direction, and one that someone on the crew might have noticed, had their flight preparations not been so rushed. But Diana would never know the details. She would never know that this particular plane had arrived earlier that day from Beijing with its crew reporting a frozen seal in the rear service door. She would never know that a ground engineer had switched the aircraft's pressurisation system to 'manual' for the purposes of his inspection, but neglected to switch it back to 'auto' when he'd finished. Neither would she know that because the system was set to manual, the valves controlling the flow of air into the cabin remained where they were – slightly open – when the engineer completed his investigation, so that as the plane climbed into the night sky, thinner air from outside seeped silently inside.

There were so many reasons to say 'if only'. An alarm sounded in the cockpit as the craft continued to ascend, alerting the captain and his co-pilot to the fact that the cabin had failed to pressurise. If only that alarm had not been identical in tone to the take-off and landing configuration warning that the pilots routinely tested before each flight. If only the pilots had not wasted crucial minutes in the cockpit with that distracting horn blaring in their ears. If only they'd realised what was really happening, instead of sending messages to their maintenance operations centre about how to turn off what they believed to be a false alarm. If only they'd recognised the beginnings of their disorientation and made recourse to their emergency oxygen supplies.

The cruel irony of oxygen deprivation is that it reduces the brain's ability to recognise the symptoms. As the pilots descended deeper into confusion, Diana woke from a dozing sleep, aware of a vague sense of unease among the passengers around her. Also, she felt strangely warm. Her toes tingled and . . . now she came to think of it, it was a little hard to catch a proper breath. She didn't understand that she and everybody else on the plane were now inside an incredibly brief window that is called – in the context of extreme oxygen deprivation – 'the time of useful consciousness'.

But if hypoxia is cruel, and deadly, it also comes with the blessing of a strange, dissociated euphoria. As the aircraft continued to climb, the temperature in the cabin fell. The air inside condensed, filling the plane with a ghostly cloud that Diana found curiously beautiful. She lifted a hand to touch it, and was almost surprised to find four pale fingers and a thumb there at the end of her arm. When an oxygen mask dropped from its overhead panel, Diana had a few seconds left before unconsciousness would claim her, but given that there was nothing she could have done to save herself, it was probably a mercy that the only thought triggered by the strange plastic jellyfish that dangled in front of her face, was the word *yellow*.

hold

IN MUSICAL NOTATION, the 'fermata' symbol – ⌢ – is an invitation from composer to musician to hold a note, a chord, or a pause in the music, for as long as the musician deems necessary. It is a statement of trust, an acknowledgement that the player will know, under the circumstances, what is best.

So hold the thought of Flight PQ108 making its way on autopilot through a cold, dark sky, not one of the 312 people aboard still alive.

After message upon message from Malaysian and Indian air traffic control authorities failed to re-establish contact with the flight, two Indian Air Force Flanker fighters were dispatched. Closing to within 200 feet of the airliner, the pilot of one of the Flankers adjusted the night-vision goggles that enabled her to confirm that both Air Pleiades pilots were in their seats, though their bodies were slumped forward over the controls.

Hold the thought of those Flankers continuing their escort, following the airliner westward, before breaking off at the far reaches of Indian airspace, where the pilots conducted a terse but professional handover to Pakistani officers, who carried on the vigil in their sleek F-16s. The stripes of the escorting planes changed several times more as the airliner made its way across the

Middle East into Europe, crossing the Caspian Sea, clipping the northern shore of the Sea of Azov.

Meanwhile, news of the ghost flight was breaking on the networks, the plane-tracking enthusiasts of the world having detected the unusual military activity in the skies. Embassy telephones rang and senior officials were pulled out of meetings or woken from their sleep as the plane followed its curving path over Ukraine, Poland and Germany, remaining for hours in a strange extended dawn, its western trajectory keeping it always just ahead of the morning's light. Fuel reserves spent at last, after fifteen hours Flight PQ108 spiralled into the Atlantic Ocean about 300 nautical miles west of the French coast.

Hold the thought of Arie Johnson at his desk at Sonder Digital late on a Monday afternoon when Richard got back to the office from a meeting with a serious face, and joined together two questions that on their own might have meant nothing much – 'Have you seen the news?' and 'Is Di already in Paris?' – but that, together, caused Arie's pulse to race. A story was just breaking, Richard said. A plane had gone down, he said. The words were still coming out of his mouth when Arie's mobile, its number listed on Diana's travel documents as the contact for her next of kin, began to ring.

The phone call over, Arie felt as if the earth had shifted and the rafters were collapsing around him and the walls were turning to rubble. Somebody who was probably Richard was asking questions, but Arie could barely hear him. Though the world was falling off its hinges, if he knew one thing in that moment, it was that Belinda Clare could not be allowed to hear this news through a telephone the way he had just done.

Arie snatched up his car keys.

Richard said, 'Mate, there's no way you should be—'

34

But Arie was already at the door.

Hold the thought of Arie driving out of the city, hoping against hope that he arrived at his destination before his mother-in-law switched on the television. He made his way to her as fast as he could, though it was necessary every now and then for him to pull over to withstand a crashing wave of grief.

Hold the thought of Belinda opening the door, of Arie uttering the words. Hold the thought of him trying to catch her as she buckled to the carpet.

Across the country, around the world, people watched the news. Some shivered at the thought of a plane flying through the night sky with nobody aboard left alive, an aerial *Mary Celeste*; others could not stop themselves from picturing the cold tableau of the plane's interior; others sent their hearts out to the people waiting for a plane that never arrived. Reports explained that the plane disintegrated on impact, that there would be no bodies to recover, no remains to be repatriated.

Hold the thought of Richard, going home to Lenka. Hold him the way he held her in their kitchen, while her sobs shook every square inch of her body.

Ten days later they sat – Arie and Belinda, Richard and Lenka – in a room made soft by gentle light coming through arched windows. There was a powerful scent of lily of the valley; at the front of the gathering there was no casket, only a large portrait of Diana. Belinda held Arie's arm so tightly that it might have hurt had he been able to feel bodily pain above the other ache, the one that racked up almost past endurance when the first of the hymns came to an end, and the congregation sang, 'Amen'.

She was Diana Clare, concert pianist and beloved of Arie Johnson, and the writer of a love song that she would never, now, play for him.

—INTERLUDE—

As BENE ROMERO stepped off a plane at Heathrow, he shrugged on a coat over the top of the thin jumper that had been all very well for Singapore, but was a long way from sensible in the January chill of London. He made his way through the terminal building to the baggage claim area where he dodged an overloaded trolley being pushed by a man too tired to be polite, and watched with amusement as a plane-load of irritable passengers jostled for position at a luggage carousel that had not even begun to move.

Bene adjusted his watch to London time, 5.30 am, aware of a pressure mounting in his chest. He didn't want to be standing here, stalled and waiting for his suitcase. He wanted already to be speeding home towards Winchmore Hill, and Beatrix. As the frustrating minutes passed, Bene became gradually aware that the people around him were no longer so fixated on elbowing their way to the front of the suitcase collection scrum. Instead, they were drifting towards various pillars in the baggage hall, looking up at the mounted television screens that were mutely broadcasting the news channel, the words of the announcers converted to auto-text.

Unconfirmed reports, Bene read, as he joined the rear of the nearest pack, *of a ghost flight over central Europe.* Moving closer to the screen, he read the words *Paris-bound* and *military escort.* There was some stock footage of an Air Pleiades jet on a runway, but the visuals were otherwise limited to the serious faces of the news anchors and that of the bow-tied former aviation engineer who was being beamed in from Seattle with a picture of Lake Washington as his backdrop.

On the faces of the people around him, Bene could see shock and disbelief, morbid curiosity, and something else, too. Relief. Yes, relief, because every passenger in the baggage hall, including Bene himself, had just now participated in the commonplace miracle of being scooped up from one point on the globe and set down only hours later in another place, far, far away.

'There but for the grace of God,' murmured a woman beside him.

Out of the airport at last, Bene found his Uber – a small hatchback whose silent driver wore a black hoodie that made him almost indistinguishable from his seat. It was not yet dawn, and as the car transported him through the winter streets, Bene had a sense of the city as a vast honeycomb in which, behind the closed doors and glowing curtained windows, people's dreams were giving way to the reality of their days.

From the radio came news of the first official confirmation that a passenger plane had crashed in the Atlantic Ocean west of France, and Bene – thinking of all those people in the world who were right now finding out that their lives had swerved catastrophically off-course – wanted even more acutely to be home with his daughter. Although he was sitting in the back of the car, he felt his right foot press down on an imaginary accelerator, as if this might somehow speed him to his destination.

Bene had been in Singapore for work, his boss at the boutique London public relations firm having sent him to meet with a key client. Bene was not entirely proud to say that the company he worked for had found its niche specialising in the green-washing of companies with less than enviable environmental credentials, but he could not deny taking pleasure in the fact that his boss was now increasingly trusting him, with his affable personality and talent for closing deals without ever becoming openly confrontational, to represent the firm in Asia.

He'd been away for only three days, but each of the days had been long because he'd been unable to contact Beatrix. This, of course, had been his own fault.

'Speak to me like that one more time, and you can hand over your phone,' he'd said, in the heat of an argument that inconveniently exploded right before he was about to leave.

Even as the words came out of his mouth, Bene knew that the chances of this tactic bringing Beatrix to heel were nil. She was, after all, his daughter.

'Confiscate my phone? Oh my God. You're so obvious.' Beatrix was fourteen. 'Can't you think of anything more original?'

Bene Romero, professional negotiator, cool-headed closer. That was him. Until he was in a power struggle with a teenage girl who could break his heart with one flex of her little finger.

'Well, I could confiscate your phone *and* your laptop.'

Beatrix yawned ostentatiously, and at that point the red cloud of Bene's anger rose up to obscure the trivial nature of the original disagreement. (He'd asked Beatrix to stack the dishwasher; she'd said she'd do it after she'd watched a movie; he'd said she needed to learn to delay gratification, so suggested she stack the dishwasher first and watch the movie second; she'd said, 'Juanita will be here in a minute'; and he'd said that was hardly the point, he wasn't having her grow up into an entitled little shit who expected other people to do her dirty work; and Beatrix, who actually wasn't spoiled – not right through to the core – said, 'All right, all right, I'll do it later'; and Bene had said, 'But when you say you'll do it later, you forget, so do it *now*'; she'd said, 'Just get off my case, will you?'; he'd said, 'If I'm not on your case, you'll spend the whole night like a lobotomised sloth', and for good measure, he'd followed up with a mime of her staring vacantly at a screen; she'd said, 'Go die in a fucking hole.')

'Right,' Bene said. 'That's it. Phone and laptop. Hand them over. Right now, Bea.'

She rolled her eyes, which didn't go down well, and by the time Bene set off for the airport, his carry-on bag held Beatrix's phone, Beatrix's laptop and the power cord to the desktop computer, plus the house modem, just for good measure. That would teach her, Bene thought, and all the way to Heathrow he felt righteous and powerful. It wasn't long, though – he got as far as his airline club lounge – before it all seemed embarrassingly petty.

In the time it took to knock back a few whiskies, Bene's remorse blossomed into full-scale guilt. He wanted to apologise, to mend the rift, but he couldn't call Beatrix because he'd taken her phone. And he couldn't email her because he'd taken her laptop. And he'd disabled the desktop and removed every means in the house of accessing wi-fi. Now, because of his own pig-headed thoroughness, his only conduit to Beatrix was Juanita.

Once, Juanita had been Beatrix's babysitter, but when Beatrix turned thirteen she insisted that she no longer needed such a thing.

'What if we just made up another name for it?' Juanita had cleverly suggested. 'You know, like a euphemism.'

'What's a euphemism?' Beatrix had asked.

'It's like a substitute word or phrase. Like "pre-loved" for "second-hand".'

'Okay then. It's perfect.'

'What is?' Juanita was befuddled.

'Euphemism. This is Juanita, my friendly euphemism.'

They had laughed, and the term had stuck.

Before Bene stepped onto the Singapore-bound plane he called Juanita's phone.

'Euphemism speaking.'

'Hey. Can I talk to Bea?'

'Why don't you call *her* phone?' Juanita asked, deadpan.

'Ah, not funny. Not right now.'

'You can't talk to her. She's asleep.'

'Is she really?'

'I don't know, Bene. She *says* she's asleep, okay?'

'Shit. Well . . . can you just tell her I'm sorry?'

'What did you do, hm? Were you a bit of an . . . arsehole?'

Bene felt weak. Being the one to ring up and beg for forgiveness made him feel like he was capitulating to a terrorist, and Juanita wasn't helping. But greater than his fear of weakness was his fear of Beatrix going to sleep with their argument unresolved. When Tess had been alive, it had been their unbroken rule to sort themselves out before they went to sleep. That meant there had been nights – oh, the sheer number of nights – when he and Tess had sat up until dawn going around and around in a labyrinth of accusation and recrimination, until they at last emerged into a clearing in which apologies were possible. And sex. That too.

From him and Tess had come Beatrix. And what had he expected, with the combination of their genes? A placid, even-tempered, agreeable child who stacked the dishwasher, peaceably, the moment she was asked? Bene knew that without a mother to see her through these turbulent years, Beatrix had no choice but to pile a double helping of attitude onto his plate. He also knew that he needed to do better, be calmer, control the fear that rose each time he sensed her hurtling away from him into a future that he wasn't yet ready to face.

Bene called again the following day from the hallway outside a meeting room in his Singapore hotel.

'She's gone out for a run,' Juanita told him.

'Beatrix doesn't run. *You* run.'

'We switched hobbies for the day. I'm just sitting here plotting ways to piss off my father.'

He called again the next day.

'She's around at Jamie's,' Juanita said.

'You let her go to *Jamie's*?'

'Chill, will you, Daddy Bear? Jamie's mother is at home. I made certain of this fact. And I will have you know that she has six thousand pounds' worth of surveillance equipment trained on the interior of Jamie's bedroom.'

Single father to a fourteen-year-old girl. It was a position that felt, to Bene, way above his pay grade. It wasn't just the weirdness, when in Tesco, of popping a packet of tampons into his shopping basket along with the milk and the digestive biscuits. Or the discomfort of standing outside a Topshop changing room, feeling like a perv with his armful of rejected B-cup bras. It was also the feeling that he'd been left with the monumental task of loving Beatrix enough for two parents, when he could only ever be one, and when he was fucking up even his part of it, royally, every second day of the week.

After another attempt at calling Beatrix in the early evening, London time ('She's got a face mask on. She doesn't want to smudge it,' Juanita had told him), Bene went to the cocktail lounge. It was late, well past midnight, but a decent number of folks were there, lounging on the rattan sofas with their drinks and their on-holiday bonhomie. Bene ordered a whisky, ignored a meaningful glance from a woman sitting alone with a complicated cocktail, and sat down to think about Beatrix.

Once, his daughter had been so small that she'd been able to sleep on her stomach while stretched along the length of his upturned forearm, her tiny skull cradled in his palm. Later, he'd been able to easily swing her off her feet, settle her onto his shoulders and walk with her that way for hours. Now, she was almost as tall as he was, and sometime in the last few years without him noticing precisely when, she had acquired a kind of solidity in her body that made him feel that she was – physically at least – fully grown.

Emotionally, he felt her pulling away from him, like a tethered boat in a storm. The ropes were creaking, and there were days when the idea of letting go of her was so tempting, to the point that it sometimes even seemed like the right thing to do. But then he would look more closely at the horizon of that particular storm and know that he had to hold on, no matter what – even if she slammed against him with all her power, even if she broke him apart.

By the time Bene realised he was listening to piano music, it seemed so much like the soundtrack to his thoughts that it took him a moment to realise that it was coming not from inside him, but from the balcony above the lounge. He tuned in to the melody, and for a time he tried to listen to it over the conversations of the people gathered nearby. Then, drawn by the song and wanting to hear it at closer range, he made his way up a flight of curving stairs.

The musician was a woman with long, pale ginger hair twisted into a single fraying braid that fell over one shoulder, and Bene saw immediately that she was no ordinary player. Her eyes were closed as her hands moved over the keys, and the expression on her face was such that Bene believed he'd have known she was playing a love song even if his ears were stopped with wax against the sound.

Behind and just to one side of her, Bene leaned against the balcony railing, cradling his whisky glass, and listened. When the woman reached the song's end, she lifted her hands and left them there, suspended above the keys, waiting for the final chord to dissolve into silence as the piano's strings returned to stillness.

She nodded, and smiled. Pleased with her song, Bene supposed. But also, he suspected, with something beyond it.

Bene held his breath, half expecting her to turn and see him, her audience of one. If she did so, he decided, he would applaud. But she didn't. Instead, she started the song again, from the beginning. The woman played the piece through several times, as if trying to perfect it, and for some time after Bene was back in his room, the song played on in his head.

The next morning, Bene checked out of the hotel, left his luggage in storage and spent a few hours shopping: new earphones for Beatrix, and a sequinned T-shirt he hoped she wouldn't consider a fashion disaster.

Returning to the hotel in the early afternoon, with hours still to kill before he needed to go to the airport, Bene found himself drawn back to the piano on the balcony. With studied nonchalance, he moved a silver bollard aside and sat before the keys. From downstairs came the hiss of a coffee machine, the squeal of cutlery on crockery, chatter, a baby crying.

In the daylight, the marks of fingertips were visible in the faint covering of dust that lay on the instrument's gleaming black case. Although Bene had played since he was a boy, he was nowhere near the league of the woman who'd sat at this piano the night before. Not wanting to disturb those enjoying their meals downstairs, he allowed his fingers to roam over the keys without pressing down, producing a rendition of 'Für Elise' that – by virtue of being silent – was as perfect as could be imagined. He thought of the ginger-haired pianist, and wondered whether or not there was a match between the music she could hear in her head and the degree of accomplishment she could produce with her hands.

Probably, he thought, a little enviously.

Then he saw it. A notebook. It was on top of the piano, its black leather cover blending almost entirely into the background. Slightly smaller than A4 size, it had sepia-toned pages printed with blank musical staves, and a length of narrow scarlet ribbon for a place-keeper. On the inside cover of the book was an address. Australia, he noted.

The first few pages of the book were taken up with the notation for various complicated fingering exercises. But then, on the pages that followed, he found it. The song. Until he saw it there on the page in front of him, its pencilled notes darker and crisper in some places than others, he hadn't known precisely how much he'd wanted to hear it again. Gently, quietly, a little haltingly, he played. The song began in the key of A, but as it transitioned beautifully through a sequence of other keys, Bene felt the melody swell inside him, resonating with his homesickness and his remorse.

Then, unexpectedly, the notation petered out. The beautiful ending that Bene had heard the pianist play the night before . . . it wasn't on the page. He concentrated, trying to remember both the sound and the feeling of the way the woman had brought her song to a close. He tried a few pathways, and a few more, until at last his fingers found the right one. It took him to an E chord, and from there to an A chord to finish.

'Yes,' he murmured with satisfaction, as the remains of the music hovered in the air around his ears.

When at last Bene closed the notebook and took it down from the piano's music desk, there was a tug-of-war going on inside him. He had a strong desire to keep the book for himself, but an equally strong desire to do the right thing. In the end, his sense of obligation sent him to the hotel's concierge desk.

'I'd like to get a message to one of your guests,' Bene told the immaculate young man behind the counter. 'She has ginger hair, very long. I think she might be Australian? Do you know who I mean?'

The young man nodded apologetically, and told Bene that the lady in question had checked out earlier in the day. Bene thought. He rationalised that if he left the music book at the hotel, and even if the staff promised to return it to its owner, it would most likely end up languishing in a lost property box. Whereas if he were to take it home himself, he could be sure to post it back to her. Tightening his grip on the notebook, he affected a crestfallen look and said to the concierge, 'Well, thank you all the same.'

On the flight back to London, Bene played the song's notes on the imaginary keyboard of his tray table. Using a purloined hotel-issue pen, he wrote the last few bars of the song onto the blank staves of the pianist's notebook. It would be like a message – of admiration, of understanding – from him to her. He was playing the song again now, in the Uber, forming the final perfect cadence with his fingers on his knee as the small black car cruised up the street where he lived.

'Anywhere here, thanks,' Bene told the driver.

At his doorway, Bene took a deep breath and remembered all his resolutions about Beatrix. He would be a better father. Pick his battles more carefully. Be wiser. Calmer. More loving. Steadier. And no matter what, he would hold on. Perhaps he would make Beatrix pancakes for breakfast. Or maybe he could give her a morning off school and take her out somewhere nice. Just the two of them.

Before Bene could unlock the door, it opened. In his hallway stood Juanita, almost insanely trim in her running kit. Dark and delicate-looking, she was the only woman Bene had ever seen who looked truly beautiful with a septum piercing. Not that this fact stopped him from wanting to tear the fine silver ring out of her nose, just in case it gave Beatrix ideas.

'Well, welcome home, o holder of all technology,' Juanita said.

Bene, stepping from the frosty street into the warmth of his house, observed Juanita's packed bags in the hallway. 'You look like you're ready to do a runner. Was she really that monstrous?'

'No! She's always a sweetheart . . . for me.'

'Yeah, thanks for that.'

'While I've been looking after your princess, though, I've been losing my form. I'm pretty keen to get a run in this morning, if you're ready to accept the baton?'

'Of course, of course. Thanks for being here,' Bene said. 'I don't know what I'd do without you. So how was she, really?'

'Oh, you know. Right after you left there was some inter-galactic rage, but by the second day I'd say we were only at white-hot fury. Last night, I think we scaled it back even further to poisonous wrath. So . . . by now, I'm guessing you're at simmering hostility or similar. She's through there,' Juanita said, gesturing to the living room.

'She's awake?'

'Asleep on the couch.'

'Really?'

'Don't think she'd admit it, but I'm pretty sure she wanted to see you as soon as you got home. Get started on venting some of that hostility.'

As Juanita moved about the house, collecting her belongings and tidying up the kitchen, Bene regarded his daughter, curled under a bunched throw-rug on the couch. As he straightened the rug, pulling a fold of it up over Beatrix's shoulder, the song played on in his head.

When he was a boy, Bene had taken piano lessons on Saturday mornings at a house in Seven Sisters. His teacher was young and unorthodox, with pigtails and denim overalls, and also a large glass jar of jammy dodgers that she'd open up at the end of a lesson – if Bene had been good. Bene had liked the jammy dodgers much more than the drills, but in secondary school when his guitar-playing mates asked him to join their indie-rock cover band, he had cause to be grateful for his young teacher's insistence.

Beatrix was musical, too. Although she had rejected just

47

about every other vestige of her childhood as her skirts short-ened and her eye make-up intensified, she hadn't given up her music. Like Tess, she played the flute, and Bene would never forget the day mother and daughter had come home with Beatrix's first instrument.

'It comes in three pieces, Daddy,' six-year-old Beatrix had declared. 'Three pieces, just like our family.'

At that time, Tess had been in the middle of her first fight against breast cancer. She'd already amassed a significant collec-tion of silk headscarves and angora berets to wear in place of her lost, sandy curls. Now those same thick curls were back, but on Beatrix's head, and at this moment they were spread out over the couch cushions in a profusion of knots and snarls.

Packed down into one corner of the living room was all that remained of Bene's life in music. An electronic keyboard, a pair of quality headphones, a meagre shelf of recording equipment, some stacks of sheet music and a small collection of dusty CDs.

Bene switched on his keyboard but turned the volume down, so as not to disturb Beatrix with his playing. Absorbed in the song, he didn't at first notice when Beatrix woke. It wasn't until she was standing in front of his keyboard, her face puffy with sleep, her hair a beautiful mess, that he looked up.

'What's that?' she asked, and Bene was relieved to see no trace in her expression of the hostility that Juanita had predicted.

'It's a . . . love song,' Bene said.

'It's really nice.'

The father studied the daughter. The daughter studied the father just as closely.

'So, do you still hate me?' Bene asked.

'I never hate you,' she said. 'Not even when I hate you.'

Bene shuffled over on his stool to make room. Beatrix sat

beside him and rested her head on his shoulder, smelling of bubblegum and sleep, and he played the love song through another time.

'Did *you* write it?' she asked.

'Is there any need to sound quite so surprised?'

'No, no. I didn't mean that. I meant . . . well, you don't . . . you haven't . . . not for the longest time.'

'I didn't write it,' Bene admitted. 'It was more like I found it.'

'It's beautiful.'

'You know, we could have a go at arranging it as a duet? The flute could play the melody?'

Beatrix shrugged, but Bene was too pleased to see her to be annoyed.

'Want to go get your flute?'

'Tired,' she said, then yawned and stretched.

'Go on,' he urged.

Beatrix grumbled, but she got up anyway, and before she went upstairs she landed a cursory kiss on her father's cheek. In a moment she would come back down again, open the flute case and fit the three pieces of her instrument together. She would warm up her lips, and the instrument itself, and together they would play.

As Bene waited for her to return, he understood that there was every chance that tonight, or perhaps even before then, there would be a fresh kerfuffle, whether it was about the dishwasher or the state of Beatrix's floordrobe, the age-appropriateness of her latest Netflix obsession or an invitation to a party that Bene thought likely to be dodgy. He knew that – perhaps even today – he would screw up. But he also knew he would then try to do better. Screw up and try to do better; screw up and try to do better. Probably, there wasn't any other way to hold on.

evie

APPROXIMATELY TWENTY MILES south-west of Bene and Beatrix's home in Winchmore Hill, an unexceptional dawn gradually lightened the historic facade of a pub on the banks of the River Thames. It was called the Noble Swan, in honour of the big white birds that fed in the waterway and stretched their wings on the banks of the nearby Isleworth Eyot.

When Evie Greenlees, the barmaid, arrived with the keys, she was met by Gordon Philpott and his aged spaniel, Betty, even though it was not yet twenty to eleven.

'Morning, Evie,' Gordon said, and as man and dog turned their rheumy eyes on her in entreaty, she couldn't see how she could possibly insist that they remain outside in the cold until opening time.

'Morning, Gordon. Hey, Betty,' Evie said. She opened the door and allowed the pair to shuffle in. Catching a combined whiff of wet dog and stale, unwashed human, she wondered just how many years it had been since Gordon had dry-cleaned his tweed coat.

Gordon and Betty took up their regular spot at a table that was equidistant from the fire that Evie would soon light and the television set that she switched on immediately. She handed Gordon the remote control, figuring that he could enjoy his darts or his snooker, at least until somebody else came in wanting to watch the football.

This morning, though, as Evie kneeled at the hearth waiting for the firelighters to wear down the defiance of the kindling, and as Betty stretched out on the floorboards and began to snore, Gordon made the surprise move of selecting the news channel.

'Air Pleiades is your lot, isn't it?' he asked.

Evie, intent on the fire, didn't hear him properly. 'Sorry, Gordon?'

'Air Pleiades. The airline,' he said.

'What about it?'

'It's like you, from Down Under, isn't it?'

It was a rare day at the Noble Swan when the fact that Evie was Australian went unremarked. The regulars made good-natured sport of her accent, told jokes in which Australians featured in place of Irishmen, and just a few weeks ago had thought themselves hilarious when they presented her with a pair of Dame Edna Everage spectacles as a Christmas gift.

'Air Pleiades? Yes, last I checked.'

'Well, you won't want to fly with them when you go home,' Gordon observed. 'Horrible business.'

'What is?' Evie asked.

'That,' Gordon said, waving the remote at the television. 'Bloody terrible.'

A few dismal twists of smoke were rising from the kindling as Evie stood to look. On the screen was a map of Europe, with a curving dotted line overshooting the French coast to end in a big, red X. The text under the image read, AIR PLEIADES FLIGHT PQ108 CRASH SITE: 312 DEAD.

'Oh,' Evie said, a hand going to her chest. 'That's awful.'

Evie had flown Air Pleiades the first time she'd gone overseas. She'd been seventeen years old and on a student trip to Japan. Although she stayed away only a month, when she stepped onto the plane for the journey home, the deeply Australian accents of the Air Pleiades flight attendants had been enough to move her to tears. She'd also flown Air Pleiades when – at the age of twenty-two – she'd flown out of Melbourne with a one-way ticket, a backpack, a wristwatch perpetually stuck at a few minutes to five o'clock, and the half-baked notion of becoming a poet. That was four years ago, and so far all Evie had to show for her travels was a bundle of notebooks filled with unpublished poems.

When she started out, she flew to Los Angeles then made her way north to San Francisco, where she got a job as a croupier on a cruise ship that plied the Mexican Riviera. After eighteen months, she stepped off and headed to Canada, where she leapfrogged the country, ski resort to ski resort, working as a chambermaid, to land in Quebec, where she boarded a flight to London. Other than life itself, eligibility for a five-year UK ancestry visa – now one-fifth used up – was the only useful gift her father had ever given her.

'Never been one for travelling, myself,' Gordon said. 'You Aussies, though, you're all travellers, aren't you? Suppose you'd want to be if you had the rotten luck to be born in a country full of murderers and thieves.'

Evie didn't react; she had long since learned to let such jibes slide. She kept her eyes on the television, where footage from Charles de Gaulle Airport showed flashes of an arrivals board and images of people in coats and scarves holding each other as they sobbed with shock and grief.

Evie – like everyone else in the world, she supposed – had a horror of plane crashes. Every time she took her seat on a plane, she half-imagined what it would be like. How would she behave? If she knew the plane that held her aloft was going to fall out of the sky, would she turn to the person next to her and say something profound? Or would she just scream, even though it could do no good at all? Or would she shut her eyes and try to disappear? At what point, exactly, would she die? And would it hurt?

By now, Evie thought, all that suffering was over for the passengers and the crew of Flight PQ108. At the same time, the distress of the people who loved them had only just begun. The idea of this was enough to make Evie choke up.

'I reckon we ought to raise a glass to the poor bastards, don't you?' Gordon said, the eyes in his wrinkled face suddenly as wide as a child's.

Evie, wiping at one eye with the heel of her hand, gave a short burst of almost-laughter. 'You dreadful old rascal.'

'Go on, love. It's close enough to eleven. What's ten minutes between friends?'

The TV news rolled on while Evie shook her head and let herself through the hinged section of the bar. She reached down the Glenfiddich, and as she poured Gordon's first nip of whisky for the day, she imagined a wedge of the Atlantic Ocean rising up in a curve like a huge, blue mouth – crying out in sadness before it swallowed a plane whole. She would have to remember, she thought, to write that down.

TWO

(two years later)

three syllables

THE SUMMER AFTER the one in which Diana died, nobody picked the fruit from the apricot trees at the far end of her mother's yard. Instead the apricots hung from the branches, getting heavier and sweeter, softer and more deeply orange, until at last they fell to the ground.

This did not seem to matter to the trees, which only shed their leaves in the autumn and proceeded to wait out the winter, so that in spring they could put forth the blossoms that would eventually transform into the hard, green nuts of the young fruits. By the time these were ripe, their pinkish-orange skins stippled with red in the places where they'd been touched by the sun, high summer had come once again and Diana had been gone for almost two years.

Mid-morning on New Year's Eve, Arie arrived at Diana's mother's old weatherboard farmhouse, and although his knock went unanswered he opened the front door, knowing that Belinda would be outside, having already begun their day's task. He walked the length of the cool, shadowed hall and, just before he reached the back door, failed to resist the temptation to glance into the section of the wraparound veranda that had long ago been closed in for a bedroom.

This space was so full of memories that it seemed to Arie that he could almost see them, flitting about in the air with the dust motes. The room was narrow, a rickety double bed taking up almost all the space between its walls. Arie remembered the dehydrated feeling of being woken too early by the sun through those thin cotton curtains. He remembered, too, the smell of old rubber pillows, and the quiet way he and Diana had to move together in that bed if they didn't want it to creak.

He looked away, took a weather-beaten Akubra from a hook at the back door, and stepped out onto the porch. He could see Belinda down at the bottom of the yard, halfway up a stepladder with a bucket under one arm. In a T-shirt and denim shorts, she looked thinner than ever.

'Morning,' he called, and she waved.

He knew the first thing he and Belinda had to do was to get through the awkwardness of a greeting. Even now, after everything they'd been through together, these stilted moments still had to be borne.

There had been hugging on the day of Diana's service, and on one – but only one – of the days when he and Belinda visited Diana's memorial in a churchyard that lay a ten-minute drive, on a winding country road, from the farmhouse. There, on the windward side of a rose garden, was a brick wall that had been specially designed to accommodate metal drawers full of ashes. The face of each drawer was engraved with a name and the dates that had bracketed a life, but Arie found it impossible, as he set down his roses or tulips or sunflowers at the base of that sunny wall, to forget that Diana's drawer was empty, and that her last resting place was a long, cold way away.

Arie crossed the daisy-studded lawn to the small orchard at its far end, and there he stood ready, just in case Belinda climbed down from the stepladder and opened her arms to him. But she didn't. She only wobbled slightly on the tread of the ladder; she too, Arie thought, was experiencing an internal battle between the instinct to reach out and fear of a cheek-kiss going astray or an embrace turning awkward.

'They're perfect,' she said instead, looking up into the laden boughs of the tree.

Arie nodded. He tried not to look down at the ground, where a scattered carpet of apricot pits was all that remained of last year's wasted harvest.

The picking was slow and pensive, Arie placing each apricot in the bucket as carefully as if it were an egg – no bruising allowed. As he gentled the fruits away from their branches, he could almost imagine that Diana was there with them, climbing up and down a nearby stepladder, singing, her pale skin turning pink in the summer sun, no matter how wide the brim of her sun hat.

'Another year gone,' Belinda said into the leaves that surrounded her face. It seemed to Arie that there was an edge of reproach in her voice, and he felt unaccountably guilty, even though he knew it was hardly his fault that the earth had once again lapped the sun.

'Making any New Year's resolutions?' Arie asked. He had a habit, when he was with Belinda, of trying to minimise conversational risk by making such small talk, even though he knew that it was just as likely to be met with a snappish response as talk of any other kind.

'Ha,' she said, drily. 'Are *you*?'

'I am. My resolution for this year is to return all the casserole dishes to their rightful owners.'

After Diana's death, the sheer number of casseroles – left on the doorstep wrapped in tea-towels or pressed still warm into Arie's hands – had been overwhelming. The influx had dwindled after a couple of months, but the chilli con carnes and the ham-chicken-and-asparaguses had lived on in the freezer for what felt like eternity. Arie had recently part-defrosted the last of these condolence meals, consigning the solid lumps of them to the garbage, but now he was left with the stress of trying to work out who belonged to the yellow dish, and who to the CorningWare with the little blue flowers on the side.

Belinda gave a faintly bitter laugh. 'At least you *got* casseroles. I suppose people thought you needed them more, being a mere male.'

'Ironic, isn't it?' Arie replied. 'If the tables had been turned, Diana really would've needed casseroles.'

'What do you mean?' Belinda's tone was brittle.

Arie knew he had blundered and should probably shut up, but he somehow found himself saying, 'Well, cooking was hardly Diana's favourite thing to do.'

'Diana could cook. I made sure Diana could cook.'

'Diana could have done anything she put her mind to,' Arie said, in an effort to appease her, even though the truth was that Diana's understanding of cooking had been mashing avocado onto toast.

'Diana certainly could.'

Diana.

That word. Three syllables that made up their own tiny melody.

It was true that in the winter Arie chopped Belinda's firewood, and in springtime unblocked her gutters. For her part, she usually sent him back to the city with jars of green tomato chutney and foil-wrapped slabs of fruit cake. But the real reason he kept coming to visit, which was also the reason Belinda kept inviting him, was that when they were together they could say those three syllables as often as they wanted. *Diana, Diana, Diana.*

In Belinda's pleasantly ramshackle kitchen there was mismatched crockery on the open shelves, threadbare tea-towels hanging over the rail of an old-fashioned wood stove, and patchy linoleum that peeled up at the corners of the floor. It was a room full of things that Diana had touched, used and loved. By the kettle was a Humpty Dumpty eggcup from her childhood. Rather appropriately, she'd dropped it and it had smashed. Rather less appropriately, Belinda had put it back together again. It had not been a professional job, and a gluggy seam of Araldite was now a permanent feature on poor Humpty's moony forehead.

Soon, a batch of apricots from the morning's harvest lay pitted and quartered on a thick pine board. A glass bowl of sugar stood warming in the oven, and Arie knew that if he opened the freezer, he would find a saucer loaded with half a dozen teaspoons. Laid out on the bench were a set of scales, several paper sacks of sugar, a bowl of lemons, a selection of wooden spoons, and a tin that spent every other day of its life in the pantry and came out only on jam day.

The Clare family's apricot jam was famous. It never caught, never burned, was never too runny and never too firm, and it kept in the jar both its jewel-bright colour and the fresh taste of summer fruit.

The secrets of making this jam were many, from the ideal size of each batch (small) to the shape of the pan (relatively shallow, with flaring sides), and from the precise ratio of fruit to sugar (it was complicated) to the best variety of lemon to provide the necessary squeeze of acid (Meyer). No apricot pips were added to the bubbling mixture; that was considered a heresy in Clare family lore. The only things that went into the jam – besides fruit, sugar, lemon juice and diligence – were the contents of the secret tin. Although if Diana had been there with them, she would have insisted on one other ingredient. Music.

'What do you feel like listening to?' Arie asked, when the first batch was on the hob.

'You choose.'

The stereo was in the living room. Diana's first piano was there, too – an upright with a mottled chestnut case and, on its front panel, a matching pair of tiny brass sconces filled with wax from another time and place. Arie opened the piano's lid to reveal a set of stained yellow-grey keys that reminded him of old people's teeth. On the floor-level corners of the piano, the timber was scarred where it had been chewed by a pet rabbit, but Arie noticed there was barely a trace of dust on or between the picture frames propped along the length of the top. Diana in white shorts at a school cross-country, holding a green ribbon; Diana with a home-administered haircut and oversized teeth; Diana with a huge rabbit in her arms, its ears half obscuring her face; Diana with a Dolly Varden birthday cake; Diana in a cap and gown.

Belinda's CD collection mixed Midnight Oil with a recording of Diana playing with the London Philharmonic, the Indigo Girls with a recording of Diana playing with the Sydney Symphony Orchestra, Tori Amos with a recording of Diana and the Staatskapelle Dresden. Arie made his choice: Clara Schumann's *Piano Concerto in A minor*. Or, to be precise, Clara Schumann's *Piano Concerto in A minor* as played by Diana Clare and the Berliner Philharmoniker.

'Schumann,' Belinda observed, when Arie returned to the kitchen to the opening strains of the concerto. 'Diana always said it was good jam-making music.'

'Stirring,' Arie said, and Belinda, in deference to the old joke, managed to produce a wry smile.

'I think we're ready,' Belinda said, peering into the jam pan.

'Are you going to do it?'

'You do it,' Belinda said, and handed Arie the tin. On its lid, in pastel colours, was a drawing room scene involving women with complicated Georgian hairdos and dresses in the shades of a washed-out rainbow.

'This was always Diana's favourite part,' Arie said.

Inside were four silver forks, all exactly alike, each with a fleur-de-lis etched into the handle. In a moment they would go into the jam mixture, where it was their special task to prevent the jam from catching and burning on the bottom of the pan. According to Belinda, these particular utensils – which had belonged originally to her great-grandmother – were the only ones in the world that could be 100 per cent relied upon to do the job.

'I was going to leave them to Diana. Now what will I do with them?' Belinda asked, and in her tone Arie caught a hint of the kind of grief-related masochism that he sometimes gave in to himself.

'I could pop them in your coffin,' Arie offered, 'so the secret of your jam goes with you to your grave.'

At this, Belinda jabbed him in the ribs with one of the forks, actually quite hard, drawing his attention to the anger that simmered in her, and not so very far beneath the surface either.

'Ow,' he said.

'Sook,' she said, and handed him the fork, which he dropped into the jam mixture along with the other three.

From this point onwards, it was Arie's job to stir – not too little, not too much – and Belinda's to supervise. Although in one sense Diana was gone from them, in another sense she was right there in the music that flowed around them, as sweet and strong as the apricot-scented vapour that rose from the pan.

After a while, Belinda fetched a teaspoon from the freezer and scooped up a small amount of jam. She tipped the spoon this way and that, gauging the speed at which the jam moved across the cold metal.

'A bit longer,' she announced.

So Arie kept stirring and the jam bubbled on.

When Diana on the CD brought the concerto to its rousing conclusion, Arie half watched as Belinda drew her fingertips beneath her eyelids, catching the smudges of her mascara. Those pale eyelashes. Like Diana's.

'You all right?' he asked, carefully.

'She should be here. This was always one of her favourite days of the year.'

'It was,' Arie affirmed.

Belinda pulled a crumpled tissue out of the pocket of her shorts and dabbed at her eyes. 'You know, my hairdresser told me the other day that she thought I'd be *out of the woods* by now.'

Arie raised his eyebrows. '*Out of the woods*, hey? Well. Apparently, I should be *over the worst*.' He signalled quote marks in the air with his fingers. 'My GP said so.'

'Oh, really? Mine said I should be *about to turn the corner*.'

'My sister reckons I ought to be *getting back on my feet* by now,' Arie countered.

'Apparently, I should be ready to—'

'Let me guess . . . *move on with your life*?'

Belinda scoffed. With vehemence, she said, 'It's all very well

64

for other people to say. They don't understand that Diana *was* my life. I had my turn, and that's what I did with it. I had her.'

Arie knew how conversations like this were supposed to go. His part was to argue, to tell Belinda that there was still time, that she was young yet, that it was impossible to know what was out there on the horizon of her life. He knew he was supposed to say all of the things that people said to him. Instead, he said, 'I know what you mean.'

'No, you *don't*,' Belinda said, and if she'd been a cat, her hackles would have risen all the way down her spine. 'You can, you can . . . just start again.'

'How?'

'It's completely different for you. I can't just go and have another daughter. But you're, what? Thirty-five? You've got your—'

'Whole life ahead of me. Yeah, yeah. Blah, blah.'

'You'll find someone else,' she said, almost accusingly.

Now it was Arie's turn to give a bitter laugh. He could no more magic up another Diana than Belinda could.

'How?' Arie asked, sounding a little angrier than he'd intended. '*Where?*'

But Belinda simply shrugged, and for a while the only sound in the kitchen was the *glop, glop, glop* of the thickening jam.

what about love?

WHEN EVIE GREENLEES dreamed of publishing a book of her poems, which she did every day, she sometimes thought the title might be *Dandelion Days*. She felt such an affinity with dandelions, those little white afros of the plant world whose seeds travelled on the wind, landed wheresoever they happened to land, and grew wherever they could. In the poems Evie wrote about her own life, they seemed to sprout up everywhere.

There was a dandelion poem inside the envelope that she held in gloved hands as she stood, late in the afternoon of the year's last day, beside an old, hexagonal postbox on Edinburgh's Royal Mile. Painted the quintessential shade of glossy red, the ornate postbox might have been Victorian, or maybe Edwardian. Evie didn't know exactly, but she had come to this particular portal of the Royal Mail because it was unusual and rather beautiful, and she felt that these two things might bring her luck.

She had been standing before the postbox for much longer than was strictly necessary, trying to ignore the dead cold that was infiltrating the knitted hat she'd pulled low over the dark bob of her hair and seeping through the seams of the unlined coat she'd buttoned right up to her chin. She wished she'd worn more

66

adequate shoes, and not the low-cut ballet slippers inside which her feet had gone numb.

The last two years, for Evie, had been a gradual drift in a northerly direction. When she'd had enough of London and the Thames-side pub with its crew of aged regulars, she found a job in a café in a medieval town on the Suffolk coast, where she landed a house-sitting gig in a tiny cottage on the edge of the village green. Then, when the owners of the cottage returned from abroad, Evie allowed the breeze to carry her to York, where she took a position as a barmaid in an old pub, lodgings included. There had been something poetic, to Evie, in the precipitous staircase that led to her attic room, in the steeply sloping walls that made her bend her neck when she sat up in bed at night, and also in the bare light bulb that hung from the ceiling, so dim that it might almost have been a candle.

Evie didn't know precisely what it was that told her when it was time to leave one place and try another. Sometimes the desire to move on crept up on her over a period of weeks, and other times it arrived like someone jumping out from behind a sofa at a surprise party, and shouting, *It's ti-ime!* That was how it was when she left York and crossed the Scottish border just as the Edinburgh Fringe Festival was getting underway. She bought a second-hand tent from a thrift shop and pitched it in a crowded campground for the duration. The festival had come to an end, then the summer, too, but Evie had stayed on as the days shortened and the temperature fell.

She stamped her cold feet on the pavement by the side of the postbox.

You don't have to do it now, she told herself. *You could wait until tomorrow.*

The envelope was addressed to a venerable publishing house, one that had put out a call for poems to be considered for an anthology called *Ten Lines*. Every poem submitted had to be precisely that: ten lines long. The one Evie had chosen to send was called 'Dandelion Clocks' and she knew it by heart, of course, since she had agonised over every last syllable. She didn't really know if it was good or not, but she did know the general consensus was that if you wanted to be a published poet you just had to keep flinging little parts of yourself out into the world until, at last, one of them caught someone's attention.

She knew all the stories about writers papering the walls of their studies with rejection slips, but so far about three-quarters of all the refusals Evie had received had arrived electronically. An email folder full of 'We regret to advise you . . .' and 'Thank you for your recent submission, but . . .' didn't seem nearly so noble, nor so graphic, as a wall covered in paper-and-ink correspondence, but the net effect was the same – as yet, none of the poems she had sent out into the ether had found itself a home.

This one, though . . . she had a feeling about it. Squeezing the envelope tightly, she silently recited the words.

Dandelion Clocks

Accurate.
Wound on the language
of wind
and the eager breath
of children counting hours
their own way,
launching fluff parachutes
into a future
that only aches
to be yellow again.

You could wait until tomorrow. New Year's Day might be luckier.

Then, she told herself quite sternly, *Stop procrastinating and just do it. Now!*

Before she could change her mind, Evie pressed a kiss onto the back of the envelope and slid it into the slot. She exhaled audibly, nodded to the postbox in a gesture of farewell, put her hands in her pockets, and set off up the street.

Edinburgh, Evie thought, was the stoniest city she had ever known. There was stone underfoot, and stone walls to every side, and stone arches to pass beneath, and high above it all a stone castle that seemed to grow quite naturally out of some stony cliffs. It seemed to Evie as she strode up the Royal Mile and turned into North Bridge that something of the architecture was seeping into the air that she breathed, which was cold and mineral in her lungs. She was aware of her feet, too, which were aching from a full day of standing behind a Starbucks counter.

By working three days a week at the café and five nights a fortnight behind the bar at the Thorn and Thistle, Evie was managing to stitch together a living of sorts. She was rostered on at the pub tonight, of course – it was New Year's Eve after all – but her shift didn't start until nine o'clock. There was time enough to go home, grab a bite to eat and change one lot of black clothes (that didn't show the coffee spills) for another (that didn't show the beer).

Today, since before breakfast time, she'd been fixing cappuccinos and doling out cookies, splitting bills and squiggling runes with a white felt-tip pen on the black plastic lids of takeaway cups. She'd taken the job at Starbucks not because of any great love of making pumpkin spice cream Frappuccinos, but because this particular branch of the franchise was located on the Canongate, on the corner of Crichton's Close . . . and Crichton's Close was the address of the Scottish Poetry Library. So that was where Evie spent her lunchtimes. There, she would browse shelves tightly packed with slender volumes, every one of them a sliver of a poet's heart. Sometimes she just stood and closed her eyes to see if she could hear them beating. Always lunchtimes flew by too quickly.

Nearing her bus stop, Evie was aware of the sounds and smells drifting her way from the midwinter markets, which had filled the East Princes Street Gardens with their fairground rides, bric-a-brac stands and food stalls. This night would be a big one for the traders, and in a few hours' time the strains of 'Auld Lang Syne' would ring out through the city.

Evie threw 50p to a kilted piper who had likely been playing 'Scotland the Brave' and 'Amazing Grace' on rotation for several hours already, and dodged a young man who'd started work early on his New Year's Day hangover, and as she walked, she mulled over something that had happened at work that day.

Just after lunch, she'd made a coffee for a customer. Nothing remarkable there, of course, except that the customer had been Slim Lorain, the poet. A few nights earlier, she'd seen him read at the poetry library. Slim had tanned skin and a white walrus moustache that obscured his entire mouth, and he wore his equally white hair in a low, thick ponytail. On the library's mezzanine floor, sitting beside Dave, Evie had listened as Slim Lorain's smooth accented voice had painted pictures of big skies and wild animals, broken hearts and the invisible touch of angels. Afterwards, Evie had quietly sipped wine and nibbled cheese and crackers, leaving it to Dave – who was also a real, actual poet – to introduce himself to Slim and say how good the reading had been.

Today, in the daylight of the café, Slim had looked a little older, a bit smaller, a touch more human. At the sight of him, Evie's Starbucks smile had switched from autopilot to genuine.

'What can I get for you?'

'Caffé Misto if you please,' he'd said in that raw silk voice of his.

'What size?'

'What do I have to choose from?'

'Short, Tall, Grande, Venti.' Evie had gestured to the model cups on the counter, and the poet had looked bemused.

'Funny world, isn't it, where "tall" is on the shorter side of things? What do you recommend?'

'I guess you could choose by what you want to be,' Evie had offered. Again, she tapped the lids of the cups as she went through the options. 'You want to be Short? Tall? Grand? Or' – she tapped the Venti – 'twenty and Italian?'

The poet laughed. 'Now you put it that way, it's obvious, isn't it?'

When Evie came back to the counter and fitted the lid over the poet's takeaway Venti, he'd looked at her closely and put his head on an inquisitive angle. 'I think I know you.'

'Oh, I doubt that.'

'I do. I do know you,' he'd said, nodding. 'Aren't you Dave Wright's girlfriend?'

Evie had blinked.

Although *Dandelion Days* was the front-runner for the title of Evie's as-yet imaginary book of poems, there were times when she thought a better title would be *A Catalogue of Unhelpful Talents*. Evie had so many of these, from a remarkably consistent tendency to dress badly for the weather to the ability to put a cherry stalk into her mouth and tie it in a knot using her teeth and tongue. Then there was this one: a complete inability to stop her face from revealing what she was thinking and feeling. She'd done the gold-fish-face-of-surprise as she stared at Slim Lorain without a clue in the world how to answer his question.

Seconds had ticked by.

'Sorry, I . . . that was presumptuous of me,' the poet had said, alleviating the uncomfortable silence. 'It's just I saw you, the other night . . . and I thought . . . I apologise.'

'No need,' Evie had said, aware that she was blushing. 'Do you want your receipt?'

Slim had shaken his head, taken his upsold coffee and gone out into the cold of the street looking confused.

Dave Wright's girlfriend, she thought, arriving at her bus stop just in time to see a number seven pull away from the kerb. *Shit*. She was already so cold that she could imagine tendrils of ice snaking up her calves.

Dave Wright's Girlfriend, she thought. Now there was another possible title for a collection of poetry. Just probably not hers.

About the only thing Evie could have said for certain on the subject of her relationship with Dave Wright was that it began at the Thorn and Thistle.

By Scottish standards this was just a common-or-garden pub, but to an Australian like Evie it was beautiful. It had uphol- stered furnishings, dusty rugs, an old timber bar and a traditional 'snug' – a tiny room within a room – which had stained-glass windows and booth seats of pleated deep red leather.

Evie's favourite nights there were the once-a-month Fridays when the small stage in the corner of the bar room was home to Poetry in the Pub. If she wasn't rostered on, she'd turn up anyway, order a shandy and a bowl of salt-and-vinegar crisps, then stow herself away on a stool in a shadowy corner to listen. That's where she'd been sitting, and that's what she'd been doing, when she first saw Dave. He'd been standing on the stage with a sheaf of dog-eared pages in one hand, trying with the other to adjust the microphone stand. Downwards, much to the loud amusement of the other poets at the front of the room.

It was true that Dave was not tall. He was small and fine-boned, with unkempt hair and an intensity – of gaze, of speech – that made it difficult to resist bantering with him. At some point in the journey of them getting to know each other, Dave, in the Scottish accent that Evie found so irresistible, had christened her 'M'lady Greensleeves'. One day, with his splotch-making fountain pen, he'd dashed off a poem for her, torn it out of his notebook and presented it with a flourish, as if he were Sir Walter Raleigh laying a cape across a puddle for the Queen of England.

The poem was a bazaar of vocabulary, full of random capital letters and suggestive, half-abandoned thoughts, and although Evie knew that it meant nothing that he'd written her a poem – he'd written similar poems for all the girls behind the bar at the Thorn and Thistle – she kept it anyway.

Then one night he'd come to her at the bar, straight from the stage. He'd had to make his way past some hand-shakers and a few back-slappers, but then he was leaning forward on the bar. In his grey eyes, Evie could see . . . what? An invitation? Mockery? A dare? With Dave, it was always hard to tell.

'Good gig tonight, Dave,' Evie had said, without fawning. 'What'll you have?'

On Poetry in the Pub nights, the performers got a drink on the house. But only ever the one.

'*Wine comes in at the mouth,*' he said, '*and love comes in at the eye; that's all we shall know for truth, before we grow old and die.* So says William Butler Yeats, in any case.'

'But he was wrong, of course,' Evie said, wiping the bar in front of Dave and studiously avoiding his ambiguous gaze.

'Was he indeed?'

'Love comes in at the *eye*?' She straightened up and looked at him now, crossing her arms across her chest. 'Surely a poet would prefer the ear.'

'I don't know. I could imagine someone smitten with you at a glance, M'lady Greensleeves.'

Evie was far from new at the business of working in a bar. 'Well, this isn't getting you a drink, is it? Did you say it was wine that you wanted?'

'No, whisky,' he announced. 'Your best, if you please.'

Evie unstopped a particularly expensive drop, poured a generous nip, and watched as Dave swirled the amber liquid until it made a whirlpool.

'So, I heard on the grapevine,' Dave said, 'that you're in need of a place to live.'

Evie raised her eyebrows. This was true. The tent in the campground had been all very well during the festival, but she'd soon become tired of carrying around all the possessions that she wanted to be protected by more than her tent's front zipper. The flat she was now sharing with a crew of near-strangers was about to be re-occupied by its owner, and – being new to Edinburgh – Evie hadn't exactly developed an extensive network of friends with spare beds or couches.

'Happens I have a room to let,' Dave had told her.

Evie had known that it was stupid to be attracted to a man who smelled of late nights, Scotch whisky and a sensitive ego, and she had known that it would be even stupider to move in with such a man, particularly if the precise nature of the arrangement was not entirely transparent. But when Dave took centre stage, and even if

Evie didn't fully grasp every word that he spilled, crooned, whispered, shouted into the microphone, there was something special about the way the words went together, and Evie couldn't help wanting to be closer to him.

Dave's place, a soot-stained townhouse in the general vicinity of Leith, a short bus ride from the Old Town, belonged to an elderly woman who no longer had any need of it.

'Her chosen form of arts patronage, bless her lilac rinse, is to allow the place to become run-down under the benign neglect of a young poet,' Dave had explained, and Evie had suspected her face may have betrayed something of her bemusement at Dave's use of the word 'young'. Dave was what you would get if something cruel had restarted Peter Pan's internal clock and accelerated him to an age somewhere in the vicinity of forty.

What Dave hadn't needed to explain to Evie was that the rent he received from a flatmate would become a handy, if unofficial, part of his income – which otherwise consisted of dole payments and increasingly rare arts grants, cheques for the reviews that he infrequently penned, and the occasional sum for a poem that found a home in a broadsheet newspaper or literary journal.

The room he showed to Evie, which seemed to have been last decorated in the 1970s, had floral wallpaper, mismatched floral curtains, and carpet marked with evidence of parties past. The room was on the street side of the house, with a view of clusters of identical houses pressed tight together and punctuated here and there by cheap and cheerful restaurants, a nail boutique and a shop selling cut-price mobile phones. The street was so narrow that when double-decker buses passed Evie's window, she felt like she could almost step out onto the tops of them.

On her first night at her new address, Dave had stood beside her at the kitchen sink, drying the dishes from their first at-home dinner together. When the job was done, he had taken Evie's hand and pressed the back of it to his lips, but the way he looked at her was no longer teasing. He seemed fragile, and although Evie had known that it was a stupid idea to sleep with her new flatmate, she'd known all along that she was going to do it anyway.

In the four months she'd lived with Dave, they had established an odd sort of arrangement. Sometimes it involved sex, usually in Evie's room, after which Dave would leave her to sleep and return to his own bed. As well as having separate bedrooms, Evie and Dave had separate schedules and separate friends. When they were both at home in the evenings, one would cook for the other, but they shopped for groceries haphazardly and alone. They almost never quibbled and absolutely never fought, but there were periods of days on end in which he withdrew entirely, sleeping alone and shutting himself away in the den with a bottle, pen and paper. Evie had come to accept that Dave, rather like a cat, would engage with her on his own terms, and no others.

Dave and Evie did not, as a rule, discuss poetry other than Dave's. Occasionally, Evie considered confiding in Dave about her writing, perhaps even asking him to read her work, but deep down she already knew that the outcome of this was unlikely to be good. Once he'd told her that two poets in a relationship had about as much going for them as two drowning swimmers clutching at each other's throats. She'd replayed the comment over and over in her mind, trying to analyse its tone and work out whether or not it was evidence that he thought they *were* in a relationship.

There were times when Evie thought that Dave did think of her as his girlfriend. When they ventured out together to a play or a book launch, Dave would hold Evie's hand as they walked the streets, and whenever he stopped in at the Thorn and Thistle for a drink, he would lean over the bar and kiss her. But then there were times when she was fairly sure he didn't think of her that way. When he introduced her to someone he knew, he'd only ever say, 'This is Greensleeves.' It had been a while now since he'd bothered with the prefix 'M'lady'.

Evie let herself into the house but didn't take off her coat. She found Dave in the den, sitting in semi-darkness, his feet up on the coffee table, a can of Guinness in hand, and a scarf wound multiple times around his neck. Since the fright of the most recent bill, they'd been keeping the heating turned down as low as they could manage.

'What does *everyone* like, Greensleeves?' he asked, glancing up to where she stood in the doorway.

Oh, my day was great, thanks for asking. A Guinness? Thanks, that would be lovely.

'Why do you ask?'

'I need to write something popular,' Dave said. The coffee table was copiously littered with newspapers and magazines, flyers, pamphlets and mail, both opened and unopened.

'What for?'

'For this,' he said, hauling himself upright to grab a familiar flyer. It was for *Ten Lines*, and identical to the one she'd picked up from the counter at the poetry library several weeks earlier.

With a slight twinge of guilt, Evie thought of her 'Dandelion Clocks' lying in the belly of that bright red postbox, and wondered what Dave would think if he knew that she had already submitted a poem for the same anthology.

There wasn't any real cause for guilt, of course. She had the right to send a poem wherever she chose; she didn't need to ask Dave's permission. And yet . . . she felt awkward about the way she'd always kept her own poetry to herself. If you shared a house with someone, and a bed sometimes, too, shouldn't you at least want to tell them about your hopes and dreams?

'*Ten Lines*,' Dave scoffed. 'I wouldn't bother with something so bloody gimmicky, except the money's good. Who knows how you're supposed to make a living as a poet without going in for this kind of crap?'

Evie thought, but didn't say, that the world actually didn't care about 'supposed to' for poets, or anyone else for that matter.

'So, what's in the zeitgeist, Greensleeves?' Dave asked, flicking the flyer in the direction of the coffee table. 'What is everyone thinking and talking about right now?'

'Climate change?' Evie suggested.

'Who wants to read about *that* shit? Everybody just wants to ignore *that* shit. It's the only way we can go on. Thinking about climate change is like thinking about your own death. It's just one great big bummer. What *else*?'

Nice attitude. 'Scottish independence?'

'Yawn,' Dave said.

'Well, what about love?' Evie offered. 'Everyone likes love.'

'Greensleeves, I'm after an *in*teresting suggestion,' Dave said, and Evie knew that when he was in a mood like this one, there was no sense trying to shift it.

'Well,' she said, 'you'll work it out.'

Upstairs was no warmer than downstairs. In her bedroom Evie shivered, wishing that she was already undressed and dressed again and could skip the part where she was hopping about trying to put her tights on, her bare legs puckering to gooseflesh from the chill.

Between the parted curtains, she could see the flashing from the bright lights that encircled the window of the phone shop across the road, and she could hear a festive note in the voices of people calling to each other across the street. The old year was coming to an end, and a new one was beginning. Out there in the city, resolutions were being made; new leaves were about to be turned.

The turn of a year was a strange and fragile time, Evie always thought; it seemed to require you to look honestly at yourself, to take stock, to ask yourself if you were where you ought to be, or at least travelling the right road. Several times lately she'd dreamed of a fog-filled house that felt like it might be her own, where she lived with a partner whose face she couldn't quite see, and some mist-edged shapes that might have been children, but whenever she tried to bring them into focus, to touch them, to claim them as her own, they were swept away from her – partner, children, home, all – as if they were nothing more than clouds on a windy day.

When she woke, she would come hurtling back to reality and find herself alone in her ugly, street-side bedroom, where the posies of flowers on the wallpaper looked in the half-light like the faces of goblins. In the not-quite-warm-enough bed, she would remember that she was twenty-eight and far from home, and that the years were sliding by all too quickly and easily.

She hadn't meant to travel forever. When she'd left Australia, she'd imagined she was going for a year, maybe two, and while there was a part of her that now wanted to stop drifting and put down roots, there was another part of her that didn't quite know how it was done. What she did know, though, in those soul-bare moments in the half-light, was that if she didn't change some-thing soon, she might easily drift right past all the parts of the life that she'd supposed she'd one day have.

Right now, it was summer back in Australia. In Melbourne, where she'd lived before leaving the country, the sun was sometimes hot enough to warp the tram-tracks in the middle of the streets and turn patches of asphalt to liquid, while in Perth, where some of Evie's scattered family lived, the sky could be a perfect shade of cobalt for sun-soaked weeks on end. Evie had grown up in Tasmania, which was where her closest half-sister, Stella, still lived. There, a summer's day could just as easily be mild and tranquil, or cranky with ice-laden squalls. Or both.

Six years she'd been away, and all she really had to show for it was a stack of notebooks filled with unpublished poems. She crouched at her bedside and opened the cabinet where she kept these notebooks out of harm's way. Some were tall, some short, some expensive, some cheap. The last couple of times Evie had packed up and moved on, her notebooks comprised the greater part of her luggage; it wouldn't be long, now, until her own thoughts would become too heavy for her to carry on her back.

The notebook she withdrew at random was a pretty one she had bought for herself as a treat at London's Victoria and Albert Museum, its cover richly embroidered with doves and roses. The moment she opened it, she could almost smell the era of her life from which it had come: the pungent mud of the Thames at low tide, the cold ash that filled the bar room of the Noble Swan on winter mornings, the yeasty pong of dishcloths used to mop up spilled ale, the unmistakeable whiff of the dogs – spaniels, terriers, hounds – who dozed under the tables at their owners' feet.

Still wearing her coat, she sat down on the bed again with the notebook and flicked through its pages. There were messages she barely remembered leaving for herself, and poems she had rewritten so many times that they'd taken on the texture of overworked dough. But here was something she remembered: a description of a plane falling from the sky, the sea below crying out with a great big blue mouth as the silver craft plunged down into its gullet. The Air Pleiades crash. Was that two years ago already?

Most of the poem was terrible – Evie could see that now – but one or two of the lines were quite good. She took a pencil from the top of her cabinet and underlined the parts she thought might be worth salvaging. So absorbed was she in her thoughts that, at first, she didn't notice that Dave had come into her room.

'You working tonight?' he asked, sitting beside her on the bed, and bumping her shoulder with his in a just-good-mates fashion. 'Or are you free to see in the New Year with me?'

Bashfully, Evie put a hand over the open pages of her notebook. 'I'm due at the pub at nine.'

Idiot. If she hadn't put her hand over the page, he'd never have looked.

'What are you doing?' he asked, amused.

Evie could feel her cheeks burning as Dave pushed her hand away, uncovering the words on the page.

'Looks serious,' Dave said, a laugh in his voice. 'Oh! Poetry, no less. Really?'

'Dave, don't—' Evie began.

'What's this here? *A billowing keen of grief*? Whoa! Careful you don't go overboard.'

It was an accurate hit. He'd picked out exactly the phrase that she had loved the most, and even though the most sensible parts of herself counselled her to pay no heed to whatever Dave said next, the most fragile parts of herself waited, like an unshelled snail, for the boot.

When at last he spoke, his voice was so patronising that Evie was surprised he managed to stop short of reaching out to ruffle her hair. 'Never mind, Greensleeves. Writing poetry's not for everyone.'

elevator music

IT WAS AFTER dinner, but still light, when Arie drove back to the city from Belinda's house with six jars of apricot jam and a New Year's Eve radio special for company. Although Prince's '1999' got his fingers tapping against the steering wheel, it wasn't enough to get him in the mood for the party Richard and Lenka were hosting at their place.

The previous day, Arie had messaged Richard to say that he was going to give the occasion a miss, but Richard had fired back a text that read: *Unacceptable. See you 9 pm, latest. You'll have fun once you get here.*

If it had been anyone else's party, Arie would have stuck to his decision and stayed home with the expensive bottle of Scotch whisky that his middle sister, Lotte, had bought him for Christmas, much to the disapproval of his mother and two other sisters. But while all of Arie's friends had rallied around in the months after Diana's death, it was Richard and Lenka who had really gone the distance. They continued to insist that he eat with them once a week, and about the only Wednesday they'd missed so far was the one when Lenka had been in hospital after having Marek.

Predictably, Lenka had turned out to be one of those insanely capable women who took to motherhood as if she'd been changing nappies and settling crying babies her whole life, and the no-nonsense approach she took to her baby was similar to the forthright way she dealt with Arie's grief. The times Arie lost his shit and ended up sobbing at the dinner table, she had simply sat beside him, rubbed his back with the flat of her hand, and said, 'It's just awful, Arie. That's all there is to it. It's just awful.'

Unlike his oldest sister, Sara, and his younger sister, Heidi, who were prone to dishing up pep talks and handing over the business cards of grief therapists, massage therapists, Bowen therapists and aura therapists, Lenka didn't pretend there was any easy fix.

'Get up in the morning, breathe all day, go to bed, repeat,' she sometimes said. She listened to his most self-defeating drivel without rolling her eyes, occasionally forced him into a game of tennis, and if on a Wednesday night he inadvertently poured himself a third glass of wine, she'd drive him home.

Home. Where Arie had installed a television in his room so he could go to sleep each night with ancient episodes of *Doctor Who* mutely flickering at the foot of the bed. Home, where Arie now parked his car out the front. Indoors, he stacked the jam in the almost-empty pantry, and went upstairs to change. What did one wear to a New Year's Eve party? More specifically, what did one wear to a New Year's Eve party that one didn't especially want to attend?

Before reaching for the handle of the wardrobe door, Arie took a short, sharp breath. But brace himself as he might, it never saved him from the stab of pain that came each time he swung the door open and found himself face-to-face with Diana's clothes hanging beside his, just as she'd left them – a selection of her famous red dresses, some black dresses, winter coats, drifty summer shirts and

84

long, tiered maxi dresses. All these garments, Arie often thought, had once held her body.

The trouble with parties at Richard and Lenka's place, these days, was that they were full of people just like Richard and Lenka themselves – couples in their thirties, deep in the earnest years of childrearing. By arriving just after nine, Arie successfully avoided the part of the night when the backyard patio was full of dads with babies on hips and mums blowing on pieces of barbecued sausage to cool them down. He hadn't been forced to try to talk with Lenka while she simultaneously supervised little Marek, who at eighteen months old was given to striking out on kamikaze adventures around the garden furniture whenever his mother's attention strayed for a nanosecond, nor had he been called on to admire someone's toddler's new-found ability to 'wave night-night'.

When he got to the party, the children had already been taken indoors by the babysitters. Now the light beer and mineral water was flowing in earnest as inoffensive lounge music pulsed through the warm, summer air. In the flickering light of some high-tech garden torches, and with a full-strength beer in hand, Arie searched around for someone to talk to, preferably somebody who wouldn't talk his ear off about childcare policy or infant neuroscience, or excuse themselves from the conversation every few minutes to duck inside and check on their kids.

'Arie?' a female voice said.

He turned to find himself looking into the face of a woman, a little shorter than him, with feathery light brown hair, overbright lipstick and a nervous smile. Somewhere in the softness of her face were the bones of a woman he hadn't seen for years. Arie remembered Diana commenting, uncharitably, that this friend of Lenka's had a charm so understated that it was easy to miss it. What was her name? Sally or Sophie or something.

'It's Sylvie,' she said, bailing him out.

'Of course, yes, hello.'

'It's so good to see you again.'

It is?

'Look,' she went on, 'I just wanted to say how sorry I am, to hear about Diana. I saw you on the television. You were . . . oh my God. You know, I've never liked flying. It always makes me imagine what it would be like . . . Anyway, I can't imagine what it must have been like for you. But on television, the way you spoke about her? I couldn't stop crying.'

On the first anniversary of the crash, Arie had given an interview to a current affairs program, and it sometimes seemed to him that half the country had watched him cry on live, national television.

'I'm so sorry for your loss,' Sylvie said.

Arie never quite knew what to say when people said they were *sorry* about Diana. In the past two years, however, he'd learned that diversion was usually a safe strategy. He asked, 'So . . . what about you?'

'Well, I was married,' Sylvie said, confidingly, 'but it didn't work out. I've got a three-year-old son. He's gorgeous, of course. Being a single mum, it makes working really difficult. Anyway, my parents are great. They help me a lot. You and Diana didn't have kids, did you?'

Arie shook his head.

'Look, Arie, if you ever want to have a coffee, and maybe, I don't know, if you ever need anybody to talk to?' she offered, gesturing awkwardly with her wine glass.

Arie was stunned. If he were to make a prioritised list of the people he was likely to choose to *talk to* about Diana, then Sylvie wouldn't have rated in the Top 500. He was relieved to sense Richard's presence at his side.

'Sylvie, *hi*,' Richard said. 'Look, sorry, but can I just steal Arie from you for a minute?'

'Of course,' she said.

When they were out of earshot, Richard whispered, 'So, rule number one of being the most eligible bachelor at a party is that you don't commit to anything until you've had a good look at your options. All your options.'

Eligible bachelor? What the actual fuck?

'Do you remember Grace McLean?' Richard went on.

'Grace Mc*Lean*? As in, from school?'

'Uh-huh.'

'As in, the head girl from our school?'

'The very same.'

'Didn't she laugh every time you got your head flushed down the toilet?' Arie asked, bewildered.

Richard waved a hand in the air to indicate the insignificance of this. 'She's in the same yoga group as Lenka. They've struck up a bit of a friendship. And she's . . . here on her own.'

Arie felt himself being lightly steered across the patio, Richard's hand on his upper arm.

'Here he is,' Richard announced. Grace, turning to greet them, smiled more warmly than Arie remembered her ever doing at school. As a girl she'd been pretty, but as a woman she was beautiful, with freckled olive skin and serious, dark eyes. Her bronze dress suited her well and it had a plunging neckline that played to the rather obvious asset of her cleavage.

'Arie,' she said, kissing his cheek. 'Happy New Year.'

At school, Grace McLean would no more have kissed his cheek than eaten a frog sandwich.

'So, what are you up to these days?' he asked.

'I have a little importing company, and a couple of gift shops, although the biggest business is online, of course. Richard was telling me that I really ought to get the two of you to take a look at my website.'

'She should, shouldn't she?' Richard added.

'Of course. We'd love to take a look.'

Now that he had introduced them and seen them safely through a few exchanges, Richard made his exit, excusing himself to go and see to people's drinks.

'Do smile,' Grace said, as Richard – walking away – glanced back over his shoulder. 'The dear little Cupid. He's so excited to throw us together.'

'Sorry?'

'Leukaemia widow,' Grace said, as if this was how she introduced herself. 'Two and a half years.'

It took Arie a few seconds, but then he caught on.

'Right,' he said, with a droll laugh. 'So, ah . . . plane crash widower. Coming up for two years.'

'Yes, I knew all that. I mean, Richard told me, but even before that, I saw you on the television.'

'Ah.'

'No, you were really good. Great. Very moving.'

'Thanks. I think.'

'You're welcome,' she said. He recognised this brittleness of hers; it reminded him of the way Belinda conducted herself in the world, with a kind of forced good humour that was always threatening to crack. Perhaps, he thought, this was how public grief was supposed to be done.

'So,' he said, deciding to have a go at it himself, 'those extra six months . . . do they make any difference?'

'Oh, you'd like a report from down the track?' she asked, and sipped her wine. 'Hm, what can I tell you? Well, to state the obvious, at any social event you're almost guaranteed to be shepherded into the company of somebody else who's single. Your friends start inviting you to dinners with other random, single souls. You can expect an increase in those sorts of events. But then they dwindle again when your friends all get shitty that you haven't jumped at their first offerings.'

'Right, thanks, good,' he said, trying to match her bantering tone. 'That's all good information.'

'What else? Let's see. Oh, I know. About a month ago, there was this day when I realised that I'd got through an entire twenty-four-hour period without crying. That was a big one.'

He could feel her pain. It was like his own, just in a different colour scheme, maybe.

'Well,' he said, 'congratulations.'

'Thank you,' she said, affecting a gesture in the vicinity of a curtsey. 'How are you doing, on the crying front?'

'Crying's not really my thing. That's just something I do on television, apparently. No, for me it's the way I lose time. I'll be in the middle of something, and time just seems to slow. Like watching a movie one frame at a time. But then I look at the clock, and I find that an hour's gone by, and I can't for the life of me remember what I've done with it.'

Grace nodded. 'I'm afraid that doesn't stop. At least, it hasn't for me.'

'Righto then. Better get used to it. Anything else I should know?'

'At your next birthday, if you haven't managed to get yourself

89

hooked up with someone, not one but several of your girlfriends will buy you a sex toy.'

'Excellent,' Arie said, trying to remain nonchalant, although in truth he was feeling slightly dizzy.

'Well, maybe that won't happen for you,' Grace said. 'In a nutshell, I'd say . . . there are still good days and bad days, but the overall trend is generally upwards. I'm a walking stock-market report.'

They talked for a time, then, about what they remembered of each other from their school days, and from there found their way into a conversation about what it was like to be childless at a party full of parents. After a while, Lenka and another of their yoga friends came to join them, and – in the way that so often happens at parties – their conversation came to an end by circumstance rather than intent.

By the time Richard called out for everyone to charge their drinks to see in the New Year, a cool breeze was blowing through the garden, stirring the leaves in the young trees that had been artfully planted around the fence-line. Arie watched as the approach of midnight reshuffled the party, groups dispersing and re-forming as partners moved quietly to each other's sides, as if by some kind of magnetism. As he looked around for a shadowy spot to disappear into, Grace arrived at his side, a light scarf draped around her shoulders for warmth. She was not drunk, but it was evident that she'd had a few glasses of wine. He imagined he would have appeared much the same to her.

She stood beside him, shoulder to shoulder, so that they looked out over the rest of the gathering as if from the sidelines – a pair of spectators.

'In two and a half minutes,' she said, gesturing with her wine glass, 'everybody here will be kissing.'

'I know,' Arie said, and took a deep gulp of his beer.

'Shall we give them a thrill?' she asked, without looking at him.

Arie took a moment to be sure he understood. She was offering to rescue him from his situation, but also asking to be rescued. It was a fair enough proposition. Except for the fact that the idea of kissing somebody new filled Arie with anxiety. For so many years he had kissed Diana, and only Diana. What if he no longer knew how to do it with anyone else? What if the way he and Diana kissed was entirely specific to them? What if he did something wrong? And as for making love . . .

'I haven't . . .' he began.

'Kissed anybody yet?' she asked.

'Not since Diana,' he confirmed. 'Have you?'

'Yes.'

'What was it like?'

'A bit like trying to tune in to a radio signal from Mars. It might be that I've lost all my receivers.'

Arie, who sometimes wondered if he'd lost the full spectrum of feelings in his heart, the way some people lose the range of motion in a limb after surgery, knew exactly what she meant.

'Don't worry,' she said. 'I'm not expecting the earth to move.'

As Richard began the countdown to midnight – 'FIVE! FOUR! THREE! TWO!' – Arie felt his pulse speed up.

'ONE. Happy New Year, everybody!' Richard shouted, Lenka under his arm, laughing and totally at ease with her own body and his, in a way that Arie remembered but didn't know how to replicate. All around the garden it was the same; couples embracing, kissing, as if it were the most natural thing in the world to do.

He turned to Grace, and she reached her brown freckled arms around his neck.

'It really is okay,' she said, and for a moment the banter was gone and he caught a flash of something deeply real in her dark brown eyes.

Arie put his arms around her waist, closed his eyes and kissed her. They managed something a little more substantial than a peck, although it wasn't much more, in the end, than a pressing together of their lips. They drew apart.

'Happy New Year,' Grace said, with a sad smile.

'Happy New Year,' Arie said. He knew that while neither of them was in the place they really wanted to be, they had just shared a moment, and he was grateful.

Arie arrived home just after midnight to find a party going on noisily in the front yard of the conjoined house next door. As he made his way up the path through his own front yard, one of the revellers leaned on the fence, beer can in hand, and called, 'G'day, neighbour! Give us a yell if we're bothering you, all right? Or, you know, come over and join us, yeah? More the merrier, hey?'

Arie responded with a noncommittal thumbs up.

Once, the homeowners of this street had overwhelmingly been pensioners and middle-aged couples with empty nests. When Diana and Arie had moved in, they had been something of a novelty for the neighbours, but things had changed since then. Now, the owners were just as likely to live out of town, or in another state or country altogether. Arie didn't know exactly how many of the street's cottages and terraces had become Airbnbs, but these days hire cars were as common a sight on Tavistock Row as were people towing wheeled suitcases while looking out for street numbers.

Arie no longer knew the people who owned the house next door to his, but he'd checked out the listing online. The house rules included 'No Parties', but Arie knew from his experience as an Airbnb neighbour that lists of house rules weren't worth the electricity needed to generate the pixels they were written in.

He wasn't drunk, but even so it probably hadn't been wise for him to drive home. There was no need for restraint now, though, so he fetched himself a beer from the fridge, the door of which was still covered with the souvenir magnets for which Diana had such a weakness – a windmill from Amsterdam, a rabbit in a kimono from Kyoto, a tango-dancing llama from Buenos Aires.

Stuck to the fridge with a plastic Eiffel Tower was a picture of Arie holding Marek in a christening robe. It had been taken eight months after the plane crash, and although Arie had thought he'd borne up pretty well that day, the evidence showed he'd gone to the happy event as the hollow-eyed godfather of the apocalypse. Below the picture, affixed with a blue police-box magnet, was an invitation – handwritten on handmade paper – for his youngest sister's wedding.

Weddings, christenings, the world going on without him. Arie felt a wave of pain so strong that he returned the cold stubby to the fridge and reached for the half-empty bottle of Scotch on the kitchen bench. He searched out a tumbler and headed upstairs.

On the landing, Arie paused at the open glass doors of the piano room where Diana's Steinway stood, framed by the bay window. For the first time in months, he went inside. Setting the whisky and tumbler on a corner of the instrument's wide lid, he sat on the piano stool. Inside the room there was no sound, but through the window he could hear a muted version of next door's party.

Arie lifted the smaller of the piano's lids to expose the keys. He placed his thumb on the A key just below middle C, and his fourth finger on the D just above. A for Arie, D for Diana. He couldn't recall, though, how the chords were otherwise constituted, the ones that made up the plagal cadence, the ones that sang *Amen*. Nor could he remember anything at all about those other chords, the ones that made up the perfect cadence.

If only he could play, it might have been that the piano was a transmitter, a device by which he might talk to Diana, wherever she was. If he could talk to her, he could ask her, *What now? Who am I, without you? What do I do, without you? How should I go on?*

If only he could, as in a movie, enter an accelerated montage sequence and come out the other end with the power to work this machine and make it release its own memories to him. The night before Diana left, she had been playing a song, but its melody was lost to him now, like a word in a foreign language. He couldn't play it on these keys, or sing it, or hum it. All that remained to him of that song was the feeling it expressed. Love, yes, but love of a shot-silk kind that changed colour when you looked at it from a different angle.

The room was stuffy in the summer heat. Arie got up from the piano to hinge open one of the angled panes of the bay window, allowing in the sugary smell of the flowering jasmine and a few extra decibels of the party. The late evening air was so mild that he couldn't even feel it on his skin. From where he stood, Arie had a clear view over the neighbours' nicely designed yard. Unlike his own front yard, which comprised some thirsty grass, an ugly path and a single eucalypt tree, next door's was a circular courtyard of heritage bricks surrounded by tiered herb gardens and a border of bright green, well-tended lawn. The glowing bulbs of fairy lights peeped out from the passionfruit vines that grew thickly over the latticed fence on the far side.

The partygoers stood together in clusters, sat on the low brick wall of the herb gardens and lolled on the banana lounges. Everywhere he looked, Arie saw couples, arms entwined, hands clasped, heads rested on shoulders, one lover sitting in the other's lap. The chorus of the Zombies' 'This Will Be Our Year' blended with their laughter and talk.

You'll find someone else, Belinda had said, but Arie didn't know how it was even possible to fall in love again. Did he first have to work out a way to grow a new heart to replace the one he'd given away?

He thought back over the events of the night. Kissing Grace . . . it reminded him of the way it could all too easily be when you first bought a new music album. You pressed play and started to listen but you just didn't really know any of it, and although it washed over you perfectly pleasantly, none of it really grabbed you. Maybe, just maybe, over time you might become familiar with the tracks and maybe, just maybe, they might begin to mean something to you. But more likely it would always be that no matter how many times you played the album, it would never sound like anything more than elevator music.

Arie turned away from the window and poured himself a whisky. He was thirty-five years old, and the miracle of his life was over and done with. He could see no reason to believe that the universe might yet deliver him another.

—INTERLUDE—

ON AN EARLY morning express train from London to Edinburgh, Beatrix Romero, at sixteen, having just spent a quiet half-hour watching the January scenery scroll by, turned to her friend Olivia and said, 'They'd better not *all* be duds this time.'

Olivia shrugged. 'I'd like to say they couldn't possibly be as bad as the last lot, but I'd be lying.'

'One hot boy. Is that too much to ask?'

'Maybe it's like the ideal car parking space. If you want him to turn up, you have to start thinking about him now. You know, like, *visualise*.' Olivia closed her eyes and put her fingers to her temples. 'I'm picturing a luscious Scot-boy with a gorgeous set of . . . bagpipes.'

'Ew,' said Beatrix, her mind leaping simultaneously to images of haggis, and to the jangly habit of not wearing jocks under kilts.

Beatrix and Olivia had been going to music camps together, twice or three times a year, since they were twelve. This camp would bring together – for three days and two nights – music students from three specialist performing arts schools: Beatrix and Olivia's private London college, a school in Vancouver, Canada, and the host school in an inner suburb of Edinburgh.

Half the passengers in the carriage were from Beatrix's school, and the luggage racks were crammed with instrument cases in all shapes and sizes.

It was usual for Beatrix and Olivia to share a room and, for the last two years, they'd had an agreement about giving each other space in the event that either of them got lucky. So far, however, the arrangement had been entirely to Olivia's benefit.

Olivia – with jet black hair and flawless skin passed down by her father, and striking blue eyes inherited from her mother – was stunning. She played the violin and this gave her the opportunity to show off in public another of her signature features, which was that she possessed possibly the most beautiful wrists in the history of hands being attached to arms. Being around Olivia made Beatrix horribly aware of the slight squish of her stomach, the fuzzy down on her forearms and the wild, thick mess of her hair.

'The odds are always going to be worse for you,' Olivia observed, not without a hint of smugness. 'Music boys are geeky.'

'Why does it have to be like that, though?' Beatrix moaned.

Olivia, inspecting her fingernails, shrugged. 'Just a law of nature, I guess.'

Beatrix didn't know how Olivia managed it, but every camp, quick as a fox, she would work out who was who. Before the second day was over, she'd have found a girl to flirt with during breaks and entertain in their twin-share room at night while Beatrix sat up on some shabby armchair in a cold common room, watching late-night television or reading a novel, waiting for the time on her phone to tick over to the appointed hour when she would knock softly on the door to be let back in.

When she'd packed her bags this time, Beatrix had put in not one novel, but two.

Typically, she'd left packing to the night before she left. Her father had been working late, but he'd called Juanita and had her come over to – as he put it – 'be a presence in the house'. Forming her lithe body into yoga poses while at the same time reading out the packing list, Juanita had sent Beatrix off to various parts of the house to retrieve the items needed. Getting towards the end of the list, she'd read out, '*Pillowslip.*'

Then – but only once Beatrix had been to the linen press and come back again – she added, '*Single bed sheet.*'

'What's the euphemism for sadist?' Beatrix had asked, and upon returning with the sheet, she'd flung it good-naturedly at Juanita. 'What else?'

'*Bring your instrument. Somewhat obvious, I'd have thought. And any necessary instrument-specific supplies . . . reeds, valve oil, extra strings, picks, blah, blah. And . . . manuscript notebook, or loose-leaf manuscript paper.*'

Beatrix went upstairs and came back empty-handed. 'I left my manuscript book at school.'

'Too late to go to the stationery shop, but you might find something over there,' Juanita said, gesturing to the shelves behind Bene's keyboard, draped in its black dust cover.

As Beatrix stood at the shelves, hands on hips, it was tempting to imagine that one particular item on the shelf wriggled its way forward just a little.

'Aha,' she said, yanking out the book, which had a black leather cover and a scarlet ribbon for a bookmark. She flicked through from the back and saw that most of the pages were blank. It was her dad's book, but she needed it. What was she supposed to do? He wouldn't mind.

'Manuscript notebook: check,' she told Juanita. 'What else?'

'As far as the list goes? Nada,' Juanita said, getting to her feet. 'But here, have these.'

From a pocket of her handbag, Juanita produced a handful of condoms, bright as sweets in their crinkly foil wrappers. Beatrix blushed deeply.

'I know your dad would rather I gave you a nice little razor-encrusted chastity belt. But since they didn't have any of those at Sainsbury's, I got you these instead. Better safe than under-supplied. I used to go to music camps too, you understand.'

The first afternoon went the way first afternoons at music camp usually did, with bags being dropped off at a 'hotel' that had an institutional-looking dining room and two vinyl-covered beds to a room. From there, the entire group travelled by bus to the host school's auditorium. There were speeches, one of which, predictably, was cheesy and welcoming. The other, equally predictably, was about rules and safety, and contained hints about the dire disciplinary consequences of mucking up.

Like everyone else, Beatrix barely heard a word that either of the teachers said. In her line of sight was a boy, not from her school, who had blond hair, beautiful cheekbones and a French horn case at his feet. It didn't take long, though, for her to observe both the rainbow wristband and the fact that his roving eye was taking pretty much the same route as hers.

When the speeches were over, Beatrix braced herself for the icebreaker activities. It was a strange affliction of Beatrix's that whenever she was forced to introduce herself in a situation like this, she became terrified that she would lose the ability to pronounce her own name.

'So, everybody,' said the chirpy teacher who'd delivered the welcome speech, 'find somebody you've never met before, say hello –'

In her Scots accent, this came out sounding like *haloo*.

'– and then I want you to play a little game together. You might have heard of it. It's called Two Truths and a Lie. The rules are simple. You make three statements about yourself, two of which are true and one of which is . . . not. The other person has to guess which one is the lie. Rightio. Off you go, then.'

Beatrix turned to Olivia to complain about the cringeworthiness of the challenge, but her friend had already tapped the shoulder of a girl in the row in front of them. With a sigh, Beatrix swivelled in her seat to look behind her for a partner in mortification.

And there he was.

Beatrix had the sense that she was back on the train again, rocking ever so slightly from side to side. What *had* she seen, this morning, when Olivia had told her that she ought to visualise the person she wanted to meet? Whatever it had been, she couldn't remember any more because it was already overtaken and overwhelmed. Whatever it had been, it ought to have been *him*.

Although he was sitting down, she could see that he was tall. His dark red hair wasn't artfully cut or even brushed – it was just a regular short haircut that had been let grow wild until it had passed his collar. His eyes were large and on the browner side of hazel, and while there was something soulful about them, they were also smiling eyes. Around his neck was the finest gold chain she had ever seen – its shape made asymmetrical by the interruption of his collarbones. Resting against the seat beside him was a cello case. Of course he was a cellist. What else would he be, with hands like that? They were like the oversized paws of a puppy. A Great Dane, perhaps. No, something less sleek, she thought, as she watched him run a hand through the well-worn tracks in his hair. Maybe a wolfhound.

'So, *haloo*,' he said.

He wasn't from her school, and that wasn't a real Scots accent. Canadian, then.

'Hello,' Beatrix said, not trusting herself to do the accent back at him.

'Felix.' He held out one of those cello-playing hands.

'Beatrix,' she said, feeling a little light-headed at the touch of his hand, which was warm and dry and not at all sweaty and gross the way boys' hands sometimes were.

'Beatrix,' he repeated, nodding in what seemed to be approval. 'So, if we started a band, we could be called something like the X Factor.'

Beatrix wished she had his easy confidence. How did it happen that some people were just blessed with it?

'Or, Sealed with an X?' Beatrix offered, trying not to look like she thought that was a pretty clever comeback.

'Ni-i-ice,' Felix said, looking at Beatrix so directly that it made her blush. 'So this truth/lie thing, you want to go first?'

Having never in her life wanted so badly to sound fascinating and exotic, Beatrix turned to her mental larder only to find its shelves completely and utterly bare. If she told him two truths, what might they be? *I have a thing about red hair? I'm already thinking about what it would be like to kiss you? If you tell me that you have a girlfriend, it's going to break my heart?* She had to find a way to stall.

'International visitors first, surely,' she said.

Felix sat back in his chair, arms crossed, and thought for a moment.

'So,' he said, affecting a serious face, 'my first statement about myself is that I was born in the year 1512.'

Okay, so if he's going to make it that easy to pick the lie, what game ARE we playing?

'My second is that I don't have a phone.'

You what? Seriously?

'A-a-and, my third is this: everyone from our school is getting let out on the town for a few hours tonight, and I'm kind of curious to know if you are too.'

He threw her a smile then, as big and bright as a beachball, and in that moment – if she hadn't already – Beatrix Romero fell in love.

On the twelfth day of Christmas, the midwinter festivities in the East Princes Street Gardens would come to their end. For now, though, tired stallholders continued to plate up hot waffles and drench them in chocolate sauce, and to ladle spiced cider and mulled wine into corrugated paper cups. Meanwhile, ever more generous markdowns were applied to holly wreaths, hearthside stockings and delicate Christmas tree baubles.

As Beatrix and Olivia made their way in the early winter dark through the city's narrow closes and cobbled streets towards the market, they passed gift shops with names like Thistle Do Nicely, with windows that glowed in shades of amber and lemon, lighting up the displays of tartans and shortbread within.

'Oh my God, will you slow down?' Olivia pleaded.

'Can't be late,' Beatrix said, striding up a steep street in her knee-high, fleece-lined boots.

'For heaven's sake,' Olivia said, trotting a few steps in her high heels in an effort to keep up. 'Can't you just text him? A couple of minutes aren't worth *dying* over.'

'He doesn't have a phone, so we're doing this old school,' Beatrix said. 'Eight o'clock at the Scott Monument. I have to be there.'

'He doesn't have a *phone*? What's wrong with him?'

'Nothing's wrong with him.'

'So . . . what? He has Amish parents?'

'He just doesn't like phones. Says he's never had the need for one.'

'What the actual fuck?'

'Liv, can we talk about this later? And can we hurry? Please?'

'Honestly,' Olivia said, 'you need to chill out.'

'I can't, Liv. He's perfect.'

Olivia raised one of her beautifully shaped eyebrows so that it disappeared beneath the rim of her knitted hat. 'That is a big call. Especially on the basis of, what, a quarter of an hour's acquaintance?'

'He is, though. Perfect.'

Reaching a rise, Beatrix saw the market. Beside it, the Gothic spire of the Scott Monument stood out against the deep, deep blue sky, a historic contrast to the Star Flyer, the fairground ride that rose into the air beside it, sending plastic carriages spiralling on long lengths of chain around a central column that pulsed with a multitude of neon lights.

The girls arrived at their destination precisely on time, leaving Beatrix with the challenge of watching out for Felix

103

without appearing to do so. She came up with the solution of browsing at a clothing stall not far from the monument, shoving her own woollen hat into her pocket and trying on tam-o'-shanters to pass the time. She had set a tweedy tam at a fetching angle on her head, and was pulling a pouty expression for Olivia's phone camera, when a pair of gloved hands covered her eyes.

In the sudden darkness, she caught a sharp drift of boy deodorant.

'*Haloo*,' Felix said, and his close proximity alone was enough to set off the butterflies in her stomach. He took his hands away from her eyes, swiped the tam-o'-shanter and perched it on his own head.

'A little closer together, please,' Olivia instructed, aiming her phone at the pair. This was the very first photograph to be taken of Beatrix Romero and Felix Carter. There would be more – many more, in the years to come – not that either one of them knew this as Beatrix introduced Felix to Olivia, and Felix introduced his friend Charlie, and Olivia and Charlie tactfully made themselves scarce, leaving Beatrix and Felix standing alone together, awkward and speechless for a moment.

'So,' Felix said, breaking the silence at last, 'hot chocolate?'

Steaming cups in hand, they strolled the markets together and shared stories. Beatrix learned that Felix lived with his mother and father and a Russian blue cat called Kilmauski, and in most ways he was an only child, like her, except that he had a much older half-brother, who was only sixteen years younger than their mum.

'Sixteen,' Beatrix said, and gave a low whistle. '*I'm* sixteen.'

'Me too,' Felix said. 'Seventeen in April.'

'August, for me.'

She also learned that while Felix had brought his acoustic cello to camp, back home he usually played an electric one. On weekends he went busking, and he was starting to turn a decent trade.

'Given my new-found affluence,' he said, gesturing at the Star Flyer ride, 'it would be my treat.'

Beatrix looked up at the Star Flyer's chairs, spiralling through the night sky.

He held out a hand to her. 'So, are we going to do this thing?'

She smiled, thought for a nanosecond, and took his hand. 'You bet.'

From where they stood, the Star Flyer looked fairly harmless. It wasn't until the chairs lifted off the ground and began to spin, while the lights flashed to the beat of a thumping bassline, that Beatrix became aware of the colossal scale of the thing. Increment by increment, the chairs went higher, and faster. In other chairs, people rode with their arms in the air, squealing with delight, but each time Beatrix felt herself being winched to the next level, she clung tighter to Felix's hand. The higher they went, the colder it became, the speed of the whirling chairs turning the wind to ice on her cheeks and her nose. As the speed increased, the angle of the flying chairs became more acute, and as she and Felix careened towards the stone spire of the Scott Monument, Beatrix was almost sure that they were going to be ploughed straight into it.

'Hey, you okay?' Felix asked.

'I'm not entirely sure,' Beatrix said. 'It's scarier than I thought.'

'I know what you mean,' he admitted. 'It looked pretty tame from down there, hey?'

'Uh-huh. I don't suppose it will last forever though,' Beatrix said, wishing they'd chosen instead to take a sedate turn on the Ferris wheel that she could see twinkling in the near distance.

'Try keeping your eyes up, hey?' Felix suggested. 'Watch the castle. Don't look down.'

She did as he said, fixing her gaze on the shape of the fortress on the hill, but soon the ride spun her around so that the castle was at her back.

'Okay, so . . . look at me instead,' Felix said.

For the rest of the ride, she didn't so much as glance at the ground, or the city, or its lights. As she stared into Felix's large, hazel-brown eyes, he pulled faces that made her laugh, and although her face felt stiff from the cold and her fear, she returned the favour as best she could. In his eyes, she could see his determination to keep her safe, to quash her fear. Or, at the very least, to hold on to it for her.

'I think we're going down,' Beatrix said, without taking her eyes from Felix's.

'I think you're beautiful,' Felix said, over the music and rushing air.

'You do?'

'You have a flute player's lips.'

'Is that a good thing?'

'It's the best. Can I kiss you?'

That was how and where Felix kissed Beatrix for the very first time, and his lips – to her – were exactly right, not too warm and not too cool, not too forceful and not too wimpy, and his tongue touched hers just gently, not too little, not too much. The way he kissed her made her feel like there were fairy lights strung along the underneath of her skin, making bright tracks all over her body, and by the time the ride brought them back to earth, Beatrix had entirely forgotten that the Star Flyer had been anything other than perfect.

The second day of the camp went pretty much the way the second days of music camps usually did, with the students divided up into their various orchestral sections. Because the different groups took their breaks at separate times, Beatrix did not see Felix at morning tea, or lunch, and this made Beatrix violently regret her childhood decision to take up a stupid woodwind instrument like the flute, when clearly she ought to have picked the violin or the viola. Hell, she'd have signed up for a lifetime of lugging around a double bass if it had meant that today she could be with Felix, and not sequestered away from him with a bunch of oboists, clarinet players, bassoonists and a handful of other flautists, while suffering from the knowledge that her best friend, who didn't even *like* boys, was spending the entire day in the same room as Felix, just because she'd had the good sense – when she was, like, five years old – to pick the violin.

Although Beatrix's body was present in the practice room, and although she was ostensibly playing along with some bouncy little scherzo for woodwind choir, her heart and soul were still sixty metres off the ground, turning 360 degrees above the night-time city. Physically, her lips were on the mouthpiece of her flute, but in every other way they were still pressed against the lips of Felix Carter.

Her playing wasn't anything to write home about, but she got through to the end of the scherzo without stuffing up in any obvious way, and when she felt her phone vibrating in her pocket, she did not react with any particular excitement. After all, Felix didn't have a phone. Beatrix left it in her pocket all the way through to the end of the session. It wasn't until the final break of the day that she took it out and read the message from Olivia. *So, F and I have talked. You lovebirds can have our room from midnight to 2 am if you like. Y or N?*

By midnight, Olivia – having made arrangements with a Scottish viola player who lived only a short distance from the school – was already gone. She'd slipped out the door with her boots under her arm so that she could tiptoe past Ms Kay's door in stockinged feet.

Alone in their room, softly lit by a bedside lamp with one of Olivia's silk scarves thrown over the shade, Beatrix could neither sit nor stand for more than five seconds at a stretch. She sat, then stood, then smoothed the bed coverings, as if that made any kind of sense. She twirled a length of her hair around her finger, paced the short distance from one end of the room to the other, and then – for the umpteenth time – went into the bathroom to check that her lipstick was on straight. As if that made any kind of sense, either.

In the vanity mirror, Beatrix studied her face as if trying to remember it. As the seconds ticked down to midnight, she wondered if, tomorrow, her face would have gained some new way of looking. Or if it would have lost an old one. Or neither. Or both.

At precisely midnight, Beatrix heard a soft tap on the door. She took a deep breath, and as she stepped out of the bathroom, her mirror-self slid sideways out of the frame.

She opened the door no further than was necessary, and Felix sidled in, tall, thin and almost inconceivably gorgeous. He had not come far, only from the floor below, where the boys slept two to a room with their male teachers stationed in rooms at either end of the corridor. He was wearing loose pants and a T-shirt. It was the first time Beatrix had seen him like this, and there was something undressed about him that drew her particular attention to the sharp bones of his elbows and wrists and clavicles.

'*Haloo*,' he whispered, once the door was closed behind him.

'*Haloo*,' she whispered back, and for a moment she wished she was armless, like the Venus de Milo, so she didn't have to worry about where to put her hands. She didn't want to let them creep into her pockets, or reach up and start fiddling with her hair, which was what they seemed to want to do, but they felt all weird and wrong just hanging by her sides.

All the ease of the night before had gone. The casual, sparky flirtatiousness that she and he had shared as they'd walked the market and talked had now disappeared. The omnipresent fact of what they might be about to do had filled the room to the point where it didn't seem to leave space for much else. Like talking. Or even breathing. Or moving in any way. They were still standing, face-to-face and almost paralysed, just inside the door.

It was Felix who managed to break the spell, reaching out with one of his cellist's hands so that his fingers disappeared into the thickness of Beatrix's curls, and his thumb was gently caressing her cheek. Beatrix, melting on the inside, closed her eyes.

Then they were kissing. They kissed standing up, and then they kissed sitting side by side on the bed. And then they kissed lying down, and soon Felix was lying on top of Beatrix, and just the weight of his body on hers was enough to make her light-headed. Soon clothes were coming off, item by item, and her breasts were in his hands and in his mouth. Only a few more moments passed before there were only underpants left between them, and also the single sock that Beatrix couldn't manage to wriggle off with the bare toes of her other foot.

Beatrix tugged at the waistband of Felix's boxers.

'Wait, wait, wait,' he said. 'We can't.'

'We can't?'

Felix, his nose just inches above Beatrix's, shook his head.

'I had this plan to skip out of dinner and go find a drugstore, but all the teachers were stressing because a couple of people got busted going outside to smoke. I couldn't swing it, and so I don't have any—'

'It's okay. I, um, have some,' Beatrix said, extracting a little red packet from the bedside drawer. 'Oh God, now you're going to think—'

'That you actually are a goddess,' Felix said, kissing her again.

So it was that after a bit of only moderately awkward fumbling – during which Beatrix had cause to be grateful for Juanita, and some lessons in condom application that had involved an overripe banana – that Beatrix and Felix made love for the first, memorable, sweet, sticky, slightly painful and absolutely exhilarating time.

It was only the next day, in the late afternoon, when the English and Canadian students were shepherded to Edinburgh's

Waverley Station. But love moves fast when it is all brand new and has no barnacles on it to slow it down, and by the time Beatrix and Felix were sitting beneath the domed ceiling of the station's waiting room they had already exchanged addresses and promises, and made a thousand plans about how and when they would see each other again.

'I want you to have this,' Felix said, unclasping the gold chain from around his neck. It was so fine that when the entire length of it was all puddled together, the metal took up less than the space of a penny in Beatrix's palm. 'My mother gave it to me, when I was really little. I've had it almost all my life.'

Beatrix closed her hand for a moment, and felt the preciousness of the gift.

'She won't mind you giving it away?'

Felix shrugged. 'If I told her how I felt, I'm sure she'd understand. Can I put it on for you?'

Beatrix bundled her hair into her hands and held it out of the way while he slipped the chain around her neck and fastened it. She could feel the warmth of his breath on the back of her neck and sense his concentration. When he was done, she let her hair fall, and turned around to kiss him. 'I won't take it off,' she said.

Through the waiting room's loudspeakers came the announcement that flooding on the tracks had caused an hour's delay to the ScotRail service that was to take Felix and his schoolmates to Aberdeen. While a ripple of annoyance passed through the waiting room, Beatrix and Felix reacted as if they'd just had news of a stay of execution, kissing each other with the kind of passion that made Ms Kay – sitting at the far end of their row of seats – look up from her magazine and cough, meaningfully.

'I love this,' Beatrix said, putting her hand to her throat. 'I wish I had something to give you in return.'

She thought through the contents of her overnight bag, remembering how much he'd liked her socks, the ones with the little pizza slices on them, but that was a stupid idea. He'd given her a necklace that he'd worn for most of his life, and she was proposing to give him some socks that were almost certainly manky and in need of a wash?

'Wait,' she said, remembering. 'Wait, wait, wait.'

She'd seen it during the morning's workshops, when the woodwinds had been given a composition task to do in their manuscript books – that song, that love song. There had been this little phase in her life when she and her dad used to play it together, she on her flute and he on his keyboard. It must have been a year or more since they'd done this, but its melody was part of the musical library in her mind, and every now and then, she would find herself humming it.

Beatrix tugged the manuscript book out of the smaller of her two bags.

'Here,' she said, opening the book to the right page. 'It's the best I have.'

Felix kissed her. 'Will you play it for me?'

'It has two parts,' Beatrix said.

'Just the melody, then?'

Beatrix took out her flute and fitted its parts together. As she played the notes of the treble clef, Felix's eyes moved from Beatrix to the sheet music and back again. By the time she had reached the end, he had taken his cello from its case and begun to play the notes on the bass clef, improvising to fit the piano music to his own instrument.

In twenty-seven minutes from now, the final call would come

for Beatrix to get on the train to London. She would be crying while she kissed Felix goodbye, and not gentle little sniffs either, but great big racking sobs that made her worry she was going to get snot on his face. And then the doors would close, and Felix would be left to stand there, nothing in his hands but a leather-bound manuscript book, watching the train haul its many carriages out of the station and away, ripping his heart out of his chest and towing it behind as if on a string, a sad little red thing bouncing along on the tracks.

But that wouldn't be for twenty-seven minutes yet. For now, Beatrix returned to the beginning of the song, and Felix followed her lead. As she played, she glanced up now and then from the sheet music to watch Felix's fingers pounce from string to string, effortlessly and unerringly finding their mark. To Beatrix, the song was familiar, but for Felix this was true sight-reading – *a prima vista* – and yet the two pieces of the song fitted together as if they had always been meant to be played together on a flute and a cello in a waiting room in a cold train station, where backpacking couples unburdened themselves of their luggage and stood rubbing their shoulders, and men came out of M&S with bunches of flowers to take with them on their journeys by way of apology or seduction, where business people towed tidy little suitcases as they hurried on through the concourse and an elderly lady sat with a dachshund on her lap, its coat made from the same tartan as her shopping bag.

THREE

as simple as that

WHEN EVIE WOKE, she had no sense that this day would be significantly different from the one before, or the one before that. Although the morning sky was still dark when she threw back her ugly floral curtains, she knew that it would lighten only to the motley January-grey colour it had already been for weeks on end. And while there was a pile of clothes on the floor beside her bed, the clothes were all – as usual – her own. Not a single visual clue remained to confirm that Dave had even been here in the night.

It was often like this, so much so that Evie had become accustomed to waking up with the idea that she might only have imagined him. Sometimes it seemed to her that the Dave she knew in the darkness – tender and fragile – was some kind of dream-creature and not a real man at all.

Evie showered and dressed in her coffee-making blacks. Downstairs, Dave was sitting at the kitchen table with a pen in hand, a notebook splayed open in front of him, and the slightly wired aura of someone who had consumed the entire contents of the large coffee plunger that stood empty on the table. Probably he'd been awake since the time he'd left her bed in the early hours.

'Morning,' she said.

'Working,' he replied.

How did I sleep? Not bad, thanks. You? Evie thought, flicking on the kettle.

'The milk went off,' Dave said, without looking up from his notebook.

Evie registered the carton sitting in the sink. Without milk, there was no coffee that Evie could be bothered with, so she took a clementine from the fruit bowl. She put her thumb through the skin of the little soft patch at its crown, peeled it, and ate it segment by segment. Still, Dave said nothing, but neither did he write any words on the blank page in front of him.

If Dave *was* actually some kind of fairy-tale character, Evie thought, then he was probably one of the sort cursed to go about in the daytime inside a prickly pelt that he could only throw off after dark. If he and she were in a fairy tale, then maybe there would be a way to release him from his curse. Perhaps she would be able to find his discarded skin and throw it in the fire. Or something.

Dave tilted in his chair, just ever so slightly, enough to allow a fart to escape from beneath one cheek of his bum, and Evie's thoughts of fairy tales evaporated. Instead, she thought that maybe her relationship with Dave was more like that of a long-married couple, except that she and Dave had skipped the part where they'd fallen in love and believed in a happily-ever-after future, and just fast-forwarded themselves to the bit where they no longer reserved for their partner a single cup of coffee out of a full-sized plunger, and where it was fine to fart out loud and not excuse it. Maybe it was some kind of strange blessing that there had been no passionate love affair that had hollowed out or gone sour, and no golden age to look back on and regret having lost.

Evie gathered up all the little orange scabs of clementine peel from the table, and as she walked past Dave on her way to the rubbish bin, she thought about how normal it would be for most people, in a moment like this one, to drop a kiss onto their lover's head; at the very least to deliver a tiny touch to their shoulder.

Evie's morning at Starbucks was standard, and her visit to the poetry library at lunchtime was pleasant but unremarkable. She worked steadily through the afternoon, smiling approvingly at the customers who remembered to bring their keep-cups and shrugging ruefully along with the much greater number of customers who forgot. When the day was done, she walked to her bus stop and had been standing there for a few minutes, waiting in the cold, when a very ordinary thought occurred to her. *Milk*.

While Dave could be relied upon to replenish the house stores of beer and whisky, it wasn't wise to trust that he'd go out to the shops for milk. If Evie wanted coffee the next morning, she'd have to provide for herself; the nearest shop she could think of was the M&S in Waverley Station.

The chill of the January afternoon seemed to chase after Evie as she descended on the steep escalator into the station's heart. After locating the full-cream milk amid the bewildering array of low-fat and no-fat milks, she paid for her purchase at one of the self-service booths that both pleased her introvert tendencies and made her worry about being complicit in the layoff of supermarket staff. She made her way out into the ticket hall, and that was when she heard it.

Evie didn't know if she heard the cello first or the flute, or if she heard them both together, but the picture her mind immediately made out of the two sounds was of a pale silk ribbon twining around the branches of a dark-wooded tree. Her eyes quickly sought out the source of what her ears had already found, and there they were. A pair of teenagers, he playing the cello, she the flute.

On those unexceptional railway station chairs, the two musicians sat as close to each other as their instruments would allow, their bodies angled inwards, a book of music propped open on the seat between them. The young man was almost ridiculously good-looking, his dark red hair overgrown and his long limbs both lanky and fluid as he played. She, too, was beautiful, with thick sandy-blonde curls and a poised way of holding her body – shoulders back, chest open – that seemed to be all of a piece with the way the music flowed through her and into the flute and out into the hallway.

Evie moved closer, feeling the way the music made something inside her rise and fall in accord with its rhythms. The cello's part ascended and descended in a discernible pattern while the flute's part darted and soared. Evie could feel the song reaching into the very middle of her, tugging on different threads. If she'd had to describe the feeling, she'd have said it was something like the bittersweet feeling of wanting to cry for happiness.

But if Evie was honest – and she always tried to be – watching these two, listening to them, was also bringing out in her the bright green sting of envy. Evie could see in the set of their bodies, and hear in the notes of their music, that the cellist and the flautist were in love. Not just any kind of love, either. What they were feeling, what they were playing, wasn't tepid love, or friendly love, or practical love, or sympathetic love, or convenient love. Flowing between them in the music was passionate love, all-or-nothing love, a-little-bit-dizzy-in-the-head love – love of the kind that Evie had only ever seen from the outside. It hurt her even to admit how much she wanted to feel it for herself.

What was it, Evie wondered, that made some people fit for a love like that, and left other people wanting? Was love like a radio signal, and you just had to be lucky enough to be born with your heart's dials tuned to the right frequency? Or was it something that could only happen to you when you were young and fearless? And, if so, had Evie already grown too old and too scared? Had she already missed her chance? Or was there still time?

When the music stopped, Evie watched the cellist lean in to kiss the flautist: a hold-nothing-back kiss that caused a woman reading a magazine to look up with a supervisory air, and cough. Evie could see that although the musicians pulled away from each other, they remained connected, the invisible traces of the music still moving between and around them.

That, she thought. *I want that.*

She walked back to the bus stop with the carton of milk under her arm, aware of the width of the chasm that lay between the kind of love she'd just witnessed and the sad, decaffeinated thing that passed for love in her life with Dave. Her bus arrived, and even before it had delivered her to Leith, Evie had decided. It was time. Not just to go, but – this time – to go home.

It took just over a month for Evie to cast off all her ties. She felt a small amount of regret when she gave her notice at the Thorn and Thistle, but none at all when she quit her job at Starbucks.

For all the time Evie had been travelling, she'd had an amount of money in her bank account which she chose to regard as equivalent to zero. The sum – which was enough to get her home and allow her to live for a couple of months without an income – had sat there in case of an emergency. However, the fact that she'd regarded it for all these years as a kind of calcified deposit didn't, in the end, make it difficult to spend.

By way of a series of easy swipes and clicks, she booked herself an off-peak train ticket to London and a night in a cheap hotel near Heathrow. The February airfares to the east coast of Australia were blessedly low, but the same could not be said of Melbourne's summertime accommodation prices.

She was going to need a couple of weeks in 'Tram Town': time enough to retrieve and sort through the belongings she'd left in storage there, and also to work out which part of the country to head for next.

When Evie had left Australia, she'd not been able to bring herself to sell her 1960 pastel blue Volkswagen Beetle, so she'd treated it like an oversized suitcase and crammed it with as much as would fit, before driving it into a rickety garage in the backyard of an old friend of her brother-in-law's. And there it remained, out of registration and most likely undriveable by now. For all she knew, mice might have made their homes in the seats, and silverfish might have eaten the clothes and books she'd been unable to discard. She hardly remembered what else she'd stacked away on that long-ago day when she'd been about to set off to see the world.

In her last week in Edinburgh, Evie made sure to visit all of her favourite haunts – the Library Bar in Teviot Row House, the Writers' Museum, Calton Hill and, of course, the poetry library. She returned her borrowed books, used up the last of her shampoo and conditioner, and took several shopping bags full of winter clothes to a charity shop. At last, all that remained was to say goodbye to Dave.

She left it as late as possible. On the morning of the day she was to take the train to London, she moved slowly through the small, gloomy rooms of Dave's house, collecting up the last of her things. Everything she did felt significant because she knew she was doing it for the last time. This would be the last time she walked up these stairs, the last time she opened this bedroom door, the last time she had to look at that awful wallpaper.

Her notebooks went first into the deep belly of her backpack, and her few remaining items of clothing filled the spaces around the edges of them. Evie hefted the pack onto her back, secured its clasps and went downstairs, keys in her hand. Dave was in the kitchen, not long back from the off-licence. There was a bottle on the table, still in its paper bag, and his coat gave off the street's familiar scent of mossy coldness. He looked at Evie, and then looked more closely, his expression of surprise amplified by his halo of unkempt hair.

'I'm tempted to say you look like you're going somewhere,' he remarked.

'Yes, well. I'm going home,' Evie said.

'Home? What do you mean, *home*?'

'I mean, home home.' She set the house keys on the table.

'As in, Australia?'

'Yes.'

'What? *Now*?'

'More or less,' Evie said.

'Wow, I . . . uh. I kind of didn't see this coming. Should we *talk*?'

Evie, her shoulders feeling the strain of the heavy pack, smiled sadly. 'What would we say, Dave?'

'What about your jobs . . . the café? The pub?'

'I quit.'

'Just like that?'

'They won't miss me. At least, not for more than five minutes.'

As these words landed on Dave, Evie saw they'd struck him as personal.

'And, what, you think that's the same for me?'

'Isn't it?' Evie replied, gently.

'Pissed at me, are you?'

Evie shook her head, and quite truthfully said, 'No.'

There was no use being pissed at Dave. He was what he was, after all. He was a boy wonder who'd grown up loved and lauded. Then he'd grown up some more and things hadn't gone according to plan. Instead of changing the plan, though, he'd only kept looking in the bottom of a bottle for the plan that he originally had, the one that everyone promised.

'It's time I went home, Dave. Got myself a life,' she said. 'That's all.'

'Shit, Greensleeves,' he said, and he reached out for her hands. His were cold, and she wrapped her fingers over the top of his to impart some of her warmth. 'Shit, shit, shit,' he repeated.

'Yeah,' she agreed.

'I'm kind of blown away here. Australia? Fuck.' Genuinely bewildered, he asked, 'Was it something I did? Is this about New Year's Eve? About that thing I said, about your poetry? Look, I was an arsehole, I admit it. I'm sorry. But you shouldn't take anything I say too—'

Evie leaned towards Dave and kissed his cheek.

'Dave? Do you know what's going to happen to me next in my life? I'll tell you. I'm going to meet somebody. Somebody nice. Somebody really nice. And they're going to want me. Really, properly want me, not just kind-of. And it's going to be as simple as that.'

Dave looked at his feet. 'I'm sorry it wasn't better than it was.'

'It doesn't matter,' she said.

He opened the front door for her, and she stepped out into the street, feeling ungainly under the weight of her backpack.

'Maybe I'll come visit you one day,' Dave said.

But Evie knew he didn't mean this; it was just the kind of thing you said at a time like this, when there was really nothing else left to say.

dark mode

ALONE IN THE offices of Sonder Digital on a Saturday afternoon, Arie was deep in the inner workings of the website for an artisan brewery called Humulus.

'I want something special,' the brewery owner had said, and Richard and Arie had nodded, knowing how often clients wanted 'something special', but not the price-tag that went along with it. Richard had diplomatically explained this.

'No, no – I *really* want something special,' the owner said. 'And I expect to have to pay for it.'

Back at the beginning of their partnership, Arie would have built the back end of a site like this one, and Richard would have tackled the design interaction and front-end experience. Arie's meticulousness and Richard's flair had got them a long way. But Arie was no slouch in the creative department either, and these days Richard was so tied up in client liaison and managing the staff that it was rare for him to have time for the dreaming and experimentation needed for a job like this one. Arie, therefore, had decided to take on Humulus as a pet project of his own.

Although Sonder had grown, it was still small-scale compared to most of its competitors. The workspace was not superbly renovated, and despite the diffuser sticks that several of the staff kept on their desks – creating a weird mélange of lime, basil, grapefruit and gardenia – there was no hiding the smells of engine oil and ink that were an ongoing legacy of the building's printing press days.

Almost a year ago, a couple of the staff had hit upon the idea of putting Sonder's main room into dark mode by replacing the plain light globes with purple LEDs. It gave the place the nocturnal feel of a bar or a nightclub. Dark mode wasn't a decor decision Arie would have made himself but he had to admit his staff were right – the purple globes made the dodgy plaster walls and fraying carpets less obvious, and none of the clients who came to Sonder headquarters for meetings ever failed to comment on the lighting.

Not everyone liked it, however, and Richard was among its detractors. Arie, though, had taken the concept and run with it, installing a huge light box on an otherwise empty wall and allowing the staff to use it for random words or inspirational messages. Right now, owing to an ongoing joke between two of the junior developers, the words on the light box were: FEAR ME, FOR I AM THE SPAGHETTI CODER OF THE APOCALYPSE.

Once, Arie wouldn't have been alone at the office on a Saturday afternoon, but the arrival of little Marek in Richard's life had changed his view on overtime. In fact, Richard had become evangelical about the staff knocking off promptly at the end of a day. At 5 pm on the dot, he'd stand up at his desk, announce the hour and start shepherding everyone out the door. Arie wasn't exempt from Richard's nagging, but his position as a partner in the business enabled him, mostly, to ignore it.

Over the past two years, the staff had settled into a particular way of behaving around Arie. He sometimes felt as if there was a forcefield extending a couple of metres around him and that when his colleagues stepped inside its radius, they felt the need to tread more softly, move more slowly, talk more quietly.

He dropped out of the table-tennis roster when he realised that everyone was letting him win, and that the game's usual soundtrack of laughter and cheerful abuse never reached its normal volume when he was in the room. He also knew he got away with swearing in a way that nobody else did. One of the designers, Lee, was a zealot when it came to the swear jar, charging fifty cents per 'shit', a dollar per 'fuck', and two dollars per instance of blasphemy, regardless of the deity. Although she had the ears of a bat, she never seemed to hear a bad word come from Arie's lips.

The desk closest to Arie's belonged to Jenavive, a junior developer cursed by her parents to spend her life spelling out her name. She was a pale young woman who sat – in the months of autumn, winter and spring – with a granny-square rug over her knees to keep out the cold, and her niche of the office was decorated in a style that Arie imagined she had cribbed from a craft magazine, involving a good many succulent plants popping out of unexpected objects including a hot pink stiletto and an old rotary dial telephone. She was talented and hard-working, but she had the slightly irritating habit of making Arie cups of undrinkable tea. She never let the teabags steep for long enough, but at least dark mode made it possible for him to surreptitiously tip cold tea into the soil of a forgiving umbrella plant.

Weekends were Arie's favourite time to be at work. On Saturdays and Sundays there was no nagging from Richard, no cat-piss cups of tea from Jenavive, and nobody speaking to him in careful don't-upset-the-grieving-man tones. He could just work in solitude, for as long and late as he wanted, disappearing as deep as he liked into the alternative dimension of code, sinking hour after hour into the unique websites that made Sonder Digital's services pricey, but sought after.

Arie had no sense of what time it was when he heard the turning latch of the door in the foyer adjacent to the main room where he was working. It was Richard, no doubt. Looking up from his screen, Arie blinked and stretched. From the ache down the left side of his body, he knew that he'd been slouching at his standing desk again, and from the insistent throb of 1980s throw-back electronica in his ears, he knew that the junior developers had once again been much too instrumental in the composition of this week's Spotify playlist.

He was surprised to see that it wasn't Richard who'd arrived, but Lenka. She was looking decidedly weekend-ish, in a casual skirt and T-shirt, her light brown hair pulled back into a ponytail. She had a basket with her, and an air of purpose.

'Hey,' Arie said.

She set her basket down on Richard's desk.

'Thought I might find you here.' Lenka glanced up at the purple light globes. 'I don't know how you can work in here. When was the last time you saw sunlight?'

'I haven't been here that long,' Arie lied. 'I had an idea for this site, the Humulus thing. Thought I'd catch it before it disappeared on me.'

Aware that he was justifying himself to Lenka, and that actually he didn't have to, he waited for her to explain what she, herself, was doing here. She wasn't exactly a stranger to the place; she often called by to take Richard out for a lunch date, and sometimes she brought Marek in to say hello to Daddy. But for her to call in on a Saturday, without Richard?

She came over to sit at Jenavive's desk, right near Arie's.

'The reason I'm here,' she said, 'is to find out why *you* are here.'

'I told you, I—'

'No, Arie. Why are you here? Outside, the sun is shining. It is a beautiful day.'

She was speaking to him, Arie realised, the way she spoke to Marek. Slowly, deliberately, her slight middle-European accent more pronounced than usual.

'Did Richard tell you to come here and send me home?'

'Richard is worried about you, yes. But I made my own choice to come. I made a promise, you remember.'

He did remember. Many times, Lenka had invoked the promise she made to Diana on the night before she went away. *I'll feed him and water him. Make sure he occasionally gets fresh air and sunlight*, she had said. *I promise.*

'Lenka, I'm fine. I—'

'You are not. This is bullshit.'

He looked at his friend, and in her hazel eyes he saw a certain steeliness. He'd glimpsed this part of her in her interactions with Richard, but he'd never before been on the receiving end of it.

'You cannot stare at screens forever. You will make yourself sick.'

Again that slow, enunciated speech, like he was eighteen months old.

'I really do have work—'

'This is crap. You work too much. And you know it. *Why* are you here?'

'I don't . . . like being at home on the weekends,' he admitted.

'And why is that?'

'The place is so quiet.'

'Then you have to make noise,' she said, simply.

'It's not just that. It's—'

'No, I know. But you didn't call me yet,' she said.

'No, I'm not—'

'Arie, it is now February.'

What she meant by this, and Arie knew it, was that a month had passed since the second anniversary of Diana's death. On that day, Lenka and Richard, and Marek too, had accompanied him on his journey to the cemetery. For the last stretch of the drive, Belinda had been with them as well – she and Arie squeezed into the back seat of Lenka's small European car on either side of Marek's car seat. It had smelled of curdled milk, baby wipes, and the huge bunch of Asiatic lilies that Lenka held on her lap while Richard drove. That day, Lenka had offered to help Arie deal with Diana's things – the wardrobe, her jewellery, the things in the bathroom. Lenka would come, she told him, with boxes and bags, and together they could go through it all and she would take away whatever he wanted taken away, so that he never had to think about it again. All he had to do, she'd told him, was call her and name the day.

'I love you, Arie, but I think I am no longer keeping my promise if all I do is say *there, there*. It is true – she was remarkable, and you loved her. It is also true that she is gone. It is sad and unfair, and it is shit, Arie. Total shit. But you have wallowed long enough, now. It's time.'

'For what, exactly? To start dating?'

'I don't care if you date or drive yourself to Timbuktu. I'm not going to tell you what to do, except for this one thing.' She leaned towards him and took his face in one hand, a thumb and a forefinger on each of his cheeks, the way his mother might have taken hold of him when he was little. She looked at him, almost fiercely. 'Live now.'

She stood up and walked away from him, as if she had surprised even herself with the level of her intensity. Onto Richard's desk she unloaded the contents of her basket, making a stack of boxes. They contained, Arie realised, light globes.

'One more thing, actually,' Lenka said. 'Get rid of the fucking purple bulbs. This place needs some light.'

That afternoon, Arie went home earlier than he would normally have done. In the comparatively calm streets, he paused for other drivers to reverse in a leisurely Saturday fashion into parking spots on streets lined with cafés and clothing shops. Lenka had been right; it was a beautiful day.

When he turned into Tavistock Row, he noticed a woman walking down the street, dwarfed by the enormous pack that she carried on her back. She walked the way that travellers so often did, glancing down at the piece of paper in her hands, then looking up at the houses, searching for a number or a sign.

Her hair was almost black and cut into a bob that swung into points at either side of her jaw, its colour contrasting sharply with her winter-white skin. She wore a corduroy skirt and what appeared to be woollen tights, and her long sleeves were pushed up to the elbow. The boots she wore were for hiking, large and heavy-looking, but her legs were long and thin, so that there was a hint of Olive Oyl to her silhouette.

When Arie stepped out of his parked car, she was standing on the street, looking confused. He would have been willing to place a bet on why.

'You after the Airbnb?' he asked her.

'Yes,' she said. She looked tired and hot; there was a hint of dampness at her hairline. 'Apparently I'm looking for 12, which is *that* one. But this message from the host says it's the place with the courtyard in the front, which is *this* one. But this is 12A?'

'12A's the one you want,' Arie said, 'but for some reason, the A gets dropped off the address all the time. I have a lot of people showing up on my doorstep thinking they're about to move in. The key safe's not easy to find, either. It's behind the pot plant.'

She smiled with relief. He had the feeling that she was all out of energy for obstacles and challenges. She walked up the path to the front door and pushed aside the foliage of a climbing rose.

'Got it?' Arie checked.

'Thanks!'

'Welcome.'

She referred again to the piece of paper in her hand, punched in the combination to the key safe, and let herself inside. Idly, Arie wondered how long she'd be staying.

do you spark joy?

THREE DAYS AFTER Evie arrived at the Airbnb on Tavistock Row, she stood in the middle of the living room and acknowledged to herself that she had wrecked the joint.

When she'd first come into this room, it had been the picture of *Vogue Living* perfection. The walls were white, the windows were covered with white louvred shutters, and sparse mid-century Danish furniture had been artfully arranged. The polished floorboards were partially covered with a cowhide rug, and a few fashionable novels and non-fiction titles had been stacked in symmetrical pyramids on the shelves of narrow white bookcases. It had been hot outside when she arrived, but the cleaner had left the air-conditioner ticking over, and the radio softly playing ABC Classic FM, so that the place exuded a cool, studious calm.

Now, though, the living room looked like a bad day at a charity shop. There were cardboard cartons closed up with perished and peeling tape, opaque plastic tubs with cracked lids, battered suit-cases, a rusty ironing board, a rolled Persian rug, a sewing machine and a guitar, both in their latched-up travelling cases. Evie had pulled all of this out of her Beetle and ferried it back to the Airbnb in a rent-a-car. The Beetle itself – dusty and cobwebbed – would have to stay where it was until she could replace its tyres and get it re-registered, or try to sell it.

The owner of the garage was a middle-aged and tightly be-denimed guy known only as Crosby; he'd once been in a pub band with Evie's brother-in-law, Reuben. With some difficulty, he'd flung up the tilting garage door to reveal Evie's Beetle, parked next to a motorboat that looked like it hadn't seen the sea in a decade.

Crosby had nudged one of the Beetle's flat tyres with his toe. 'She still goes. I checked her now and then, turned the engine over. Lucky you didn't leave it too much longer, though. I was only going to give you one more year, then I was going to scrap the bloody thing. You know, if Reuben and Stella didn't want to deal with it.'

But when Evie hefted a case of cold Crownies into his arms and thanked him repeatedly and enthusiastically for his trouble, he'd looked pleased and told her that it really hadn't been a bother at all.

'How are Reuben and Stel, by the way?' he asked. 'Haven't seen them for bloody years.'

The same was true for Evie.

'They seem to be fine,' she said.

Crosby nodded. 'Where are you going to go, now you're back?'

Evie had shrugged and smiled. 'Not sure yet. I'm just going to . . . take it as it comes.'

Now, hands on hips, hair held back with a headscarf, Evie stood in the centre of the mess she'd made and wondered where and how to begin the task of sorting through the possessions that her past self had considered worthy of bequeathing to her future. From a suitcase she'd exhumed the crumpled summer skirt she now wore, and from a shoebox she'd extracted the Amy

Winehouse CD that was playing on the house stereo. It was time to get seriously Marie Kondo.

'Do you spark joy?' she silently asked the Husqvarna.

'I do,' the trusty old sewing machine confirmed, reminding Evie of dresses past. It would be nice to make herself some new clothes, whenever, wherever she settled. Evie moved the heavy case to the side of the room she intended for the 'to keep' pile.

Next, she identified which of the cardboard cartons contained the china dinner service that had been handed down to her mother, from her own mother. When Evie's mother had died, Jacinta – the eldest of Evie's half-sisters – hadn't wanted the china, and neither had Stella. Evie had been only eight years old at the time, and Stella had decided to pack the boxes away in case Evie grew into the kind of young woman who would one day want a Royal Worcester dinner service.

Evie undid the packing tape and peeled the yellowed newspaper away from a teapot with a fussy, gilt-edge floral pattern. As she did so, she glanced at her wristwatch, which was, as ever, reporting that the time was a few minutes to five o'clock, even though mid-morning sun was shining in bright beams through the gaps in the shutters. Evie, feeling an old familiar sadness, breathed out and then forced her lips into one of those smiles that were supposed to make you feel better if you faked them for long enough.

'Do you spark joy?' she asked the boxes full of china.

'Actually, no,' was the answer from the dinner plates and the side plates, the soup plates and the bowls, the teacups and the saucers and the matching salt-and-pepper shakers. 'We give you guilt and a storage problem.'

One of the things she had known before she had begun this task was that it was going to require her to make hard decisions about the physical objects that were all she had left of her mother's life. Evie sifted through the faded, moth-eaten memories of her early childhood, but she didn't think she had any real, actual memories of her mother using the Royal Worcester. Fine china had never really been her mother's thing.

'I'm sorry,' Evie murmured to the boxes, and moved them to the side of the room for things that had to go.

She sighed, summoned another modicum of strength, and approached a series of cardboard cartons clearly marked BOOKS. Inside, she knew, there would be novels and poetry, plays and non-fiction, old books, new books, books, books, books . . .

'Do you—'

'Don't you dare even *ask*,' the cartons replied, and Evie moved them all to the 'to keep' pile.

Next was an archive box, and written in her own long-ago handwriting on the side were the words SENTIMENTAL STUFF. Evie, trying to remember what she might have classified in this way, peeled away the tape.

Here was her first pair of shoes – a pair of tiny doeskin moccasins, stored inside lemon-coloured tissue paper in a decorative cardboard box. And here was a pair of pink silk ballet slippers. Evie had never been a dancer, not for a moment, but at the age of sixteen it had been her fashion statement to wear them everywhere, their tatty ribbons criss-crossed up her calves. Reuben had glued on a pair of makeshift leather soles to help them last.

There was a pair of beloved jeans, patched until they were composed more of patches than denim. Her first passport. The first pot she'd thrown in ceramics class at high school – lumpy, but with a beautiful midnight blue glaze. Beneath these odd treasures were her diaries.

Just like the notebooks that filled her backpack, they were a haphazard collection. The earliest were covered in bright-coloured contact paper, presumably by Stella, while the ones from her teenage years were her own creations, their covers decorated with intricate collages of magazine pictures – actors, singers, roses, mermaids, swans, scraps of paisley print. Evie opened the earliest of the books and began to read.

In the childhood handwriting she'd once thought so grown-up was a story called 'The Girl with Six Sisters and None at All', and another called 'The Seven Princesses of Peregrine'. Book by book, as the writing settled into something Evie recognised as her own hand, the imaginative content gave way to self-examination (*why must you sulk, go quiet and retreat, instead of saying what you want?*), dreams (*one day I will live by the beach with a very small dog and a very large cat*), accounts of loves begun and ended, scraps of song lyrics and charts for guitar chords, stanzas of dreadful poetry, and doodles of dying roses.

Hours passed. Occasionally Evie got up to go to the bathroom, get herself a drink or make yet another round of the Vegemite toast on which she was subsisting, but mostly she sat, cross-legged on the cowhide rug, and read. There were so many stories, so many thoughts, so many feelings . . . but she could hardly remember having any of them. Between the pages of these books she had pressed, like flowers, herself as a dreamy child, the introverted teen-ager, a young woman on the edge of adult life. The eight-year-old child wanted her mother back, the fourteen-year-old girl wanted to kiss Will Daintree, the twenty-two-year-old woman wanted to see the world. Every page so different, and yet every one of them a private record of the same thing . . . *I want, I want, I want.*

Evie wasn't sure how diaries so full of anticipation, hope and ideals had been written by the same person who had ended up thinking it was a good idea to move in with Dave Wright, just because he had a spare room and the ability to spin life into words like straw into gold. She wondered, as she read, if the process of growing up was the process of learning not to want, or to squash the wanting deep down inside you where it couldn't be seen and could only be felt dimly, until something happened to sharpen its edges. Like hearing a love song in a train station.

By the time Evie came to the last page of the last diary – *I am casting off into the world, I wonder what I will find there* – the light coming in through the shutters had the golden tone of late evening. She felt drained. Diaries, after all, had a habit of sifting out the average parts of life and leaving only the extremes, but sixteen years' worth of highs and lows was a lot to absorb in a single sitting. She loaded the diaries back into the archive box and replaced the lid.

'Do you spark joy?' she asked the box.

'What a dumb question,' the box replied. 'I hold the archive of your heart, Evie Greenlees – its joys *and* its sorrows.'

Adding the small box to the 'to keep' pile, Evie became aware of just how little progress she'd made on sorting through her belongings. Her neck was stiff, her eyes felt dry, and she'd been cooped up in this room all day long.

Since arriving in Tavistock Row, she'd been contemplating the prospect of the banana lounges in the brick-paved courtyard in the front garden, and now seemed like the time to try them. On her way out the door, she picked up her guitar case.

'Do you spark joy?' she asked it.

'Cheeky cow,' the guitar said. 'You know I do.'

'Just checking.'

Outside, the sky was a greyish-blue with cloud-strokes of yellow. The scorching heat of the day had dissipated, and the air was mild. Arriving back in the country, she'd found she'd become re-sensitised to the dusty mint of eucalypt trees, and she could smell it now, along with the fragrance of the jasmine that was rioting all over the front of the house next door.

Evie perched on the edge of one of the banana lounges and settled the guitar's curvy, symmetrical concert-style body into her lap. As ever, she was pleased by its rich sunburst pattern which moved through shades of reddish brown to amber to pale gold. Once, this guitar had been Reuben's. Evie was thirteen when Reuben had upgraded to a new guitar, and the old one she'd loved had disappeared – sold and gone forever, she imagined. Then, when Christmas came, the old steel-string was under the tree for her and Evie had played it all day long – the same three songs over and over – until she had blisters on her fingertips.

Evidently, she'd been diligent enough to loosen the strings before putting the instrument in storage, so it took a while to get it back in any sort of tune. She hadn't played at all the entire time she'd been away, but although her fingertips felt soft and unfamiliar on the strings, her left hand shaped itself into chords on the fretboard without too much trouble. As a few elementary finger-picking patterns emerged from the muscle-memory of her hands, she found that she still knew how to play the songs that Reuben had taught her – old folk songs that told sad stories, like 'Scarborough Fair', 'Wild Mountain Thyme', 'Danny Boy' and 'Barbara Allen'.

Evie had only ever been the most amateur of guitarists, and usually confined her playing to the moody privacy of her own bedroom. All the songs she'd written had either been love songs with repetitive, boppy chorus lines, or break-up songs in a minor key. Now, just as she had done as a teenager, Evie wished she were a better musician. If she were, she might have been able to replicate the love song she'd heard in Waverley Station, played on the cello and the flute.

Since the day she'd heard it, little grabs of that song's melody had repeated themselves in her memory. She couldn't remember it all, just a couple of phrases. Closing her eyes, she hummed one of them, then tried to produce the same sequence of notes on the guitar. *Close*, she thought. *Not exactly, but close.* Gradually, little by little, the sound the guitar was making moved closer to the sounds she could hear in her memory. She wondered where the song had come from, whether it had been written by the red-haired boy, or the sandy-haired girl, or someone else entirely.

Playing just these shreds of the song didn't give her the same feeling as the one she'd experienced in the train station. But – sitting there on the banana lounge that evening, imperfectly finger-picking the barest bones of a song on her old guitar, while mosquitoes grazed on her ankles – she was able to summon up a trace of it, at least.

Evie would have been the first to admit that the notes she was playing were a pale imitation of the song in its full glory. They were a wisp of the real thing, at best. And yet, they drifted upwards like a thin trace of smoke, past the star-shaped flowers of the jasmine vine, to brush against the glass of the bay window on the upper storey of the house next door.

It was fortunate that the window was open just a little, because it allowed the notes of the song to slip into the piano room, slide across the gleaming top of the Steinway, and sneak under the frame of one of the frosted glass doors to the landing. But that was about as far as they could carry on the still air of that summer night. There, the song could do no more than wait and hope to be heard.

—INTERLUDE—

WHEN TOM WENDALE was on the road and found himself with a night to spare in Vancouver, he rarely bothered to alert his mother, even though she lived in a beautiful home in the West End and would for certain have wanted to know he was in town. Rather, it was Tom's style to slip into the city undetected – doss down for the night on a friend's sofa, or even just catch a few Zs on the floor at whatever party or jam session he'd managed to find – then slide out again without a trace. Today, though, a combination of sentiment and guilt had made him hump his guitar case and duffel bag all the way from Waterfront Station to Haro Street, where he found himself standing across from a pretty-as-a-picture nineteenth-century weatherboard with a front yard full of magnolias and Sitka spruce.

Tom crossed the road and stepped onto the verge, sending a grey squirrel scurrying up the trunk of a tree where it paused, furry little arms outstretched, claws gripping the bark, as it watched to see what this slightly roguish-looking man would do next. Tom took a deep breath and opened the gate. He lugged his gear up a wide flight of steps, set it down on the front porch and knocked on the door. While he waited, he observed that the house was freshly painted – its boards in an elegant shade of slate blue, its trimmings as white and bright as royal icing. Ruched curtains hung in the windows of the boxy bay window that protruded out onto the porch, where an outdoor table of white-painted wrought iron was surrounded by matching chairs. Three of them. Even the doormat was pretty, its patterned threads in a blue that matched the colour of the house.

He knocked again and waited some more, but it seemed there really was nobody home. It occurred to him that he could head back into town – just pick up his guitar and his bag and be on his way without Cassie ever being any the wiser. She'd just keep on with her weekend, oblivious to his proximity, being all tied up with her wealthy husband and her second son and her market basket full of fresh sourdough and big bunches of jonquils, or whatever it was that Cassie did on Saturdays nowadays. But while the thought of absconding gave him some kind of self-defeating pleasure, the walk from the station had been tiring, and his luggage was heavy.

Just visible beneath the fronds of a hanging plant at the side of the front door was a key safe. Cassie was fond of key safes. Back when she'd been a single, working mum and Tom had been her only kid – her latch-key kid – she'd usually installed one outside the front door of their apartment. There had been many apartments over the years of his childhood: apartments that were never freshly painted, and – no matter the city – never in the kind of neighbourhood where you'd just go ahead and leave an expensive matchy-matchy doormat lying around outside.

Tom considered the key safe.

Was it possible that he knew the code?

He scrolled the tiny dials until they made the combination

1812, four numbers that nodded to Tchaikovsky's *1812 Overture*, but were also one way – of Canada's many ways – to write Tom's birth date: 18 December.

Tom had a guitarist's fingernails – short on the left hand for finding the notes on the fretboard, long on the right hand for finger-picking – and he used one of his long nails to flick the small catch on the safe. It slid easily and the safe door popped open, revealing the key; which proved, Tom supposed, that at least in this small four-digit way he was still a presence in his mother's life.

Inside, hats and coats and scarves were hung on a row of hooks, all the garments artfully tossed together like something out of a magazine spread. Tom supposed you couldn't go far wrong if everything you bought was blue or grey or cream and cost a bomb. He took off his boots in consideration of the plush dove grey carpet, but suddenly his creased black stovepipe pants, his denim jacket, and indeed all the rest of him, felt dusty and shabby and road-worn.

Once upon a time in this house's history, a weary traveller might have been shown to a room with a washstand, and given a big pitcher of warm water and a freshly laundered towel. Instead his welcome was a noise that sounded something like *yerr-rrrowwwellll*. It took Tom a moment to realise that the sound was coming from the smoosh-faced Russian blue cat that had appeared in the hallway, her tail curled into a question mark, her smoky coat toning beautifully with the carpet.

'Hello, cat,' Tom said. 'I hope you know you're only decor.'

Tom gave the cat a cursory pat on its head and passed through into the living room. Here there was art, and this was Henry's doing. Tom's stepfather was seriously into art, although he chose his pieces according to some kind of organising principle that Tom couldn't understand. The walls were cluttered with specimens, but Tom couldn't identify the connection between the abstract pieces with their inch-thick paint and the dainty pencil drawings of ugly children, or the huge silvery photographs of women, glamorous as Hollywood starlets, who were shown all in black and white except for one or two strange, watercolour details – like a salmon-coloured fish-fin for a hand, or a lemon yellow duck's bill for lips. On the other hand, Henry's music collection was easy to understand; on a previous visit, Tom had flicked through his CDs and taken almost no time to understand that the connecting factor was that all the music was popular and a little bit cheesy, fitting neatly within what Tom called 'the Neil Diamond spectrum'.

It wasn't until he reached the kitchen that Tom detected his mother's influence. A floor-to-ceiling cork wall panel was covered with colour photographs – hundreds of different images from every era of her life, all jumbled together. There was a picture of herself as a baby right next to one of Tom as a toddler, a recent picture of her and her husband and her younger son at some kind of blue-sea-blue-sky resort next to an image of her teenage self dressed as a Halloween vampire. Best of all, to Tom, there were pictures of him and her sitting in the back of her Kombi van. Along with Cassie herself, that vehicle was the one constant of his childhood. They used to pack it up and take it with them whenever it was time to move cities, whenever his mother's heart had been broken, or her latest job had reached its inevitable dead-end. Always there would be a new apartment, with leaks and draughts in new places, and eventually a new batch of hand-me-down furniture.

It wasn't until Tom was grown up and gone that his mother met Henry and stepped into the pages of *Vogue Living*. Tom was already eighteen, but Cassie was only thirty-four when she had her second child, and after Felix was born, Tom found himself straying further from home and coming back less often.

The truth was that everything hurt him, even though he didn't want it to. He wasn't the materialistic sort, or at least he didn't like to think he was, but it stung him: the way the birthday party invitations matched the serviettes at Felix's third birthday, the goose-down parkas that kept Felix toasty through Canadian winters, Felix's brand-name shoes, the fine gold chain around his perfect little neck, the cello lessons (Tom had taught himself guitar out of a library book), the cello itself (Tom had delivered catalogues for years to buy himself a crappy, second-hand steel-string), and maybe worse than any of that, the way his mother and Henry would sit together at Felix's recitals, eyes shining with pride.

'He's a real talent, isn't he?' Henry would ask Tom, slapping him on the back with a vigour normally reserved for someone choking on a piece of unchewed steak.

Henry was a skinny guy with an oversized head and eyes that stuck out just a bit too much, and it wasn't until he grew his beard and it came out thick and bright red that you could see where Felix's colouring had come from. That was another galling thing about Felix. Somehow, in the split-millisecond of conception, the little brat had managed to sift out every one of Henry's good features and every one of Cassie's, and stitch them all together in such a way that the result was far more than the sum of its parts. Felix was the baby that stopped people in the streets, the kindergartener chosen to be photographed for the school brochure, the token boy on the birthday party invitation list of every girl in his primary school, the heartthrob of his high school.

The most annoying thing about Felix, though, wasn't his designer clothes or his poncy cello music, or his thousand-watt smile, or how quickly and easily everyone loved him. It was the fact that Felix loved Tom, adored Tom, revered and idolised Tom with a sick devotion that made Tom feel like the most unworthy pile of shit ever to be produced in the entire history of faecal matter.

Tom thought kids were supposed to have some amazing sort of sixth sense that told them when somebody didn't like them, but Felix – although he seemed to be smart as paint in every other department – somehow managed to miss the fact that Tom radiated irritation and hostility whenever Felix stood too close to him, breathing on him with his hot little breath, touching him and his stuff with his sticky hands.

For his younger brother's whole life, Tom had hated – most of all – the ungenerous way that Felix made him feel, because he, Tom, was not an ungenerous person. He never passed a person living on the streets without giving something – a coin, a sandwich, the jacket off his back. Among his friends, he never shirked his round at the bar; on stage at a gig, he never hogged the limelight. Tom knew himself to be a person with a big heart, who gave. He gave things and he gave of himself, but when it came to his brother he somehow turned into a miser. Occasionally, when he was travelling he'd send Felix a postcard from some far-flung place, or he'd throw a CD in the mail. The truth was, though, that he didn't really do it for Felix. He did it for Cassie, who wanted nothing more than for Tom to love Felix even half as much as Felix loved him.

Cassie.

She'd been so much younger than all the other mums. In Tom's childhood, she'd never told him off for swearing, and she never brushed his hair in public. She didn't make him tuck his shirt in, or take to his grubby chin with a licked hanky. She'd let him sleep in her bed if he was feeling sick, or just for any old reason really, and she'd let him watch cartoons on a Saturday morning for as long as he liked. There were a lot of nights when she served up a bowl of breakfast cereal for dinner.

If it was that version of Cassie he could visit, Tom thought, then he'd never breeze through Vancouver without stopping by. He'd love to see *that* Cassie again, to spend some time alone with *her*, way more than he wanted to see the Cassie whose key he could now hear turning in the front door lock. He could imagine the way she'd look, fifty-one years old and trim in her denim jeans, but with her hair made straight in some way that wasn't quite natural, and coloured a deep burgundy to cover up the beginnings of her grey.

'Hey, Cassie,' he called out.

That was how he referred to her – Cassie – and he'd been doing it since he'd worked out, at the age of eighteen, that it irked her. It was a way of taking her job away from her, minimising her role. It was his way of saying, you're not my mom any more. Why had he been so nasty?

'*Tom?* That you, honey?' she said, coming into the kitchen with a market basket full of ripe tomatoes and a huge bunch of white roses.

'Prodigal son,' he replied, aware of the slightly hunched figure he was cutting, there in front of the photo-board.

Cassie put the basket down and came towards him with her arms already outstretched. When his mother held him, held him tight the way she always did, he sensed the little shudder in her breathing that was not a million miles away from tears, and Tom felt the weird twin emotions that he always felt in

148

these moments: the longing to sag into her and cry, and the need to pull away.

'How are you, love? How long are you in town? Are you staying? Can I get you a coffee? Hey, I have banana bread. You want some? Are you tired? You look a little tired. Not that I mean you look bad. You don't look bad, you look gorgeous. You're a sight for sore eyes! Have you been travelling? Where have you come from? Oh, listen to me . . .'

'Coffee would be awesome,' Tom said, with a sideways smile.

'Just coffee?'

'Straight black.'

'Nothing to eat? I can't feed you anything?'

Tom shook his head. 'Where is everyone today?'

'Henry's out *sailing*,' Cassie said, in a *bless-his-heart* way. Tom knew his stepfather had recently gone thirds – with two other art-collecting medicos – in a racing yacht.

'And how's Felix?'

'Felix is excellent,' Cassie said, with a sigh and a roll of her eyes.

'Oh?'

'In love.'

'I see,' said Tom, who was not in love, and who – at the age of thirty-five – was already wondering if being in love was just some glorious trick of the hormones that happened to you when you were young and then, when nature was all done with your bloom, *bang*, you lost the hang of it altogether. 'So, who's the lucky girl?'

'She's English. He met her in Edinburgh.'

'Edinburgh?' Tom raised an eyebrow.

'Yeah. At band camp.'

'Many a cherry's popped at band camp,' Tom said, accepting

the steaming cup of coffee his mother held out to him. 'So I hear.'

There was a silence.

'I know, love. I do know. I wish I'd been . . . when you were younger. I wish I'd been able to give you all the things I've been able to give Felix,' she said, and her sincerity was a million times more effective at bringing out his guilt than defensiveness would be.

Tom knew he shouldn't have said that. *So I hear.* Why was he *still* so nasty? If he had bad feelings about his little brother swilling around in his gut, that didn't mean there was any excuse to let them bubble up through the cracks where Cassie could see them.

'Hey,' he said, 'you were an awesome mom. Are, as well.'

Cassie's smile was tight.

'So where is our young Romeo?' Tom asked.

'He's down on Granville Island. Busking. It's how he spends his entire weekend. Saving up for a plane fare to London, you see. Hey, we could go down there. You want to go check him out? He's pretty amazing.'

Tom shrugged. Poncy cello music wasn't really his thing, but the look of entreaty on his mother's face was enough to turn his shrug into a reluctant nod.

When his coffee was finished and the smell of his mom's banana bread – toasting – had got up his nose so that he'd accepted a piece after all, Tom and Cassie walked up the rise and down the other side to the waterfront in the crisp spring-time sunshine. The only other passengers on the tiny little ferry were a pair of middle-aged tourists, earnest in their brand-new outdoorsy clothes and brand-new Canucks scarves, studying their unfolded maps like they were any minute going to be made to sit an exam on the topography of the Vancouver water-ways. Tom and Cassie exchanged a mildly amused look that was all the conversation the two of them needed to have on the topic, and Tom remembered that this was how it was when he was with Cassie – they could say a lot to each other without so much as opening their mouths.

Tom knew that the ramshackle-ness of Granville Island was as carefully curated as the stalls inside its marketplace, but he loved it anyway. The place was a patchwork of corrugated iron buildings coloured deep red and turquoise, umber and silver grey. In the middle of everything there was a place for buskers, a semi-circle of pavement rimmed with rustic timber benches. And there sat Tom Wendale's little brother, Felix Carter, with his electric cello between his lanky knees. Felix sat on a chunk of tree stump, the spike of his cello driven into a gap between the interlocking pavers, with a battery-powered amplifier at his feet. Cassie nodded in Felix's direction, and the nod meant something like, *there he is, right there, isn't he great?* And Tom nodded back that yes, there he was indeed.

But this wasn't the Felix that Tom remembered. There wasn't a single poncy thing about this tall, red-haired young man in his green combat boots, his ripped trousers and his slightly grotty parka. He didn't look, any more, as if his mother dressed him. Or cut his hair. Or insisted that he shave that bit of russet-coloured facial hair that Tom could see drifting down around the sideburn region and creeping along his chin. His brother. His *little* brother. *Well, holy shit.* Felix was turning into a man.

The music wasn't poncy either. The electric cello was strange – a lean, mean, black and skeletal version of its acoustic cousins. Something about its shape made Tom think of a stingray, and somewhere underneath the cello's fretboard a tiny red light blinked like a heartbeat. Felix was playing a classical mash-up, while his amplifier thumped an accompanying beat that radiated outward like a thick, dark but friendly cloud, drawing in the passersby. There were couples and families, tourists and locals, their toes tapping, their hands reaching into their pockets. Felix's cello case was, Tom saw, nicely sprinkled with paper notes and coins.

Tom felt his mother's hand slip into his own. When he was little, she'd had this thing where she'd squeeze his hand twice in quick succession, and that was code for 'I love you'. She did it now, and Tom returned the message.

Felix swayed as he played, side to side, his eyes closed as if nobody at all were watching him. After a while Tom heard a hint of something new creeping into the backbeat, a hint of Asian bells – *gong, gong, gong* – which gave the music a whole new texture. It was, he had to admit, a pretty cool touch. A guy with market bags full of groceries strolled up and threw a five-dollar bill into the cello case, and Tom watched the way Felix somehow knew it was the right moment to open his eyes and, not so much smile as *glow*, by way of thanks. When the mash-up came to an end, the gathered crowd – including Tom and Cassie – applauded.

'He's all right, isn't he?' Cassie said.

'He's all right,' Tom agreed, still clapping.

'Hey, I've got some stuff to do at home. You want to stay here? Come back with Felix when he's done?' Tom could sense his mother's uncertainty. 'You know you're welcome to stay. The night, the week, as long as you like. You know that, right?'

Tom watched Felix fiddling with his phone and amplifier, getting ready to play a new song. Looking at that was easier than looking at his mother's face. *Shit*, Tom thought. Were those tears in her eyes?

'I know, Mom,' he said. 'I do know that.'

'All right. See you when you get home?'

Home.

Felix kicked an effects pedal, launching into the air a rich, techno backing track. For a moment, the young cellist let that sound fill the circle around him, and then he began to play his instrument, plucking the notes of a bittersweet melody.

Then Felix touched the pedal again with his heavy boot and switched from *pizzicato* to bow. Now there was more reverb in the techno track and the volume was going higher.

As the beat built in speed and volume, Felix began to play faster and faster, as if he was scribbling sound on the air, like someone writing with a sparkler on the darkness, and when at last the song came to an end, Felix's face creased with some kind of emotion that Tom didn't fully understand. The last time Tom had seen Felix he'd been maybe fourteen, but that gangly boy was gone now, all grown up.

When Felix opened his eyes, he caught sight of Tom and put his cello down with the kind of haste that Tom wasn't sure was good for an instrument so expensive. Leaving his cello and his case unattended, he headed straight for his brother, and Tom – who'd busked in cities all over the world – wanted to tick him off for being so careless, but there was a light in Felix's eyes as he stepped easily over a timber bench that made Tom feel . . . what was that feeling . . . *chosen*?

Felix didn't hug; instead, he grasped Tom by the whole forearm.

'Hey, man. What're you doing in town?' he asked, delighted.

Tom shrugged. 'Got a gig playing slide on a few tracks for

some buddies. Nothing huge. Thought I'd swing by and say hi to you and Mom. And Henry.'

'Hey, can you hang out? I can go pack up my stuff?'

The big brother sized up the little brother. Felix was tall. He'd pass for nineteen, surely.

'Come on then. I'll buy you a beer.'

Tom saw a tiny speed wobble in Felix's new-found grown-up-ness, but he recovered with style and said, 'Awesome.'

When they reached the island's brewery, Felix – to be on the safe side – took a seat in a far corner of the taproom while Tom ordered from the bar. They raised glasses full to sloshing point.

'So, Mom tells me there's a girl. An English girl.'

'Part Spanish.'

'Whoa! Fiery.'

Felix blushed. 'Her name's Beatrix. She lives in London.'

'London's a long way away, buddy.'

'I'm saving for an airfare. Going over there again this summer.'

'So, it's serious then?'

'I love her,' Felix said.

The open-heartedness of him struck Tom as something dangerous and wild, like a creature he really ought to warn Felix about. *You'll get scratched, little bro.* But all he said was, 'Sweet.'

'So, you got a girlfriend, or anything?'

'Anything?' Tom repeated. 'What are you asking?'

'It's not good to assume,' Felix said, a little too seriously.

'Man, things have changed,' Tom said.

'So? Girlfriend?'

'No, buddy. I reckon I might have grown out of love.'

'I don't believe that,' Felix said, tapping a rhythm on his knee.

'You don't?'

'Nope. I don't believe anybody grows out of love. No matter how old they get.'

'Hey,' Tom said, 'that last piece you played?'

'You liked it?'

'You wrote that?'

'I wish, hey? It was a gift. From Beatrix.'

'She wrote it?'

'Nah. Her dad heard someone play it somewhere, apparently.'

'Well, it was awesome.'

'There you go then,' Felix said, grinning. 'You can't have grown out of love.'

'Why so?'

'That piece? You know what we call that piece?'

'All right . . . tell me.'

Felix grinned. '"Love Song".'

Later that afternoon, Cassie Carter stood at her kitchen bench surrounded by all the things she needed to make a big hearty braise. Kilmauski was threading through her ankles, begging for the scraps of beef, and through an archway, in the living room, Tom and Felix were jamming. Cassie couldn't for the life of her name the tune they were playing; she only knew that there was pressure at the corners of her eyes and that she had never before been so grateful for onions, because they meant she could cry for a perfectly good reason, and not because it made her so insanely happy that her big son and her small son were making music together, Tom with his slide guitar on his lap, Felix right beside him on the cello.

Cassie listened to the glittery, shimmery sound of the slide guitar. Underneath it was the smooth, stout-and-melted-chocolate voice of the cello. She didn't recognise the tune, but she knew the feeling that it spelled out, and her swollen heart was singing along.

FOUR

the last thing we forget

WHEN THE SONG arrived on the landing at Arie's house that warm February night, the space was otherwise quiet and still. The frosted glass panels of the piano room doors caught traces of streetlight, refracting them into a soft glow that touched on the timber banister, the half-open doors that led into other rooms, and the framed photographs that were mounted on the wall of the stairwell.

There was a picture of Diana – pensive, hands clasped together behind her back – outside the front of Carnegie Hall in her famous red dress. And one of Arie, in sunglasses, resting on the oars of a dinghy in Central Park, with flowering trees and skyscrapers behind him. And one of Diana and Arie together, kissing, the picture taken so close up that the famous Duomo of Florence had been reduced to nothing more than a smudge of Tuscan colour in the background.

The stairs leading down from the landing fell gradually into the shadows of an empty hallway rimmed with closed doors, and behind one of these was Arie, sitting on a stool at the kitchen bench. A stubby of beer stood open at his elbow, and his sister's wedding invitation was propped against the screen of his laptop.

Arie could picture Heidi, at her table in Sydney's Blue Mountains with her stack of freshly handmade paper, dipping her fountain pen into a bottle of ink. She'd have been wearing a pinafore most likely, made of something homespun, and a pair of house slippers she'd fashioned herself out of a repurposed woollen jumper and a bicycle tyre. Or similar. Their father described Heidi as the 'mung bean' of the family, and she'd met her match in Greg, a park ranger with a headful of remarkably tidy dreadlocks.

The wedding was to be held in an orchard close to their home, some nine hundred kilometres to the north of Melbourne. Although Arie had been well aware that he needed to get on with the business of arranging his journey, it was only tonight, when he'd looked again at the date on the invitation, that he'd come to the acute realisation that the event was now less than two weeks away. He hadn't needed to look at the calendar to know that between now and then lay the minefield of 4 March. Diana's birthday. This year, she'd have been thirty-five years old.

Arie wondered if he and Diana would have had a wedding by this time. After everything he'd said to her on the night before she left, would she have come home with an answer for him? Would that answer have been *yes*? Or would Heidi and Greg have beaten them to the altar, even now? What would Diana have been like at the age of thirty-five? Would she have begun to hear the ticking of her biological clock by now? Or would she have been one of those women for whom the clock somehow remained dormant?

He brought her face to mind, in extreme close-up. He considered himself lucky that he had spent so much time studying it. He could easily picture the small indentation at the tip of her freckled nose, the uneven lay of the individual hairs of her pale ginger eyebrows, and the many different colours between amber and green that jostled about in her irises. It would have been nice to know which parts of her a child would have inherited, and which parts of him, but Arie knew this was thinking that did nothing but hurt. He tried to refocus himself: on Heidi's wedding, on practicalities.

The rest of the Johnsons had already booked their flights and arranged for their hire cars, and Arie knew that his parents and his older sisters, their partners and children, were all bunking together in the same sprawling guesthouse, where the cousins would be able to run riot together in the hallways and gardens.

His mother and older sisters had been on his case in recent weeks, urging him to get organised, but each time they asked how he was planning to get to the wedding, and where he was intending to stay, Arie had been evasive. If he told his mother that he was going to drive, then she might come up with some kind of ruse to ensure he had company on the ten-hour journey, and if his sisters knew, they might embark on a campaign to persuade him that it was time to start catching planes again.

It wasn't that he was afraid to fly, exactly. It was that everything to do with air travel – advertisements on billboards, spam emails about flight sales, the sight of jet streams in the sky – had a tendency to set off his own personal movie reel of the last minutes of Diana's life. As far as he could, he avoided driving anywhere near the airport, because this only reminded him of the morning he had driven Diana there and just . . . let her go. Going anywhere near that place made Arie feel negligent. He couldn't fathom how he'd taken her there instead of taking possession of her passport, or why he'd kissed her and waved her farewell instead of begging her, *begging* her, to stay.

On his laptop, Arie searched for the guesthouse whose name his mother had messaged to him. Several times. It turned out that there was a room available – a single on the top floor – but when

Arie paused to imagine the combined force of all his nieces and nephews, from the sulky tween to the toddler, he clicked open a new browser window and launched a search for nearby alternatives. The place he eventually settled on was a cottage of sorts that had once been a barn. The online pictures showed rustic timber interiors, an open fire, and geese grazing on a stretch of green grass beyond the windows. Given the season, he wouldn't need the fire, and neither would he need the second of the two bedrooms, but the place looked comfortable, and – more importantly – it was staggering distance from the wedding venue.

Reaching the part of the payment page where he needed to give his credit card number, Arie felt for his wallet in the back pocket of his pants. It wasn't there, but he knew where it would be: on his bedside table. He stepped into the darkened hallway and took the stairs two at a time.

The music reached him just before he set foot on the landing, and although it seemed to be coming from the piano room, it was not the sound of a piano. It was a stringed instrument . . . possibly a guitar. What he heard was nothing more than a series of notes, being played in a halting way, but even so this was enough to make him stop. He stood for a moment, his feet bare on the carpet of the landing, his shirt half untucked. He listened to the way the music began purposefully before dwindling away into nothing . . . and then started again.

He pushed open the glass doors. Inside the piano room, the dark lid of the Steinway gleamed like the surface of a lake. One of the angled panes of the bay window had been left open, and through the narrow gap between sash and sill, the phrase of music came again – soft and tentative, and somehow familiar.

Standing in the half-hexagon shape of the window, Arie looked out over the front yard of the house next door. The woman he'd seen arriving in her winter-weight clothes with that massive pack on her back looked entirely different now, sitting on the edge of one of the lounges with a guitar on her lap, wearing a light summer skirt and a pale camisole top, her dark hair held back with a headscarf. Her bare legs were crossed at the ankles, her head was bent in concentration over her guitar, and as he watched her play, it seemed to him that she gave off an air that was at once entirely self-sufficient and just a little lonely.

She played until the song petered out again, as if she had followed a thread as far as she could and had now come to its frayed end, leaving a special kind of expectant silence in its wake. Arie had a sense that he knew this song, and that he knew how it ought to continue, but he couldn't grasp it well enough to sing it, or hum it, or even really to picture it in his mind. It was like playing hide and seek with a ghost, or trying to catch a cloud with a butterfly net.

Arie wasn't good with music; not in that way. He was nothing like Diana. All she'd ever needed was a short string of notes, and then she'd be singing the rest of the tune as if it were the simplest thing in the world to draw that particular ribbon of song out of the hundreds, thousands, she kept in her musical memory.

'Listen!' she'd say to him in good-natured frustration when he was unable to name a song. 'You *know* this one. You've heard it *before*.'

Once, when they had been together for a few years, Diana had taken him with her to a nursing home not far from her mother's house, to visit her first music teacher. The woman was ancient and almost frighteningly frail, and although she had not been able to remember Diana, precisely, she had been perfectly pleased to have young visitors. Arie and Diana had helped her into a wheelchair and taken her to the recreation room, where she had sat beside the piano and happily sung along to every single song Diana played for her.

'Music is the last thing we forget,' Diana had later explained. 'I read a book about it. Apparently, we have this special place in our brains for remembering music, and it's completely separate from the parts where we store every other thing. And when we hear music that we know, our brains light up in completely different ways than when we hear music we don't. We're wired up to feel something special when we hear music that reminds us of something.'

Was his brain lighting up in that special way right now? *Did* he know this song, or was it only his imagination that it sounded something like the song Diana had played, here in this room, on the night before she went away? Was it the same song, or was it only the fact that he was standing here in this particular room, on a summer night, that made him think it could be? For the life of him, Arie would not have been able to say, but he wanted to know.

When the light was on outside 12A Tavistock Row, as it was that night, a semi-circle of brightness spread outwards from the portico at the front door. The curve of light swept over the courtyard with its matched pair of lounges, over the well-kept garden beds and lawn, and ended at the low wall which separated the yard from the footpath. This wall was broken by a gap in the brickwork where you might have expected a white picket gate to swing, although none did.

When Evie looked up from her guitar, she saw that someone was standing in that gap, just on the far side of the rim of light, and it took her a moment to realise that it was the man from the house next door. The way he stood – slightly awkwardly, one hand at his chin – gave Evie the impression that he wasn't quite sure how to proceed. He looked as if he'd have appreciated a door to knock on, but instead had found himself standing at a threshold made only of warm summer air.

Although it was past ten o'clock, he was wearing what looked to be a work shirt, mostly untucked. His sleeves were rolled halfway up his forearms, and he wore a pair of sandals that Evie suspected might have been an afterthought, put on as he left the house.

When she'd encountered him on her first day here, her fleeting impression had been that he was one of those men who were good-looking quite by accident. He was lean, with longish dark-blond hair, brown eyes and gentle features – not at all one of those sharp, put-together types who were out to make an impression in their shiny shoes and fashionably cut pants.

She placed a silencing hand over the sound-hole of the guitar and smiled at him curiously.

'Hello,' she said, in a way that was both a greeting and a question.

He smiled back, although the expression around his eyes appeared anxious, as if he had something difficult or awkward to say to her.

'I, um . . . you were playing the guitar,' he said.

'Oh,' Evie said, colouring now that she understood. He'd come to tell her the noise was bothering him. 'I'm so sorry. I meant to play quietly, but I can stop.'

Evie made a move to put her guitar down, but she could see he meant it when he quickly said, 'No, no. That's not . . . that's not it at all.'

'I'm sorry,' he went on, 'but . . . you know how it is when you hear a song, and you can't quite place it? I heard you playing, and I felt like I knew the song, but . . . I wasn't sure. I just came over to ask what it was.'

Evie was taken utterly by surprise. 'The song I was playing just now? This one?'

She played a few bars, even more tentatively now there was somebody watching her.

'Yes,' he said, taking a step within the boundary of the property, into the semi-circle of light.

'You *know* it?' Evie asked, sparking up with hopefulness. For all she knew, it was a song that half the world was familiar with, but one that had somehow passed her by. If he could tell her what the song was, then she'd be able to find it and listen to it again properly. 'What *is* it?'

'I have no idea. I just thought I might have heard it once. That's all. I was hoping you'd . . . be able to tell me.'

'Ah, I see,' Evie said, realising that this was not going to be simple after all. 'I wish I did know.'

'Where did you come across it?'

'In a train station, strangely enough,' she said. 'I heard a pair of kids playing it. I mean, I say "kids", but they were teenagers. One of them played the cello, the other one the flute. It was so beautiful, and I've been trying to piece it together, but I'm not even close to doing it justice. For one thing, it had two parts, and this is just what I can remember of the melody.'

She played through the scrap of song again, then let her hand fall away from the guitar. 'I'm sorry. That's as much as I know.'

'Train station?' he asked.

'Edinburgh.'

He nodded, although he seemed more lost in his thoughts than present. Now that the anxiety had disappeared from his face, Evie could see something else in his expression. It was in the lines at the sides of his mouth, and the faint hollowness around his eyes. She knew that look – had known it in her own face. Sorrow. She wondered what it was that had put it there.

'I'm sorry I couldn't help you,' she said, plucking one string of her guitar, 'with the song.'

'I guess it's just going to remain a mystery.'

'I guess so.'

He seemed to shake a thought away. 'Well, it was probably just my imagination. The song . . . I probably don't know it.'

A silence settled between them then, but rather than rush to fill it, Evie counselled herself to sit quietly and see what he would do next – keep the conversation going, or just let it drop like a rope into a river.

'Well, I should go,' he said.

Evie gave a small wave of farewell, while somewhere in her imagination a rope went *splish*.

blank pages

IN THE DAYS and nights that followed, Arie listened out for the sound of guitar music from the house next door, but it never came. Instead, the song played on his mind, the insistent companion to his thoughts as he stood in the shower, waited in queues for coffee, and climbed the stairs to the offices of Sonder Digital. The song was like a nagging question, and part of him wanted to search out the answer, to solve the mystery. Another part, though, already knew that this was a quest doomed to failure. He was all too aware that there were some things you could never find by determination alone.

In a moment of confidence, though, he downloaded a song-recognition app onto his phone. He sang the notes he could recall into the microphone, feeling like an idiot as he did so, but the only soundbite he could manage was too short, so the technology could give him no answers. He tried a different app, and then another, and by the time he was willing to admit the complete hopelessness of the enterprise he'd been at it for over two wasted hours, behaving like a thirsty man in a desert, intoxicated by a mirage.

While the song eluded him, though, the woman in the house next door seemed constantly on the edge of his consciousness.

It wasn't that he did anything as deliberate as watch out for her, but he found that he was very aware of her, there on the periphery of his life.

On Wednesday morning, he noted that she had remembered to put the garbage bin out on the street on the correct day, and also that she was a conscientious enough guest to clear the junk mail from the mouth of the letterbox. That night, coming home late after dinner at Richard and Lenka's, he saw that she'd put the light on in the front yard, and was sitting out on one of the lounges in the balmy, late-summer evening. She had no guitar this time, but was instead writing feverishly in a notebook. Arie realised he'd quite like to talk with her again, but although he swung open the gate to his yard as noisily as he could, she was so deep in concentration that she didn't look up from her page.

The following morning, he saw her sitting on the low brick wall, wearing a crumpled dress and a hat with a broad brim, the twin points of her dark hair framing her face beneath it. He noticed that her forearms and calves were now not quite so white as they had been, and that her shoulders under the straps of her dress were pink with sunburn. Arie waved to her, and she waved back, and as he slid behind the wheel of his car, he considered asking if she needed him to drive her somewhere. He was still trying to decide if this was a good idea or not when a car pulled up to the pavement in front of her, and she spoke for a moment to the driver through the wound-down passenger-side window before opening the door and getting in.

Friday morning there was no sign of her, and it occurred to Arie that she might easily have come to the end of her time at the place, and that the next people he would see letting themselves into 12A would be the husband-and-wife cleaning team, with their buckets and mops and white stacks of fresh linen. When there was no sign of her again that evening as Arie got out of his car and went indoors, it began to seem even more likely that she had gone.

But then, when he'd been home less than ten minutes, and was upstairs in his bedroom, having thrown off his work clothes and buttoned up a pair of jeans, he heard a knock at his front door. Pulling a T-shirt over his head as he hurried down the stairs, he had the fleeting idea that it might be her, although he quickly told himself how unlikely that was. But unlikely or not, there she stood on his doorstep, holding a parcel.

'It's for you,' she said. 'The delivery guy came around lunchtime. I was out the front, and you weren't here so I signed for it. Otherwise they were going to take it back to the depot and leave one of those pesky cards.'

Arie took the freight satchel from her, feeling the crackle of bubble wrap inside the plastic, but it was only once he caught some of the words written on the docket in the clear envelope on its front that he remembered the internet order he'd placed late one night, on impulse, as a gift for little Marek.

'Thanks, that was—'

'I really hope you don't mind,' she interrupted, clearly wanting to explain herself. 'He probably shouldn't have let me do it. I could have been anybody, but I got the impression he didn't really care as long as he had a signature.'

This was the first time Arie had been quite so close to her, and now that he was, he could see that she was almost exactly his height. She seemed fresh, as if she'd just taken a shower, the skin of her face plump, her lips newly glossed. The denim shorts she wore made her legs look especially long, and from her hair he caught the bright scent of mint.

'No, that's great. Thanks.'

'No worries,' she said, and turned away.

If she'd not signed for the parcel, he'd have had to call the freight company, only to have them re-deliver at another time when he once again – most likely – wouldn't be there, or else he'd have had to drive out to the depot, which was in an awkward part of town. Perhaps she was generally just a very thoughtful person. Or perhaps, Arie thought . . . perhaps she, like he, had been looking for a way to connect.

She had taken only a few steps up the path to his front gate when he called out to her, 'I should have said, *thanks*.'

She looked over her shoulder at him, smiling. 'You did.'

'I maybe didn't say it well enough, though. I do really appreciate it.'

She took a step back towards him and he watched her think, a series of thoughts playing out on her face like ripples on the surface of water.

'Not that I was sticky-beaking or anything,' she said. 'And not that I accidentally happened to read anything written on your parcel, but I just want you to know that I definitely will not be next door tonight, envisioning you over here playing with your . . . Dalek plush toy.'

He saw the teasing look in her blue-green eyes, but there was nothing arch in it, nothing sharp. He almost said, *It's for my godson*, but he knew the only response to that was, with a knowing nod, *Of course it is*.

'It's not just a Dalek plush toy,' Arie said, with mock indignation. 'It's a talking Dalek plush toy.'

'Let me guess. *Exterminate*?'

'I'll have you know this is an advanced talking Dalek plush toy. It has no fewer than three phrases.'

'What are the others?' she said, laughter in her voice.

171

'To tell you the truth, I can't remember,' Arie said. 'It was late, there was whisky. What I was actually looking for, originally, was a K9 piggy bank, but I couldn't find one and then I got suckered by this 10 per cent off deal. So now I have an advanced talking Dalek plush toy.'

All this was true. Arie had imagined that a piggy bank was a responsible sort of gift for a godfather to give. Promoting saving, teaching the delay of gratification. All that. The shape of the Doctor's little metal dog would have lent itself nicely to a piggy bank, he'd thought. But although a great many things you could dream up now existed, and were available for purchase somewhere in the world, a K9 piggy bank turned out not to be one of them.

'If it makes you feel any better,' she said, one eyebrow arched, 'I can confess to having a thing for the TARDIS. You know how some people are very good at the kind of forward planning that involves life insurance and things like that? Well, I'm *not*, but even when I was very little, I knew it would be important to have all my wishes mapped out, just in case I ever accidentally rubbed a lamp and let a genie out. It hasn't happened yet, but if it ever does, then I'm totally prepared. And . . . my first wish will be for a TARDIS.'

'That is a good plan. Can't fault that.'

'My second would be for a Babel fish.'

'As in, from *The Hitchhiker's Guide to the Galaxy*?'

'That's the one.'

'Stick it in your ear and you understand every language ever?'

'Exactly.'

Arie pondered. 'You know, you might be wasting a wish there. A TARDIS has a built-in translator. Probably just as good.'

'Harder to stick in your ear, though,' she countered. 'Not so discreet, when you're eavesdropping.'

Arie laughed. 'Good point. And your third?'

'I believe the honourable thing to do is to reserve one wish so you can set the genie free. One can learn so much from television and movies, don't you agree?'

She was funny, this woman, and sweet, and as Arie bantered with her, it occurred to him just how long it had been since he'd met someone entirely new.

'How much longer are you staying?' Arie asked, reaching for a way to keep the conversation going. 'Next door, I mean?'

'A bit over a week.'

The other night she'd mentioned that she'd been in Edinburgh, but she wasn't Scottish; her accent was Australian. 'Where are you from?' he asked.

'Hard to say, really. I've been out of the country for six years, so I'm not really sure any more.'

But before Arie could ask any further questions that might detain her, he heard the ringtone of the house phone in the kitchen. The only person who ever rang the landline was Belinda Clare, and Belinda was not somebody who could be ignored.

'I should get that,' Arie said apologetically.

'Of course.'

As she turned to leave, Arie impulsively said, 'I don't know your name.'

'It's Evie.'

'Arie,' he offered in return.

She gestured to the parcel in his arms and gave a mischievous smile. 'I know.'

The phone kept ringing, persisting beyond the number of rings most people would think reasonable, so even before Arie picked up the receiver he'd got a sense of the call's urgency. Such a call was not unexpected. The approach of Diana's birthday was one of those times of year – along with the lead-up to Christmas, and the days before the anniversary of the crash – when Belinda was especially fragile.

'I'm afraid this is one of *those* calls,' Belinda said, and Arie could tell from the overly controlled tone of her voice that she was trying not to panic. Yet.

'The computer?'

'It's crashed, Arie. The screen got all these narrow vertical lines on it and then it went completely black. I can't restart it. I can't get any sense out of it at all.'

This did not sound good, but drawing on skills honed from years as a tech trouble-shooter, Arie took a deep breath, and tried to exude calm down the phone line.

'Have you tried—'

'The photos, Arie. My photos. I'm worried about my photos.'

Just about anyone would be anxious if they thought they'd lost their photographic archive, but Belinda's fear went beyond most people's. She had so little of Diana that she felt it was crucial to hold on fiercely and tightly to every piece of evidence that remained.

'Even if we can't fix the computer,' Arie said, 'the photographs will be fine. Do you remember we backed them up to the cloud?'

'I don't like this cloud thing. I don't trust it.'

Arie gave a silent sigh; he had heard all this before. Belinda had made prints of her photographs, but her terror of losing their high-resolution digital versions was almost impossible to assuage, and the fact that she was a technophobe didn't help.

'I don't even know where this bloody "cloud" thing *is*,' she went on, becoming increasingly shrill. 'I mean, what if it goes kaput?

It's all very well if they say "oops, sorry", but those photos . . . they can never be replaced!'

'We backed them up to a hard drive too, though – remember?'

Actually, Arie had backed Belinda's photos up to two separate hard drives. He'd left one at her house and brought the other back to his.

'I read somewhere that those things can get corrupted, but I can't even check. I can't open the hard drive, because I haven't got anything else to plug it into,' she said, and Arie thought she might be about to cry. 'Oh God, I wish we still used negatives. I could put them in a fire-proof box or something. I don't like . . . I just feel like, it's all going to . . . Arie, if I lost her again. If she just faded away . . .'

'Belinda,' Arie said, 'it will be all right. I promise.'

'Arie . . . could you . . . could you come? Please. I know I'm not being totally rational, but I just don't think I can sleep tonight unless I know that they're all right. Can you bring *your* computer, so I can check the hard drive? I just want to know if they're definitely there. Can you come? Please?'

Arie, knowing that she meant *can you come right now*, breathed another silent sigh. An hour and a half out to her place, an hour and a half back. At least it was Friday, so there was no need to be at work early in the morning.

'Of course,' he said. Because what else would he be doing? 'I'm leaving now.'

'Oh God, what would I do without you? Thank you, Arie,' she said, and the relief in her voice was palpable. 'I know it's a long way. I'll make up the guest bed in case you want to stay.'

Arie put his computer, a jumper and a toothbrush into an overnight bag. As he drove out of Tavistock Row, he caught a glimpse of the woman next door – just her silhouette – in the bay window of the upstairs room. He wondered what her Friday night held in store. He'd have quite liked, he realised, to have talked with her some more.

For the last two years, almost everybody he'd talked to for more than a couple of minutes – including Grace on New Year's Eve – knew his story. He hadn't realised, until tonight, just how weary he was of the strange careful-clumsy manner that people tended to use when dealing with the bereaved. People were overcautious around him, as if his grief were some kind of unpredictable dog that might any minute get off the leash and bite them. And the intense way they tried to avoid upsetting or offending him seemed only to make it twice as likely that they would do so.

In the presence of the woman from next door, though, Arie – for the first time in a long time – had not felt like the sad man. She was from outside his circle of friends, acquaintances and colleagues, and beyond that, she'd been overseas for years. She was like a blank page, and this had made Arie feel as if he could be one, too.

the map of where to next

At 12 Tavistock Row, Arie and Diana had dedicated the room with the bay window to the Steinway and installed themselves in the rear-facing room across the hallway, but the owners of the near-identical number 12A had configured their place quite differently. When fixing it up for an Airbnb, they'd decided to keep one room for storing personal effects, locking its door when they had guests, and to fit out the bigger, street-side room for their guests to sleep in.

It had polished floorboards, a painted fireplace with a dark timber mantel, and a high queen-sized bed covered in bright white bedding. By mid-morning that Saturday, the mercury was rising steeply and the blue of the sky was singed with the faint orange tint of heat-haze. Evie kneeled on the upholstered cushions of the bay window while she worked the plastic chains to partly close the blinds and block out some of the sun.

Evie loved this window seat, this room, this house, but she knew that very soon she would have to move on to a more realistic environment. Once her savings were exhausted and wherever she ended up choosing to settle, she wouldn't be living in a house like this one. Unless she was house-sitting. If she ended up having to rent, then she'd be back to the type of accommodation that she could afford on whatever wage she could cobble together from her usual combination of low-paid McJobs.

Today she would haemorrhage yet more money. Her plan was to get an Uber out to Crosby's house, stopping on the way to pick up four new tyres for the Beetle. It was going to be hot in that rickety shed of his, where she would face the task of remembering how to change a tyre.

While she'd managed to get a temporary permit that would allow her to drive the Beetle back to Tavistock Row, it would still have to be checked over by a mechanic before it could be fully re-registered, and Evie was in no doubt that this, too, would be an expensive process. Perhaps she should have just sold the old car, or even junked it; she could easily have picked up a small, cheap car for less than it was going to cost her to make the Beetle road-worthy. But she and the Beetle had been fellow travellers for quite a few years before she'd left it behind, and she felt as if she owed the car some loyalty. Sometimes, she mused, it could be expensive to have a sentimental soul.

Below her, the front yard of 12A looked like a landscape architect's drawing, with its circular brick courtyard, timber lounges, and the wedges of grass kept green by the electronic watering system that clunked and hissed into action every other day in the pre-dawn hours. This yard was a stark contrast to next door's, which was cut through with a cracked cement path and sprouted nothing but a single flowering gum tree that dropped its leaves and flowers onto parched and patchy grass.

Whoever he was, this Arie Johnson who lived next door, and whatever he did with his time other than sit up late at night drinking whisky and making random purchases from The Who Shop, it was obvious that gardening was no part of it. Over the past few days, Evie had begun to think that Arie probably lived alone. She hadn't seen anyone but him going in or out of the front door of number 12, nor spotted another person driving the slate-blue Renault that was parked most of the time out the front – although it was not there right now. From their two brief encounters, Evie had come to the conclusion that he was nice. Possibly even very nice.

So what? she asked herself sternly. Nice was only one part of the equation.

Since leaving Edinburgh, Evie had reflected a good deal on romantic failures, her own especially. It was easy – in retrospect – to see how often and how quickly, in the past, she had given her heart to people who didn't want it. Or at least, not enough.

Before Dave there had been Michael, a history academic in London, who'd broken up with her by email even though he lived just around the corner from the pub where she worked. Before Michael there had been Ben, a fellow Australian on board the cruise ship where Evie had been employed, who'd told her he was separated from his wife, though he later explained – as he said his goodbyes to Evie before going back to that same wife – that it had really been more a case of him taking some 'long-service leave'.

Whatever Evie did next with her rather open heart, she resolved that it wasn't going to involve giving it away to anybody who didn't fully and completely want it.

Evie made the bed with care, tugging on the white linen to get rid of all the wrinkles. Then, on top, she spread out a map of Australia. It was old and the paper had thinned at all the folds; undoubtedly, some of the rose-pink roads that snaked over the contours of the continent of Australia would have changed course by now. She'd found the map in one of the boxes she'd exhumed from the Beetle. It was dated but still perfectly adequate for her purposes.

You could go west, Evie suggested to herself.

Her eyes travelled across the wide span of the Nullarbor Plain. While it would hardly be a joy to drive for three days, in March, in a rattling VW Beetle with no air-conditioning, the west was fresh country, a part of Australia she'd never been to before. She wouldn't want to live right in Perth, but Fremantle was a possibility. Or she could go further south to Margaret River, or Augusta, or Albany. Scanning this sector of the map, she spied the word Esperance, printed in neat round letters on the edge of the country's south coast. *Esperance.* A word for hope, left behind by French explorers. There were worse ways to choose a destination than by its name.

Evie had no map pins, but she did have earrings, so she put a small silver star stud through the paper at Esperance. The next earring, a crescent moon, she pushed into the township of Bellingen in the New South Wales hinterland, for no other reason than because this was a profoundly pretty part of the country – lush, green and hilly, yet not all that far from the coast – and because she had passed through there a few times and liked the atmosphere. She could imagine sliding with ease into a job in a laid-back café, spending her days in sandals and light clothes, needing few possessions to get by in the mild, easy-going climate.

Where else?

Stella and Reuben wanted her to come back to Hobart. Evie looked at the island of Tasmania, which she might have described as a triangle, or a heart-shape, or the face of a devil with a pointed chin. As a teenager, Evie had ached to leave the place behind, but that was long ago. Now that she was older, she could picture herself living, once again, under the snow-sugared mountain that curled its foothills around the small capital, reacquainting herself with the changeable weather that so regularly altered the colour and texture of the river that divided the city. Stella had a friend who was looking for a house-sitter, too. His place was one in a row of ramshackle boathouses just out of the city, most of which had been done up as tiny residences. It was an appealing idea, spending winter evenings rugged up and watching the sun set from one of the timber jetties that jutted out into the yacht-filled bay.

The island also had a drawcard that no other place had: not only Stella and Reuben themselves but their children, too. Matilda and Oscar were ten and eight, and Evie knew that there was time yet to be a proper aunt to them, to help out with school pick-ups and sport, spend time baking, or taking photographs, or sketching, or reading, or whatever it was they were interested in doing. The first thing she would have to do, Evie realised, if she chose Hobart, was to find out exactly who they were, these two children whose lives she had so far almost entirely missed.

She pressed a third earring, a tiny silver heart, into the southern tip of the island.

Now there was just one more earring, an arrow, in her palm.

Darwin? No, she decided quickly. Too hot.

Mooloolaba? Possibly. Its name had a beautiful rhythm.

Magnetic Island? Too small.

Sydney? Way too big.

But what about . . . right here in Melbourne? Evie considered the prospect. She'd enjoyed living here, had loved this place for its blend of sportiness and artiness, the way its women dressed sharply in coats and boots in the winter-time, the trams and the cafés that lined Degraves Street, the haberdashery in the Nicholas Building and the Athenaeum Library, which was the perfect place to secrete herself away to write. But she'd *done* Melbourne. Hadn't she?

There were a lot of advantages to the idea. She knew her way around; it wouldn't be hard for her to work here; she was already *here*. And, although she wouldn't be in the same city as Stella and Reuben and the kids, she wouldn't be that far away from them, either.

Through the bay window, Evie caught sight of the blue Renault coming along Tavistock Row. It reversed into the vacant parking space in front of 12A, and Evie saw Arie get out of the driver's side, then reach through to grab a bag from the back seat of his car. He was wearing the same T-shirt and jeans as the night before, and his hair looked a touch sleep-mussed. Wondering where it was that her neighbour had spent the night, she stepped back and out of view as Arie came closer to the house.

She returned to her map, and counted on her fingers: Esperance, Bellingen, Hobart, Melbourne. She felt a little thrill at the prospect of choosing a whole new adventure.

There was a small office set-up downstairs in one corner of the Airbnb's living room. Evie, who hadn't yet got a new Australian SIM card for her mobile, had been grateful for the landline telephone, and also for the slimline computer that gave her access to the internet. She jostled the mouse, waking the screen. Her usual routine when she was about to make a move was to run a series of searches: jobs + place, house-sitting + place, poetry + place, place + what's it really like. She opened a browser window, but what she typed into the Google search field was none of those things. Instead, it was: Arie Johnson + Melbourne.

What are you doing, Evie?

Just . . . looking, she told herself.

If he was anything like her, there would be nothing to see. Even in this day and age, it was still possible to remain near enough to invisible in the online space, although to do so you had to live a life like

Evie's – one that remained in the middle of the bandwidth, having neither any major highs nor any major lows that would make you the subject of other people's interest. But Evie very quickly came to understand, as the search results scrolled down the screen in front of her, that the man next door had not been able to do this.

Her eyes moved quickly from the official Sonder site at the top of the list, further down to the place where she saw all the words that explained the sorrow she'd seen in his face . . . *PQ108, the ghost flight, Air Pleiades, Diana Clare.*

'No,' she murmured.

She remembered the poem she had written and abandoned, and pictured again the image that had driven her to pick up her pen in the first place – an image of the sea opening itself up like a big blue mouth and swallowing the plane whole.

Evie had vaguely followed the British television coverage of the plane crash, and although she remembered the faces of the UK victims appearing in the newspaper pages, she had not known until now that an Australian concert pianist had been among those who died.

Soon, Evie was watching her on the screen – Diana Clare, in a red dress with a plunging V-neck, playing the piano on the stage of a concert hall, an orchestra ringed around her. Evie didn't know what the music was, but it was big and powerful. Diana Clare's bare arms rose and fell; her whole body swayed with the tide of her music, her long ginger-blonde hair and red dress accentuating all her movements, giving her the look of a beautiful, exotic sea creature. So this was the woman Arie Johnson had loved – this dramatic, accomplished, celebrated musician.

'Oh my God,' Evie murmured to herself, feeling suddenly mortified. She had played music in front of him. He would have been used to the kind of music that Diana Clare could play, and

Evie had sat innocently in front of him, plinking at the strings of her guitar like the complete amateur that she was.

On the second page of search results was an interview with Arie himself. He sat with one elbow resting on the closed lid of a piano, his face lit from the opposite side by the light from a window. Eighteen months had passed since the segment went to air, and Arie's face on the screen was gaunt and sallow compared to the way Evie thought it looked now, but the voice captured by the footage was familiar. His was a surprising voice, slightly deeper than you might expect from looking at him, and textured with an accent that – although clearly Australian – seemed to contain a whisper of something European.

'Diana was always travelling,' he said. 'Her music took her all over the world, and I'd taught myself not to worry about it. To repeat that old mantra – getting in a car is the most dangerous thing we do every day, far more dangerous than boarding a plane.

'It's hard to know which mornings are the worst. Sometimes, I think the worst mornings are the ones when I wake up with a vague sense that something terrible has happened, but I can't yet tell – in that half-awake state – whether that something is real, or just from a dream. And then, as my brain, or my memory or whatever it is, comes into focus, I remember that it's all true. I have to go through the discovery of it all over again.

'But then, I think . . . no. The worst mornings are the ones when I wake up from a dream of something good. I'm waiting at the airport in Paris when she steps off the plane. Or I'm at my desk at work when she calls to tell me she's missed the flight.'

It was clear that he was finding it hard to continue, that he was getting through by leaving spaces between the words so that he could steady himself, breathe. As he brushed away a tear, she could see that by some miracle there was no apparent anger in him – only pain.

'Or else, I am on the plane with her. I am beside her when the oxygen runs out and her eyes close. I am holding her hand. In the dream it seems so real, but then, when I wake up, it's not. On those mornings . . . those are the worst mornings. On those mornings, I start the day by falling from such a great height.'

On screen, he swallowed audibly, and Evie – watching him – did too.

That day was fiercely hot and in the early evening, when Arie went out to pick up some takeaway for dinner, the breeze in the street felt as if it were being pumped through a furnace. As he got into his stifling car, he noticed an unfamiliar vehicle parked outside 12A. It was a Beetle – a vintage original with patches of rust here and there on its body, but with conspicuously brand-new tyres.

It wasn't until he returned, though, that he realised the car must belong to Evie, for there she was, out in the street, with a bucket of sudsy water at her feet, wiping with a dishcloth at the Beetle's dusty panels. There were black marks on her forearms and thighs, and also on the striped playsuit that she wore, one shoulder of it falling off as she worked.

Arie dawdled, walking around to the back of the Renault to check if there was anything in the boot that needed bringing inside. He saw Evie move from the pavement side of the Beetle to the curving slope of its bonnet, splashing through a soapy puddle as she went, although the wet footprints from her bare feet quickly disappeared from the hot asphalt.

Once again, in her bearing he sensed that odd blend of self-containment and longing, as if she was quite happy to be doing what she was doing, and content to be doing it alone, but also waiting for the arrival of whatever it was that she was missing. There was something about her that unsettled him, though he couldn't name it precisely. It occurred to him that her self-containment made him feel unnecessary, though why this should bother him – why he should want to be necessary to her – he didn't know.

She looked up and saw him, smiled and offered a wave of her grubby dishcloth, and that was enough invitation for him to walk over to the blue Beetle.

'You bought a car?'

'Retrieved it,' she corrected. 'It's been in storage, the poor old thing.'

He walked a circle of it, taking in the vehicle's exaggerated wheel arches and the small triangular windows that could hinge outwards. The handle of the back-end engine compartment looked like a Frisbee that someone had flown into the car's body.

'When I got my licence, all my friends were buying these sleek, brand-new little things, with CD players and air-conditioning. But not me. I wanted something old and groovy. Let's just say it was not a particularly practical decision. I hate to think what this thing's cost me over the years.'

'It's a classic,' Arie said, peering in through the soap-bubbled windows at the old-fashioned dashboard dials and leather-headed gear lever.

'Hey, I don't suppose you have a hose, do you? I found a tap just by the fence there, but no hose. I mean, I could make do with the bucket, but it would be great to be able to do a proper rinse-off.'

Arie thought. 'I might. Let me go take a look.'

'Oh, you were about to eat,' Evie said, gesturing to the plastic bag in his hand. 'It can wait.'

'It's okay. It won't take a minute,' he insisted.

As he passed through the house, setting his takeaway curry on the kitchen bench, he tried to remember the last time he'd opened the little tin shed in the backyard. However many months it had been, it was long enough for the bolt lock to have seized up so that Arie had to yank on it, hard, to get it to open. Inside, a dormant lawnmower hunkered in a corner beneath shelves that contained hopeful things like potting mix, fertiliser and lawn seed.

Taking up most of the space, though, were two bicycles – his old mountain bike, and Diana's cruisy street bike with its wide handlebars and front-mounted basket – their pedals and spokes all intermeshed so that he couldn't move one without the other. At the sight of them, he felt a familiar tide of sadness begin to rise inside him.

'Hose,' he murmured to himself, trying to stay on track. 'Hose.'

There it was, hanging in a coil from a rusted nail in the wall, stiff with disuse. It could be perished by now for all he knew, and the orange plastic fittings on either end were probably so brittle that they'd crack under any kind of water pressure, but this was the best he could do.

He held up his find for Evie to see and then set to work attaching the hose to the tap in the front yard of 12A. Arie tested the pressure, then twisted the nozzle closed. Gradually, the water and the heat did their work on the creaky rubber, so that the hose partially unkinked itself as he dragged its length out onto the street and handed it over to Evie.

The heat was still oppressive, and there was something about the way the skin on her forearms was slick with water, and the smell of hot concrete, and the way the puddles beneath the car were evaporating into a faint haze of steam, that made Arie wish that he, too, was barefoot in a puddle, or running through a sprinkler. He wished he knew Evie well enough to flick water at her, and watch soap bubbles settle on her hair.

She examined the nozzle. 'Do you just . . . ?'

'Yeah, twist,' Arie said, miming.

He stood back, close to the brick wall, while Evie squirted water over the curving top of the Beetle, sending rivulets of suds down its sides and into the gutter.

He didn't see it coming. When the spray of water hit him full in the chest, he looked up in total surprise to see Evie grinning at him from the far side of the car. As he stood there, rooted to the spot, her grin faltered, and Arie could see that she couldn't quite believe what she'd just done. The look of embarrassment on her face deepened to mortification.

'Oh God, I'm so—'

She might have been about to follow with 'sorry', but Arie – feeling a little rush of exhilaration – had already taken two big steps towards the bucket and caught up its handle.

'Right,' he said, and Evie, relief palpable on her face, dashed away to the back of the Beetle as he came charging around the front. But she'd found herself at the end of the hose's length and couldn't get any further away from him unless she abandoned her weapon. She turned the hose on Arie as he swung the bucket in her direction, and his aim was good – the soapy water fanned up and out of the bucket's lip, drenching Evie from head to mid-thigh. At the same time, the hose spray hit him again, saturating his clothes entirely.

He backed away, all out of ammunition, and when he reached the pavement, he turned and leaped over the low fence. Reaching the tap, his sopping shorts and T-shirt dripping onto the grass, he turned it off.

Evie flicked her wet hair from her face as the last of the water drizzled out of the hose onto the pavement. Arie tried not to notice the way her playsuit now clung to her slender figure, the wet fabric plastering tightly to her breasts.

Eyes up, eyes up, he told himself.

'Truce?' she said. 'I'm not quite finished.'

'What? You think I'm just going to turn this tap back on?'

'Um . . . yes?'

'I don't think so.'

'You can trust me,' she said, her eyes wide with mock innocence.

'Tell you what. You give me the hose, and *I'll* finish rinsing the car.'

'But can I trust *you*?' she asked.

'It's a mystery,' he said.

Laughing, she approached him, and handed him the business end of the hose. Holding her hands in the air, she looked down the length of her wet body. 'Seriously, do your worst. I can't get much wetter now anyway.'

Arie spun the tap so the water flowed again, but other than giving Evie a light spray in the face, which she received quite happily, he did as he had promised and rinsed off the car.

'There you go,' he said when he was done. 'One washed car.'

They stood together, and Arie noticed that she – like he – was breathing just a little more heavily than usual.

The expression on her face was both mischievous and sincere when she said, 'I really am sorry. If that was childish. But it's just so . . . hot. If I'd really thought that you'd mind, I wouldn't—'

'If you hadn't have started it, I would have done,' he said, although he knew this probably wasn't true.

'So, can I get you a drink?' she asked.

Evie went into the kitchen, leaving a trail of water along the hallway, and returned with two ciders and a bottle opener. She levered the tops off and handed one of the frosted bottles to Arie, who was already sitting on a lounge in the courtyard.

'Cool change is coming,' he said, and she followed his gaze to the southern sector of the sky where scudding puffs of cumulus were massing on the horizon.

'Hallelujah,' she said. 'There were a couple of times today when I seriously thought I was going to get heat-stroke. It's been a long time since I've seen weather like this.'

Evie settled herself onto the second lounge so that she was resting her back against its wooden slats and looked over at Arie, reassessing, curious to know if she could read anything new in his face, now that she knew so much more about him. All she saw, though, was the same faint cast of sadness to his features. Grief certainly left its marks.

'So tell me, what was it you were doing all that time you were away overseas?'

'Just travelling,' she said with a shrug.

'You must have worked,' he observed.

'Enough to get by. I changed a lot of sheets. Babysat quite a lot of children. Poured a great deal of beer.'

'I thought I observed a certain level of expertise in the bottle opening.'

'Yep. Champion bottle-opener, me,' she said.

'So what brings you home then?'

The memory of a song played on cello and flute flitted through her mind, but all she said was, 'Oh, nothing in particular.'

'And what will you do now? You and your little blue Beetle?'

'I haven't got anything you'd call a plan. I suppose I'll pick a corner of the country, go there, and work out what to do next.'

'Where's home though?'

'Home?' Evie repeated. She hardly knew.

'Where does your family live? Where did you grow up?'

'I grew up in Hobart,' she said, not answering the first of his questions; the answer was too complicated. 'As soon as I could, I started travelling around Australia. Before I left, I'd been living in Melbourne for a while. That's why I came back here. To get my car, and all the other stuff I left behind.'

'And now you're just going to pick a place to live? Simple as that?'

'Yes.' She smiled at his expression of genuine bewilderment.

'That sounds . . .' he began, and then frowned slightly, trying to find the word for it.

'Disorganised?' Evie suggested.

'No, the word I almost said was "foreign". It's just that I . . . I can't imagine what it would be like to be so free.'

'Well, you actually are that free. Really and truthfully,' Evie said, then hoped that this had not been tactless.

It was true, though. He could, if he chose, drop every single thing he believed was confining him – whether that was his house, his job, his mortgage – and do something different, go somewhere different, strike out on an entirely different path. Something Evie had learned on her travels was just how many people were locked in cages with invisible, imaginary bars, and constrained by rules they had made up for themselves. Equally, though, she'd learned how lonely you could get when you stepped through those bars and dismantled all the rules.

'I have a business,' he said, mildly enough, though Evie detected a hint of defensiveness that made her think that she might have accidentally sounded a bit preachy.

'What kind?' she asked, hoping to make up for it.

'Tech,' he said, and took a sip of his cider. 'I'm a computer geek.'

Of course, Evie thought. She could see who he was, and who he must have been at school – one of those gentle and almost-invisible boys, the sort who listened and asked questions, the ones she'd always liked so much better than the competitors, the charmers and the crowd-pleasing hot-heads.

'What species?' she asked.

'Developer,' he said. 'A friend and I, we're in business together. Sonder Digital.'

'Sonder?' she asked, clarifying.

'Yes, it's—'

'From the *Dictionary of Obscure Sorrows*. I know. A word for that feeling you have when you realise that everybody in the world has a reality as amazingly complex as your own.'

His eyebrows shot up. 'I think it's a first that someone's defined it for me.'

Evie, pleased, shrugged. 'I like unusual words.'

'Try me.'

'Solivagant.'

Arie thought.

'Nope. Don't know it.'

'It means to ramble alone.'

'Nice word,' he said, nodding.

One cider turned into two, which turned into Arie fetching the takeaway curry from his kitchen bench, reheating it and dividing it into two bowls. By the time they'd finished eating, they'd been talking for a couple of hours, but Arie had made no mention of Diana, although he'd said quite a bit about Richard, his friend and business partner, Richard's wife and their son, Arie's godson. Evie understood, though. She too was leaving things out; in the expurgated version she'd given him of her travels, she had mentioned nobody called Ben or Michael or Dave.

While they had been talking, a bank of ink-dark clouds moved in over the city. Soon, exploratory drops of rain were falling – big, fat drops that landed and spread on the warm bricks of the courtyard.

'It's going to bucket down,' Arie said, peering up at the heavy sky.

'You're right,' Evie said, knowing that – once again – they faced a moment of choice. But she had done her risk-taking for the day; she had been the one to turn the hose on him, and now it was going to have to be Arie's turn. If he wanted to keep talking, she decided, then he would have to be the one to say, *Let's go inside*.

'What time is it?' he asked, and a few more raindrops fell.

Evie rolled her wrist over to look at her slender, silver watch.

'It's almost five,' she said.

Arie looked puzzled – an hour or more had passed since sunset, and he knew, and she knew that he knew, that five o'clock was long gone – but he didn't press her for an explanation.

'I should let you . . . get on with your evening,' he said.

That was a phrase that Evie herself would never have used. On the telephone, she would never say, *Well, I should let you go*, because when people said those words to her, it wasn't usually that they were being considerate of her, but looking for a polite way to tell her that they felt the conversation had already gone on for long enough. It was rare for Evie to feel that way. When she wanted to talk to someone, she could easily talk all through the night, but she knew that there had been men in her past who had found this aspect of her needy, or overly intense. It was something that she'd learned, over the years, to curb.

A spray of rain came with a gust of wind, and she and Arie got to their feet.

'Thanks for your help with the car,' she said.

'And thank you. For the impromptu shower,' he said.

She grinned. 'Any time.'

Once he left, the rain began to fall in earnest. It fell all across the city, flushing the stuffiness out of the air, rinsing the heat off the roads and the buildings, and restoring parched grasses and wilting trees. Meanwhile, in Tavistock Row, Evie Greenlees sat cross-legged on the cushioned seat of the bay window watching the patterns change on the water-veined glass and listening to the sound of the rain, which was heavy and steady on the roof. On her lap, a diary was open. About this day she'd written many things, but the last of them was: *He is nice. Very nice.*

3.46. It was a sequence of numbers so familiar to Arie that he'd come to regard it almost as an old friend. He was also closely acquainted with 3.44 and 3.45, not to mention 3.47 and 3.48. But when he sat bolt upright in bed on that particular Sunday morning, it was 3.46 that was shining greenly back at him from the display on his bedside clock.

The way he always did when he woke with his heart beating too fast, Arie turned to the muted television at the foot of his bed, where the world of *Doctor Who* waited to take him in. This morning, the screen showed trees thickly clustered with pink blossoms. In the distance, through the gaps between the branches, was the Eiffel Tower.

Soon the image cut away to the top of the tower where the Fourth Doctor and his Time Lord companion, the sailor-hatted Romana, were taking in the view. Arie didn't need to turn up the volume to know what they were saying to each other – he'd seen the episode more times than he could remember – and no words at all were necessary to spell out the chemistry between the actors. Back in the Paris springtime of 1979, Tom Baker and Lalla Ward had been in love.

Arie had been awake during enough early mornings to know that it was best only to hope, but not to expect, that he'd be able to get back to sleep. But this wasn't one of his lucky days. After an hour of lying in bed with his eyes closed, trying to get comfortable first on one side, then the other, then flat on his back, he gave up, increased the volume on the television and watched *Doctor Who* until birdsong, and eventually dawn light, sifted into his room.

One small benefit of having close friends with very young children, Arie had discovered, was that they tended to be up and about almost as early as he was. When he set out on his recently rediscovered bike to Richard and Lenka's house in the neighbouring suburb, the shadows on the grassy lawns were still long and cool, and the rolled-up Sunday papers only freshly scattered. Puddles of the previous night's rain still remained.

'Well, look who else couldn't sleep!' Lenka said, opening the door to Arie with Marek in her arms. The toddler, wearing nothing but a nappy and a singlet, was a writhing mass of plump, dimpled limbs and semi-masticated rusk, and he beamed at Arie with an unmitigated pleasure that Arie hoped one day to be able to return with sincerity.

As things stood, Arie was slightly terrified of Marek, with his raw desires and the speed at which he could transition from cheerful to inconsolable. Nevertheless, Arie bravely took his godson from Lenka's arms and spoke to the child in the sensible, adult tones that he had promised himself he would always maintain. 'Morning, Marek. Making decent progress on that rusk there, I see. How are the fangs coming along?'

Arie reached past the wriggling boy to kiss Lenka's cheek.

'Coffee's made. I can get you breakfast too if you want, but I don't think there's anything very exciting.'

Arie followed Lenka into the kitchen, observing the havoc that a single child had wrought on a once-immaculate house. The place was now a maze of thigh-high safety gates, the sink was lined with sippy cups, and the floor was a carpet of wooden toys. On the fridge, crinkled sheets of paper were covered in primary swirls of finger-paint.

'Richard's gone back to bed,' Lenka told Arie. 'Nobody got much sleep around here last night, I can tell you.'

In her dressing gown, and wearing spectacles in place of her usual contact lenses, Lenka looked tired but not unhappily so. She took Marek back from Arie and set him down on the kitchen floor, giving him a set of brightly coloured measuring cups to play with before pouring Arie a cup of good, strong coffee.

'You look like you have something on your mind,' she said, as perceptive as ever.

Arie nodded. 'That might be so.'

'Well?'

'I need you to tell me what to do.'

'Go on.'

Arie took a gulp of his coffee. 'I've forgotten how to ask a woman out. Actually, that's a total lie. I don't think I've ever known. With Diana . . . well, you know what she was like.'

Lenka made a sad smile. 'Dear, dear Diana. I imagine that she would have decided what she wanted, and . . . poof! . . . your little mind would have been blown apart.'

'That's pretty much how it was.'

'So, there's someone in particular that you want to ask out?'

'There is.'

'Well, this is good, Arie. Isn't it? Who is she?'

'She's staying next door.'

'In the Airbnb?'

'Yes.'

Lenka processed this information, and then something occurred to her. 'Oh, I was going to get you breakfast. You want Weet-Bix? I think it's that or Marek's rice porridge. It's a little bit Sunday in our cupboards.'

'Weet-Bix is fine, but only if you've got enough milk. I can eat later.'

'No, no – we have milk.'

Arie watched her do the particular dance of her kitchen – box from the pantry, bowl from the cupboard, spoon from the drawer, all the while stepping around Marek on the floor. 'So, she's travelling, then?' Lenka asked.

'Which is ideal, I think.'

'How many Weet-Bix do you want? Two, three, four?'

'Three.'

Lenka put the cereal in the bowl, then looked at Arie, her brow furrowed. 'Why is it ideal that she's travelling? I don't follow.'

'Well, it's kind of safe, don't you think?' Arie said. 'We could go out to dinner, talk. I could just be this normal . . . person.'

'What do you mean by "normal"?'

'I mean that for five minutes I could be somebody other than the miserable guy who lost his girlfriend in a plane crash.'

Lenka raised her eyebrows as she contemplated this. 'You are thinking you can go out to dinner with this woman and not tell her about Diana?'

'There wouldn't be any need, would there?'

'I see. You're thinking there is no need, because you will have one date with her and then she'll be gone?'

'I thought you'd be pleased I was, you know . . . taking a chance.'

Lenka gave him a penetrating look. 'Do you think any woman wants to go on a date with someone who regards her as a skill-building exercise?'

'It's not like that,' Arie protested.

'It's not?'

'No. I like her. I really like her. I mean, I hardly know her yet, but she seems—'

'Why?' Lenka challenged. 'Why do you really like her?'

So Arie told her about the guitar music, and the parcel delivery, and the way she'd asked him to borrow a hose and then drenched him with it. 'She's funny, and thoughtful. She has this really expressive face, too. I reckon she'd be dreadful at poker. I don't know . . . she's just . . . perfectly herself somehow,' he concluded.

Lenka smiled proudly. 'You do like her,' she diagnosed. 'But if this is so, why wouldn't you give it a proper chance?'

'Oh, come on, Lenka. This would be my first date . . . since. The law of averages says that—'

'How long is she staying for?'

'About a week, I think.'

Lenka pulled a thinking face, then went to the fridge, got out the milk and poured it onto his cereal. 'I think you should keep your mind open. Keep your heart open. I do not think it is wise to go into such things any other way. And, by the way, I am not expecting you for dinner this Wednesday, am I?'

Wednesday was Diana's birthday.

'No, that's right, I'll be out at Belinda's,' he said. *For the second time inside a week*, he thought.

On Diana's birthday last year and the year before, he and Belinda had laid flowers beneath the empty drawer in the memorial wall, then gone back to her house to drink weak tea while listening to music. He imagined it would be the same this year. He'd ask if she needed anything done around the house, and then he would drive home with a freshly bruised heart.

Again, with the accent, and in the serious-mother voice, Lenka said, 'You have not asked me yet, about the wardrobe.'

'That's true,' Arie said distractedly. 'This week . . . there's Diana's birthday. And I have to take Friday off too, to drive up for Heidi's wedding. Maybe it's a bad idea to ask Evie out this week. Maybe this is the wrong week.'

'Evie? That's her name?'

'Yes.'

'But next week she will be gone, yes?'

'Yes.'

'Then it will have to be this week,' Lenka said, as if this were now firmly decided.

'But how do I do it? What do I even say?'

'You say – would you like to have dinner with me?'

'That's it?'

'Yes, Arie. It's as simple and as difficult as that.'

'Would you like to have dinner with me? That's all I have to say?'

'Correct.' Lenka set his breakfast in front of him, and Arie looked down to see that the Weet-Bix in the bowl had been cut with the edge of a spoon into tiny chunks, the way you might prepare it for a toddler.

'I know I'm a bit remedial in some areas,' Arie said. 'But I think I can manage breakfast cereal.'

Lenka peered into the bowl, and then laughed.

'Oh, shit,' she said. 'I really am tired.'

how to tell (the time)

WHEN EVIE OPENED the door to Arie, and they exchanged greetings, she noticed that he looked more brushed and combed than usual. For once his shirt was tucked in all around his middle.

'So, I was thinking,' he said, squinting a little, as if whatever came next might hurt. 'Would you like to have dinner with me?'

'I'd love to.'

She could see in his expression that he'd not expected it to be so easy.

'O . . . kay. Great,' he said. 'Which night?'

'I'm free any night this week,' she said.

'I can't do Wednesday,' he said. 'Or Friday.'

She thought through the options. That left tonight, tomorrow, or Thursday. Thursday seemed too far away, but Evie didn't quite have the guts to say, *How about tonight? Right now?* So she picked the middle path.

'Tomorrow night?' she suggested.

'Great. I'll pick you up at . . . seven?'

Now that this was settled, Arie seemed to need to leave right away. Perhaps to breathe out, which Evie was fairly sure he had not done properly the whole time he'd been standing at her door.

The restaurant, built on a curve in the narrow river that snaked through the suburbs, was called Chopsticks, and at Lenka's suggestion, Arie had reserved a table for two on the back deck. In the twilight, the lightly rippled surface of the water shone in shades of indigo and rose gold, and on the table, a citrus-scented candle burned, supposedly keeping the mosquitoes at bay.

From the outside, it probably appeared all so very simple: a man in his mid-thirties, out for dinner with a pretty woman, who was – he guessed – in her late twenties. She was beautiful, in a simple black scoop-necked top and a pair of black pants that emphasised her narrow waist. Her silver hoop earrings were very fine, but large in circumference, so that their curves followed the edges of her bobbed hair. She wore more make-up than he'd seen her wear before, but it was mostly concentrated around her eyes. He couldn't say that he really understood eyeshadow, but whatever she'd done, it had made her blue-green eyes look larger and even more intense.

Arie wondered what the people sitting around them would see, observing the pair of them. They were not touching; there was no casual clasping of hands on the table, and no meeting of feet underneath it, so they probably didn't come across as an established couple. Probably, they looked like exactly what they were: two people out on a first date, on best behaviour, slightly nervy and very solicitous of each other. They were engaged in a conversation that moved about like a skittish foal – tentatively coming in close, then shying away. Piece by careful piece, they were getting to know each other.

'So, is Evie your full name, or short for something?'

'Neither,' she said, taking a sip of her white wine.

'Then it's . . . long? For Eve.'

'Yes. And what about Arie? It's not exactly a common name. Not here, anyway.'

'My mother's Dutch,' he explained.

'Ah. That would explain the smidge of an accent you have.'

'Accent? I have an accent?'

He already understood that Evie was someone who watched and noticed, but he was just now coming to understand how closely she had been watching and noticing him.

'It's subtle,' she said, 'but it's there.'

'Mum would be pleased to hear that. She's quite Dutch, although she only gets *really* Dutch around Christmas time.'

'I'm guessing . . . oliebollen?' Evie asked.

'That's New Year, but yes. My sisters all make them, too. Turns out I didn't get the gene.'

'How many sisters do you have?'

'Two older, one younger. The youngest one's getting married this weekend.'

'Is that . . .' she began, and then kept going, '. . . another thing you didn't get the gene for?'

Arie knew she was testing, but only gently.

'I'm not sure,' he said. 'I . . . got close to married. Once. But it wasn't to be. You? Ever married?'

Evie shook her head, the thin silver of her earrings catching the candlelight. 'I've never even been to a wedding.'

'What? Never?'

'Nope.'

'Do you have siblings?'

'In one sense, yes, I have heaps of them. In another, I'm an only child.'

'You're going to have to explain that,' Arie said.

'I have two older half-sisters, Jacinta and Stella. They're my mother's daughters, but not my father's. Then I came along, but I was only a baby when my parents split up. Dad remarried pretty quickly, and courtesy of him I have another four half-sisters, including a set of twins.'

'An only child with six sisters?'

'That's me.'

'Seven girls? Sounds like a fairy tale,' Arie observed.

'Funny you should say that. When I was unpacking all the stuff I left behind in Melbourne, I found this old story I wrote when I was a kid. Kind of embarrassing, really. It was called "The Seven Princesses of Peregrine". They all had special talents,' she said, laughing at herself.

'And when you say "they", you mean "we"?'

'Of course.'

'So, what was yours?'

'Ah. Mine was very special.'

'Are you going to tell me?'

He could see her consider whether or not she wanted to share.

'My special ability was that I could turn back time. Get things to turn out differently.'

Arie felt these words go through him like a sword, and he saw that Evie had seen it happen. Concern furrowed her brow, but he shot her a smile he hoped was convincing. 'More wine?'

'Thank you,' she said, and he poured.

'So,' he said, searching for a way to steer the conversation back to safe ground, and remembering the night he'd seen her lost in concentration with notebook and pen, 'do you still write?'

This, Arie saw, set something sparkling a little more brightly in her eyes.

'I do,' she said.

'What do you write? Fiction? Non-fiction?'

'Nothing so sensible,' she said. 'I write poetry.'

'I've never met a poet before.'

'Well,' she said, 'I wouldn't be getting ahead of yourself just yet.'

A waiter swerved in beside Evie, as if on silent roller-skates, and placed a plate of ginger duck in front of her, then coasted around to Arie's side of the table to deliver a prawn laksa, which Arie now regretted ordering. All that awkward potential for things to drip and leave turmeric-coloured splotches on his pale blue shirt. He was grateful for the thickness of the napkin he settled in his lap.

When dinner was done, Arie suggested a walk on the narrow pathway that led away from the restaurant along the water's edge. The night was mild, and the path empty except for one or two other couples strolling hand in hand, and the occasional cyclist standing high in the pedals while swooping around the many bends.

As they left behind the haze of light from the restaurant, Evie felt the release of a small amount of pressure now that they were walking side by side rather than looking at one another constantly in the eye.

'What's the time?' Arie asked.

Evie didn't even look at her watch. 'It's still a few minutes to five.'

'It's not, of course,' he said.

'Not here, I guess,' Evie said. 'Or not now.'

'I hazard a guess that there's a story behind that watch.'

If Arie had been an archaeologist, Evie thought, then he'd just decided to dig a layer deeper. She said, 'That's true.'

'Is it a story you tell often?'

'Almost never.'

'Almost never. But not absolutely never.'

'Correct.'

'Will you tell it to me?'

So, this was where it happened, Evie thought. Here, with the dark river at their feet and the lights of the city hovering just beneath the ripples of its surface – this was where she traded her story for his. This was where she told him why she wore a stopped watch, and he told her why it was that he had never married. Evie took a breath.

'It was my mother's watch. She died, though.'

'What happened?'

'It was an accident.'

'How old were you?'

'Eight.'

'That's so young. What kind of accident?'

'She was an aid worker with Médecins Sans Frontières, a nurse. She went to Sudan.'

'Hang on. You just said you were *eight*? Where were you when this happened?'

Evie felt warmed by his incredulity, even at the same time as she didn't want him to think badly of her mother.

'My mum . . . she was kind of done with the mothering thing by the time I was born. My big sisters are quite a bit older than me, and she was over it, really. The only reason I was born was because my dad wanted me, apparently, but then he left to start a whole new family' – *he didn't want me* that *much, as it turned out* – 'so there was my mother with this little baby, when what she really wanted' – *what she wanted more than she wanted me* – 'was to go overseas and help people. She had a calling, I guess. She waited until I was eight. The plan was that she was going to go for a year. Just a year.'

'She must have been brave.'

'She was,' Evie said, even though she knew herself to be surmising just as much as Arie was. Her memories of her mother were twenty years old or more. Only a handful were crisp and vivid. The rest were either shapeless things, colourless, or else they looked suspiciously like the photographs that had survived from the first seven years of her life.

'So, what happened to her?'

'It was a landmine. She was in a Jeep, with two colleagues. They were driving in convoy, and the car my mother was in . . . it was in the lead. They were blown apart, all three of them. It was the driver from the car behind. He was the one who found her watch, and sent it home with all her other things. But it had stopped.'

'At almost five o'clock?'

She nodded, and then averted her thoughts from the track they were travelling down. Sometimes, in dreams, Evie couldn't avoid all the images that came along with the story of her mother's watch.

'I really don't know very much more than that.'

This was true. What Evie remembered of the time when she was eight years old was that the surface of her existence had yawned open and swallowed her mother whole, but then – like the sea after a tidal wave – it had all smoothed over again, and life had gone on, with her wondering what the hell had happened and if it would ever, could ever, happen again.

Half a heartbeat before Arie reached out to take Evie's hand, she knew both that he was going to do it and that she wanted him to. His hand made hers feel small, and the warmth of his skin made her realise that hers was a little cool.

It was so weird, Evie mused, the way things like this happened.

His hand, her hand, curled together – it was at once very innocent and entirely intimate. He and she had just crossed a line together. This was the first time they had touched. And yet they had just kept walking, and the moment had gone unremarked between them. Although, she supposed, one way of thinking about it was that the touch stood in for the words. *I like you. I want to be closer to you.*

'What was it like for you, to lose your mother?' Arie asked.

Evie sighed. It was not a question with a simple answer. They walked in silence for a moment while she thought of the best way to answer it.

'Have you ever heard of the Mandela Effect?' she asked.

'As in Nelson Mandela?'

'Yes.'

'He has an effect?'

'He does. It's this thing about collective misremembering. It got its name because there are a large number of people who claim to have *remembered* hearing about Nelson Mandela's death in prison, back in the 1980s. Which, of course, never happened. But there are people who are sure, really sure, that it did. They're even convinced that they remember seeing footage of his funeral on television.'

'What does that have to do with your mother?' he asked – curiously though, not impatiently.

'Nelson Mandela's death is only one example. There are lots of others. The children's books, *The Berenstain Bears*? People will swear black and blue that in their childhood, they were called the Beren*stein* Bears, with an e. And the logo on Ford cars? There are people who vow that the Ford logo is *wrong*, that the way it looks now doesn't match their memories. And it isn't just that the logo's been changed recently, they say – if they look at old photos, they claim the logo has been changed in those old photos, too. That the photos are wrong.'

'But how is that possible?' Arie asked.

'I don't know if it's possible or not. But the point is that people see the Mandela Effect as evidence of a . . . of a . . . what would your Doctor say? A tear in the space-time continuum? They say it could be proof that the multiverse exists. Maybe the Mandela Effect happens because there's some kind of crossover between this version of the world – the one where Nelson Mandela lived and was released from prison and went on to govern South Africa – and another version of it, where he died in prison before any of that was possible. Or maybe it's proof that people are time travelling and changing the course of history – you know, saving Nelson Mandela's life, but not erasing everybody's memory of his death. Or just messing about with details, like the Ford logo, or the way you spell "Berenstain Bears". But what it means to me is that I'm at least allowed to dream. To imagine that somewhere . . . somewhere out there, in another reality, on another version of Earth, my mother was in the second Jeep, and not the first one. Which means in that other reality, there's a version of me who has a mother. Somewhere to go home to. I like to think of that version of me, sometimes.'

'A different version of the same life,' Arie said.

Evie nodded. And waited for Arie to tell her about Diana.

They had come to a small timber platform built out over the river-bank, where a pair of park benches offered a place to sit and rest. Arie and Evie did not sit, but let go of each other's hands and stood, almost touching, as they leaned on the railing. Out on the river a late-night water taxi chugged past, leaving behind the diagonal pulses of its wake and a short burst of an overplayed pop song.

Arie looked up at the city's sky, smudged with smog and all the light it trapped. It had been a long time, he thought, since he'd seen a proper night sky, clear and black and filled with stars. Was it possible that somewhere out there, beyond the fug, beyond the stars even, beyond all that was known, beyond all that could so far be proven to exist, there lurked facsimiles of this Earth orbiting facsimiles of this Earth's sun?

Right now, Arie supposed, would be the perfect moment to tell Evie about Diana. He could tell her that somewhere, on one of those other Earths, his beautiful and talented girlfriend went away on a concert tour, first stop Singapore. Then, uneventfully and quite safely, she flew from that city to Paris, where she played Prokofiev's *Concerto No. 2* and the audience gave her a standing ovation. Onwards she travelled to Salzburg and Prague and St Petersburg, and then she came home to him, and they were married.

For several enjoyable months they tried for a child, and although Diana was very sick in the early months of the pregnancy, she glowed during the second and third trimesters, and although it hurt her to turn down the many invitations she received to perform in the far-flung corners of the world, and although she shed a few tears over the hiatus in her career, it didn't matter so much when she gave birth to their . . . daughter? Son? Arie didn't know. There was no telescope in the world long enough or powerful enough for Arie to look into that world and find out.

Yes, the way was open to tell Evie all of this. But Arie didn't want to. Not yet.

'So what do you think?' he asked.

'About what?'

'About the multiverse? Alternative worlds? Do you believe in all that?'

'Probably not,' Evie admitted. 'But I like to think about it. I like to think of that other me, out there on her other Earth.'

'You find it comforting?'

'Absolutely.'

But Arie wasn't sure this was how it was for him. Thinking of himself and Diana living on in another reality made him feel as if he'd been abandoned here on this particular, benighted Earth, while his actual life went on somewhere else.

'It doesn't make you feel as if the real you is gone, and it's only the husk of you that's been left behind here?'

He saw Evie smile in profile.

'Oh, no. I imagine that we're both quite real,' she said, still looking out over the river. Then she turned to him, just one elbow on the railing now. 'That other me? She's out there, doing her own thing. I'm here, doing mine. We just got dealt different hands, that's all.'

'But there are winning hands and losing hands, aren't there?'

'I know winning is the point when you're playing cards. But in life, I'm not so sure it's always the best goal.'

'So, how are you different, you two?'

Evie thought. 'She has more confidence than I do. She's stronger.'

'Because?'

'Because her mother didn't go forever, only for a while. Because her mother did whatever she needed to do and came home again. They had time, that Evie and her mother, to replace whatever was missing.'

'And what about *this* you?'

'This me?'

'Yes, this one right here. What's her story?'

'Me? Oh, I'm just blowing in the breeze.'

She looked so wistful saying this that Arie acted entirely on impulse. Without thinking at all, he reached out and touched his hand to Evie's face, his palm against the pretty curve of her jaw, her silver earring brushing the back of his hand. She didn't pull away, but closed her eyes and breathed out. He felt a vague heaviness as she allowed his hand to take up a fraction of the weight of her head. With his thumb, Arie stroked her cheek, and she opened her eyes and smiled at him.

'Is this all right?' he asked.

'It's lovely,' she said.

When he kissed her, it was nothing like the stilted kiss he'd shared with Grace on New Year's Eve. This was real.

Eyes closed, heart beating, he could smell mint in the foreground, and in the background the scent of the gum trees that hung their leaves down over the water. He could feel the warm softness of the front of her body pressing against his chest. To his happy surprise, as one hand slipped up under her hair and the other rested on her hip, pulling her gently in to him, he found that he remembered exactly what to do.

Do you know what's going to happen to me next in my life, Evie had said to Dave. *I'll tell you. I'm going to meet somebody. Somebody nice. Somebody really nice. And they're going to want me. Really, properly want me, not just kind of. And it's going to be as simple as that.*

And Arie did want her. Evie could tell from the way he kissed her. His story, any more of her story . . . that was all forgotten for the moment. As the kisses became deeper and deeper, Evie knew that she was right. He really, properly and truly wanted her. And it was going to be as simple as that.

night vision

ALTHOUGH IT WAS quiet inside the Renault on the drive from the restaurant car park to Tavistock Row, it was the opposite of quiet inside Arie's head. He didn't want to be presumptuous, but at the same time he'd felt what was inside and underneath that kiss, and his mind was reeling with it.

He watched the road but was aware of Evie in the passenger seat, fidgeting with the moonstone ring she wore on the middle finger of her left hand. He didn't know for certain what was going to happen next – she might not want to take things any further, she might decide *no*. Equally, she might really want to. He had remembered how to kiss her, but that part was easy in comparison. It had been nine years since he'd made love to a woman for the first time, and over two since he'd been with anyone at all.

Whether or not they ended up in bed together, Arie was almost certain they weren't going to say goodbye out on the street. He tried to think of a way to make sure they went to her house and not his. At his house, there were pictures of Diana on every second wall, and an entire room devoted to a piano that he didn't play. Diana's winter coats, her hats, her umbrella . . . they were all still hanging on the rack just inside the front door.

Arie hadn't been into 12A since it had been renovated, although he and Diana had taken the opportunity to look inside during the open home when the place had been on the market. Perhaps he could tell Evie he'd like to see what the owners had done with the place.

As he turned the car into Tavistock Row, he was aware that he felt more alert than he could remember feeling in a very long time – awake in a crisp, fresh kind of way. It was the complete opposite of the drained, lead-heavy wakefulness of the insomniac in the early hours of the morning.

But as he approached the stretch of the street where his house stood, he saw that there was a car already parked out the front, and his sense of anticipation turned swiftly into a different kind of anxiety. It was as if his fizzing nervous pleasure had undergone a chemical reaction and changed its colour to guilt. The car was small, and white, and familiar to him. The interior light was switched on, and in its glow he could just make out the shape of somebody sitting in the driver's seat. It was Belinda Clare.

Evie saw the car, too. There was nothing remarkable about it, but she felt Arie react as if he'd been given an electric shock. She glanced over at him and saw that his jaw was tight with stress.

There was room to park his car right outside number 12, even if the white car had possibly made the gap a little tight. As they came closer, Evie caught a distant glimpse of the rear-view mirror inside the car. The person reflected there, she was fairly sure, was a woman with short fair hair. Evie expected Arie to slow to a stop and reverse into the free space, but instead he hit the brakes, threw the gear lever into reverse, and backed into the driveway of the nearest house before retreating along Tavistock Row in the direction they'd just come.

'Is everything all right?' Evie asked.

'Not . . . really,' Arie said.

'What's going on? Is there something wrong?'

He turned the car out of Tavistock Row, left into the nearest cross-street, his hand clenched tight around the steering wheel. He pulled up at the kerb and looked at Evie, his face pained.

'I'm so sorry. This is really not . . . look, I can't explain everything right now. There's a woman in a car outside my house. She's . . . look, she's not . . . it's nothing like you might think, but she just can't see you. Not right now. Not . . . tonight.'

Evie felt as if she'd been lying in a warm bath, and then someone had sucked away all the water at some incredible speed. Her limbs felt suddenly heavy, and her skin cold.

'There's a woman in a car outside your house,' she repeated, 'and she can't . . . see me?'

'Not tonight she can't. Another time it would be different, maybe. Evie, can you just cut me some slack here? I have to go see to her, okay? I just need five minutes.'

Evie tried to remain calm and to be understanding, but her brain was having trouble pulling all the pieces of this situation together. Five minutes. Did he need five minutes alone with the woman, and then he'd come back? Or did he mean something else?

'I don't understand. What exactly are you asking me to do?'

'I am so sorry. I know this is entirely shabby. Worse than shabby. I need you to get out of the car, and just give me five minutes. Just wait here for five minutes until I can take her inside. That's all I need. Just five clear minutes. Then you can just walk back to your place.'

'I can *walk back to my place*?' Evie said, her sense of humiliation beginning to override her desire to understand. '*Can* I just? You give me permission? Thanks a million.'

'Please, Evie. I can explain everything, but not right now. If she's here, she'll be a mess. I'm so sorry. Please?'

Evie nodded, because really what else was there for her to do? There wasn't anything, she realised. Or at least, nothing dignified. She reached for the door handle.

'Thank you for a lovely dinner,' she said tersely.

'I'm sorry, Evie.'

'So you keep saying.'

Evie stepped out into the street and closed the car door behind her, being careful not to slam it. She slung her small handbag – containing nothing but the house keys, her wallet and a lipstick – over her shoulder, and crossed her arms against her chest.

The late-night breeze that rolled down the cross-street blew easily through the thin fabric of her cotton top as it fully dawned on her that she was standing alone in the street, while the man she thought she was about to go home with made a tight U-turn and drove away from her.

Evie's watch told her only that it was a few minutes to five o'clock. Its hands would not move in the next five minutes, or ever again, and since Evie had no phone to tell her the time, she had no way of measuring the minutes, except within herself.

She went up the cross-street, but no matter how fast she marched only one part of her was warm, and that was her flaming cheeks. She continued until it seemed like a good idea to turn left, and then walked some more, sending a cat on the footpath streaking away underneath a car at the sound of her footsteps. So much for her prophecy. There was nothing simple about this situation after all. Nothing.

Evie walked for a long time, until she had eventually traced a wide circle that brought her back to the bakery on the corner of Tavistock Row. From there, she could see the stretch of street outside 12 and 12A. There was no sign of Arie or the woman on the footpath or in his front yard. The white car was still parked on the street, its interior light now switched off; the Renault was parked directly behind it. As Evie approached on soft feet, all was quiet, all was peaceful, and it seemed to her in that moment that everything was in its place and as it should be. Except for her. As she had been so many times before, she was the extra piece, the wrong piece, the piece that didn't fit.

FIVE

mirror in the mirror

AT NUMBER 12 Tavistock Row, Belinda Clare sat in the middle of an armchair, her thin body compressed into a posture that seemed designed to minimise her even further – feet together, shoulders tight, elbows resting on her knees, chin in her hands. Her eyes were rimmed red, and there were crumpled tissues on the coffee table next to a mug of milky tea that had gone cold.

Several times over the last hour she'd said the same thing, in various ways, through tears: 'I just wish we'd been able to bury her. I hate having to think of her at the bottom of that bloody ocean. I hate that we lost every part of her.' But Arie had been able to do nothing for her pain but brew the tea, place a box of tissues within easy reach, and search out the pillows and sheets and blankets needed to make up the sofa bed.

Finally, Belinda's tears had stopped, and Arie had put on some music. It was Arvo Pärt's 'Spiegel im Spiegel', which Diana had recorded with her cellist friend, Naomi Koh. Out of all Diana's recordings, this was perhaps Arie's favourite, and it was the most soothing thing he could think of to play for Belinda this night.

Diana had once told him that the name of the piece meant 'mirror in the mirror', and she had made him pay attention to the progressions of notes and the way they moved away from each other, then converged again, like mirror images, although they were subtly different each time.

The long, slow bowing of the cello and the simple sequences from the piano – which sounded like soft plinks of dripping water – flowed around and through him, and Arie remembered Diana's pale wrists rising and falling, and the way she closed her eyes as she played, making herself into a conduit between the place the music came from, wherever that was, and the ears of the listener.

Pärt's composition was gentle and inexpressibly sad, and as it played Arie's thoughts shifted to Evie. This house and the neighbouring one were separated by nothing but a single wall, a handspan's worth of paint, plaster and brick, and for all he knew she could well be in the mirror-image living room, only metres away from him.

He could see how it must have looked through her eyes: a woman in a car outside his house, his panic, the shameful way he'd driven her around the corner and left her there. If he'd thought calmly for a moment instead of reacting blindly, he could have handled the situation in a hundred different ways. A hundred better ways. He knew he needed to apologise and explain. But how? And when? Tonight, Belinda would be here, and tomorrow – Diana's birthday – was spoken for.

On the stereo, 'Spiegel im Spiegel' slowed to a halt. Arie remembered that although Diana had generally not liked music without what she called a 'proper' ending, this was a piece for which she had been prepared to make an exception.

'I don't think you're meant to believe that it really does end there,' she'd told him. 'I think you're meant to believe that it goes on and on, forever and ever, although maybe in another room.'

In the wake of the cello and the piano, the room fell silent.

After a moment, Belinda said, 'It wasn't me, you know.'

Arie didn't know. 'Sorry?'

'It wasn't me. I was never the musical one,' Belinda said, and Arie felt something opening between them. Something new. 'She didn't get the music from me. She got it from her father.'

'You've never talked about Diana's father,' he said carefully. '*Diana* never talked about her father.'

'No, she didn't. She went easy on me,' Belinda said. 'She asked me about him only once, and I told her what I could. After that, she dropped it. It was this strange, tacit thing. She just . . . left it alone. We had each other, and that seemed to be enough.'

The questions in Arie's head wrestled with each other to be the first in line. Who? When? Where? How?

Belinda bit her thumbnail, and a small spark crept into her eyes. 'I met him in a pub when I was travelling around the country with a girlfriend. In her panel van, if that tells you something about the time in my life it was.'

Arie tried to imagine a young Belinda on a road trip. Sandy feet on vinyl seats. The smell of coconut-scented sunscreen. Pulling on tight jeans in a space where it's impossible to stand up, laughing.

'Did he ever know about her?'

'No. Never, nothing.'

'You don't ever think of looking him up?'

'I don't know that I could.'

'Because?'

'I don't have much to go on.'

'How much is not much?'

'He played in a band, and his name was Rory. Don't look at me like that, Arie. I was so young.'

'I'm not looking at you like anything,' Arie protested.

'You are.'

'All right, maybe I am,' he said, risking a smile. 'It's just that I hadn't pegged you for a groupie. I'm trying to imagine you in a mosh pit.'

'He was pretty gorgeous,' Belinda said, with a smidge of pride.

'And you've really never thought of finding him?'

'When she was alive there was never any need. She never pressed me about it. And now, after everything that's happened, it seems like a pretty miserable thing to do. What would I tell him? You had a beautiful, talented daughter. But you'll never meet her.'

Belinda let this thought hover for a moment, then said, 'I should let you get to bed.'

'Want a hand with that sofa?'

'No, I'm fine with it.'

'Well, night then.'

Arie stood, and as he passed Belinda on the way to the stairs, another to-hug-or-not-to-hug moment passed between them, resulting in Arie making an awkward gesture that was somewhere between a salute and a wave. When he was almost out of the room, she said, 'Arie, I do know this isn't how you planned to spend your evening.'

Arie, feeling a little stab of guilt, looked back to scan her face, but it didn't appear that she was referring to any specific circumstances; she had only meant to say that she was sorry if she had inconvenienced him.

'It's fine. Really.'

'I know I'm fortunate,' she said. 'That you're here for me.'

'Always,' he said, and while he meant it, he also suspected there was a mismatch between her expectations of him and what he could truly promise. One day, he knew, he was going to disappoint her. It had almost happened tonight.

No music played in the living room of 12A. All Evie could hear, as she stood looking at her map of Australia, was the faint electronic hum of appliances and the swoosh of her own blood in her ears.

Either the map was large or the table was small – or both – because the northern tips of the Australian land-mass listed off the edge of the table and drooped, Dalí-esque, towards the floor. The four markers she had pushed into the paper were still there, but now Evie removed the small star from Esperance. It was such a far-away place, and tonight the prospect of crossing the entire country and setting herself up in a town where she knew nothing, and nobody, only made her feel unbearably weary.

For much the same reason, she plucked the silver moon from Bellingen. All the adventure had gone out of her. Now, what she really wanted was a safe, warm burrow in which to curl up, away from the world.

In the past hour, Evie's thoughts had already done several circuits of the same set of thoughts, and they began again now. First came the questions. Who was the woman in the car? And why had Arie not wanted her to see Evie? Then came the assumptions. Obviously, the woman was someone who would take a dim view of Arie being out for dinner with Evie, not to mention kissing her. Was she his lover? Or one of his many lovers, for that matter?

After that came the tempering thoughts. She shouldn't make assumptions; she didn't know all the facts; Arie didn't owe her anything. They had gone out to dinner together, that was all. One kiss was hardly a diamond ring. Men who were divorced or widowed – they never stayed single for long. Evie knew that. For a lot of women, a grieving man was a special kind of emotional challenge – a real fixer-upper. A man in Arie's situation? Women probably threw themselves at him.

Evie was well aware that dating more than one person at a time was a thing people did, although she had never done it herself. She was, and always had been, an all-or-nothing kind of person, to the point where an ex-boyfriend had once described her as 'one of those girls who bring their furniture along with them on the second date'.

Then the questions started up again. If Arie had been comfortable with whatever he was doing – if he was just playing the field in a way that seemed reasonable to him – then why had he reacted so? Why take Evie around the corner and leave her there unless he was ashamed of something? Or afraid of something? She didn't know, and maybe she would never know, because she certainly wasn't going to go next door and ask. Not tonight, not tomorrow, not ever.

There was one thing, though, that she was sure about: whatever there was, or had fleetingly been, between herself and Arie Johnson, it wasn't simple. Not at all.

With some effort, Evie turned her attention back to the map. Melbourne or Hobart? Big city or small city? Edge of the continent or south of the island? Here or there?

Not here, her heart said. *There is nothing for you here.*

The decision was made.

Half an hour later, she and the Beetle were booked on the Monday sailing of the Bass Strait ferry. Five more days and she'd be on her way.

Now the computer clock read close to midnight, but Evie knew Reuben had a habit of sitting up late at night trawling the internet and listening to songs by obscure bands on YouTube. She still hadn't organised her phone service. It was on her never-ending list of things to do, to choose an Australian provider and get herself a local SIM card. In the absence of a phone, she launched Skype.

While the familiar chimes rang, Evie tried to find a flattering camera angle for her face, but before she could – and knowing that such a thing was probably mythical, anyway – the screen opened like a doorway into the living room at Rumsfeld Street. There was Reuben, with his rockabilly sideburns, two-day stubble and lopsided quiff of sandy hair.

'Eve-star!' he exclaimed.

'Hey, Roo.'

'How's things, girl?'

'Not bad. Not bad.'

Stella appeared at Reuben's shoulder in her pyjamas, her face red from being washed and shiny with before-bed moisturiser.

'Hello, love!' Stella said. 'It's pretty late. Everything okay?'

'Fine, fine. It's just, I've got news and I thought you would want to be the first to know.'

In tandem, Reuben and Stella asked, 'What?'

'I'm coming home.'

It did Evie good to see these slightly pixelated versions of Stella and Reuben high-fiving each other with joy, but it didn't entirely take away the ache that had settled in her heart. With every beat she was reminded, *not quite enough, not quite enough, not quite enough.*

eselverue

DIANA'S BIRTHDAY HAD come and gone. Now it was Thursday evening, and Arie – head bowed in thought – was standing at the front door of 12A Tavistock Row. In one hand he held a box that was wrapped in marbled paper and tied with a ribbon. The other hand was poised in readiness to knock, its knuckles suspended a short distance from the timber. He had been standing there like that long enough to feel as though he were a living statue.

Ideally, he'd have come over and done this before now. *But it was impossible*, he told himself, in the same breath that he argued back, *Actually, you just didn't make it possible*. In his lunch hour, he'd gone to a florist. Looking around at the display, he'd realised he didn't know what kinds of flowers Evie liked, or what kinds she didn't like, so he'd walked out without buying anything.

After that he'd gone from shop to shop with the vague hope that he would catch sight of something that would say 'I'm sorry' in a way so perfect Evie would have no choice but to forgive him. Unsurprisingly, he found no such irresistible thing, although in a shop full of intricate model ships in bottles, an idea did occur to him. It had taken him the rest of the afternoon to find and make all of its parts.

The box felt light in his hand, and Arie didn't know how Evie would receive its contents – whether she would write it off as a cheap gesture, or if she would understand. Overwhelmingly, he felt like walking away, facing this at another time, or on another day, but he knew that he had to do it now. Tomorrow, he would set off on the long drive north to Heidi's wedding.

He took a deep breath. Then another. And knocked.

Silent seconds passed before Arie heard distant noises that eventually became the sound of bare feet on floorboards. When Evie opened the door, it was only to the extent that a chain-lock might allow, although no such thing was in place. She leaned against the wall inside, her calves bare below the skirt of a patchwork dress, and her hair once again held back with a scarf. Her face was completely free of make-up so that he could see the freckles on her nose and cheekbones.

In her expression he detected hurt, anger, and reservation.

'Hello,' she said, and that same mixture of emotion was audible in her voice. There was something else too, though. Something that gave Arie heart. As well as everything else, she was – he could see – curious.

'I've come to apologise,' Arie said. 'To explain.'

She raised her chin slightly, as if to say, *Go on, then*.

'Could I come in, do you think?'

He watched her features subtly shift as she considered this. Then, without saying any more, she opened the door wider.

Evie reached the dining room ahead of Arie, wishing that she was better at nonchalance – that her heart did not speed up at the slightest prospect of awkwardness, that her hands didn't shake when she felt nervous, that she wasn't so prone to blushing at the slightest provocation. She looked around the dining room for anything that needed clearing away. If she couldn't be inscrutable, she might at least stop her environment from giving too much away.

She was pleased that her dinner dishes were washed and stacked in the drainer, and that the music on the stereo was none of the compilations of schmaltzy ballads she'd been listening to in the past couple of days. It took her only a moment to fold up the map that still lay on the table.

'Have a seat,' she said, gesturing to one of a pair of white leather wing-back chairs.

Arie placed something on the table, and although Evie tried not to look at it – tried, instead, to look over the top of it, pretending it didn't exist – she saw at a glance how perfectly the gift was wrapped. She took the seat opposite Arie's, one foot tucked beneath her, and for a moment he closed his eyes, as if looking for an autocue behind his eyelids.

'The other night,' he said, 'I didn't think clearly in the moment, and I handled everything very badly. If I could go back and do it all again, I would still have turned the car around. But I could have taken you to a café, or a bar, and I could have told you everything I need to tell you now.'

Evie could see how carefully he was choosing his words, and she suspected he might be about to mete the story out to her in tiny, bite-sized chunks, when what she wanted was for him to spit it out quickly.

'The woman in the car,' Arie said. 'It's nothing like you must think. She's . . . she's the mother of someone I loved very much.'

Mother? The woman in the car was . . . Diana Clare's mother? Questions piled up on her tongue, but before she could get them into any sensible order, Arie began to tell her the whole story . . . Diana, the plane crash, his ongoing and complex relationship with Belinda Clare. As he spoke, Evie was reminded of the way he'd looked in the television interview she'd seen on the internet. He was so sincere, so vulnerable, that she knew it was going to be difficult to remain angry with him.

'Yesterday was Diana's birthday,' he said, and the smile he gave her had a twist of grief at its corners. 'That's why I've not come to see you sooner. That day . . . it's, kind of, set aside. And the other night, do you see? I knew that if Belinda had driven to town on the night before Diana's birthday, she'd be upset – and I was right about that. Seeing you would have made it worse.'

For the first time since he'd started talking, Evie suspected he wasn't being entirely truthful.

'You didn't want her to know you were out on a date,' she said. It was not a question.

Arie winced. 'No. No, I didn't. I'm so sorry, Evie.'

The woman he'd wanted to hide Evie from was not his lover, then, but the guardian of a memory. He'd felt the need to choose, and he had chosen. One dinner date, one kiss – Evie knew these had to seem like flimsy things compared to the years of history he shared with Diana's mother. He'd done what he'd done out of care. Evie understood all of this, but the fact remained that he'd humiliated her. It was all so very complicated.

'I should have told you. About Diana.'

'Why didn't you?' Evie hoped this sounded only like the genuine question it was, and not a recrimination.

'I liked the way it felt when you didn't know.'

Evie bit her lip. 'I did, though. I did know, about the plane crash, and Diana.'

'You did?'

'I may have Googled you,' she confessed, her blush refreshing itself.

Arie looked puzzled. 'You knew, and you didn't say anything?'

'I figured you'd tell me when you were ready.' She paused. 'It must have broken your heart, to lose her.'

'It did. I should have told you that, too. By the river, with you . . . it was the first time since she died that I tried to do anything with my heart.'

At this, Evie felt herself soften a little further.

'I know I've blown this thing with you. Irreparably,' he said.

Yes, she thought, *you have.*

'But maybe what I have to take away from it is that I've got a bit more work to do, on myself, before I'm really ready to move on. I hurt you, I know I did, and I'm so sorry for that. Right now, I don't feel like a very safe pair of hands.'

It was, Evie thought, a brave thing to admit.

'So, have you decided where you're going?' he asked, gesturing to the folded map.

'Not yet,' she said, realising that she didn't want him to know any more than he already did. Her anger had dissipated, but she could still feel all the edges of her disappointment. She wanted to have her walls in place, and to hide as much of herself as possible behind them.

'I had hoped to make it up to you,' he said. 'To see if I could persuade you to let me take you out for dinner again – just a friendly dinner – and see if I could do the ending part a bit better. But I have to go away tomorrow. I won't be back until Sunday.'

'I check out of here on Monday,' Evie said.

'I'd reschedule, but it's my sister's wedding.'

'I see.'

'She's getting married in the Blue Mountains. It's a long drive.'

'You're driving?' Evie asked, perplexed.

'Yes.'

'Oh, I see. Because you don't—' *Fly*.

'No.'

After a pause, Arie pushed the box towards her. 'This is for you. To say I'm sorry. I thought of flowers, but . . . I didn't know what kind you liked.'

Evie wondered what it could be. Chocolates, maybe? She untied the bow and peeled away the paper, and inside the wrapping she found a wooden box. Its lid – about the same dimensions as a postcard – was carved with an intricate paisley-like pattern.

'You and I – we talked,' Arie said, as she regarded this rather beautiful thing, 'about the *Dictionary of Obscure Sorrows*. Do you remember?'

She did.

'Go on,' Arie urged.

Evie lifted the lid and could not help but smile. The box was filled to about a third of the way up its sides with what appeared to be white sand, although the grains had a particular sparkle to them that made Evie think there might be some glitter involved, too. Wedged into the sand at an angle was a small glass vial, stoppered with a cork. Inside this little vessel was a slip of paper: a message in a bottle. Evie opened it and used the tips of her fingernails to catch the edge of the paper and draw it out. The words were – carefully, elegantly – handwritten.

eselverue

n. the desire, brought about by the knowledge that one has made a grievous error, to travel through the universe to an alternative Earth

and merge, there, with a version of oneself who had the good sense not
to have made the same error.

Evie commanded her face to be still.

'It's my contribution . . . to the dictionary,' Arie said, leaning forward, clearly anxious to know whether or not she liked it.

Evie was still processing. He'd invented a word. Just for her.

'You said you like unusual words,' he prompted.

Eselverue, Evie silently repeated. Who in the world, she thought, hadn't at one time or another – after doing a stupid or regrettable thing – felt a pang of *eselverue*?

'Thank you,' she said, moved. 'It's lovely.'

'Can you forgive me?'

Of course I can. 'Maybe. What happened was pretty shitty.'

'It was,' he said, 'deeply shitty.'

'I have had worse endings to dates, but not very much worse,' Evie said, with a laugh that went dangerously close to letting out one or two of the tears she was holding fiercely in check.

'I can't tell you how much I wish this had all gone differently. I'm sorry that we seem to be out of time.'

Despite an urge to placate him, to soothe him, Evie said nothing. Then she saw his brown eyes brighten a little as he considered something.

'You know,' he said, 'you *could* come. To the wedding, I mean.' He looked as surprised as she was, as if these words had come out of his mouth before he was quite certain that he'd intended to say them. 'I know it's insane to be driving all that way. You probably wouldn't want to, but . . .'

She thought.

'You did say you'd never been to a wedding.'

He gave what she assumed to be his best imitation of a careless shrug. It was true that it was a crazy idea, but Evie was fond of road trips. And, truth be told, she'd love to take a glimpse inside his world, to meet Arie's mother and father, and his sisters.

'So, you'd like . . . a friend,' she clarified, 'to go with you to the wedding?'

'Very much.'

'I didn't think you could invite extra guests to a wedding at the last minute? I thought there were, you know, seating plans and so on?'

'It's not that kind of wedding,' he rushed to say, and then he was rambling, about how Evie would be doing him a favour, really, since they could share the driving a bit, but only if she wanted to, obviously, and how there were two bedrooms in the place he'd rented, but if that was too awkward then she could stay there alone, and he could go to the guesthouse where the rest of his family was staying, and . . .

'When are you leaving?'

'Around nine.'

'And your sister. Are you sure she wouldn't mind?'

'Heidi? God, no. She'd be thrilled.'

The days between now and her ferry booking were empty. What else would she be doing?

'Well?' Arie prompted.

'I'll . . . think about it,' she promised.

present tense

ARIE WAS FAR from sure which way Evie would decide. But in the morning, there she was, standing in the street with an overnight bag at her feet. Coming out of his house, he saw her before she saw him, which gave him a minute to study her in her huge tortoiseshell sunglasses, white T-shirt, floral skirt and strappy brown leather shoes. There was something classic about her – perhaps it was her haircut – that made her look timeless, and it occurred to him that if the Tavistock Row backdrop were stripped away and replaced with the hillside of a Greek island some decades in the past, she could easily have passed for a tourist there, waiting for a car to stop on the dusty white road and collect her.

She's actually going to come, he thought, allowing himself for the first time to understand just how much he'd wanted her to.

'You're joining me then?' he asked, trying not to seem over-eager.

'Looks that way.'

'Take your bag, madam?'

'Why thank you, sir.'

By the time they'd stopped to grab takeaway coffees and croissants, Arie had worked out that if Evie was holding on to any bad feelings about the Belinda Clare situation, she hadn't brought them with her on the road. Instead, she'd packed an iPod with a ready-made playlist – 'a very long one', she told him.

As they passed through the city fringe, he was profoundly aware of her in the passenger seat beside him – of the reflecting light that bounced off the lenses of her sunglasses, of the strawberry birthmark on the side of her right calf, of the way her lips moved ever so slightly to the words of the songs. A few flakes of croissant pastry clung to her T-shirt and littered the fabric of her skirt. She'd put her bare feet up on the dash, so that there was now a subtle, smudgy line of toeprints along the inside of the windscreen.

On her playlist, there were songs he knew and a lot he didn't, but all of them were joyful in a mellow kind of way. While the music played, not too loud, not too soft, Arie and Evie talked easily, their conversation fading in and out without any pressure to keep up the chatter. She didn't ask him to share any more about Diana, and for his part he didn't press her on the subject of her future plans. What he felt, and almost wanted to say to her, was risky as a compliment. But if he'd gone ahead and said it, he'd have meant it as high praise – there was nothing about her that irritated him.

She burst open a bag of jelly babies. 'What colour do you want?'

'Green.'

'Seriously? You like the green ones?'

'You don't?'

'No. Yuck. I only like the red and orange ones. The purple ones are okay.'

'Nah – green and yellow, all the way.'

'My God,' she said, with a burst of disbelieving laughter. 'How good is this? Wide open road, music on the stereo, and a perfect match of jelly-baby preferences.'

In glances, Arie observed her. It was clear that her sunglasses were cheap, that her skirt was handmade from thin cotton, and that the shoes she'd discarded on the floor of the car had seen better days. She reminded him of the girls he'd known as a student – the ones who'd been able to cobble their style together on the most threadbare of shoestrings. But in the time he'd spent with her, he'd never had even the vaguest sense that she was in any way discontented with her lot. She was one of those lucky people, he thought, who were easily delighted by the small things in life.

They ate dinner on the road and arrived at their destination at twilight. The owners of the cottage, who lived in the nearby homestead, had left a couple of the interior lights switched on, so that the casement windows appeared as lozenges of amber set into the dark timbered walls. The honeymoon effect was not lost on Evie, at the wheel now, as she carefully threaded the Renault through a narrow gate and brought it to a standstill on the gravel patch that lay a short distance from the cottage. Nearby, a flock of geese nested like a scattering of white boulders in the grass.

A sensor light flicked on as Evie and Arie approached the front door, so they could see the large old-fashioned key waiting there in the lock. Indoors – where the timber of the walls and furniture was everywhere softened by tasteful rugs and cushions – the scene was no less inviting, nor was it any less clear what assumptions the owners had made when Arie had messaged to say there would now be two guests instead of one. A lamp had been left on in the loft bedroom, which had steeply sloping walls, so that a triangle of light glowed at the top of a rustic timber staircase. A pair of deep-bowled wine glasses and a bottle of local Shiraz stood on the kitchen counter, along with a handwritten note that said, *We hope you have a magical stay!*

Evie gravitated to the bookshelf while Arie loaded their provisions into the fridge, then opened various of the downstairs doors to locate the bathroom and second bedroom. They had been so easy with each other for all of the car journey, but now they had arrived in this new space, Evie could feel a charge of tension in the air. There were things to navigate and negotiate, and in response to this they had both become awkward and quiet.

'Which room would you like?' Arie asked.

Evie didn't mind, but she knew that if she said so, this could only be followed by Arie saying he didn't mind either, and so it would go, each of them trying to be more considerate than the other.

'I'll take the loft room,' she suggested.

'Great. I'll, um, have this one.'

Evie took her bag upstairs, where a dormer window set into the rough-timbered walls gave a view over the semi-darkness of the grassy yard. On the foot of the low futon bed, a pair of bath towels had been set out, their corners overlapping. A silver-wrapped chocolate had been placed on each side of the invitingly turned-back covers.

It would have so been nice, Evie thought. That is, if she and Arie had been the guests they were supposed to be.

The loft bed was soft in a feathery way that made Evie feel extravagant, and its yielding mattress dragged her down into a deep, deep sleep. When she woke, it was to the smell of coffee and frying bacon. She got out of bed and peered down over a railing into the kitchen below, where Arie, believing himself all alone, was humming a thread of song as he supervised eggs poaching in a pan and bread toasting under the grill.

He'd set the table for two, including a couple of orange marigolds in a water glass, and everything Evie saw returned her to yesterday's atmosphere of holiday, escape and calm.

'Morning,' she said, coming down the stairs.

'Morning,' Arie said, smiling up at her. 'I made you coffee, but I don't know how you take it.'

'Just white.'

'Easy to remember, then. Same as me.'

There was an incongruity about the situation that made Evie smile. On the one hand, there was something ridiculously intimate about standing there with Arie in that small kitchen and having him pass her a steaming mug of coffee. At the same time, though, she was such a stranger to him that he didn't even know if she took milk or sugar.

'So, I've been worrying,' she said, watching him expertly plate up the toast, poached eggs and crispy bacon.

'About?'

'My clothes for the wedding. Everything I own has either been in a garage for several years or else it's spent half its life scrunched into a backpack.'

He handed her a plate and gave her a reassuring smile. 'It really won't be a fussy kind of wedding. Promise. You could come in a hessian sack if you wanted to.'

'Well, that's probably fortunate.'

The ceremony wasn't to be held until mid-afternoon, but Arie was expected in the late morning at the guesthouse where the rest of his family was getting ready. After breakfast, and having taken

240

lengthy turns in the bathroom, Arie and Evie emerged from the cottage.

She'd chosen a well-travelled favourite of a dress – simple and sleeveless – that held a subtle shimmer in its deep green fabric. From her stored clothes, she'd retrieved a black wrap of fine wool; back at Tavistock Row she'd sat down with a needle and thread to repair a couple of moth holes in order to make it presentable. The shoes, too, had come out of storage, and although they were pretty – black and strappy with a kitten heel – they hadn't ever fitted all that brilliantly. She'd straightened her near-black hair until it shone, and while she'd kept the rest of her make-up subtle, she'd run amok with the most dramatic mascara she owned.

'Perfect,' Arie told her.

He looked comfortable but a little dressy in a pair of light brown pants and an off-white linen shirt, tucked in, but with no tie. She could smell some kind of scent and it struck her as warm and expensive, like honey and petrol together – but in a good way.

Under different circumstances, Evie thought, this would have been the perfect moment – here on the grass, outside this quaint little cottage – for Arie to offer her his arm, or to reach out and take her hand, and from the look on his face, she thought he knew it, too. As if trying to keep himself out of trouble, he slid his hands into his pockets.

'Ready?' he asked.

'As I'm ever going to be.'

They set off along a country road that led past the orchard where the wedding was to be held, and where a small marquee had already been erected in a clearing between long-established plantings of apple and pear trees. Nearby on a low stage, a band was doing a sound check, startling some nearby cows with sudden bursts of guitar and squeals of feedback.

The guesthouse was further on, and before Arie and Evie were even three-quarters of the way there, she had an inkling that these particular shoes had been a mistake. But, in the time-honoured fashion of women everywhere, she convinced herself that they were going to be totally fine.

As they turned into the driveway of the guesthouse, Evie could hear the shouts of the children Arie had referred to as the *neven en nichten*, his nephews and nieces: the many children of his two elder sisters. She followed as Arie searched out his parents' room, where Malcolm Johnson – spectacles low on his nose – was yanking inexpertly on the zipper pull of his wife's bright, floral dress.

Ilse Johnson was a tall and generously proportioned woman with large blue eyes and the look of someone who'd spent the morning at a salon. Her fair hair was sprayed into submission, although a few carefully controlled curls had been allowed to escape from the elaborate bun at the nape of her neck.

Malcolm was altogether more angular, with dark hair and eyes the same brown as Arie's, and also that same smooth olive-toned skin. Glancing from one parent to the other, Evie understood that Arie looked more like his father, but that his mother's contribution to his appearance was a certain softening of his features. He had, in Evie's opinion, done rather well in the genetic stakes.

'Oh, look at you, handsome thing,' his mother said, catching sight of Arie in the doorway. 'And this must be Evie?'

'Hello,' Evie said.

Arie's dad glanced over the top of his glasses. 'You're a patient soul, to put up with such a long drive.'

'It's fine. I actually love a road trip,' she said.

'Well, we're glad you could come,' Ilse said. 'So glad. But for heaven's sake, Arie, can *you* do my zip? This *boerenkinkel* is going to tear my frock open in a minute if he's not careful. Ow!'

Malcolm walked away from the situation with some relief. 'All yours, mate.'

'It fitted two weeks ago,' Ilse complained.

Arie wriggled a segment of trapped fabric out of the teeth and took the zipper pull back to the bottom to start again, and as Evie watched, she was visited by an image of him helping Diana into a red gown. Evie could imagine her holding her hair out of the way while Arie wrangled the zip. Diana would have needed two hands for all that hair, and Evie could picture the way it would have fallen in a ginger-blonde mass when she'd let it go.

'The secret is to breathe out, Mum,' Arie said. 'Not in. *Out*. Okay, ready?'

When he was done, his mother turned from side to side, looking at herself in the mirror, pleased. She kissed Arie's cheek.

'Where's everyone else?' Arie asked his mother.

'Outside with the photographer. You go on. We'll be down in a minute.'

In the grounds of the guesthouse, a photographer was training a long lens on various small children, some of them climbing the low, inviting branches of the gum trees that lined the driveway, others investigating a flowerbed where, so they were all shouting, there was a blue-tongue lizard. Eschewing it all was a tall girl in the vicinity of twelve or thirteen years of age, who sat listlessly on the seat of a tree-swing, clearly wishing that she was anywhere else in the world but here. Evie could remember that time of her own life. One day, this girl would look back on this phase too, possibly with the help of the photo Evie saw the photographer take from a distance.

The little boys wore tweedy waistcoats and bow-ties, and the girls wore chocolate-brown linen dresses with broderie anglaise frills at the hem. There was, however, one notable exception.

A thin girl of seven or eight, her white-blonde hair cropped close in a pixie cut, was wearing nothing but her underpants and singlet. A clump of brown linen and broderie anglaise lay on the gravel beside her, and she was shrieking at a tall, buxom woman who looked the way Evie imagined Arie's mother would have looked in her late thirties.

'No!' the child yelled.

'Put it back on, right now,' the woman demanded, but Evie could see that the battle lines had been well and truly drawn. The child's tear-streaked cheeks gave Evie the impression that there had already been several failed rounds of entreaty, threats, bribery and steely determination.

In a low voice, Arie told Evie, 'So that would be Sara and her youngest, the indomitable Imogene.'

'I'm guessing Imogene's none too pleased with her frock.'

'Imogene doesn't really do conformity,' Arie said.

'You can't make me!' Imogene yelled, and she dashed away in a flash of silky hair and flushed cheeks, like a furious fairy – past Arie and Evie and into the guesthouse.

'Argh!' Sara exclaimed, walking in their direction, the crumpled dress in her hands. 'That child. Honestly. Hello, dear you.' She kissed Arie's cheek, then turned to Evie. 'I'm sorry you had to see all of that. She isn't always so vile. Just mostly.'

Arie introduced them, and Evie could see Sara was trying her hardest to be polite and interested, even though she was preoccupied with the problem of her daughter's role in the wedding party.

'She's supposed to hand over the rings. I guess she'll just have to miss out. One of the others will have to do it,' Sara said. 'And one day, we'll all be looking at the photos from Auntie Heidi's wedding, and Imogene will say, "Where am I?" and I'll say, "Chucking a tantrum, as usual!"'

From somewhere indoors there came the sound of a slamming door.

'I could have a try,' Evie offered.

'You're a brave woman,' Arie said. 'I wouldn't be going there.'

'Sometimes strangers have diplomatic immunity,' Evie said.

'Oh God. That would be amazing,' Sara bundled the dress into Evie's arms. 'If you can do anything to get her into it, anything at all, you'll have my eternal gratitude.'

Evie found Imogene in an attic room on the top floor, hiding in plain sight in the space beneath a tall, *Bedknobs and Broomsticks*-style bed. The little girl, upon seeing Evie arrive with the dress, decided to take the upper hand immediately.

'You can't make me either, whoever you are,' she said venomously.

Evie sat cross-legged on the floor at a respectful distance. 'Actually, I was just hoping you could tell me what's wrong with the dress. I figured there must be a problem.'

'It's prissy and I hate it.'

'Ah, prissy. Is it this bit that makes it prissy?' Evie asked, indicating the ruffle of broderie anglaise at the hem. 'This lacy bit?'

Imogene sniffed disdainfully. 'Yes.'

Evie examined the seam that held the broderie anglaise in place, and then, in one swift decisive movement, she ripped it away. Imogene's blue eyes went very wide and she made a stifled laugh of disbelief.

'Does it look better now?' Evie asked, holding the dress up at the shoulders.

Imogene considered, and Evie could tell she was wondering just how far this game could go. 'It's brown.'

'Hm. Can't do anything about that part, I'm afraid. Is there anything else?'

'It's too long.'

'Well, we can probably fix that.'

Evie went downstairs and from the guesthouse owners she begged a pair of scissors, a needle, and a roll of red cotton that wasn't ideal but would have to suffice. When she returned to the room, Imogene was surveying the dress that Evie had left lying on the counterpane.

'How much shorter do you want it?'

Imogene fixed Evie with a look that was also a dare. 'Here,' she said, indicating a spot just beneath her ribs.

Evie frowned seriously. 'I think that might be a bit too short. But here's the thing. I used to have a pixie cut, so I know what goes with them. Girls with pixie cuts look really good in clothes that finish mid-thigh.'

She drew an imaginary line on her own leg, and Imogene tilted her head, assessing.

Twenty minutes later, Imogene was dressed in a re-styled brown smock dress. It would have taken a close inspection to reveal the tiny dots of red cotton that showed through on the right side of the garment from the hemming stitches. Imogene had, quite tastefully in Evie's view, decided that the new version of the dress would look best with skinny jeans and a pair of brown elastic-sided boots. The shoes she'd been expected to wear were a stiffly brand-new pair of black Mary Janes, and Evie wasn't at all surprised that Imogene said they pinched.

In the ensuite bathroom, Evie washed the tearstains away from Imogene's face. It was something she remembered her own mother doing: rinsing a facecloth under very hot water, then squeezing it out and laying it on Evie's upturned face. Doing this for Imogene, Evie felt a rush of tenderness for the stubborn, independent child.

'Did you come with Uncle Arie?'

'I did,' Evie said, locating a hairbrush in one of the toilet bags on the vanity.

'Are you his girlfriend?'

'No, just his friend.'

'I thought that,' Imogene said, in a tone that sounded wise beyond her years.

'Oh?' Evie prompted, curious. She turned the little girl to the mirror and carefully brushed her fairy-floss hair until it looked neat, but not too neat.

'My mum says Uncle Arie will never fall in love again.'

'Is that so?'

'Auntie Lotte says he just hasn't met the right woman yet. But Oma, she says the right woman would have to be someone who knew how to share with Diana.'

Evie felt stung. But she asked, 'Oma?'

'It's Dutch for Grandma,' Imogene said, with a sigh that indicated this was something she'd had to explain quite often in her short life.

'You seem to know rather a lot about Uncle Arie's love life,' Evie observed.

'You know what adults are like.' She gave another of those exasperated sighs. 'They *think* we're not listening. But *obviously* we are.'

'Do you want a bit of lip gloss?' Evie offered, reaching into her handbag.

'Yes, please.'

She showed Imogene how to apply it, and then treated her to a tiny helping of mascara on her pale lashes. The little girl looked at herself in the mirror, turning this way and that, obviously pleased.

'I wish you *were* Uncle Arie's girlfriend,' she said.

Evie smiled at her. 'You look beautiful. Ready to have your picture taken now?'

'If I must,' she said, with an eye-roll for emphasis, but she skipped ahead of Evie down the stairs and out of the back door, where she rushed to join her siblings and cousins, eager to show them her modified flower-girl outfit. Evie had her fingers crossed behind her back as she re-joined Arie and Sara, hoping that Arie had been on the level when he'd told her this wasn't a fussy sort of wedding.

'Sorry about the dress,' she said.

'At this point in time,' Sara said with a pragmatic grimace, 'I'll call that a win.'

Evie breathed a sigh of relief.

'Brilliant,' Arie whispered.

'I'm just going to go and tell the photographer only to shoot her from the waist up,' Sara said, striding away. But, quietly, Evie hoped that the photographer had the good sense to ignore her.

Heidi and Greg were married in front of a stand of gnarly old apple trees festooned with the red baubles of their ripe fruit. Heidi – in flat shoes and a cream dress with bell sleeves, a garland of flowers in her hair – was a beautiful bride.

One of Arie's nephews read from Dr Seuss's *Oh, the Places You'll Go*, and at the right moment Imogene handed over the rings with an appropriately theatrical bow. Heidi herself did a reading from *Captain Corelli's Mandolin*, her voice quivering at times with emotion. The words she'd chosen were about the difference between being in love, which the author said could happen to just about anybody, and real love.

'Those that truly love,' she said, looking up from the page at Greg, 'have roots that grow towards each other underground, and when all the pretty blossoms have fallen from their branches, they find that they are one tree and not two.'

Arie felt an ache in his throat. He heard a sob catch in his mother's, and was fairly sure Evie was holding her breath in an effort not to cry.

'De Schoonfamilie,' Ilse said, embracing Greg's father and stepmother after the ceremony. *The in-laws.*

The wedding feast, mostly vegetarian and served up on mismatched casserole dishes and plates, had been provided by various of Greg and Heidi's friends, and the wedding cake took the shape of a mountain. It was covered in chocolate ganache at its base and had snowy white icing on its peak. A walking track with many steep sections, zigzags and backtracks had been marked out in shards of wafer biscuit. Two tiny figures – Heidi and Greg – stood at the bottom of this long and winding journey.

As the day's light fell away entirely, the paper lanterns hung in the boughs of the apple trees began to glow. After the cake had been cut and the speeches made, the dancing began. Heidi and Greg chose Bright Eyes' 'First Day of My Life' for their song, and Arie couldn't think of anything that would have more perfectly captured the mood of the wedding. Then, as the band took over from the recorded music, more people drifted onto the section of grass that had been marked out for a dance floor.

Arie wasn't a natural dancer, nor did he dance that often, but every now and then the mood or the music struck him in exactly the right way, or a few glasses of wine made him just disinhibited enough to enjoy it.

The band was a bunch of local guys at the outer margin of middle age: a well-oiled unit, happy to have a tilt at whichever requests came their way. Their cover of Fleetwood Mac's 'Everywhere' was the first tune to hit a collective nerve. Arie, seeing his mum and dad hit the dance floor with some moves that would have been bang on trend in the late seventies, searched for Evie.

When he held out a hand of invitation to her, he saw a flash of wariness in her eyes, but it seemed to dissolve when they began to dance – close, but not too close. She'd taken off her shoes, so he knew he'd have to be careful of her feet.

Evie's hair swung forward in two dark curves as she let the music move her, her dress slipping easily over her hips and thighs. Arie's hands only brushed the shimmery green fabric, and although she didn't reach for him at all, she kept contact with her eyes. In his peripheral vision, Arie caught sight of his three sisters watching and conferring, and he didn't have to wonder what they were talking about.

The night wore on, and while Evie wasn't always at his side, Arie seemed always to know which way to turn to find her again. He watched her on the dance floor teaching Imogene the moves for the Nutbush. When next he looked, she was dancing with the best man, Greg's younger brother – a deeply tanned surfer type – and although Arie saw that they made a handsome couple, he also noted the way she kept just a little more distance from him than she had from Arie. Every now and then, too, he saw her look about to locate him, as if her attention was lightly tethered to his.

His sister Lotte came towards him, wine glass in hand, her long brown legs visible beneath the short hem of a burgundy shift dress. She'd inherited their father's angular features, and was the most polished of his sisters, the only one given to hair colour or nail polish, and tonight she looked the kind of elegant that would have fitted right in at the horse races.

250

She stood beside him and poked the point of her chin into his shoulder the way she might have done when they were teenagers, just to let him know she was there, and remind him that she still retained a slight advantage, both in age and height. He and she were the closest, in years, of the four siblings. Sara was three years older than Lotte, and Heidi six years younger than Arie, but only fifteen months separated the middle pair. While Sara had marked out her territory as the classic oldest child – bossy and ambitious – and Heidi had been a quintessential youngest – unconventional and idealistic – Lotte and Arie had competed for every inch of the middle ground. They'd not always had an easy time of it when they were children – they had assayed the equivalence of every slice of cake, every glass of soft drink and every Christmas gift of their young lives – but it remained the case that Lotte was the sister who knew him best.

'I like her,' Lotte said, glancing out towards Evie on the dance floor.

'Yeah. Me too.'

'It's a good woman who can capture Miss Imogene's heart.'

'I know.'

'So, will we be seeing her again?'

'I wouldn't get your hopes up.'

'Why not? She seems perfect.'

Lotte was tougher than him, more practical, and always had been. If he tried to tell her that his heart felt weak and out of practice, she'd only tell him to 'person up' and get on with it. Instead he told her, 'She's quite the traveller. Only passing through, I think.'

'I see. And you're just going to let her go, are you?'

It was well past midnight when Heidi and Greg said goodnight to their guests, and Arie and Evie set out on the walk back to the cottage. The moon was maybe one night or two short of full, and while Evie wasn't in the world of drunk, exactly, she had for some hours been hovering in its tipsy borderlands. She carried her shoes by their straps and hobbled a little in her bare feet when the grassy bank got too steep and forced her back onto the edge of the gravel road. Altogether, she felt warm, mellow and careless.

'So, what did you make of your first wedding?' Arie asked.

'I thought it was beautiful,' Evie said. 'Really beautiful. There was something . . . I don't know . . . I want to say "ancient", about it.'

'Ancient?'

'Maybe it's the wrong word. Maybe I mean "pagan". You know, the tribe all coming together to celebrate. Did you see the older couples, the way they were with each other? It was like they had this beautiful thing to give to your sister and Greg, this *knowledge*, but at the same time, tonight was about them, too. They were giving their blessing, but they were getting something as well. Maybe they were remembering their own weddings, but it was more than that. They were looking back on it, but from this new, deeper place. It's like they really know, now, what they were doing back *then*. They understand it now.'

Her head felt cottony and she was aware that she was talking too much, and possibly not making a lot of sense.

'You sound like you might write a poem about it.'

'I just might,' she said, pleased that he had noticed. 'What about you? Did you have a good time?'

'I had a really good time,' he said, 'and I still am.'

When he reached for her hand, she allowed her fingers to lace through his, and for the rest of the walk to the cottage they didn't talk, despite the fact – or perhaps because – both of them knew what was coming next.

In the seven years he and Diana were together, Arie had come to know her body like the intricate, temperamental machine it was. He knew how to speed it up and slow it down, and where every one of its sweet spots was located. Every time he'd thought for more than a minute about how it would be to make love to another woman, he'd worried that it would be embarrassingly awkward, that he wouldn't know the first thing about how to touch her. Maybe he'd do things she didn't like. Maybe he'd do things too fast, too slow, too hard, too soft, too much, not enough.

But it wasn't like that with Evie. At all. From the moment just inside the door when she dropped her shoes to the floor and turned to place her palms on the front of his shirt, he knew what her body wanted. They stood there for quite a long time, with the outside light sifting in through the glass to the otherwise dark interior of the cottage. She undid the top button of his shirt, and he kissed her. Another button, another kiss. When his shirt was all the way open, he easily undid the zip at her back and pushed the green fabric off her shoulders so the silky dress slipped down onto the floor, making a haphazard circle around her bare feet.

Arie wasn't sure this was the right thing to do, but it felt inevitable now. When she stepped out of the puddle of her dress and moved towards the stairs, looking back over her shoulder to make sure he was following, he absolutely was. In the loft room, another pair of silver-wrapped chocolates had materialised on the turned-back covers of the neatly made futon, but they fell to the floor when Evie pulled aside the duvet.

Arie wasn't worrying any more about knowing what to do; now he was worrying that this could all be over in a heartbeat, because he was beginning to understand that in one sense, it had begun hours earlier. Every time he'd glanced at Evie across the orchard, all the time he'd spent sitting beside her at dinner, while they'd danced together on the grass, as they'd walked back to the cottage – he'd already been partially here, lying beside her, feeling her bare skin down the length of his body, smelling her hair but also the warm scent of the dance-floor sweat that had dried on her arms and her chest.

He was right – it didn't last. Before long, she took his earlobe between her teeth and said she was coming, and that undid him, too, but for the short time he moved inside her, her hips like liquid and her mouth tasting of wine, he didn't think or worry about anything at all. While it did last, Arie lost every trace of the past or the future inside the raw tenderness of making love in the present tense.

wake

THERE WAS NOTHING new, for Arie, about waking in the early hours of the morning with his heart beating too fast. It was something that happened to him most nights of his life, but this time there was no flickering television set at the foot of the bed to catch him as he fell from the world of sleep and landed in a reality where the first thing he had to do – every time – was remember it was true that Diana had gone. He felt it now, the sensation of his heart plummeting down through his body.

Arie sensed a stirring beside him. Evie. In a cascade of images and memories, his mind reconstructed her and everything he had ever thought or known about her. In the low light, he could see the lovely curve of her jaw beneath the dark shadow of her hair, and the jutting outline of her shoulder. He pulled the duvet up over her bare skin and pressed a silent kiss on her hair.

As quietly as he could, and with his heart rate not yet steady, he got out of bed. He put on his boxer shorts and went downstairs, trying to keep his footsteps light. When he reached the far side of the front door, the sensor light activated and Arie cursed himself for forgetting to turn off the switch. He glanced up at the window of the loft bedroom and hoped he had not disturbed her.

The night air was cool on his skin and the grass dewy underfoot. He felt the beginning of a headache at his temples, and in his gut was a feeling that was not precisely regret, although it was somewhere in its ballpark. Because here is the thing about moments of pure present tense – they come to an end.

Being in the present, and only in the present, is like standing between the two halves of a sea that's been parted. By whatever species of divine intervention, grace or magic you happen to believe in, the weight of all that water is pushed back on both sides to reveal a pathway to the safety of the other shore, a new land. The past and the future, though, are powerful forces that can only be held back for so long, and Arie hadn't quite reached the far side when they had come crashing back together, knocking him sideways, sending him tumbling in a turbulent ocean of thoughts and memories.

From the past, there came Diana – from a thousand different moments that he hadn't known he'd stored away so perfectly. Diana: astride him in that bed in the sleep-out bedroom at her mother's house, one finger across her lips warning him to be quiet and still while she moved her body against his, but only to the precise degree that didn't make the bed creak. Diana: emerging from a bathroom in San Francisco, a white towel around her middle, which she then dropped before jumping on the bed with him, giggling. There was no sense or order to the memories. There was just Diana, Diana, Diana.

Meanwhile, from the future there came questions and fears. What if it was always like this? What if the past was always going to rise up in this way and swamp him? What right did he have to meddle with Evie's heart, if he no longer had the ability to give his to her, whole?

In her half-sleep, Evie felt the warmth of the covers on her shoulder, and also the kiss that landed on her hair, but she came fully into wakefulness when she heard Arie's footsteps on the stairs. At first, she assumed he was going to the bathroom, but then the brightness of the sensor light came through the dormer window. Had he gone to the car for some reason? Was he all right?

Evie rolled out of bed, taking the covers with her, and through the window she saw him standing a short distance from the house. He wasn't doing anything in particular, just standing there in his boxer shorts, with his arms crossed over his chest.

She went outside, the duvet trailing her like a bridal train, and when she reached Arie she stood behind him and wrapped her arms and the coverings around him, feeling how the skin on his arms and back had tightened to gooseflesh. The honey-and-petrol scent of his cologne still clung to his skin, but it was changed now, made deeper by his own scent. He put his arms over hers, and Evie could feel that he was troubled.

Are you surprised? she asked herself, already knowing the answer.

Already knowing was perhaps the greatest of Evie's unhelpful talents. When she had moved in with Dave Wright, she had already known it was a bad idea. When she had taken up residence in the cruise ship cabin of a married man, she'd already known she was asking for trouble. When she'd agreed to come with Arie on this journey, she'd already known – hadn't she? That if he reached for her, she would fall for him. That if she fell for him, she could fall a long way while he was looking elsewhere. She'd known that when he'd asked her to step out of the car the other night, and she'd known it even before little Imogene had knowingly said, *Oma says the right woman would have to be someone who knew how to share with Diana.*

He continued to face away from her, looking out over a post-and-rail fence to a paddock where some donkeys stood quite still in the moon-glazed grass.

'What are you thinking about?' she asked.

He breathed out heavily, but said nothing.

'Was that the first time . . . since?'

He made a noise that meant yes.

'You and Diana,' Evie began tentatively, 'you were never married, were you?'

'We were engaged. For a long time, but never married.'

'Why was that?'

Arie took a deep breath, and Evie felt his ribs expand inside her embrace. 'I don't fully know. I never knew whether she really wanted to . . . take that final step or not. I never really knew if I was totally, entirely what she wanted.'

Oh, I know that feeling, Evie thought, and she was visited by an image that made the poet inside her pay attention. There was Arie: fixing his attention on someone who could never, now, truly love him back. And there she was, standing behind him, doing the same. Perhaps one day, someone else would stand behind her in the same way, and someone else behind them, and on and on it would go in a conga line of misplaced desire. In order to break it, someone would have to turn around. But Arie didn't; he just kept looking off into the distance while she held him.

All trace of tipsiness gone now, Evie felt clarity blow through her, cold and certain. In another time, another place, another world, she and Arie would have loved each other until they were the same tree. But it wasn't going to happen here, or now, or in this one.

The long drive back to Melbourne was quiet. Heading north, Evie had felt buoyant and cheerful, but now she felt as if the gravitational pull of the earth was increasing with every kilometre they covered, making her limbs, her heart, her mind feel heavy and dull. She kept the music soft and mostly instrumental, avoiding anything from her library that was abrasively upbeat or too obviously heartbroken. Whether he was at the wheel or in the passenger seat, Arie was subdued and preoccupied, and the journey became an act of polite endurance.

The sun had set by the time they pulled into Tavistock Row, and when Arie switched off the Renault's engine, he sighed deeply, obviously relieved to be home. He fetched both their bags from the boot and set them down on the pavement, while 12 and 12A faced the street with near-identical expressions on their near-identical facades. Arie stood directly in front of her and took her face in his hands.

'Thank you for coming with me, Evie. Thank you for – everything.'

When he kissed her – gently, sweetly – she felt all his sadness and confusion flow through her own body.

'I'm really sorry I've been so quiet all day,' he said. 'Last night, it . . . blew me away a little bit. I'm just kind of reeling. I know we need to talk. I know we need to work out what comes next, but I need to think. Would it be all right if we talked first thing in the morning? I don't even know . . . what your plans are.'

But Evie already knew that they would not talk tomorrow. She already knew that she would be up before dawn to pack into the Beetle her boxes of books, her collection of notebooks and diaries, her sewing machine, her guitar, her two remaining suitcases of clothes, her backpack – all the things that she would take with her into yet another new chapter of her life. She already knew that by the time the sun came up, she would be at the ferry terminal, and that by the time this city had begun its Monday in earnest, she would be sailing out across the bay.

'Goodnight, Evie,' Arie said.

She kissed him one more time and wondered if he was really listening when she said, 'Goodbye, Arie.'

Arie didn't sleep any better that night. For several hours, he lay on his back watching with tired eyes as the television at his feet played its silent pictures. He didn't turn up the volume, because the soundtrack interfered with the thoughts that were on endless rotation inside his head. He managed to get to sleep again just before dawn, and it was the distinctive sound of Evie's Beetle pulling away from the kerb that woke him.

From the window of the piano room, he scanned the street; the little blue VW had already reached the corner. During the morning, he checked several times to see if the car had returned. He knew she was supposed to be checking out today, but he didn't think for a moment – not yet, anyway – that she would leave without saying goodbye.

Instead of going to the office, he worked at home, so that when Evie got back, he would be able to go next door and tell her all the things he'd been thinking on the drive, and all the things that had been circling his head in the night.

I'm still a bit broken. I'm still going to need some time. I'm going to need your help. But if you can put up with me, if you can be patient . . . I'm not sure, I don't know for certain, but I think, I think, I think . . .

He thought she would understand. Wherever it was she

decided to go, they could keep in touch, maybe they could meet for the occasional weekend.

At last there was movement next door, though the car that pulled up outside was not a Beetle but the small red hatchback belonging to the cleaners. They gave him a neighbourly wave, then went on with the business of getting out their mops and buckets and armloads of white sheets. As they let themselves into the house, Arie understood that she'd gone, and that he didn't have the first idea where.

−INTERLUDE−

'WILL YOU BE all right?' Felix Carter asked the small version of Beatrix Romero that he held in his hand. FaceTime couldn't quite keep up with the way she tossed back her mane of curls, so for a moment the screen of his phone was filled with a swish of blonde-brown pixels.

'How many days did you say you're going for?' she asked.

'Three.'

It was early morning his time, mid-afternoon hers. The pair of them were too young to consider it amazing that they could, from their respective homes in London's Winchmore Hill and Vancouver's West End, pour so much data about their lives directly into each other's palms, but they were young enough to know that nobody in the history of the world had ever loved anybody quite so much as they loved each other.

Around the edges of Beatrix's hair, Felix could see aspects of the room he had come to know through digital means. He had mapped it in his mind, so that when he thought of her – which was pretty much all the time – he could picture her doing homework at her desk, or getting ready for school in the morning, or lying amid the large and unsmoothed quantity of quilts she kept on top of the bed, which featured particularly prominently in his dreams.

'Three days? That's for-fucking-ever! And, what, no phone at all?'

'Father–son time. Dad's intense about it. The phone doesn't even get to go in the car.'

This trip was an annual event in the Carter household, and every year before this one, Felix had itched to spend three days alone with his dad – rock-climbing, camping or hiking. This time Henry Carter had decided on a sailing weekend, but for Felix it was complicated: he still wanted to go, but he didn't know how he was going to go for three whole days without a single text.

If everything went according to plan, he'd see Beatrix again in the summer holidays; he was stashing away just about every penny of his busking takings to pay for a flight to London. But it was still only March, and for the next few months the telephone would be their lifeline.

'Felix!' his mother called. 'Time to get in the car.'

'Gotta go, babe,' Felix said with a sigh.

'Love you,' she said.

'Love you too,' he said.

'Love you more,' she said.

'Love you to the max,' he said, and this went on for some time, but at last – after his mother had yelled again – Felix ended the call and bounded downstairs. Out front his father was waiting, the car already loaded with provisions and brightly coloured waterproof bags. In the driveway Cassie Carter hugged her husband goodbye and stood on tiptoe – this hadn't yet ceased to strike her as strange – to kiss her son.

'Have an awesome time,' she told them both.

It would have been an exaggeration to say that Cassie went up to Felix's room the moment the big 4WD backed out into the street. In truth, she gathered her supplies first. Garbage bags, a plastic carton, the big vacuum cleaner for the carpet, the hand-held vacuum cleaner for the skirtings and other poky places, bucket, cloths, disinfectant.

Although Felix was aware that his mum usually did a bit of tidying up while he and his dad were out of town, it would be some years yet before he understood that giving his mother the opportunity to do an annual spring clean in his bedroom was the unspoken underbelly of the father–son bonding trip.

Cassie had enough good humour to imagine herself swaggering into the war zone of Felix's bedroom, snapping her rubber gloves against the insides of her wrists in readiness, spray-wipe holstered at her waist. But again, the truth was that the first thing she did was sit on the end of his unmade bed and pick up the phone he'd been forced to leave sitting on his desk.

One of the rules of Felix owning a phone was that Cassie was kept informed of his access code, although he remained blissfully unaware of how often she used this information. She punched in the numbers and scanned through his recent messages and photos, including the hidden photos file that mercifully still contained nothing more alarming than a few pictures of Beatrix Romero's cleavage and some shots of Felix's muscled torso that had been taken in the bathroom mirror. She found a bit of talk about weed from one of his schoolfriends, an exchange with his cello teacher about a forthcoming recital, and a lot of lovey-dovey mush – nothing much to worry about. Cassie, digital tour of duty over, put the phone down and readied herself to tackle the room.

She found a crusty bowl lined with the remains of a spaghetti bolognese dinner from several weeks earlier, and a breakfast smoothie that had been left on a shelf to grow inventive patterns of mould. She scooped up the clothes and shoes from the floor and went through the wardrobe like a dose of salts, throwing out holey socks and past-their-best underpants. Beneath the bed there lay an accretion of stuff: loose papers covered in musical notation, essay plans, bent-open novels, socks, a Rubik's cube, and many other dusty and long-forgotten things.

It was here that Cassie applied the six-month rule: a rolling program of decluttering that had been in operation since Felix was a baby. Anything in his room that she considered border-line went into a plastic tub. The plastic tub went into the back shed, and if – within six months – Felix asked after any of its contents, she was able to produce them, with a smile. But when the time was up, all that remained went into a charity bin.

At the end of a long, dirty couple of hours, Cassie closed the door on Felix's clean and fresh-smelling bedroom, and crossed the lawn with the heavy plastic tub in her arms. She shoved it under a low shelf in the shed and went back indoors for a well-earned cup of tea and slice of cake. And somewhere in the middle of that tub was a half-full and beaten-up music note-book, bound with black leather, and with a strip of red ribbon for a placeholder. Within its pages – written in pencil – was a love song in the hand of Diana Clare.

On the east side of the North American continent, where the day was a few hours older than it was in the west, Lucie Doran was taking a bath. Her tub wasn't the sort in which stretching out was possible. Rather, it was the sort that fitted into the bathroom of a cramped apartment on New York's Upper East Side: so small that she had to dangle her heat-reddened legs over the ceramic edge while she soaped her calves and got ready with the lady-pink Schick. But before Lucie swiped away the stubble, she wrote something in the whiteness of the lather.

One word. Two letters.

NO.

By the time Lucie got out of the bath, the sky beyond her window had taken on a pretty pink-and-orange glow. She dressed carefully. In track pants. Ha! Take that! However, if she was truthful, the track pants she'd chosen were her best: dusky pink and high-waisted and just nicely clingy around a butt that was keeping its shape pretty well considering it now belonged to a woman of almost thirty-seven years of age.

Yes, this year, Lucie Doran, lead singer and banjo player for Lucie Doran and the Curious Lovers, would turn thirty-seven. The precise date in October when this would occur was firmly on her horizon and had been for much of her life – for such was the fate of a girl whose name was a soundalike for that of a pop song heroine. Ever since little Lucie had misheard Marianne Faithfull singing 'The Ballad of Lucy Jordan', she'd regarded the age of thirty-seven as some kind of landmark, a deadline by which time she had to have her shit together.

While Lucy Jordan had longed for Paris, and a sports car, and a warm breeze blowing through her hair, Lucie Doran – being a girl from Prince Edward Island – wasn't overly fussed about convertibles. And since her band had hit the medium-time (not the big-time, yet), she'd been to Paris, more than once, and a lot of other cities besides. No, Lucie Doran didn't want a soft-top and a baguette. She wanted not to be dicked around, not by anyone, but especially not by men, and most especially not by *him*.

She and Elijah Tripp had history, and a lot of it. Lucie and Elijah had been twenty-three (her) and twenty-two (him) the very first time they'd met, on a cold summer's day in the dance hall of an Alaskan resort hotel under the shadow of a snow-capped Denali. He was tall, thin and elfin, with almost-black hair and eyes of heartthrob blue. He was standing by the stage when he called out, 'Hey, banjo girl! Can you come over here and give me a hand?'

She hadn't known his name, but she'd seen him around – with a tray in the line-up at the resort canteen, leaning on the railing with a beer in hand and taking in the view, crouching down in his black pants and cowboy boots by the hot tub talking to the cruise ship girls. She'd also watched him play the fiddle on stage with a bluegrass outfit that was, other than him, made up of guys with silver hair and impressive moustaches. He played the kind of music that made something inside of her want to sing, and the way his face looked while he played – eyes closed, brow creasing in new ways with every note – told her that there was one hell of a big, deep well of feeling inside of him. If he wanted a hand with something, then twenty-three-year-old Lucie would oblige.

'What d'you need, fiddle boy?'

'Jump up there a minute,' he'd said, indicating the stage. 'I just want to see if the stage is level.'

So she'd stepped onto the stage in her long skirts and tall boots, unsuspecting, her banjo hanging across her body by its strap.

'Now what?' she'd asked.

'Can you play a bit?'

Eager to impress, she'd launched into the Beatles' 'Norwegian Wood'. Lucie played the banjo clawhammer style. She'd learned it from her grandfather, Kit Doran; on the Atlantic coast, that was a name music people knew. While she played, fiddle boy had stood down on the floor, tapping a toe on the boards and grinning.

'So,' she said, over the notes of her own music, 'how is this supposed to help?'

'You must know, banjo girl.'

'Know what?'

He winked at her, creasing his whole face. 'What I was always told about how to find out if a stage is level, is that it's when the banjo player's drooling out of both sides of their mouth at once.'

In the moment all she'd been able to do was call him an ass-wipe, but she'd got him back properly a few days later by sneaking backstage at the dance hall and unstringing his fiddle right before a gig.

The pranks had gone back and forth for a week before Lucie found herself in Elijah's bed doing tequila laybacks and singing drunken harmonies to campfire songs. That wasn't the only thing they'd done in his bed, of course. That was the problem. From the very beginning it had seemed that Lucie's body knew Elijah's, and his knew hers, like those bodies had been sneaking off together for years to practise without the brains or hearts within knowing a single thing about it.

For nearly fourteen years, that's the way it had been. There had been some periods of time when he had some girl-friend or another, or when she was seeing someone else, but just about every time their paths crossed that old electricity would arc up and they'd find themselves between the sheets. Lucie was ashamed to admit that there hadn't always been a clear demarcation between her relationships with other men and her dalliances with Elijah Tripp. He'd been the cause of her breaking up with several serious guys, with serious intentions – not because her lovers had found out about her infidelity, but because being with Elijah always had the side effect of making other men seem kind of . . . colourless.

But any time in her life she'd tried to pin Elijah down – ask him what their relationship was all about, suggest they try to coordinate their lives so they saw each other more often on the road – all she'd got for her troubles was a cheeky grin, a kiss goodbye and a promise that she'd see him again, somewhere down the track.

Lucie blow-dried her hair – shoulder length, fair and wavy – and took to it with the straightening tongs, half freaking out about and half enjoying the faint smell of singeing it caused. She put green paste under her eyes to conceal the bagginess there, and smoothed foundation over the top. She spent a good fifteen minutes on her eyeshadow, but before she traced the curving outlines of her lips, she took the liner pencil and wrote herself a little message on the bottom corner of her mirror. NO.

'No,' she said to her reflection, over-enunciating. Then, 'Uh-uh. Nope. Nah. Not happening. Never again. No, no, no, no, no, no.'

Somehow, the last six syllables started to sing the doo-dah-days from 'Camptown Races', and then Lucie Doran was humming, putting her make-up away in the cupboard, checking the pasta sauce in the pot – nothing fancy, mind. And there would certainly be no dessert.

She tweaked the alignment of the cutlery on the table, and

had to admit that the setting looked kind of cosy. But then, what could you do in an apartment that was only big enough for a table the size of a postage stamp, and where you were better off with stools than chairs on the basis that they took up less space?

When she heard the knock at the door, Lucie felt a surge of nerves, but she took herself in hand and breathed. With the help of a sticky note fixed to the back of her front door, she rehearsed, quietly.

'No.'

And then she opened the door to Elijah Tripp.

In the many years they'd known each other, Lucie Doran had opened a lot of different doors to Elijah Tripp. Doors that belonged to resorts up and down the Alaskan coast, doors in the homes of people who were kind enough to billet her at folk festivals in Woodford and Cygnet, Stornoway and Telluride, the Brecon Beacons and Ballyshannon. Hotel doors, motel doors, doors of rented apartments, the downstairs door at her mom and dad's house on PEI.

No, Lucie reminded herself. *No*.

'Well, hello Lucie D,' Elijah said, leaning in to kiss her on the cheek.

'Good to see you, friend,' she said. *Friend*. Say after me, *friend*.

It had been six months since she'd last seen him – six months since they'd shared a stage at the Celtic Colours Festival, and a bed in an old and pretty hotel in Baddeck on Cape Breton Island. At that time Lucie had just turned thirty-six, which meant she'd been thinking a lot about how there was only one year to go. That fact had made her panicky, which was why she'd launched, probably stupidly, into a version of 'The Talk'.

'Come on, Lucie D,' he'd said to her, with an acre of the hotel's frilly, floral bed linen rucked up around his naked hips. 'We've got a good thing, haven't we? Don't go getting all serious on me.'

Now, here he was standing on her doorstep with his fiddle case in one hand, his duffel bag in the other and a bottle in a brown paper bag under his arm.

'Say, Luce – why don't they have banjos in *Star Trek*?' he asked.

'Because it's the future,' she said flatly.

'How do you *tune* a banjo?'

Lucie yawned. 'Nobody knows.'

'So, tell me. How can you tell one banjo song from the next?'

'Yeah, yeah, yeah. Heard that one, too. By their names. Now shut up and come inside.'

Lucie hadn't lived here long, in New York City, and she wasn't planning to stay either. It was only where she'd decided to base herself while she wrote the tracks for the new Lucie Doran and the Curious Lovers album, and where she and the guys would be recording it, starting in just over a week. She was still short of a track or two, but she had faith that she'd find a couple more songs somewhere – at the bottom of a Starbucks takeaway cup, maybe, or stuck to her shoe after she'd gone for a jog through Central Park.

'So, what brings you to town?' she asked him. 'Gig?'

'Nope. Just came to see you.'

'Right,' Lucie said, making no effort to hide her disbelief.

She watched Elijah scan the apartment, taking in the tiny table with its two stools, the kitchen the size of a yacht's galley, the cowhide rug on the floor, the two-seater couch and the three different banjos lined up on their stands. He put down his luggage, screwed the bottle out of its paper sack, and set it down on the table. Tequila. He took off his jacket and fished two big, fat lemons out of the pockets.

'I'm trusting you've got the salt,' he said, and pulled up a stool at the table.

In the kitchen Lucie found a small dish filled with salt flakes, and a plate and sharp knife for the lemons. From behind her came the sound of the bottle cap being twisted free, but from the cupboard she took only a single shot glass.

'Here you go,' she said, placing it in front of him.

'Hey,' Elijah said, frowning. 'What's the story?'

'No story,' Lucie said. 'Just . . . not tonight.'

She studied the squinty look on Elijah's face. There was puzzlement in it, certainly, and some disappointment, too. But what was that other thing there in the mix? Lucie couldn't for the life of her say.

Elijah put the cap back on the bottle.

'You don't have to do that. You can go right ahead if you want.'

Elijah shook his head. Sadly, she thought. 'Wouldn't be any fun without you, Luce.'

And that was more or less how dinner went down, that night. Elijah tried all the usual ways into their old routine, and Lucie found new and interesting ways to block the path. He pulled a face and slurped his pasta like a three-year-old, but Lucie only smiled back at him like an indulgent, slightly bored adult. When they stood together at the sink washing up the dishes afterwards, he put soap bubbles on her nose, but she just calmly wiped them off with the tea-towel and didn't take the bait. Lucie Doran, aged thirty-six-and-a-half, thought she was doing pretty well. Until Elijah Tripp said, 'Hey, there's this song I want to play you.'

A song is not so very different from a recipe. After all, who invented bolognese sauce? Sure, it was Pellegrino Artusi who was the first – in 1891 – to publish its recipe in a book, but we can be fairly sure that the meal itself had been travelling, from stove to plate, from host to guest, for a long time before that.

Once released into the world, songs, too, have a tendency to make their own way, each new musician reinventing them: removing an ingredient, adding a wild new flavour, changing the balance of the spices.

So it was that when Felix Carter's big brother, Tom Wendale, left Vancouver with a love song in his guitar case and took it to Seattle, it sounded a little different there, when he jammed with his friends on their acoustic guitars, slide guitars and keyboards. It picked up a lilting tone when it travelled to Osaka with one of Japan's most famous Irish fiddlers, and it got more up-tempo down in Buenos Aires where it went on the road with the guitarist from a mariachi band.

It developed an electronic vibe in San Francisco, where the producer of an acrobatic circus seized on it as the perfect theme song for his trapeze-flying lovers, and it turned out all cute on a ukulele in Vanuatu, where just a handful of its notes would eventually be heard through the radio speakers of the archipelago as the jingle for a new local brand of icy pole.

The song had developed a little bit of a bluegrass accent by the time it flew east to Toronto, and was carried off the plane and into the city by the members of a folk band who were that night playing in a Leonard Cohen tribute concert at the Danforth Music Hall. That's where Elijah Tripp first heard it: out the back after the gig, while the musos from half a dozen different bands chilled down with a few drinks, instruments never far from their grip.

There was a decent sprinkling of rosin dust on Elijah's shirt-front as he sat examining the shredded horsehair of his bow, and his plaid shirt was wet at the armpits and down his back because of all he'd sweated under the stage lights that night. He felt like he'd been on the road for a long time; in fact, there had been days lately when he'd felt like he'd been on the road forever. He was getting tired – not in a regular way, but in a right-down-deep-in-the-soul kind of a way.

That was how he was feeling – tired and spent – when a bunch of musos began to play. Some of them were his old friends, some he knew at a distance, and some he'd never seen before, and the fabric of the music was tight already without him. Before long, though, his toe was tapping, and soon he'd picked himself a spot in the weave where he could slide in the sound of a fiddle.

The way some people look funny without their glasses, and other people are harder to recognise without the hat they always wear, Elijah somehow looked just a little bit more like himself once he'd settled his instrument into his body. He'd pushed his stool back to give himself some room while Lucie stayed where she was, elbows on the tabletop. As she watched him finetune the fiddle, she noticed that there was a slight tremor in his hand. What was this? she wondered. Because this was weird.

Never before in her life, not in all the backstages and green rooms they'd ever shared, had she seen Elijah look nervous.

He resettled the fiddle under his chin, and started to play. Nothing Elijah ever did with a fiddle looked like it caused him any trouble. His left hand moved about the fretboard, finding the notes so effortlessly that he didn't even seem to be pressing down on the strings, and his right hand on the bow looked loose and relaxed no matter how fast or hectic the notes. He played just the way she'd always loved to see – eyes closed, forehead creasing up with what it cost him to dredge his feelings up out of the deepest parts of him. He continued, sprinkling the melody with delicate grace notes, and Lucie knew that what she was listening to was a love song, but she didn't expect for the life of her that Elijah would begin to sing.

His wasn't a strong voice, but it was tuneful and clear, and the texture of it made Lucie think – for no particular reason that she could work out – of hazelnuts.

'Hey Lucie Doran,' he sang. Lucie waited for the lyric to turn into a joke, or for Elijah to somehow work in an insult about banjo players, but to her amazement his face was utterly sincere.

'Do you want,' he sang on in his hazelnut voice, 'do you want . . . do you want to do this thing, for real?'

Still Lucie waited; for the sting in the tail, the punch in the solar plexus, the moment when this performance of devotion dissolved into what it surely had to be – one of Elijah's pranks. But Elijah kept playing, and no joke arrived to pierce the mood.

Then the song ended and Elijah's bow came to rest. Now all Lucie could hear was a muted version of the New York City melody: sirens, zooming motor vehicles and honking horns.

Elijah looked at Lucie, and Lucie looked at Elijah.

At last, she said, 'Give me that fiddle.'

275

She took the instrument out of his hands and laid it carefully on the couch. Then she went back over to where he sat. Expectant, vulnerable. Just sitting there, empty handed, in his blue jeans and plaid shirt. No boots; he'd taken them off. He was looking up at her, waiting. Waiting. Then Lucie lifted one foot and kicked him full in the chest. Taken entirely by surprise, he toppled, landing heavily on his back on the floor while the stool flew out from under him. But Lucie wasn't all that practised at kicking. She lost her balance too and went sideways, hitting the floor with her hip. Ow, that was going to bruise.

'Fuck, Luce! What was that for?'

'For being a total ass-wipe,' she said.

Still on his back, Elijah groaned.

'It's not nice to dick around with a woman's heart,' Lucie said, teary and almost yelling. 'Especially not a woman who's about to turn thirty-seven.'

'I'm not dicking around. I promise you.'

'Fuck off, Elijah. You think you're being funny?'

With some difficulty, he propped himself on his elbows. 'Tell me. Where do you want to live, huh? Where do you want to call home? I mean really home. San Francisco? Quebec? Fuckin' Fairbanks? We'll move there. Anywhere you name, I'll go there. I'm yours.'

'Shut up.'

'How many children do you want to have? I don't care. We'll have as many as you want.'

'Fuck you.'

'Two? Three? Seven? Tell you what, go get a piece of paper. Let's write their names down right now. You pick whatever you like. Even, you know, weird hippie noun names if you want. River, Ocean, Forest. I'll just roll with it.'

'Will you *stop* teasing?'

'I'm not teasing!'

Lucie put her hands over her ears. 'E-li-jah!'

'Okay, here's a deal for you,' he said, her hands hardly even muffling his words. 'You say yes to me, and I will never. Ever. Never, ever again, for as long as we both shall live, make another banjo joke. That is my proposition to you.'

Lucie snorted, half laughing, half crying. 'That is not a promise you can keep.'

Elijah's face was serious. Really serious. 'It is if you say yes.'

For the briefest interval of time, Lucie allowed herself to consider that he might actually be for real. She pictured them at folk festivals. They'd be one of those music families where the kids ricocheted from parent to parent during and between gigs, ending up asleep on the lap of their harp-playing godmother before being given a shoulder ride by their mandolin-playing godfather. Lucie had seen those kids at festivals. She'd seen toddlers chewing on electrical leads, watched how fast they learned to keep their fingers out of the stomp box. They were always cool, those kids, having become accustomed to staying up late dancing to reels at the front of country halls, their feet bare, their faces painted with flowers and rainbows and puppy faces.

'Luce, I'm saying I want to do the whole thing. All of it. With you.'

Lucie cried, 'You're a jerk. You know that?'

'I'm a jerk who loves you.'

'You love me? You love me *now*?'

'I've always loved you, you crazy banjo girl,' he said.

'But you always run away from me!' Lucie cried.

'Yeah, that's true. I used to do that,' Elijah said, nodding. 'But I won't do it any more.'

'So, what's changed?'

'I'm ready.'

'Well, what if I was ready for so long that now I'm unready?'

'Are you telling me it's too late? I don't want to believe that.'

'I don't know, Elijah,' Lucie said. 'I promised myself . . .'

Elijah was on his knees beside her now, and he pulled her up so she was on her knees, too. He kissed her, and she kissed him and the feel of his mouth on hers, and the warmth of his hands on her waist under her T-shirt made her want to kiss him more, and more. They kissed for the longest time. He kissed her tear-streaked cheeks and he kissed her in the middle of her forehead, and then he kissed her on the mouth again and her body hummed, and she could feel his body harmonising.

She opened her eyes. 'Did that just happen? Hang on, what just happened?'

'I asked you to marry me.'

'You did?'

'I did.'

'I think I missed that bit.'

'Okay, so there can't be any mistakes. You ready? You listening?'

She nodded.

'Lucie Doran, goddess of the banjo, love of my life, most outrageously sexy woman alive, will you marry me?'

'No more banjo jokes. Not one. So long as we both shall live?'

'Not one,' Elijah agreed.

Lucie's heart said *yes*; Lucie's body said *yes*; even Lucie's mind said *yes*. Still, it seemed a shame to waste all that rehearsal time. She tossed back her straightened hair, looked Elijah full in the face, and – just like she'd practised – said, 'No.'

His eyes went wide. 'I thought . . . Are you *serious*?'

'No,' Lucie said, grinning with happiness. Twice she'd been able to say *no*, and this time she really meant it. 'No, Elijah Tripp, love of my life, I am not serious. Not at all.'

SIX

autumn

MARCH DWINDLED ON and slipped into April, and every day Arie thought of one reason or another that he might have called Evie, if only he'd been able to. He'd have liked to tell her that he'd been asked to build a website for a pair of graphic artists calling themselves The Mandela Effect, and to share the fact that the *Dictionary of Obscure Sorrows*, which had so far been found only on the internet, was now apparently going to be published as an ink-and-paper book.

Arie had assumed that as the days went on, she would fade from his mind, but if anything the reverse was true. Increasingly, it seemed to him that he was passing just about every thought he had through the lens of Evie. What would Evie think? What would Evie say? Would Evie like this/that/those?

Easter arrived, and on the Sunday Arie turned up alone at his parents' home for a family gathering. Although his mother never failed to mention how she missed the Easter daffodils and hyacinths of her childhood, she had adapted her traditions to Antipodean conditions, decorating the table with a red-leafed autumnal branch, and hanging its twigs with blown eggs that had been dyed to russet shades using onion skins.

Everyone was there but Heidi and Greg, who were still on their trekking honeymoon in Bhutan, and after lunch, when the children were outside hunting for eggs, and Malcolm was watching from the sunroom window and fearing for his beloved vegetable garden, Ilse handed around Heidi's wedding photos on her iPad.

Arie flicked through images of Heidi getting dressed, of the flower girls and page boys climbing trees and standing amid flowerbeds, of his eldest niece sulking in a tree swing. There were photographs of the ceremony, several trillion of the bridal couple, and all the predictable groupings – Greg's family, the Johnsons, the families combined, the entire gathering. Although Evie had done her best to absent herself from all the photographs but the one of the whole crowd, the photographer had found her nevertheless.

In one candid image, Evie was kneeling opposite Imogene so that their noses, in profile, were level; woman and child were smiling into each other's faces, and the quality of mischief in their eyes was identical. There was another of Evie by herself, standing with an attitude of listening; it must have been taken during the dinner-time speeches. Although Arie knew that nothing Evie had been wearing that night had been expensive, she had looked lovely in that simple green dress with the black wrap looped through the crooks of her elbows. He remembered the sound of that dress's zip opening, the fabric falling to the floor.

She had fitted in so perfectly at the wedding. Nothing about the way she looked or behaved had asked to be especially noticed or remarked upon. She hadn't sought any attention, nor too obviously tried to avoid it. When Imogene had thrown a tantrum, Evie had been the one to resolve it, and during the speeches – the evidence was here, in this photograph – she had listened with wholehearted happiness for other people's joy.

'Why didn't Evie come today?' Imogene asked, parking herself on Arie's lap and noticing the photograph he was looking at. The corners of the little girl's mouth were smudged with Easter egg chocolate.

'She's gone away, Im.'

'Where?'

He gave a helpless shrug. Like most citizens of the digital world, Arie had believed that he lived in an era when an internet search would turn up at least some small detail about almost anybody. But when it came to Evie, the great god Google had failed him.

The search 'Evie Greenlees' returned nothing except some telephone directory results from the USA. There was no Evie Greenlees on Facebook, and although he telephoned every Greenlees who still had their number listed in the dwindling Australian White Pages, none of them had ever heard of Evie. He tried to recall the number plate of her Beetle. It had been a Victorian plate; he remembered that much. There had been a K somewhere in the mix. The numeral 3, possibly.

Remembering that she'd grown up in Tasmania, that she had a sister there, he'd gone back to Google and tried 'Evie + poet + Hobart', 'Evie + poet + Tasmania'. Getting more and more desperate, he dropped the 'poet'. In the results pages that this generated, he found many Evies from Tasmania, but search as he might, none of them was her.

'Where's she gone? I wish I knew,' Arie said, tucking a lock of white-blonde hair behind the child's ear. 'I really wish I knew.'

So, where *was* Evie?

To get to the place where she was, Stella, Reuben, Matilda and Oscar, carrying the makings of an Easter Sunday lunch, had to pick their way down a steep, shaley path. At the bottom they reached a walkway which stretched around the edge of a wide bay, and which gave access to about thirty small timber boatsheds.

The sheds were of similar shapes and dimensions, but in different colour schemes and various states of repair. They had been built above the water and rested on pylons, some of which were made of timber, some of concrete, and some – most dubiously – cobbled together from rickety stacks of bricks. Each of the sheds was unique. Some had corrugated iron fireplaces jutting out from their sides, others porthole-style windows; one was plastered with pictures of silver screen icons, another decorated with pieces of driftwood. Their front doors were reached by short jetties that stretched from dry land across water that lapped around seaweed-covered rocks.

The shed Evie was minding, while its owner was overseas, was a shade of deep terracotta with a black tin roof. Inside there was a single room with a rudimentary kitchen, a fold-down double bed, a pleasant cluttering of eclectic furnishings and knick-knacks, a well-stocked bookshelf and a chest full of board games. There was nothing much to take care of except for a couple of pot plants, but Evie's main task was to be visible, coming and going, so that nobody got the idea the tiny home was lying vacant.

'This place is awesome, but why did you have to look after it in *autumn*?' eight-year-old Oscar complained when he'd passed through the room and out to the back deck, where yachts and catamarans leaned back on their moorings in a chilly breeze. His stretching legs were those of a soccer player, and no matter the weather he always wore short pants. He was right about the season: in summer, this deck would have made a beautiful diving platform, but today the water beyond it was a disappointing and choppy grey.

'Because, stupid – people leave here when it's cold and go to warmer places,' said ten-year-old Matilda, using the scathing tone Evie had noticed she reserved solely for her brother.

Matilda was the same height as Oscar, although it was possible that he was going to fully overtake her in the next five minutes. She had a slender figure and thick, mid-brown hair, and was presently in the business of growing into her teeth. Evie could see, though, that all of this was going to blossom into something special when Matilda hit her late teens. She was a lovely kid – a deep thinker who wrote poems and songs and had decided that the ultimate in fabulousness was to sleep over at the boatshed of her newly reappeared aunt.

Because they had all agreed that it was too much of a hassle to cook, lunch was a case of cold chicken and ripped segments of French bread, plum tomatoes and avocado, ham and various kinds of cheese. Reuben pulled the cork out of a bottle of sparkling wine and filled three of the boatshed's plastic flutes, while Stella poured pink grapefruit juice for the kids.

'To you, Eve-star, to "Dandelion Clocks", and to the many, many, many more poems you will publish,' he said.

It had been a good week for Evie. Not only had she exchanged a very casual job behind the bar at a grubby pub for a guaranteed five shifts per week at an upmarket wine bar, she'd also had an email from Edinburgh, from the publisher of *Ten Lines*, telling her that 'Dandelion Clocks' was to be included in their anthology, which would come out later in the year.

'How much do they pay you?' Oscar asked.

Evie laughed. 'Not much, Oscar. If they pay you at all.'

Oscar screwed up his face. His plan was to become a world-famous soccer player. Or a cricketer. At a pinch, an AFL star would do. 'So why would you *do* it?'

'It's a mystery, buddy,' Evie said, ruffling his hair, which was dark like her own. 'Although, there's this poetry competition I heard about while I was in Melbourne, and if my poem's chosen, I get one . . . thousand . . . dollars.'

Oscar's eyes lit up at the word 'competition'. 'That's cool. What's your poem about? The one you're entering?'

'I haven't decided yet.'

'Make sure it's a good one,' Oscar advised sagely.

They ate indoors because of the cold breeze on the deck, and also because the local silver gulls were daring creatures. When the food was eaten, the sparkling wine gone, and Reuben and the kids had started a predictably fractious game of Monopoly, Stella suggested she and Evie take a walk along the foreshore.

'It's great having you home,' Stella said, slipping an arm through Evie's.

The soundtrack to their walk was the tink of halyards against mainmasts and the rhythmic lap of waves.

'You have beautiful kids,' Evie said wistfully.

They walked in silence for a while, but when Stella said, 'So, tell me,' Evie knew that she'd walked smack into an opportunity for one of Stella's famous heart to hearts.

'So, tell me why it is that someone who's wanted to be a published poet for as long as I've known her, who really ought to be very happy right now . . . *isn't*.'

It was a good question. The surge of excitement Evie had felt when she got the news about 'Dandelion Clocks' had quickly fizzled out in the absence of anyone to share it with. There was really only one person she wanted to tell, and although she got as far as looking up the number of Sonder Digital with her newly activated phone, she took herself in hand before she dialled it. There were reasons, she reminded herself, that she was here, and not in Melbourne.

'What makes you think I'm not happy?'

'Come on, Evie,' Stella said, in the maternal tone she had every right to use on her little sister. 'What's the problem, girly-bird?'

Evie turned her face to the wind so that it blew back her hair. 'I got hurt.'

'By that Dave character?'

Evie laughed. She'd lived with Dave for months but thrown him off like an unwanted coat, and without a backwards glance. On the other hand, she'd known Arie for just over a week, and her tangle with him had left her feeling like half her heart had been torn away. 'No, not Dave.'

'Well?'

'I met a guy in Melbourne. I slept with him once, and I can't stop thinking about him.'

'What happened?'

'Well, he liked me. I know that much. But . . . there's someone else. Someone he can't quite let go of.'

'Bummer,' Stella said.

'Huge bummer,' Evie agreed.

'So, what are you going to do now?'

'I am going to . . . write poems, read books, pour wine, regrow heart, and hang out with the *neven en nichten*,' she said.

'The what?'

'It's Dutch,' Evie said.

'For?'

'For Oscar and Matilda.'

The sisters walked until their cheeks were pink and their fingers bloodless, and when at last they returned to the boatshed, Oscar had worked his way up to hotels on Trafalgar Square, Bond Street *and* Park Lane.

Make sure it's a good one, Oscar had said, and that night Evie trawled through the scribbled notes, vague ideas, fragments and first drafts that filled her notebooks. When she came upon an embryonic description of a plane falling into the sea, she lingered there.

Studying her own words, Evie saw how she had tried to capture an image of the plane twinning itself in the moments before disaster so that only one of its selves plummeted towards the ocean, while the other rose up and went . . . where, exactly? Her unfinished poem didn't say. The instinct behind the poem was to offer a vision of hope, but Evie could see that the image wasn't the right one, that the words on the page were not yet hitting the mark.

Sometimes poetry felt like extraction – a kind of mining that involved hunting in the dark for seams of brightness, and working out how to bring them up to the light – but she could now see that with this poem she had been digging to one side of the place where the gold lay.

She tore out the page so she could lay it alongside a fresh one and begin again. She tried and failed, tried again. On scrap paper she free-associated, scribbling down every relevant word she could think of, no matter how obvious. *Flying, flight, flew, wings, feathers, wax* . . . and then, there he was. He had flown right into her vision: Icarus, son of the inventor Daedalus. Icarus: the boy who'd flown too high, and fallen when the sun's heat melted the wax that glued the feathers to his wings. *I start the day by falling from such a great height.* That's what Arie had said, on that television interview. Evie wrote those words down, too, and at last she was beginning to see how her poem might come together.

She added words and took them away. She sharpened her pencil, added more words, then erased them. Then began again.

It was frustrating work, both wonderful and mystifying. It was so strange, she thought, the way poetry worked – the way words from one draft of a poem pushed through into the next, hard as jewels, while the rest crumbled away. Pictures wafted past your mind's eye whispering a childish dare: catch me if you can.

'Yes,' she whispered when at last she believed her poem was done.

turning

ARIE, FINDING EVIE nowhere in the virtual world, was reduced to watching for her in the real one. He looked for her in crowds and developed a habit of slowing down when he passed long lines of people queuing for coffee. Cutting through the heated domains of department stores in his lunch hour, he watched for her at shop counters and looked for her on escalators. He scanned the faces of people at tram stops and sought out her shape wherever crowds gathered to listen to a busker finish a song, or a magician finesse a trick. But she was never there.

Wandering the city blocks one lunch hour, Arie paused at the window of an outdoor shop, where backpacks and wet-weather coats were on display in their confident and unisex colour schemes. He didn't want to buy any of these wares, but he did want to imagine for a moment what it would be like to be the sort of person who disappeared into the mountains and the stretching plains that loomed all over the shop's billboards, to shrink all his necessities down to what he could carry on his back.

Well, you actually are that free. Really and truthfully. That's what Evie had said to him, and perhaps she had been right. Arie was realising that so many things he had come to consider essential were, in actual fact, only essential to a version of his life that no longer existed. He'd put so much time and effort into laying down its cornerstones – buying the house in Tavistock Row, and building up Sonder Digital to provide financial security. But all of this was predicated on a life he no longer lived. The house with the bay window had been Diana's dream, not his. Sonder Digital was now big enough, strong enough, that were he to walk away from it, Richard would simply carry it on.

These thoughts were new, and they made Arie's pulse speed up a little, as if he really were standing on that trackless tundra, with every shred of his known world swept away and out of sight – nothing but tawny grass all around him, nothing to hold on to, no path to follow, no map in his hands. When he blinked his actual life back into focus, feeling the familiar shapes and structures rise up around him, he felt safer again, but he also had a sense of being hemmed in, and maybe a little bit bored. He wanted to tell all of this to Evie, but Evie was nowhere to be seen.

As April slipped into May, and May gave way to June, temperatures fell and rainfall increased. Deciduous trees raised bare branches to the sky, and Arie, going to his wardrobe for the first time in the season for a winter coat, knew that the time had come.

He phoned Lenka.

'I'm ready,' he told her.

What happened the day before she came, though, was something Arie did not expect, and it happened on the only Saturday of the year – the one belonging to the Queen's Birthday long weekend – that Arie allowed Richard to drag him along to the football. Arie had ended up with his team the way some people got first names or titles: it had been handed down from his grandfather to his father, and in turn to him.

Arie did nothing to maintain his allegiance, other than own a red-and-navy-blue scarf and go to the footy with Richard on the June long weekend, when Arie's team played Richard's in an annual blockbuster. Since Richard's team had been looking good in recent years, while Arie's had been languishing near the bottom of the ladder, Richard was especially keen.

They spent the afternoon drinking overpriced beer that tasted like horse piss in plastic tumblers and eating pies with innards so hot that Arie ended up with a burned tongue. Richard's team won, which was an excellent outcome because it made him stupidly happy and didn't bother Arie at all, whereas the alternative outcome would have made Richard morose and brought Arie only minimal pleasure.

After the game they piled onto a tram so crammed Arie couldn't get a handhold, either above his head or on the corners of any of the seats. He had to rely on the crush of bodies to keep him vaguely upright as they hurtled around bends. That's where he was when he saw it. Through heads topped with black-and-white beanies, and heads crowned by red-and-blue polar fleece dreadlocks, he saw her name in print on the wall of the tram. *By Evie Greenlees.* At least, that's what he thought he saw. A guy with a face-painted kid riding on his shoulders had shifted position, blocking his view.

Arie craned, trying to see. There were several poems – part of some kind of public art competition – and they scrolled down the curve between the tram's ceiling and its walls. Each time the tram took a corner and its passengers swayed sideways, he was able to catch a little more . . . *when Icarus fell . . . Strange that to be found . . . the tide of night.* His pulse was speeding.

They were not far from Richard's house now, only a block and a half from their stop.

'Ready, pal?' Richard asked, squeezing himself through the crowd towards the door.

'You go. I'm going to stay on.'

'What? Your car's at my house, you great numpty.'

'I'll double back,' Arie assured him.

'What the—?' Richard began, but he was swept off the tram with the outgoing tide of passengers.

Stop by stop the tram emptied, until Arie was able to stand right beneath the poem.

Turning
in memory of PQ108

Some say the sea wept
when Icarus fell,
a billowing keen of grief
and still
the idea of flight remained.

Strange that to be found
we must first be lost,
the sun every day rising
somewhere
turning the tide of night.

Lenka arrived in Richard's station wagon, not with a roll of garbage bags but with a stack of brand-new packing boxes – not too big, so they didn't get too heavy. She'd also brought a copious quantity of tissue paper, and a plan to do the job with the maximum of love and respect. Together, she and Arie chose an album of the cheeriest music they could stomach, a compilation of 'feel-good' songs, and turned up the stereo to a distracting volume.

Out of the wardrobe they pulled dresses and shirts that had once smelled of Diana but now smelled of clothes stored too long in a closet. There was no better person than Lenka to help with this task. As Arie lifted garment after garment off their hangers and passed them to her, he thought how awful it would have been if he'd mistakenly asked for the help of somebody who wanted to try things on, or who too obviously wanted some souvenirs. Lenka, oxen in her determination, just put her head down alongside him, without pressure and without subtext. Together they folded and wrapped and stacked, taped the boxes closed when they were full, and carried them out to the station wagon.

'Where will you take them?' Arie asked.

'Away. Where they can be of use, and where you won't have to worry about seeing Diana's favourite jumper on another woman's back.' And this – as Lenka had clearly intuited – was all that Arie really needed to know.

At last, Diana's drawers stood empty, and with the exception of Diana's dynasty of famous red dresses, the wardrobe now contained only his own clothes.

'You are going to keep them?'

'No,' Arie said.

'So what are you going to do with them?' Lenka asked, touching a hand to a fold of scarlet.

'I'll tell you when it's done,' he promised.

Lenka nodded and did not pry. 'I'm starving. You?'

Downstairs in the kitchen, Arie felt duty-bound to join her in a soulless lunch of celery, carrot and tahini, all washed down with strong coffee.

'Can I see this poem, then?' she asked.

Arie had told Lenka the whole story of Evie, leaving out only two things. One was the part about putting Evie out of the car after arriving home and finding Belinda on his doorstep. He'd not have been able to bear the look of disgust that Lenka would have been justified in giving him. The other thing he kept to himself was the night he'd spent with Evie after Heidi's wedding. That had seemed much too private to share.

'Of course,' he said, handing her his phone. She magnified the photograph he'd taken and her brow furrowed as she read, and re-read, Evie's words.

To Arie, the poem was a kaleidoscope. It seemed to shift, allowing him glimpses of new angles, new perspectives. At first it had seemed only to be a poem about the plane crash, but then his attention was drawn by another part of the poem, the part at the end of the first stanza: 'and still/the idea of flight remained'. Even if Icarus had fallen from the sky, and even if he had flown too close to the sun, the idea of flight hadn't been extinguished. And Evie, Arie knew, was trying to say by extension that even if we're burned by love, even if its heat melts the wax that holds our feathers to our wings, that's no reason to stay forever grounded.

'You see these lines here,' Arie said. ' "Strange that to be found, we must first be lost".'

'Yes. What are you thinking?' Lenka asked.

'It's not about Diana, is it? It's about *her*. Is she telling me she's lost?'

'Isn't she telling you more than that? Isn't she telling you that she's waiting to be found?'

solstice

THE SUN WAS setting on the longest night of the year as Evie stepped out of the boatshed and locked the door behind her. The inky waters of the bay swished about beneath the planks she stood upon, and the brackish scent of the estuary was sharp on the carrying breeze. A harmless dragon, she breathed pale mist as she took the path behind the sheds, her knitted hat pulled low over her ears and sheepskin coat zipped high under her chin.

Each time she reached a gap between the sheds, she glanced out over the bay to check on the sunset, the colours of which were changing by the second. The scrubby bank on the far shore of the bay was an indigo silhouette, feathered at the tops with the outlines of individual gum trees. Away to the west, the sun – having already disappeared behind the mountains – was throwing a last few beams of brassy light at the undersides of the clouds, and this same light dripped down onto the bay, where it caught and quivered on the surface of the rippling water. Tomorrow, which was the shortest day of the year, was Evie's birthday; she would be twenty-nine years old.

Although the solstice shuffled its date around on the calendar from year to year, it couldn't move very far, so for all of her life Evie had celebrated her milestones in concert with one of the

Earth's. For all the years she'd lived in the northern hemisphere, she'd had a midsummer birthday instead of a midwinter one, and this had never seemed quite right. But now she was home again, where the nip of the cold wind, the salty scent of the water, and the fast-fading colour-work of the setting sun made her feel like this really was her time of year.

As she walked, Evie checked her watch, which told her – probably reasonably accurately – that it was just a few minutes to five o'clock, and she felt a surge of nerves squeeze at her chest. A couple of weeks ago, when this particular June Saturday had seemed very far in the future, she'd put her name down to perform in a poetry event called 'Fly by the Seat of Your Pants'. But now that the day had actually arrived, Evie couldn't think for the life of her what had possessed her to volunteer. It was no small walk from the boatshed to her destination, but she figured the exercise might stop the nerves from taking hold of her body and paralysing her brain.

In the years Evie had been away from Hobart, the city had changed its mind about how to do midwinter. Nowadays, instead of hiding away in their suburban homes, turning up their heaters and worrying how on earth they were ever going to pay their electricity bills, the locals had accepted the invitation of an eccentric gambler and art fancier to turn the solstice into the party of the year, complete with irreverent performance art, Bacchanalian feasting, poetry readings and huge-scale light installations. Visitors flooded in so that the city's Airbnbs were at capacity and it was hard to get a seat on a flight or the ferry.

The centrepiece of Hobart's midwinter festival that year was an installation called Spectra. It was as simple as it was impressive – a single brilliant column of light, generated by a bank of powerful globes, that rose fifteen kilometres into the sky above the city. On clear nights, its luminescence seemed eventually to dissipate among the stars, while on hazy nights it projected an enlarged circle onto the underside of the clouds, giving it a resemblance to a sweeping, Gotham City search-beam.

Tonight Spectra had a blue tint to its light, and where it intersected with a thin band of high cloud it set off a glow, so that the whole thing looked like an enormous wand casting a spell. As Evie neared the city on foot, she felt like she was part of a pilgrimage. Coming down the steep streets of the suburbs as if drawn by the light were couples walking hand in hand, groups of teenagers already primed for excitement, and adults with children wrapped in puffer jackets, beanies and scarves.

Evie's poetry event was on the fringe – both of the festival and the city. It was to be held in a stolid old corner pub with an open fire, a low stage, and some canny advertising for cheap drinks that had successfully detained a lot of the pilgrims who would eventually press on to the heart of the city when the festival got going in earnest, later in the night.

When Evie arrived at the pub with pink cheeks and a sense that her make-up had been blown off by the breeze as she walked, the Mistress of Ceremonies was on the stage adjusting the standing mike. Her name was Viv, and she was an eccentric middle-aged woman whose business card announced her as a 'cobbler of both shoes and words'. She wore a tailcoat that had no hope of being fastened around her comfortable girth.

Evie took in the stage setting: a long table with a white cloth, three chairs, three writing pads, three glasses of water and three ridiculous ostrich-feather pens. The deal was that Viv would throw prompts at the poets, and they would have just a few minutes to hurl together a poem in response. Evie felt the urge to turn around and walk straight back out of the door.

'Evie!' Viv boomed into the microphone. 'Come on up, come on up.'

Viv wiggled the mike out of the holder and thrust it into Evie's hand.

'So, you've used one of these before, right?'

Evie nodded.

'So, rock star, okay? Not ice cream, right? Show me?'

Evie gave her a baffled look and Viv took back the microphone.

'Rock star is like this,' she said, demonstrating, holding the device horizontally to her mouth. 'And ice cream is like this.' She turned it vertically in front of her chin and put out her tongue as if to lick it. 'So none of the ice cream business, okay? It's rock star all the way. Now go and pop some more lippy on. Bit more eyeliner too if you've got any in your bag – the stage lights'll wash you right out.'

Evie did as she was told and by the time she returned, the other poets had arrived. She'd not met either of them before. One was a nervous young man – a boy really, barely out of his teens, Evie thought, from the patchiness of his facial hair and the loose, al dente look of his long limbs. The other was a neat middle-aged woman with a button-up cardigan and a smooth auburn bun, but a look in her eye that made Evie suspect there was something less tidy underneath the surface.

In the first round, the smooth-haired woman went first and Evie realised she had been quite right about her. The poem she performed – in response to the prompt 'moist' – was entirely, delightfully smutty. The boy, though, surprised her with a gust of unexpected rage as he recited an angry poem in response to the prompt 'fickle'. As for Evie, she thought she managed passably well to come up with a vaguely coherent few lines that responded to 'quiver'. Her poem was, or at least was supposed to be, about both archery and affairs of the heart.

Viv was announcing that they were ready to get on with the next set of poems. In front of Evie, Viv placed a small slip of paper, and when Evie turned it over the word written there was 'match'.

Evie picked up her feather-pen, and time – mercifully – slowed. 'Match' was a word that offered multiple meanings. A contest. A pairing. A tool for making fire. But when the nib of her pen touched the paper, Evie understood that this one didn't require conscious thought. Somewhere inside herself, she had been writing this poem – or a version of it – for months.

Every time she sat down with notebook and pen, there he was: Arie. She pictured him wet from head to toe on a sun-scorched street while she held the hose, and cupping her face in his hand by the side of a river full of drowning lights, and asking her to get out of his car on a side street – oh no, she had not forgotten that. Urging her to open a box containing a word in a bottle, dancing with her at a wedding, standing in front of her on damp grass while she wrapped a duvet around his cold skin.

And then Viv announced that her time was up, and Evie found herself standing at the microphone, her sheet of paper shaking visibly. The stage lights were hot and bright, and within seconds of coming to stand beneath them, Evie could feel sweat on her upper lip and underneath her hair. But while the heat was uncomfortable, the brightness was a blessing, because it reduced the crowd to shadows.

The room was not silent. Evie could hear the talk and laughter from the next room, the occasional clink of colliding eight-balls, and hoots of celebration. But the people in this room were paying attention. She could feel but not see their eyes on her; she had a sense of the room's collectively held breath.

'Hello again,' she said into the microphone, and although she

302

had whispered out of nervousness, the microphone somehow translated the texture of her voice into something nearer to sultry. 'My topic for this round is . . . match.'

Evie felt the powerful way her voice leaped, like a creature of its own volition, out of her mouth and into the whole room. She took a breath and glanced at her page, although she barely needed to, for this was the poem that had been cooking inside her. She hadn't seen the words in print until just now, until they'd come flying off the nib of that ostentatious feather-pen in her own handwriting, but the emotion they contained was well rehearsed.

> 'I am a solitary
> wooden match,
> all out of patience
> with this interminable tilt
> towards light.
>
> Scratch
> and my fire
> would burn down our walls
> and cast us together,
> displaced persons
> in the wilderness
> of desire.
>
> There is so much
> more
> for our hearts
> to know.'

Evie surprised even herself with the depth of feeling that had come through as she spoke the words on the page, and when she finished, the room was hushed. Her heart was in her throat now that she had come back from whatever place her poem had taken her to, and she was unsure, for a time, whether she had in fact done something shocking, or if her poem had been just plain terrible.

She had the same feeling as the one she sometimes had in dreams, when she realised she had been going about all the business of her regular day while wearing not a stitch of clothing. She was relieved when she glanced down and realised she was actually wearing a dress. The hush seemed to go on and on. Then someone's whistle went off like a loosed cork, and the room filled suddenly with a burst of applause.

As he drove out of the city towards Belinda's house, Arie watched the sun retire early behind the distant mountains and knew that the year's longest night had begun. His car towed a full trailer-load of firewood that caused it to labour on the uphill stretches and gather momentum on the downhill. When he was only a few minutes away from Belinda's, he phoned ahead so she could be waiting for him at the gate that led into the paddock beyond the apricot trees.

Bordered by wire fences on one side and thick bushland on the other, the paddock was grazed not only by sheep, but also by the marsupials that came down from the hillsides in their dozens each night. Arie pulled into the paddock and saw in the last of the day's light that Belinda – her small frame dwarfed by a large plaid jacket – had done just as she said she would. She had selected a patch of close-cropped grass suitable for their purposes, and collected enough dry leaves, she-oak needles, sticks and fallen branches to provide a solid bed of kindling.

With all the competence of a city driver, and grateful for the forgiving expanse of the paddock, Arie backed the rented trailer up to the site, following Belinda's impatient hand signals as he half understood them in his rear-view mirror. Getting out of the car, he felt the give of soft earth under his feet and caught the scents of eucalypts and the cold.

She nodded a greeting, and Arie handed her the smaller of two pairs of gloves he'd bought that day from a hardware store not far from the firewood depot where he'd filled the trailer to capacity.

'Very thoughtful,' she said, accepting them, and Arie knew that in Belinda-speak this was close to effusive praise.

'You ready?' he asked.

'Let's do it,' she said.

Arie liked the feeling of this physical work – grasping the roughly split chunks of timber in his gloved hands and piling them on top of the kindling. He and Belinda made no attempt at an elaborate structure for their bonfire, but tried as best they could to make sure there was space between the logs for air to flow.

When the trailer had been emptied, the wood pile on the ground was as high as Arie's middle. Belinda reached into the pocket of her jacket and drew out two boxes of large matches, then handed one to Arie. Silently, they began – on either side of the pyre – making their way slowly around and, at intervals, holding their small flames to the kindling.

It was a relief to have something to *do*, and Arie thought this was something he and Belinda had in common. They were both better off with actions to take, motions to go through, challenges to achieve. They were good at getting apricots into buckets, jam into jars, logs into heaps, sparks into flames.

Arie lit one last match, and the sandpaper scrape of the head against the striking strip loosened something inside him. Then the flames began to creep – a hot, bright vine of orange and yellow and red – up through the stack of firewood until the entire structure was well alight. From another deep pocket of her coat, Belinda brought out a leather-jacketed hip flask, unscrewed the lid, took a slug of the contents and handed it to Arie. Rum, he discovered, as the liquid fire hit the back of his throat.

'So are we going to do it?' she asked.

'Now?'

'Good a time as any.'

Arie went to the back of his car and drew out an armload of scarlet fabric. Four famous red dresses, each one of which had been worn in the great concert halls of the world, each one of which had held the beloved body of Diana Clare. He gave two to Belinda and kept the other two for himself. He noticed that he and Belinda mirrored each other's movements, holding the dresses first to their faces and then tightly against their chests.

It was their plan, in the morning, once the fire had reduced all of its fuel to ash, and once that ash had chilled against the midwinter ground, to come back to this place and scoop up a portion of what remained. Then they would go to the cemetery, and there, inside the walls of the rose garden, they would remove the screws in the four corners of Diana's silver plaque to reveal the drawer hidden away inside the brickwork: the drawer that they would no longer have to think of as empty.

And so, in the darkness of the longest night of the year, they threw the dresses onto the flames. It was barely any time before the flimsy things had dissolved into heat and nothingness, but for a moment their fabrics caused the flames to flare – high and bright – and while it lasted, Arie took a chance putting his arm around Belinda's shoulders and holding her tightly. He felt her relinquish just a little of her tension and lean into him as together they watched this too-brief and beautiful spectacle, and remembered the fire that was Diana Clare.

'There's something I want to tell you,' Arie said after quite a long time, although the truth was he didn't really want to tell her at all.

'I think I already know.'

'You do?'

'You met someone.'

Standing beside her, his arm still around her shoulders, Arie couldn't see her face. He wished he had a better sense of the thoughts that were going on inside her head. 'What makes you think that?'

'Well, I figured there had to be a reason you wanted to do this, to say a different kind of goodbye.'

'Well, what if I had? Met someone?' he asked, feeling the heat of the fire on his cheeks.

'Will I like her?'

Arie gave a bitter laugh. 'I don't think we'll ever find that out, unfortunately. The chance I had with her' – he winced at the memory of it – 'I wasn't ready for it.'

'So, what happened?'

'She went away.'

'And?'

'Now I can't find her.'

Belinda took a slug from the hip flask and handed it to Arie.

'We have a special talent, don't we?' she said. 'For losing people.'

'We do,' Arie agreed. 'We sure do.'

−INTERLUDE−

JUST BECAUSE RORY 'Red' Somerled drove a Mercedes-Benz was no good reason to think he was wealthy. He'd owned the big, beamy station wagon for nigh on thirty-five years, and it had been second-hand when he'd bought it.

Red had chosen the Merc, all those years ago, mostly because it was big enough to take a five-piece band's guitars, amplifiers, cables and mike stands, as well as his portable keyboard. But he couldn't have denied that the purchase was also in part down to the influence of the Janis Joplin song, which was one of the few covers that the Locksmiths ever played. 'Mercedes-Benz' was, in Red's view, the perfect song to pull out when you found yourself in front of a crowd that was just itching to sing along.

Red lived in North Fremantle, a suburb sandwiched between the Swan River and the Indian Ocean and graced by the iconic Dingo Flour silo, but once again it would have been a mistake to regard his address as a marker of financial success. He'd bought the house – a tumbledown limestone worker's cottage with a sun-faded tin roof – not long after he'd bought the car, in the days just before the America's Cup turned the world's eyes to Freo, beginning the gentrification process that would surely and steadily change the port city from a cruisy back-water to a place with a café strip and its own team in the AFL.

Deep inside, in a part of himself he didn't choose to look at too often, Red knew that he'd fucked it. Life, that was. Thirty-five years ago, he'd had a shiny blue Merc and a full head of hair, a band with songs in the charts and every reason to think his life's trajectory would be steady and upwards. But then, somehow, he'd stalled. Year by year, the Locksmiths diminished in popularity and notoriety, until they were barely able to fill a local pub to three-quarters of its capacity. It was Red's cross to bear that he'd been given a great start, but somehow failed the test. He hadn't converted. He hadn't capitalised. He'd coasted.

Such thoughts were dangerously close to the surface of Red's mind that chilly June morning, when he sat behind the wheel of his Merc trying to coax the old beast into life. In Freo, winter really only lasted for about six weeks, but this day felt like the very heart of it. The wind that was whipping the Indian Ocean into a frenzy was so Antarctic that Red could smell penguin shit on the breeze.

The car spluttered and choked, then – finally – fired up. Red revved the engine, blew on his hands and considered what music to play on the way to work. In his car, Red kept a bunch of CDs he'd burned for himself, and they were catalogued not according to artist or genre but curated according to mood. He had songs for being angry and songs for being wistful, he had songs for being bored and songs for being lonely. What did he need today?

It wasn't precisely anger that he felt, although he was pissed off. It wasn't precisely wistful that he felt, although he certainly longed for the past. It wasn't precisely lonely that he felt; it was more like broken and useless. He'd been feeling this way, acutely, for the past three weeks, since Louise Trethewey, who was now his boss, had called him into her office and served him up the news. With a sigh, he picked out the CD he kept for his most forlorn moments and slid it into the stereo – once the height of technology, now an outmoded piece of crap.

Today was a day for Leonard Cohen, if ever there was a day for Leonard Cohen, so Red forwarded through the tracks until he hit 'Hallelujah'. He cranked the volume until it reached the sweet spot, loud enough for the song to drown out every other thought in his head, and drove out onto the highway, where the wind pushed the big old Merc sideways with every powerful gust. He listened to the lyrics and he sang, not giving a single flying fuck that he could be seen through his car windows and in his rear-view mirror. Even when he had to stop at the lights, and he knew that he was some freaky mime show for the people in the car beside him, he didn't stop belting it out.

In the East Perth studios of the Australian Broadcasting Corporation, Red stood in the canteen queue and fished for coins in the pockets of his too-tight black jeans. He knew there were only so many times he could wink at Barb-behind-the-counter and have her chalk up his coffee – black, three sugars – to the never-never. Besides, if Kimmy-behind-the-counter ended up being the one to serve him today, then the wink would be useless.

It was yet another sad fact of Red's life that the wink now only worked on women north of a certain age. With those women, there was a chance they'd once ridden on their boyfriends' shoulders in a mosh pit at a Locksmiths gig, or sticky-taped one of those posters to their wardrobe doors – the ones in which Red had appeared at his keyboard with his big ginger-blond hair. The hair had lasted Red through his forties and even into his mid-fifties before the uncompromising combination of a fluorescent light and a mirror-lined elevator had told him that the gig was up. It was ten years now since Red had deposited his crowning glory on a barbershop floor. These days, the most youthful attribute Red could boast was that he'd never since his glory days gone up more than a single size in black jeans.

By hanging back in the queue, he was able to make sure that Kimmy served the person ahead of him, and that it was Barb, slamming the cash register drawer closed after her last trans-action, who turned to him and said, 'Cold enough for you out there, darl?'

'Yeah, bit chilly today, isn't it?'

'I'll say. So, what's news with you, Red?'

'Haven't you heard?'

'Heard what?'

'They're canning my show, mate.'

'Nah,' Barb said in a *you're pulling my leg* tone.

'Yeah.'

'She wouldn't.'

She was talking about Louise Trethewey.

'Actually, she would.'

'*Disc & Co*? She can't! That program's a nationwide institu-tion! Your listeners will freak. You having coffee, darl?'

Red nodded. 'Institution or not, it's on the way out, I'm afraid.'

Barb plucked a cup from the top of a stack and set it under the outlet of the coffee machine. 'But why?'

311

Red gave a shrug of deep bewilderment. Over the churning of the coffee maker, Barb asked, 'So what are you going to be doing around here now?'

'I'm not.'

'What?'

'I'm not going to be doing anything around here now.'

'They're letting you go?' The spoons of sugar Barb tipped into Red's coffee were on the generous side of things. 'She can't do that.'

'Well, she has.'

'I'm sorry, Red. Really sorry to hear that.'

'Yeah, me too, mate.'

'When's this all happening?'

'End of financial year, Barb. Because that's what it's all about, right? The *dólares*.'

'Shit, Red. So when's your last show?'

'Next Friday night.'

'That's a real shame, Red,' she said, passing over the steaming cardboard cup.

Red put on a sheepish face. 'I've only got a dollar on me,' he said, holding out a gold coin in his palm. And just for good measure, he winked.

'Oh, go on with you,' Barb said. 'You bloody rascal. I'll put it on your account.'

Red carried his cup along corridors and upstairs to his desk, pretending not to notice each time coffee slopped onto the carpet. It wasn't, after all, carpet that he was going to have to live with.

He walked past Louise's office. He could see her through the glass, sitting in the chair she'd occupied on that particular Friday afternoon, the one when she'd called him in for 'a talk'.

312

He could see, too, the chair in which he'd sat while he listened to her deliver her pronouncement.

'It's not my job to be popular, Red,' she'd told him. 'It's my job to do the most we possibly can with the resources we have available.'

Red had argued. He'd cited his show's impressive nationwide ratings, and reminded her that *Disc & Co* had blazed a trail through the earliest days of the podcast market. He repeated back to her some things she'd said herself about how important it was for some of the national broadcaster's content to come from the west, so the country's vision of itself wasn't entirely produced by the eastern states.

But when she'd responded, picking her words out of a limited set of Big Brother-approved phrases, he'd known that she was performing. That their meeting was not, for her, primarily about the end of his career, but how well, how seamlessly, how professionally, she was managing her ugly little task. Passing her office now, Red allowed a particularly generous splash of coffee to land on the carpet tiles.

Red's desk was in a far corner of a large open room, by a window. Having been the presenter of *Disc & Co* for fifteen years, and of various other music programs before that, he had amassed a sizeable collection of CDs. Stacks of them rose, three rows deep, from his desktop to the height of his cubicle divider. Although enough room had been left under the desk for feet and knees, the space was otherwise taken up by towers of cardboard and plastic cases. Along the full length of the window beside Red's desk were milk crates, shamelessly filched from the canteen and stacked floor to sill, every one of them packed to capacity. So, when Red arrived back at his desk to find a couple of letters and a small, square parcel sitting on his keyboard, there was really no great mystery about what the parcel was likely to contain.

Red noted the long strip of Canadian stamps and the way his name and address had been written out by hand. The shape and height of the sloping capital letters faintly kindled something in his memory.

Even after all these years, and even after all the many thousands of parcels Red had received from record companies and eager self-starting musicians, he still got a little buzz when a fattened envelope landed on his desk, and he still opened parcels like a kid at Christmas time. This CD, Red saw as he tugged it unceremoniously out of its wrapping, was in a cardboard case – one of those pesky tri-fold things that, like a pair of new shoes, were just a bit too tight until you'd had a chance to wear them in. *For Real*, it was called, by a group called Lucie Doran and the Curious Lovers. The cover was all grainy and romantic, with a windswept blonde girl in a dusky pink dress standing on the edge of a jetty. Waves the colours of blurred ink and whipped cream were trying to jump up at her feet; in her arms was a banjo. Doran, he thought. Lucie *Doran*.

Red put to one side the folded letter that had slipped out of the parcel and concentrated on winkling the disc out of its casing. He slipped it into the slot on the side of his computer and settled his big plush headphones over his ears. When the first track began in a rush of Acadian banjo-and-fiddle folk, Red's memory coughed up the connection. Lucie Doran. *Kit* Doran: banjo player with the Salt Strings, and later with Mercy Reid's backing band. Kit Doran. One of nature's gentlemen, if he was even still alive; Red hadn't thought of him for twenty years or more. Toes tapping, Red unfolded the letter.

Dear Red,

I imagine this letter comes to you out of the blue, although I cannot work out if it seems to me a very long time ago, or only yesterday, that you and I were playing pubs by night and terrorising the fish by day. I fondly remember your boat – what was it you used to call it? A tin dish? I have never forgotten how kind it was of you to take me, an old man even then, under your wing, and just for the record I never did find a fish that pickled half so well as your West Australian herring.

I don't even play the banjo much these days as my hands have got too old. Same can't be said for little Lucie, though, my grand-daughter. She's doing well with her band the Curious Lovers, as you will see from the enclosed CD. The Guardian over here writes that her music is 'perfectly positioned at the crossroads of folk and pop', which I think might be cribbed from an article written about the Locksmiths some thirty years ago. What it really means, I think, is that people are oftentimes surprised to find themselves enjoying folk music as much as they do.

This month, which I always have to remember is the middle of your winter, Lucie's touring your part of the world, and I promised her that I would send a letter to you, my friend, on the chance you could do something or indeed anything at all to promote her gigs.

It's hard to believe that our little Lucie is not so many years shy of forty. Although the mathematics say that I'm eighty-seven already, I sometimes struggle to remember that I'm any older than forty myself. Lucie is soon to be married, which I am pleased about because she gave all of her young years to her music, and it was hard not to feel somewhat responsible for that. Her man is a fiddle player whose people are from B.C., but we won't hold either thing against him because at least he is a devout fan of the Montreal Canadiens.

In other news from the Doran clan, Margaret is no longer with us, which is a cause of sadness to me every day, though I am pleased to have the comfort of her voice on all those Salt Strings albums. I sometimes hear her voice in Lucie's, too – that same trueness. If I was to direct you to any of the songs on Lucie's album it would be to the title track, 'For Real'. It has a quality that I can't put my finger on, but it's something ghostly and when I listen to it, I could almost swear that Margaret is right beside me again. But you will be thinking these are the ramblings of an old fool, so I will sign off now and send you my very best, my friend. I hope you will enjoy Lucie's music, and that you and I will meet again one day.

Your friend in music,
Kit Doran

Well, Red thought, letting the letter fall to the desk. Kit Doran. Red had met Kit somewhere in those years that followed the Locksmiths' nanosecond of national fame – the years in which the band played up and down the coast to fans of their music style, which was a little bit pop and a little bit rock, but had something acoustic and folksy in its roots.

Kit Doran, Red thought, remembering the Canadian's relaxed clawhammer banjo style and his elegant backcast, a dance so often reflected in the still waters of a trout-laden lake.

They'd talked, Red and Kit, as they'd stood on wave-washed rocks and knee-deep in rivers, and dangled their legs over the edges of jetties and trolled for herring in Red's tin dish. Kit talked about his wife, Margaret, with a kind of down-to-earth reverence that Red had never come across, not at all, in any man of his acquaintance, and which he certainly never expected to see in a man who could also gut a fish with three strokes of a sharp knife and put a bullet in a bunny on the far side of a farm dam. Red had decided that it must be a north American thing, or at least an unobtainable thing. There were plenty of women, after Locksmiths gigs, in hostel dorm rooms and the backs of panel vans, but Red Somerled never did marry, or settle down, or partner up, or have kids. God knew he was never too careful, so he occasionally allowed himself to wonder if it would ever happen that some ginger-haired individual would turn up on his doorstep with the words 'I'm your daughter' or 'I'm your son'. It hadn't happened yet. Maybe the truth was that he shot blanks.

On Kit's advice, Red toggled the CD forward to the track called 'For Real', and what happened next to Red Somerled was something he'd never in his life be able to explain. There weren't too many words in 'For Real'. For the most part it was an instrumental piece with a bottom end that rose and fell in sequences of three, and a top end that strummed Red's heart-strings in such a familiar way that he could have sworn this was a song he already knew. Even, it seemed possible, from the way the song harmonised with some deep-down twist of his musical DNA, it was a song he not only knew, but a song he had *written*. Was that right? Or was it maybe the case that the song was already written on him?

Red didn't hear the words, but even if he had, he wouldn't have needed them to tell him that this was a love song. But not *only* a love song. For the life of him, Red wouldn't have known whether this song belonged on his compilation for wistful, or his compilation for lovesick, or even on his compilation for lonely. 'For Real' seemed to him to jump across all the categories. Or else, it needed one all of its own.

Red didn't know he was crying until Ann Cooper from the weather desk was beside him, tugging a lace-edged hanky out of her bra, and he couldn't stop even while she patted his shoulder, or even after the song had finished and he'd pushed his headphones back down around his neck. Head in his hands, elbows on his desk, Rory 'Red' Somerled, at the age of sixty-four, cried and cried until the little hanky was all wet through, and until everyone in the room was either watching him cry or studiously *not* watching him cry.

He cried for love, and he cried for loss. He cried because he hated Louise Trethewey with a passion, and because he detested every smug syllable of her weasel-worded bureaucratese. He cried because *Disc & Co* was being dragged off the air after fifteen years of solid ratings, and because he'd never see Kit Doran again, and because Lucie Doran sang with a voice like a half-fallen angel. He cried for all these reasons and a hundred more he couldn't name. He cried because he was human, and because it was only human to cry when bittersweet music ran – loud and clear – through your veins.

SEVEN

through the ether

IN THE CAR park at the far end of the boatshed track, Evie switched off the Beetle's engine and sat for a moment in the sudden stillness. She'd worked for the last five days straight, and this had been a busy Friday – full of businessfolk taking long lunches to the extreme, after-work drinkers putting the week behind them and midwinter festival patrons getting a jump on the night. Now it was almost ten o'clock, and although she was tired, Evie didn't relish the prospect of the quiet weekend that stretched out ahead of her. It took energy and optimism to keep loneliness at bay, and right now she wasn't sure where she was going to find either one.

At last she forced herself to leave the warmth of the car for the chill of the outdoors, and when she looked up into the sky, she saw the beam of Spectra emerging from behind the low mound of the Queen's Domain. Shreds of cloud drifted around and through its pillar of brightness as she made her way carefully down the sloping path to the water's edge.

Opening the boatshed and stepping inside was the opposite of coming home to company and a warm house. Everything inside the boatshed was quiet, cold and still, and tonight the place seemed especially desolate. Evie turned on the gas heater and flicked the switch on the small transistor radio which sat on a shelf above the kitchen sink.

The radio was small and battery-operated, quite old, with a close-fitting leather case with holes for all its buttons and dials, and a circle of large pinpricks for the part that covered the speaker. Standing at the sink, still in her coat, Evie scrolled through the stations, catching snatches of sound – the frenetic tones of a horse-race caller, a burst of orchestral fanfare, the shaky voice of an elderly man recalling a memory, a few bars of jazz, a song played on the fiddle, banjo and guitar. But not just any song. It was *the* song.

The radio wasn't perfectly tuned to the station, but Evie pulled her hand away from the dial, scared that if she altered anything she might lose the transmission altogether. Suddenly unaware of the cold, she stood staring at the small radio, listening hard, as if she could turn her own body into a receiver. No, she wasn't imagining it. It really was the song – the one she'd last heard being played on cello and flute in Waverley Station in Edinburgh, the one she'd tried to piece together on the strings of her old guitar.

She almost laughed with relief; hearing it again was like watching a lost bird fly voluntarily back through the open door of a cage or having a butterfly land on your hand. She held her breath, nervous that if she made a move to capture it, she'd startle the creature back into flight.

All she had to do though, she told herself, was keep listening. At the end of the song, someone would tell her its name, or at least the name of the artist. Or even if the announcer had already introduced the song before it started, Evie would be able to call the radio station and ask about it. Whatever happened, the song was now hers in some way. She had a lead on it, a thread that would allow her to find it.

It sounded different, played in this folksy combination of guitar, fiddle and banjo. Even so, it was still entirely itself, full of love and longing. Closing her eyes to listen for a moment, Evie knew that this song, for her, would always be bound up in the time she'd spent at Tavistock Row. It would always be the song that told the short, bittersweet story of the time she fell in love with a man who could almost love her back, but not quite.

There came a pause in the music, as for an intake of breath, and then a voice – a woman's voice – began to sing. *Hey, lover mine, do you want . . . do you want . . . do you want to do this thing . . . for real?* Those were all the words she sang before the instruments rose up again to take over from her voice. Evie – hooked, carried along – felt the song's building tensions as the fiddle and the banjo skirted and circled each other in an intricate, intimate exchange. It made her feel a particular kind of pain, but not the kind she wanted to back away from. She wanted to feel it, because it was all of a piece with how beautiful the music was.

Finally, the song came to an end with a sequence of chords that Evie predicted half a heartbeat ahead of time. She could already feel the shape of them, so that when the actual sounds arrived, they resonated in her chest cavity with perfect rightness.

Then a man's radio-practised voice broke in: 'I'm Red Somerled, and that brings us to the end of *Disc & Co*, not just for tonight, but for always.'

The name of the song, she thought. *Tell me the name of the song.*

'You've been listening to the title track of *For Real*, the new album by an up-and-coming Canadian folk band, Lucie Doran and the Curious Lovers—'

Evie felt the cage door swing shut, her hand close tight. *Got you.*

323

'—who are, as it happens, in Australia at this very moment. They have one final concert as part of their national tour, down in Hobart where the midwinter festival is about to wrap up. If you're lucky, you might still grab a ticket to see them live at the Avalon Theatre tomorrow night. Well, that's all from me. Now, it's news time and the end of an era. Goodnight, Australia. You've been listening, for the very last time, to *Disc & Co.*'

Evie's weekend, all of a sudden, was no longer so empty.

It had been a long time since Arie had arrived home to find music playing in the house. Tonight, he'd been out at the pub shooting pool with some of the Sonder crew, but when the others had been ready to kick on to a cocktail bar, Arie had called it quits.

He heard the music as soon as he opened the door. It was coming from the kitchen – from the radio, presumably. He must have left it switched on, he thought, as he hung his coat on a hook and tossed his keys down on the hall stand. Although that seemed strange, because he couldn't remember listening to the radio that morning.

In the doorway of the darkened kitchen, Arie stood for a moment while the equaliser lights of the radio rose and fell like a monitored heartbeat, and then he understood what it was that he was listening to. It was at once completely recognisable and strikingly new, like seeing an old friend with a radically different haircut, or an old house repainted in an unexpected colour scheme.

He took a couple of huge strides and reached urgently for the volume knob, turning the sound up until it hit that point Diana used to talk about, where the music was loud enough to fill his head entirely. But it wasn't just filling Arie's head, it was flowing all the way through his whole body, like a current, like his own blood.

In the mix of the music he heard fiddle and banjo, and in the background, guitar. It was definitely the one – the song he'd heard Evie play on her guitar.

What *was* it? Arie pulled out his phone and opened one of the several song-recognition apps he'd downloaded, back in February, to his phone. He tapped the screen and a series of concentric blue rings began to pulse in time with the music.

Listening, the screen said.

Then it delivered its verdict: 'For Real', by Lucie Doran and the Curious Lovers.

A thumbnail of an album cover flashed up alongside the words, and Arie could just make out the shape of a woman in a pink dress on a jetty, her blonde hair all blown about and a banjo strapped across her middle.

He'd found it, and all he wanted to do was tell Evie.

'I'm Red Somerled,' the radio announcer said, breaking into Arie's thoughts, 'and that brings us to the end of *Disc & Co*, not just for tonight, but for always. You've been listening to the title track of *For Real*, the new album by an up-and-coming Canadian folk band, Lucie Doran and the Curious Lovers, who are, as it happens, in Australia at this very moment. They have one final concert as part of their national tour, down in Hobart—'

Hobart?

'—where the midwinter festival is about to wrap up. If you're lucky, you might still grab a ticket to see them live at the Avalon Theatre tomorrow night. Well, that's all from me. Now, it's news time and the end of an era. Goodnight, Australia. You've been listening, for the very last time, to *Disc & Co*.'

Hobart.

Evie.

Was she there? In that small city at the bottom of the world? A traveller like her – she could have gone anywhere in the country. He knew that. And yet he felt as if the song on the radio had just dealt him a clue. It was the city where she'd grown up, the place where her sister still lived. And now it was the place where a band was playing her song.

Perhaps he was just desperate and clutching at the slenderest of straws. But, what if she was there? What *if*. . . ?

Hobart.

He could go, if he wanted to; there was nothing stopping him. What was it that Evie had said? *Well, you actually are that free. Really and truthfully* . . .

What did he have to lose? If he went, and didn't find her . . . he'd be no worse off. If nothing else, he would hear Lucie Doran and the Curious Lovers playing *that* song, live.

He began to calculate: the gig was tomorrow night. It was on the far side of Bass Strait. Then the realisation hit him: there was only one way to get there in time.

the idea of flight

LESS THAN TWENTY-FOUR hours later there he was, watching a flight attendant with an immaculate blonde ponytail move through the cabin, counting the passengers with a clicker. The silver constellation brooch that glinted on her navy blue lapel was a symbol Arie knew only too well. He couldn't quite believe this. Not only was he flying, he thought with amazement as he buckled his seatbelt, he was flying Air Pleiades.

He had made his way through the airport reasonably well, if he did say so himself, grateful that this journey required only that he tackle the domestic terminal, and not the international one where he'd said goodbye to Diana. At security, he'd calmly handed his bag to the explosives tester. In the bar, he'd sunk only two shots of whisky. At the gate lounge, he'd picked up a free newspaper and even if he'd not precisely read any of it, he'd managed to hold it in front of his face and absorb the shapes of some of the words with his eyes.

Even as Arie had walked down the airbridge to the waiting plane, what he was doing had not seemed entirely mad to him. So what if he was flying – *flying* – to Hobart to see a gig? So what if he'd heard a song on the radio, then impulsively bought a Hobart-bound flight, at a ridiculous last-minute price, and a night in a hotel? So what if the only available flight would put him on the ground with half an hour or so to spare before the gig started? So what if he'd gone to all this trouble solely because he'd imagined there was half a chance – a quarter of a chance? an eighth? one-sixteenth? – of seeing Evie again?

Until this moment, none of the above had seemed especially crazy. But now the small screen on the back of the seat in front of him was playing the safety video. It didn't matter that the video was cleverly done and beautifully shot, that the cast were lovely-looking human beings and that the locations were exquisite, and it didn't matter that the instructions were delivered with irreverent and deeply Australian humour, because there was nothing in the world that could stop him from feeling nauseated at the sight of a life jacket being tugged over somebody's head . . . *fasten the straps behind you* . . . and nothing that could stop his breathing from getting shallow . . . *with a light and a whistle to attract attention* . . . when he saw a vision of a yellow oxygen mask falling from a ceiling compartment . . . *fit your own mask before assisting others*.

The closest place Evie could find to park her car that night was a ten-minute walk from the theatre, on a side street in the city's hilly western quarter. It was windy, and as Evie made her way down a steep street to the Avalon, she had to keep a hand on her head to stop her beanie from being swept away into somebody's lavender hedge.

When Evie was little, the theatre had not been called the Avalon. At that time, it had been a huge electrical shop, known only by the name of its proprietor, but in recent years both its name and its art deco elegance had been restored. At last, Evie stepped gratefully out of the wind and into the plushly carpeted foyer, where Lucie Doran and the Curious Lovers T-shirts and CDs were for sale at a merchandise table. The nearby bar was doing a brisk trade in the midwinter festival's signature hot gin punch. It didn't seem quite right to Evie that a paper cup of the punch cost almost as much as the CD, *For Real*, but in any case she bought one of each.

Just because Evie was used to going places alone didn't mean she always liked it, and tonight she was particularly aware of herself as a spectator for those couples who swung through the front doors arm in arm, and also for the people who turned up alone but were quickly enfolded into their groups with exuberant greetings, hugs, kisses: one cheek, then the other. The gin cocktail lent her a kind of artificial buoyancy, but she imagined that if someone had cut her in half at that moment and looked at her in cross-section, they would have seen a thin layer of joyfulness around the edge but something darker and sadder at her core.

The auditorium doors were thrown open and Evie joined the rush. Within, there was a smoky feel to the old place, despite the fact that there had for decades been no actual smokers to fuel it. The flammable note of alcohol was in the air. Low-standing platforms had been installed at the sides of the room to create some different levels for the audience, and upon them stood tall, circular tables for people to cluster around. Evie chose a spot at the left of the room, on the front edge of one of these platforms, hoping for a good view.

The crowd kept coming, so that the early arrivals were pushed forward by those still pouring in through the doors, and there was music playing – folksy and electronic at once. The Curious Lovers didn't keep their audience waiting. Soon, the drummer was settling himself in behind the barricade of his kit, and the guitarists were plugging in their instruments.

There had been only one fiddle player in the band pictures that Evie had seen, but there were two on stage – a short, buxom woman in a floral tunic, and a rather gorgeous-looking man with black hair and blue eyes. Front and centre, though, was Lucie Doran herself, her fair hair shining gold in the stage light, her electric banjo strapped high and tight across her chest with a thick, woven strap.

She wasted no time on an introduction to the first track, only stamped her foot – *one, two*. This was music that you were supposed to dance to, and it was clear that some of the people right at the front of the room had come for that express purpose. Around the edges of the room, though, were people – like Evie – who were content to tap their toes and sway.

The first track was instrumental, a set of reels both joined and separated by bridges of shifting tempo and key. When it was over, Lucie Doran stepped up to the microphone.

'So, next we're going to play you a song from our new album,' she told the crowd. Her speaking voice, lightly accented, gave a hint of just how beautiful it was going to sound when it shifted gears into song. 'I didn't write this one – I wish I had, but I didn't. We don't know who wrote it. We've asked around, and the best we can say is that it seems to have been jumping from ear to ear and heart to heart, which is how all the best songs make their way across the world.'

The bass guitarist at the back of the stage leaned into his microphone. 'So, the news is that our Lucie here is going to be a bride, and I'm afraid it's kinda gone to her head, hence all the talk about hearts.'

'Well, thanks for sharing, Frankie,' Lucie said, a little bashful, her face still turned to the crowd. 'But it is true that this next one is a love song. It came to me in New York City, and before that, it came to my fiancé – oh yeah! I said the f-word! That's Elijah right here' – the blue-eyed fiddle player made a half-bow – 'and this song found him in Toronto, Canada. We don't know what this song was called at the beginning of its life, but we call it "For Real".'

Lucie played alone for a time, but then, as the rest of the band joined in, Evie felt the beat in the floor come rising up through her legs while the melody poured through her ears and amplified in the beat-box of her chest. As she knew she would every single time she ever heard this song, she thought of Arie.

The journey to the island was not a smooth one. Arie's plane passed through several pockets of turbulence, causing the flight staff to switch on the seatbelt sign and send everyone back to their seats. Each time the plane fell into a sudden patch of dead air and Arie was jerked upwards against the restraint of his lap belt, he felt his own fragility. He tried to stop himself from thinking about Diana's small frame – how it would never have stood the faintest chance against the colossal forces of wind, weather and engineering.

At last the plane began its descent, something that could hardly come soon enough for Arie. Not only was he desperately ready to step off the craft and onto solid ground, he was also aware that the flight was running behind time and it wouldn't be long until the Lucie Doran and the Curious Lovers gig began. He could only hope there would be enough taxis at the airport, that the drive into the city would be quick.

As the plane passed through a bank of cloud, Arie's porthole window filled with static before clearing to reveal a spectacular view. The outlines of mountain ranges were visible against a midnight-blue backdrop patterned with wind-blown clouds, and the city of Hobart was a spill of coloured lights split in two by the intricate black bays and inlets of the River Derwent. Not far from a bridge across the river that was picked out in spans of red neon, a huge beam of light rose up into the sky. This, then, was Spectra.

Arie had read about the midwinter festival and its light installations, but he'd not been prepared for the impressive scale of it, nor the way its presence seemed to make some sense of this lunatic mission. The beam appeared like a gigantic beacon. In the face of all his questions, the light seemed to provide some kind of answer.

But instead of descending further, the plane swooped upwards again and banked in a wide turn. A few minutes later, the pilot spoke over the sound system. 'Well, folks, as you probably worked out, we didn't make our landing into Hobart on this pass. The conditions are very difficult, with westerly winds gusting to thirty-five knots. So, if you'd be so kind, hold tight while we circle around and have another go. Rest assured, we have your safety uppermost in our minds at all times, so please sit back and enjoy what is going to be a slightly extended flight.'

'Slightly' turned out to be an understatement. By the time the pilot started his second attempt at landing, Arie knew that he'd missed the beginning of the gig. Then, instead of bringing the craft to the ground, the pilot once more pulled up and made another huge swooping turn, so that Arie had the feeling the plane was spiralling around Spectra like a chair tethered to a fairground ride. He checked his watch again and felt all the hope leach out of him.

Something Arie had always hated about air travel, even before PQ108, was that once you stepped aboard you were committed to whatever the flight held in store. There was simply no changing your mind. It amazed him that the flight attendants could cope, day in, day out, being trapped inside their workplace, all choice removed from them. Again, he tried not to think of Diana, and again, he failed.

The pilot announced he would make one more attempt at landing. If it turned out, he said, that it was still too dangerous to proceed, the flight would be diverted to the northern Tasmanian city of Launceston, a two-hour drive away from Hobart. Arie closed his eyes as the plane made its third descent, juddering and jostling in the cross-wind.

This time the plane landed, wheels hammering down hard before its big body hurtled down the runway, shimmying left and right. Eighteen minutes later, Arie Johnson was among the first off the flight, clattering down the metal stairs and hurrying across the windswept tarmac towards the terminal building.

There was a taxi waiting, and the drive to the city was as swift as Arie could have hoped for, but when he arrived at the Avalon Theatre the place was all but empty. A few groups of people lingered on the footpath outside, talking and laughing together, while inside the foyer a woman at a merchandise table was folding T-shirts into a cardboard carton. Propped on the bar was a sign advertising gin cocktails, but the lights above the bar were switched off and there appeared to be no bartender on duty.

Door staff in black clothes noted his presence as he passed by them and into the auditorium. On the now-deserted standing platforms, discarded paper cups stood on glass tables. Behind the sound desk, a guy with a huge beard stood bathed in the light from a screen; amid the abandoned instruments on stage, a couple of techs were busy rolling cables. He went back into the foyer where the mirrored walls forced him to acknowledge the stupidity of his journey.

'Can I get a CD?' he asked the woman at the merchandise table.

'I've disconnected the EFTPOS machine,' she said, 'so I could do cash, but I haven't got any change.'

The CDs were twenty dollars; Arie had only fifty-dollar bills. *Throwing good money after bad*, he thought, handing one over.

'Keep the change, in that case.' At least he wouldn't go home completely empty-handed.

Outside the venue, Arie tried to get his bearings. He'd never been to this city before, so its lay-out was a mystery to him. With his overnight bag slung across his shoulder and phone in hand, he searched for directions to his hotel. Fifteen minutes by foot, apparently, or six by car. The walk would do him good.

He turned in the direction of the arrow on the screen – left. Following the street, he began to climb, and each time he turned to look back, his view over the city was a little different, although one thing remained the same: Spectra, its light shining steadily upwards into a cloud-scribbled sky.

Behind the Avalon Theatre, in one of the city's usually disregarded and undeveloped parking lots, a pop-up bar had sprouted out of the gravel and the weeds. It had the look of a zoo enclosure, with multiple levels and rampways between them. Fires burned in glowing 44-gallon drums and sent occasional showers of sparks pluming up into the air. Beside one of these sat Evie Greenlees, sipping a furiously strong short black and silently humming a tune.

For quite some time, she watched the people with her poet's eye, capturing the vividness of their clothing, their mannerisms, their laughter, their touching. So many people, all around, and so many of them seeming to radiate with the knowledge that they would not be going home alone, as Evie would be.

At last, she pulled her sheepskin coat tight around herself and began the climb up the hill out of the city. As closed-up cafés and dark-windowed shops full of homewares gradually gave way to weatherboard townhouses and sandstone cottages, the foot traffic diminished and the gradient increased.

She had to step into the road to get out of the way of two girls – loud, tipsy and shrieking with laughter – who were walking backwards down the street because the heels of their tall, glossy boots were too high for the slope. She could feel the climb in her thighs.

At last she turned into the cross-street where the car was parked, which was – mercifully – on the level. She sought the Beetle, and found it, its familiar rounded shape glowing where she had parked it beneath a streetlight. But there was somebody beside it. A man, and he was pacing the pavement.

Nothing worth stealing in there, she thought, and felt in her pocket for the safety of her phone, though she hardly knew what she intended to do with it. Her heart rate, already high from the uphill walk, lifted another level as she watched the man stride up and down the pavement, never going further than the length of her car. It wasn't until he paused to blow on his hands, and to roll his wrist over as if checking the time, that Evie realised there was something in his movements that was familiar to her. *Wasn't it . . . ?*

It had been three and a half months since she'd left Melbourne. But Evie was wise enough to know that even if you did spend all that time thinking of someone, wanting them, longing for them, it wasn't enough to make them appear like a midnight wish by your car. *Was it?*

She blinked, expecting when she opened her eyes for her vision to have cleared.

Then he saw her.

'Evie?'

Her heart went faster still, beating *it's him, it's him, it's him.*

In her dreams, Evie was the kind of cool, calm and collected person who would somehow have the composure to . . . stroll . . . the final distance that lay between them. But in reality, she was the kind of heart-on-her-sleeve girl who had to hold herself back from breaking into a run.

When she reached Arie, she didn't stop to think. She hugged him, and he hugged her back, and for a while they stood there, chins on each other's shoulders, breathing in time. She felt that he was cold, even though his suede jacket was zipped up and his scarf wound tightly at his neck. When she pulled away from him, his brown eyes and his wide smile were the only warm things about him. His face was pale and his shoulders tight with shivering. But that smile. Those eyes.

'I found you,' he said.

Evie didn't know if the expression on his face contained more happiness than relief, or more relief than happiness – but she knew that it was all for her.

'You did. But . . . how are you even here?'

'KFP 532,' he said, quoting her number plate. 'I was walking up the hill, and it was just pure dumb luck. I looked left, and there was your car. And in there, on the seat – I knew they were your sunglasses. So all I had to do was . . . wait.'

'You're freezing. How long have you *been* here?'

'A while,' he said.

336

'But . . . how? Why? *What?*'

'I needed to tell you that I found out the name of that song,' he said. 'I thought you'd want to know.'

He pulled the CD from his pocket, then Evie tugged the matching one from her purse.

'You found it, too,' he said.

'Or it found me.'

'You were at the gig?' he asked, putting the CD back in his pocket.

'Uh-huh.'

'I tried to get there, but the plane—'

Plane, Evie processed.

'—it couldn't land the first couple of times. I feel like I'm always doing this with you, Evie. Eventually getting where I need to be, but always a bit late.'

She didn't say anything. She wanted to hug him again.

'You left me without saying goodbye,' he said.

That wasn't true, actually. Evie remembered every single thing about the moment she *had* said goodbye – the early autumn breeze gusting lightly down Tavistock Row, the faint trace of Arie's warm cologne, a sad kiss still echoing on her lips. That seemed at the same time terribly long ago but also like yesterday.

'There hasn't been a day over the last few months when I haven't thought of you, and missed you. And there hasn't been a day when I haven't asked myself what you would have done if I'd asked you to stay.'

Smiling, Evie gave a shrug. 'I would have stayed.'

'My, stupid, mistake.'

'Eselverue?' she asked.

'I think I might need a new word for this. One that means I

337

don't want to have to imagine that it's only in another place and another time where it works out for us.'

He opened his hands to her.

She regarded them.

'I'm ready,' he promised. 'This time, I'm ready.'

Evie knew that in a moment she would kiss him for the second first time. A little later, in a boatshed that no longer felt so empty, they would make love for the second first time. Tomorrow, Arie would miss his flight to Melbourne, and he wouldn't go home the next day either, nor the day after that, and in the several days that he and she would remain hidden from the world, watching the wintry waves of the bay through the boatshed window, they would marvel at their good fortune to have been listening to the radio at the same moment when 'For Real' played over the airwaves, and she would read him poems from her notebooks, including the one about the match, and he would tell her about the red dresses going up in flames on the solstice, and in the months to follow there would hardly be a weekend when Arie wasn't in Hobart, or Evie in Melbourne. There was more beyond that, too. Much more, but it was all yet to come.

For now, they were standing in a cold street, and he was holding out his hands.

This time Evie took it slowly, not because she was uncertain but because she wanted to be sure that she would remember every single thing: the feel of the wind; the tarry smell of the street; the slightly overfull feeling of her heart, which only wanted to rush. She closed her eyes and remembered her own words. *Do you know what's going to happen to me next in my life? I'll tell you. I'm going to meet somebody. Somebody nice. Somebody really nice. And they're going to want me. Really, properly want me, not just kind-of. And it's going to be as simple as that.*

She hadn't been exactly right. It hadn't been simple. Not so far. But as Evie reached out her hands, she knew that it didn't matter. Because Arie did want her, really and properly. His hands were cold against hers, but his grasp felt entirely safe. His fingers closed, tightly, around hers, as if he had no intention of letting go ever again. And if, in that moment, Evie had the slightly giddy feeling that she was placing her entire future in those hands, it was only because she was.

coda

It wasn't Red Somerled's idea to pull the Locksmiths back together for a revival tour; Tony the drummer had been the one to track them all down and talk them into it. He'd phoned up Red a couple of months after *Disc & Co*'s demise, when Red had been in a funk, sleeping late on weekdays and putting away a good deal too much Jim Beam and Coke in the evenings.

'Who wants to listen to a bunch of old losers like us?' Red had asked.

'Yeah, but here's the thing,' Tony had said. 'Who cares?'

It was a good point. Now here they were, on a tiny stage in a Fremantle pub on a roasting December afternoon. It was a far cry from their glory days, when the crowd used to press up against the edges of the stage, and Red – behind the keyboard – could feel the heat from the eyes of a hundred different women. Now each of the Locksmiths sported a bald head, turkey wattles or a gut like a belt-buckle soufflé, or all of the above, and the Sunday session crowd was sparse.

But as Tony had said – who cared? At rehearsals, the musicians found that all their old songs were still inside their keyboard-playing, guitar-strumming fingers, just waiting to be let out again. Red had forgotten how satisfying it was to play music with other people, picking up on cues, intuiting where to go next, expanding, compressing, and sometimes making mistakes the audience would never detect.

In the middle of an instrumental track named 'The Guillotine', after a surf break down the coast, the guitarists cleared a space in the music – just the way they used to – for a big, rolling swell of a keyboard solo. Red gave it everything, closing his eyes while his fingers found their way over the crests and troughs of the music. When it came to an end, he saw that a woman at the bar was still watching him, her legs crossed and her foot jiggling a little. She held a drink – maybe it was a gin and tonic – in her hand.

She was small, with the kind of light-coloured hair where the grey didn't show all that much, and her face was somewhat drawn. Even so, there was something about her gaze and her posture that rekindled in Red a memory of a much younger woman. At the end of the set, he stepped down off the stage and went over to her.

'I feel like we might have met before,' he said, hoping that didn't sound like a dodgy pick-up line.

'We did,' said Belinda Clare, 'but it was a very long time ago.'

The December day Lucie Doran and Elijah Tripp found out they were pregnant, they were on the road from Boston to Quebec City in a minivan with the rest of the Curious Lovers. They stopped somewhere in Vermont, and while everyone went off for a pee, Lucie went to a drugstore.

When they piled themselves back into the van, Lucie slipped the white stick with its two bright blue lines into Elijah's hand and his eyes went big with excitement and fear, and the two of them rode north for a while in silence, Lucie leaning into Elijah as much as their seatbelts would allow, both of them contemplating a future that was suddenly as wide open and ordinarily miraculous as everything they could see through the front windscreen.

After a time, when just about everybody but Lucie, Elijah and the driver seemed to be dozing, Lucie whispered, 'If it's a girl, I want to call her Tango.'

What a surprise: a hippie noun name, Elijah thought. 'And if it's a boy?'

'Banjo,' she said, with a smile Elijah found hard to define.

The van drove on, the road reeled by under its wheels, and Elijah laid a hand on Lucie's belly. *Please God*, he silently prayed. *Please God, oh please, let it be a girl.*

Bene Romero walked out of Heathrow, having just put his seventeen-year-old daughter on a plane to Vancouver, via Toronto, where he was trusting that she would be adequately supervised by two adults whom he had never met before: the parents of the cocky little cellist who had stolen Beatrix's heart. Although this would be the first time that Bene and Beatrix would be apart for Christmas, Beatrix had all but sprinted through the international departure gate; there had been no backwards glance.

Bene strode through the car park, his hands involuntarily clenching and unclenching, the veins in his neck popping. When Juanita – Beatrix's 'euphemism' – had announced that she was coming along to the airport, Bene had taken her insistence at face value and assumed she'd wanted to say goodbye to Beatrix. Now, though, he was starting to understand that Juanita had known he might need some supervision himself. She held out her hands for his car keys.

'You are way too hepped up to drive,' she said. 'Come on. I'm taking you out for some fun.'

Bene didn't want to have any fun. He wanted to go home and nurse his stress and his feelings of abandonment in private, but he relinquished his car keys without argument and sat morosely in the passenger seat while Juanita drove them to Camden Town. It was a place he hadn't been for a number of years, even though it wasn't that far from where he lived. His mood improved a little once he had a kebab and a mojito on board, and then a little more as he and Juanita strolled the record stores of Camden Market, flipping through bins of old vinyl and settling big, marshmallowy headphones over their ears to sample some new tunes.

Passing a store that specialised in indie folk and pop, a drift of melody curled through the air, into his ear and down into a vault where it unlocked memories of a late night in a Singapore bar, the smoky taste of whisky, and the beckoning notes of a love song that had drawn him up to a piano on a balcony. He stopped to listen.

'What?' Juanita asked.

'I'm not sure,' Bene said, because the song he was hearing – 'For Real' by Lucie Doran and the Curious Lovers – reminded him of something.

With a tickle of guilt, Bene thought of the black leather notebook he'd half rescued, half purloined from the top of a piano in Singapore. He remembered the ginger-haired pianist, and the way he'd inked in the final bars of the song as a note of appreciation. Posting the book back to the address on the inside cover was one of those many, many things that had never quite made it off his desultory 'yeah, I'll do that one day' list and onto his serious, official 'to do' list. He promised himself that when he got home that day, he'd search out the book, and at the very least put it in an annoyingly obvious spot. The pianist, if she even still lived at that address, would be surprised to receive it after all this time . . . but it was better late than never.

Something happened, though, that wiped the newly made resolution clean out of his mind and filled the next two weeks with quite unexpected delights – and, indeed, changed the course of Bene Romero's life. It was this: Juanita smiled at him – the fine silver ring she wore through her septum piercing glittering in the multicoloured lights from the record store window – and slipped one slender arm through the crook of his.

In the Value Village charity store in East Hastings Street, Vancouver, the distinctive smell of second-hand clothes shared the airspace with tunes from an optimistic, purchase-friendly compilation. Bargain hunters hummed as they expertly flicked through racks of winter coats and holiday sweaters, while back-packers traded their winter woollies for swimsuits in readiness for their next destination, and children sat down on the floor with torn books open on their laps, or rummaged through bins full of Barbies with matted or home-styled hair. Not far from the bookshelves, an old leather suitcase lay open on a table. It was packed, end to end, with sheet music. There were books full of tunes for the recorder, anthologies of popular classics and songbooks for *Oklahoma!* and *South Pacific*, *My Fair Lady* and *The Sound of Music*. Squeezed in amongst them was a black leather manuscript book with a bright red ribbon for a place-holder. It sat there, unregarded. But maybe one day somebody would pick it up and leaf through its pages. Maybe they would carry it to the counter and exchange it for the princely sum of fifty cents. Maybe the lost love song it contained would yet be found, all over again.

The bright January sun speared through the windscreen of Arie Johnson's blue Renault as Evie Greenlees steered it around a sweeping bend in a highway leading out of the city of Melbourne. In the passenger seat, Arie used his teeth to open a packet of jelly babies. He ate a yellow one before picking out two red ones and laying them in Evie's waiting palm.

Evie had been in Melbourne for the past week, having flown in from Hobart to help pack up the house at Tavistock Row. Just yesterday – by the side of the FOR SALE sign, with its big, diagonal SOLD sticker – she'd held Arie's hand, and squeezed tightly, while a team of piano removal specialists had taken the Steinway out of the house in several pieces and loaded it into a van hired by the Conservatorium of Music, where the instrument was to live out its life. Two days from now, Arie and Evie would drive the Renault onto the Bass Strait ferry, and once back in Hobart begin the search for a place of their own.

There was something to be done first, though, and it was necessary.

'What if she doesn't like me?' Evie asked.

'She'll like you,' Arie said. 'Everyone likes you. My family have told me that if I blow it with you, they're keeping you and getting rid of me.'

'But what if I bruise the apricots?'

'You won't bruise the apricots. You'll be much too scared to do that.'

'I've never made jam before. I don't know the first thing about making jam. What if I do something wrong?'

'Belinda won't let you. I can promise you that.'

'But what if she doesn't *like* me?'

Arie smiled; he wasn't worried in the least. Belinda, too, appeared to have turned some kind of corner.

There was half a heartbeat of silence on the stereo, and then some familiar opening chords came sweet and loud from the speakers. It seemed to Arie that there was no more perfect song for the way he felt right now – achingly, stupidly, in love with the woman beside him, but aware that his feelings for her flowed through riverbeds that may never have been so deep if Diana Clare hadn't carved them out first. He glanced over at Evie, and she shot him back a smile of pure present tense.

They were driving out of town under a big blue sky full of white, fluffy clouds.

And this was their song.

a note on the poems in
The Lost Love Song

EVIE GREENLEES' THREE poems, 'Dandelion Clocks', 'Turning' and 'Fire' (p. 303), were written by the accomplished poet Young Dawkins. Young was a central figure in the New Hampshire beat revival movement, where he helped found the Jazzmouth Poetry Festival, and published his debut collection *The Lilac Thief*, before moving to Scotland and becoming a regular on the Scottish performance poetry scene. He was the 2011 Scottish Slam Champion and proudly represented Scotland that year at the Poetry Slam World Cup in Paris. He now lives in Hobart, Tasmania. A regular contributor to the *Griffith Review*, he continues to amass slam poetry and storytelling titles. Knowing that only a real poet could pull off Evie's artistry, I asked Young for help. I am indebted to him for his talent, wisdom and willingness to jump on board with crazy ideas. You can find out more at https://youngdawkins.net, and if you want to know what his wife has to say about him, you can read her blog at https://dorkymum.com.

playlist

Music inspired and nourished the writing of *The Lost Love Song*. Each of the major characters had their own 'theme song' to help me imagine them, and many scenes of the book feature specific songs. More indirectly, the tunes that were on high rotation on my stereo during the writing process have lent something of their emotional tone to the story. If you're curious about what I was hearing and imagining, here's a list:

Arie's theme: 'Unsent Love Letters', by Elena Kats-Chernin, performed by Tamara-Anna Cislowska

Diana's theme: 'Piano Concerto No. 2 in G minor', by Prokofiev, performed by Yuja Wang and the Berliner Philharmoniker

Evie's theme: 'Fantasia on Greensleeves', by Ralph Vaughan Williams (arranged by Ralph Greaves), performed by the Vienna State Orchestra

Belinda's theme: 'Northern Lights', by Ola Gjeilo, performed by the Elektra Women's Choir

Bene's theme: 'Für Elise', by Beethoven, performed by the European Jazz Trio

Beatrix's theme: 'Fantasy for Solo Flute', by Friedrich Kuhlau, performed by Elisabeth Wentland

Felix's theme: 'Whole Lotta Love vs. Beethoven 5th Symphony', performed by 2Cellos

Tom's theme: 'Paris Texas', by Ry Cooder

Elijah's theme: 'Idle Jig Set', by the East Pointers

Lucie's theme: 'Home', by the Small Glories

Red's theme: 'Albatross', by Fleetwood Mac

In her chamber music performance in Singapore, Diana joins with other musicians to play the following pieces: 'Butterflying', by Elena Kats-Chernin; 'Piano Trio in D minor', by Fanny Mendelssohn; 'Piano Trio in G minor', by Clara Schumann

The soundtrack to the chapter titled 'Hold' is: '4'33"', by John Cage

At Richard and Lenka's New Year's Eve party, the background music is: *Café Del Mar Ibiza Vol. 3*

The song playing when Felix and Beatrix board the Star Flyer is: 'Party Rock Anthem', by LFMAO

At music camp, Beatrix's woodwind group plays: 'Scherzo for Mixed Woodwind Choir', by Vaibhav Mohanty

The 1980s throwback electronica Arie hears on the Spotify playlist at the Sonder office is: 'Banana Clip', by Miguel

The Amy Winehouse CD that Evie listens to in the Tavistock Row Airbnb is: *Back to Black*

The over-played pop song that Arie and Evie hear while standing on the riverbank is: 'The Shape of You', by Ed Sheeran

The first song on Evie's 'very long' playlist for the car ride to Heidi's wedding is: 'Budapest', by George Ezra

Minnie's playlist:

'Spiegel im Spiegel', written by Arvo Pärt, performed by Sally Maer and Sally Whitwell

'La Valse d'Amelie' (piano version), by Yann Tiersen

'Nulla in Mundo Pax Sincera', by Vivaldi, performed by Jane Edwards, choir, Geoffrey Lancaster, Gerald Keuneman, orchestra and Ricky Edwards

'Winter' from *The Four Seasons*, by Vivaldi, performed by Yo-Yo Ma

'Something Pocket-sized', by Lucy Wise and the B'Gollies

'Most Beautiful', by Frente

'Anthem', written by Leonard Cohen, performed by Perla Batalia and Julie Christensen

'I Know You by Heart', by Eva Cassidy

'Wild Mountain Thyme', traditional, performed by Lucy Wainwright-Roche

'Fragile', by Sting

'Linger', by the Cranberries

'While My Guitar Gently Weeps', written by George Harrison, performed by Sally Cooper

'Never Let Me Go', by Florence and the Machine

'Elastic Heart', by Sia

'Lost Boy', by Ruth B

'Yellow Rose', by Sophie Koh

'My Little River', by Jess Ribero

acknowledgements

FOR GIVING ME technical terms for vague feelings, and patiently applying her fierce intelligence to the task of untangling my woolly notions about music, I thank my dear friend, the clarinet-playing, music-writing, sock-knitting, garden-growing, cake-baking, yarn-spinning, Essendon-supporting Clare Ramsden. Musical help also came from composer Maria Grenfell and concert pianist Shan Deng, although any and all mistakes are entirely my own. The crew at Neon Jungle (Jonny and Seb in particular) provided me with a window into the world of computer coding and website design, and I confess to stealing their office's purple lighting scheme. I apologise to Sonder Digital Marketing in Brisbane for what must look like the theft of their business name. What can I say, except that this is a case of 'great minds think alike'? My dear friend Rabbit-Hearted Girl has been developing my taste in music since my early twenties, though I can only ever hope to be half as cool as she is. For advice on Prince Edward Island, I thank the poet Richard Lemm, and for telling me about the Mandela Effect I am grateful to Billie-Jo Brezhnev of the Kazakhstan Cowgirls (you can search for their alternative Australian national anthem on YouTube). For advice on aviation, I am grateful to Chris Godfrey. Jam-making wisdom came from the kitchen goddess Lou-Lou Angel.

The team behind this book includes Gaby Naher of Left Bank Literary, Beverley Cousins, Catherine Hill, Claire Gatzen, Lou Ryan, Talie Gottlieb and Radhiah Chowdhury of Penguin Random House in Australia, Dan Lazar of Writers House, Hilary Teeman of Crown Publishing, Francesca Best and Sally Williamson of Transworld, Maria Runge of Goldmann, and Camilla Ferrier and Jemma McDonagh of the Marsh Agency. I am so thankful for the energy and expertise of these consummate professionals, and also for their warm collegiality.

As ever, I am grateful for my best and most beloved reader, Freda Fairbairn, the creative brilliance of *universalgenie* Jean Hunter, the trail-blazing magnificence of Sugar B. Wolf, the lovingly pedantic genius of the Picky Pen, the treasured friendship of Pierre Trenchant, and the steadfast support of Lagertha Fraser. I thank Wallace Beery, who taught me that music is medicine, and Marie Bonnily, who patiently organised all the almost-but-not-entirely-wasted music lessons of my childhood.

At home, I am blessed to have the love of Alaska Fox, Dash Hawkins, Tiki Brown, the Noo and the Bean. To the incomparable Jack McWaters: you are no sort of dancer, my love, but you nevertheless rock my world.

book club questions

(Warning: some questions contain spoilers!)

1. Early in the book, Arie's expectations about his future are shattered. Did you see this coming? When it happened, how did you feel?

2. What did you make of the relationship between Arie and Belinda? Does Belinda have unreasonable expectations of Arie, or does he have unreasonable expectations of himself?

3. While Diana expresses herself through music, Evie expresses herself through a different art form altogether. Did you enjoy her poems?

4. Is Evie right to leave Melbourne without telling Arie where she's going? Or is that a mistake?

5. The interludes, in *The Lost Love Song*, tell of a range of different types of love, including the love between a father and his teenage daughter, first love, love between brothers, and love on the cusp of a lifetime commitment. Which of the interlude sections meant the most to you?

6. Felix and Beatrix's story is one of powerful first love. Did you experience a first love like theirs?

7. Do certain songs take you back to particular moments in your life? Do you and your partner (if you have one) have a song that you consider to be 'your song', and do you think it means the same to each of you?

8. The song at the heart of this story affects many people and travels long distances to find its way home. Do you believe in fate, or do you think the song's consequences would be better explained as a series of coincidences?

9. What do you imagine will happen next for the characters in *The Lost Love Song*?

In a parallel universe, Minnie Darke is a concert cellist, but in this one – alas – she plays no musical instruments at all. While she studied violin and piano as a child, the only real proficiency she gained was in the art of keeping her music teachers chatting. She was raised on Pink Floyd, Deep Purple, King Crimson and Loudon Wainwright III; the soundtrack to her first kiss was Dire Straits' 'Money for Nothing'; Christmas carols reduce her to tears. She whistles rather well and sings along to everything from Queen to the East Pointers, Sia to the Small Glories, Lucy Wainwright Roche to Florence and the Machine, Eva Cassidy to the Stone Roses, the Spooky Men's Chorale to the Carpenters. Her debut novel was the internationally acclaimed *Star Crossed*. She lives in Tasmania with her family, and there is always music.

STAR CROSSED
Minnie Darke

Justine and Nick are meant to be.
He just doesn't know it yet . . .

When Justine Carmichael bumps into her teenage crush, Nick Jordan, she knows she can't leave her future happiness to chance. This time, she's going to give fate a helping hand.

An aspiring journalist on a local paper, she knows Nick always reads his horoscope. So she can't see any harm in making a few alterations to Aquarius over the next few weeks . . .

After all, Justine doesn't really *believe* in the stars – it's only a bit of fun.

What could possibly go wrong?

'A joyful love story'
Josie Silver, bestselling author of *One Day in December*

'The very definition of feel-good'
Red

'Smart, compelling and different'
Daily Mail

Great stories.
Vivid characters.
Unbeatable deals.